THE HAND I FAN WITH

OTHER BOOKS BY TINA MCELROY ANSA

BABY OF THE FAMILY

UGLY WAYS

TINA McELROY ANSA

DOUBLEDAY

NEW YORK   LONDON

TORONTO   SYDNEY

AUCKLAND

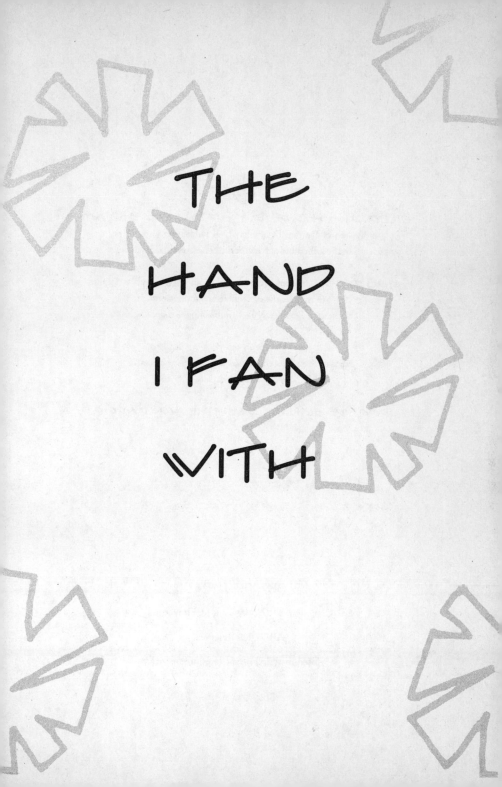

THE

HAND

I FAN

WITH

PUBLISHED BY DOUBLEDAY

a division of Bantam Doubleday Dell Publishing Group, Inc.

1540 Broadway, New York, New York 10036

DOUBLEDAY and the portrayal of an anchor with a dolphin
are trademarks of Doubleday, a division
of Bantam Doubleday Dell Publishing Group, Inc.

BOOK DESIGN BY JENNIFER ANN DADDIO

ISBN 0-385-47599-3

FOR JONÉE,
WHOSE LOVE SUSTAINS ME

ACKNOWLEDGMENTS

Blessings! That's all I've gotten in the time it has taken to write this book.

Belief in God, Spirit, Life and Redemption has been a blessing.

Lena and Herman are a blessing.

My family, who respects the time and solitude my work calls for. A blessing.

The memory of my brothers Walter and Charles who continue to run through my life. A blessing.

Zora Neale Hurston, whose wise brilliant spirit hovers lovingly at my elbow the whole time I am writing, and often exclaims "Go on, little girl!" A blessing.

My sister Marian Kerr, who led me to the title of this work, continues to be a friend and source of inspiration. A blessing.

Mrs. R. J. Shelton, my beautiful, remarkable, rediscovered grandmother, who knows me better than I know myself. A blessing.

My two editors are indeed blessings. Blanche Richardson is a good friend who became my editor. Martha K. Levin is my editor at Doubleday who has become my friend.

I could not have done it without either of them.

Michael V. Carlisle, my agent. We have, as they say, "been through things together." He is a blessing.

My island companions Zora, Ladysmith and Tuck. Blessings.

All my friends who loved, supported and understood me when I disappeared for nearly two years to write this novel.

Blessings all.

Including St. Simons Island, which continues to bless me by offering the love and acceptance of home.

CONTENTS

THE HAND I FAN WITH

PROLOGUE
CLEER FLO'

People in Mulberry had not put two and two together at first. Folks living out in the country along the Ocawatchee River hadn't, either. Nobody had. But Cleer Flo' was at the base of all the changes that were going on around town that spring after the Big Flood of '94.

Everyone in the state of Georgia knew about Cleer Flo', the newly miraculous time when the waters of the Ocawatchee River—usually, perennially, historically, almost always a red muddy, sometimes nearly ocher color—ran as cool as the dreams of a drought-stricken people, as clear as a melting glacier, clear right to the bottom. But no one connected it with the other unusual events.

All around the edge of the little Middle Georgia town of Mulberry near a gentle bend in the Ocawatchee. All around the crest and bottom of Pleasant Hill community. All around the nearly deserted neighborhood surrounding the old downtown district. All around unexpected pockets in and around Mulberry County in the spring of 1995, there was life going on and going on at a furious pace.

Flora *and* fauna.

Not only a record number of Mulberry babies were being created and born, but flowers were growing and pollinating with strange hybrids, forming new creations; long-dead perennials were coming back to life; Early Girl tomato plants grown in the muck that had been under floodwaters bore so much fruit that the plants sagged to the ground in home gardens all over town.

Migrating birds, especially ducks—mallards, teal, pintails, canvasbacks, shovelers, widgeons—were stopping in the area in record numbers. Even seabirds were being sighted on big inland ponds and lakes near town.

Birders from around the region were wildly enthusiastic. They scurried through Mulberry like coveys of birds themselves, high-powered binoculars hanging from their necks like wattles. They had reason to be excited.

The turkey buzzard population that had spent the winter at Lake Peak Park was almost darkening the sky in its migration back north and taking a few local chickens, young pigs and a newborn goat with it. The common loon's unfamiliar loud crazy yodel could now be heard frequently at dusk. The vermilion, green and electric-blue feathers of the painted buntings, which never migrated north of the state's lower coastal regions, were being spotted all over wooded spots. And in the forests around Lake Peak, the county's largest lake, twenty-two southern bald eagles were sighted where none before had ever been spied.

Some naturalists said that the increased fowl activity was probably due to bad weather up north. But the experts didn't have explanations for other happenings in nature. Albinos of all species were being born in and around Mulberry. The year after an albino buffalo was born in the American West, bringing Native American nations together, an albino doe was sighted in the woods by Lake Peak and two albino hummingbirds were spotted at a backyard feeder. Near Lake Seminole, two hunters fording a creek came across a ten-thousand-year-old mastodon's massive jawbone stuck in the muddy bog.

After the Big Flood of '94, all the receding water did not soak back into the earth immediately. The ponds and puddles and ditches of standing water gave rise to generations of mosquitoes that swarmed all over the county in the warm spring. But no one really had time to complain about the biting, stinging pests because swarms of dragonflies appeared right after the mosquitoes showed up and began eating. The dragonflies zipped through the spring air feasting on the mosquitoes so quickly, so efficiently, that the bugs didn't have time to bite and rebreed.

After a while, few folks in Mulberry paid the experts any attention. Most anybody with any sense finally laid the strange occurrences in nature to the unusual behavior of the river since the Big Flood.

The Ocawatchee was a different river *now*.

It still came meandering out of the North Georgia mountains, but by the time it eased into Middle Georgia where it usually gently sidled up to Mulberry, it had taken on so much effluence from other swollen rivers and estuaries that its old banks could barely contain it.

Preachers and ministers and evangelists all over the state used the raging Ocawatchee in their "Jesus Baptized in the River Jordan" and their "Wading in the Water" sermons.

But the river's new intensity was nothing compared to its other changes. Contrary to what the experts predicted, the state of the Ocawatchee River that rushed through Mulberry now was pristine. Although the river retained some of its old orange muddy color most weeks out of the year, now on some days it actually ran clear, a crystal-clear river green, like spring waters clear enough to drink.

Folks in Mulberry began thinking they could predict the days of Cleer Flo', but they couldn't. Cleer Flo' seemed to come and go on its own.

Other rivers in the region and to the south—the Flint, the Ocmulgee, the Green, the Withlacoochee, the Big Indian—all overflowed their banks, too, during the Big Flood of '94. On the Ocmulgee, a gasoline pipe running along the overwhelmed banks was engulfed with the floods and burst, turning the waters into a river of fire and curling clouds of black and gray smoke.

An old woman dressed entirely in white stood on high ground near the flaming waters and preached for three days and three nights straight of the fire next time. Then she disappeared.

"See, see," she had shouted, "He tried to tell you about your ways. He sent streams of water from the sky down through the valleys into the rivers to warn you. Oh, but you wouldn't listen. You wouldn't heed. Now! Now! It's the fire next time."

But neither the fiery Ocmulgee nor any of those other state rivers ever came up clear and pure. Only the Ocawatchee. And the river—Mulberry's river—began to grow in state lore. The story began to be circulated in beauty and barber shops; on street corners and at office coffee machines; over store counters in the Mulberry Mall and under shade trees outside of churches, that the new reborn waters of the Ocawatchee were miraculous waters, healing waters, good for anything that ailed you.

The county officials felt it was their sworn duty to warn the people about the danger of their new fondness for drinking from the river during Cleer Flo'. Even after county officials discovered Cleer Flo' water was purer than the water they pumped to nearly every household in Mulberry, they continued to crank out flyers and leaflets and lectures on the long-term danger of drinking the clear river's waters.

Of course, it didn't help a bit that the days of Cleer Flo', summer and winter, also brought a kind of Gulf Coast "Jubilee" to the landlocked muddy banks of the Ocawatchee. Big fat mullet, catfish, croaker and whiting showed up in angler's baskets all up and down the river, in record sizes and record catches. People who had spent their whole lives turning up their noses at anything that came out of the red muddy Ocawatchee River, people who had called mullet from the town's river "mudfish" and made faces, now practically fought with their neighbors for first pick among the ice chests of mullet and catfish that men and women in trucks and station wagons brought to sell in certain lucky, money-in-hand neighborhoods.

The spring flood changed the town. The flood changed its citizens. For a few days, coffins from low-lying cemeteries raced down the streets of Mulberry on the back of muddy orange water, bumping the doors of businesses near the old downtown river section. One plain-spoken rescue worker from Middle Georgia said on National Public Radio: "There was coffins all in the streets. But I was too busy trying to save the live ones to think 'bout the dead ones."

Looking at television news reports of the Great Flood, people would forget that this was their hometown, the streets of Mulberry hidden under all that rushing muddy water, the tops of Mulberry's trees peeking out from the new rush of a raging river running anew through the formerly dusty streets. Rushing water covering tops of cars, the tops of homes, tops of warehouses.

There were distinct signs of trauma throughout Middle Georgia and especially in Mulberry the year after the Big Flood. When the children went back to school in the fall, there were so many fights, outbursts and flare-ups in the halls, classrooms and rest rooms that school officials had to shorten the school day until after Christmas.

Children lost their way going home from school and became hysterical in the streets, throwing their books and backpacks on the ground. Some ran up on strangers' doorsteps looking for something familiar and stood there crying and banging on the front doors.

It was the worst flood Georgia had ever experienced. Potable water had to be trucked in for six weeks. The property loss was in the hundreds of millions of dollars. And when it was all over, twenty-three people turned up dead.

Lena McPherson alone, it appeared, weathered the storm that brought the floods to her hometown without any repercussions.

But most folks weren't a bit surprised at her luck. "Ain't that just the way," they said, thinking about their cheap little soggy sofas and mattresses, their portraits of Martin Luther King, Jr., and their Sears and Kodak photographs floating through the streets of Mulberry, ruined forever.

"That Lena McPherson know she got it made!"

1

BREEZE

"**Q**uit!" Lena said. She lifted one hand from the leather-covered steering wheel and brushed up the nape of her neck rapidly with the tips of her short pale polished nails a few times, briskly knocking her long thick copper braids into the air and making the large heavy gold hoops in her ears swing back and forth.

"*Quit!*"

She drew the word out long, as if she were seven years old and talking to a playmate who would not stop messing with her or to one of the little boys who used to rip and run up and down Forest Avenue and visit her brothers in the basement.

"*Quit!*"

She said it again as she drove down the long dirt road and across the narrow wooden bridge that connected her property at the edge of town with the main road, U.S. 90, that led into Mulberry.

She sucked her teeth lightly with the tip of her tongue and wrinkled her nose and tried to act irritated, though she almost had to stifle one of her deep throaty giggles as she did it. She wasn't really angry, just bothered and distracted.

So distracted that she hadn't even noticed as she drove above the river's rushing water that Cleer Flo' had started.

This early misty morning in April, however, Cleer Flo' was the last thing on Lena's mind. It was this light breeze playing around her ears and neck that had her full attention. It had been toying with her there for a week or so. The tiny gusts reminded her of tenderness mixed with lust.

Right then she felt it again across the nape of her neck at her "kitchen," where the thick sandy hair thinned and curled. She shook her head sharply, brushing her braids around her neck like a wool scarf, and that seemed to drive the breeze off for a while.

"Uhmm." Involuntarily, Lena let out a little sound.

She checked for the fourth or fifth time to make sure the lightly tinted windows were closed tightly and the breeze was not escaping into the car through the vents. She had even turned her favorite girl group from the seventies off the CD player so she could investigate just where this breeze was coming from. And she loved her Emotions in the morning.

"Come to me. Don't ask my neighbor," she sang to herself softly, absentmindedly, in her off-key voice as she pulled out of her dirt road past the bridge onto the main highway that ran side by side with Mulberry's Ocawatchee River and brushed her neck again. Glancing to her left for traffic, she caught a glimpse of her long narrow buttery brown face and full copper-tinted lips in the side mirror. A perturbed, peeved expression was playing around her nose and mouth. It surprised her to see that annoyed look still there. She half expected to be blushing.

Actually, she felt she had to stop herself from dipping her head shyly, giggling from the touch that intruded on her as she drove her dark copper-colored 450 SLK Mercedes, a car that mirrored the color of her hair and didn't even exist yet for most ordinary folks, toward her place of business in downtown Mulberry.

She was just puzzled by this breeze. It felt as if someone were playing an April Fools' prank on her. She prided herself on figuring things out. Leaving questions unanswered disturbed her. And in the last couple of days, she was beginning to feel this puzzling wisp of a wind more and more often—as she washed herself in her huge shower or deep granite tub, as she looked for something to wear in the long walk-in closet where she kept some of her mother's clothes, as she signed payroll checks at her all-female real estate office, Candace (motto: "We got on different colors, but we all look good"), as she visited former customers out at the nursing home, and as she put her head in the door at the stables at her own house out by the river to say good morning to Baby and the other horses. She had tried to pretend for a day or two that it was merely her imagination playing tricks on her. But the breeze had become so insistent against her neck and ears and hairline that it was beginning to feel that there was this real presence, vague though it was, hovering at her shoulder, blowing in her ear.

Now, as she sped along the Ocawatchee coming into town in the cool of predawn, she kept looking in the rearview mirror every second or two, but she wasn't scanning the road for a spinning blue light. She never got stopped by the cops in Mulberry, or anywhere else for that matter. She was lucky like that. Even as she threw the stick into fifth gear and felt the sweet little car inch up to 78 mph, she didn't worry.

What she was searching for was the *source* of that breeze. Maybe there's a crack where the convertible hard top meets the window in the back letting a draft in, she thought, narrowing her eyes and trying again to inspect the car's rear window through the rearview mirror.

But it seemed that the very thought of the warm breathy breeze evoked the wind itself again against her neck and, this time, to Lena's surprise, halfway down her spine, kicking up her scent of almond oil in the car.

At the touch—soft and seductive—Lena flinched sharply, drew her shoulders up by her ears and sucked in her breath suddenly at what felt like the fronds of a feather that had been lying in the sun slowly making its way down her back under the row of small pearl buttons on her downy cream-colored cashmere sweater. She felt the fine burnished hairs on her arms stand on end, and she let out a small "Ooo" with her mouth hanging open. She felt her legs fall apart at the knees below her new short satin skirt. Sinking into an orgasmic sensation, she closed her eyes, took both her hands off the steering wheel and began to slip them down the back of her sweater on either side of her neck to touch the feather-caressed spot.

Suddenly with no one at the wheel, the small car, sensitive to the slightest deviation, swerved across the yellow line and headed straight for the river's pristine waters. Lena's eyes shot open and she let out a long piercing scream. If her mother, Nellie, had heard her, she would have said, "Lord ham mercy, Lena, you sound just like Cousin Screaming Mimi."

But she did not have time for her mother's third cousin's histrionics. She had to grasp at the wheel of the car with her two hands and maneuver it smartly back within the two white lines to avoid running head-on into an oncoming honking big Mach truck.

The driver of the truck, a burly-looking fellow in a faded reddish plaid shirt, was not impressed. He leaned out of his window with scarlet veins popping in his bulbous nose and bellowed down at her, "You stupid fucking bitch!!" shaking his hairy fist at her as he whizzed past with a *WWWaaaaaaaa* sound.

Lena wanted to cover her ears with her hands and block out all the sounds of the truck and its driver's nasty voice, but all she could manage to do was keep one hand firmly on the steering wheel and the other clasped over her heart, clutching her pearls. She tried to catch her breath and find a safe wide place to pull off on the side of the road so she could break down completely. But her heart kept thumping so hard in her chest and her throat, the adrenaline rushing so wildly through her veins, she could barely see or think. Finally, she said, "Screw this," and just pulled off the two-lane highway right where she was in the dim light of dawn.

She drove off as far as she could on her side of the road through a narrow bed of gray, black and white gravel, slammed on the brakes, kicking a shower of pebbles into the air, and stopped just short of a brown wooden telephone pole. She took one deep breath and dropped her sweaty forehead on the top of the tan leather-covered steering wheel, leaving a wide stain. Panting like a dog, she breathed through her mouth, blowing noisily over her full wide lips, rustling the fine hairs over the cleft under her nose, until she could feel the stream of oxygen come and go a little more regularly.

Between breaths, she chanted, "Jesus, keep me near the cross." Pant, pant. "Jesus, keep me near the cross." Pant, pant. "Jesus, keep me near the cross."

Lena didn't know what scared her more: the fact that she had just almost killed herself in a foolish traffic accident or the fact that she had just almost come by herself in the soft tawny leather front seat of her car because of a little breeze down her back.

Shoot, Lena thought as she continued to press and massage the pounding spot right beneath the cleavage of her breasts with the tips of her middle fingers, Sister just told me last week when we were trying to hoodoo me up a man that all I needed was to have my cat scratched. Lena blew through her mouth in tiny puffs like a woman having a baby.

Thought I was so cute telling her it had been so long, whew, I indeed needed my cat, dog *and* birds scratched, Lena recalled as she still tried to breathe normally.

She brought her right hand across her forehead to wipe away the beads of sweat that were threatening to trickle down her narrow face and saw that her unadorned hand was trembling. She couldn't stop it, and that scared her even more. She rested her face in her quivering cupped palms and inhaled her own carbon monoxide.

If I nearly kill myself just 'cause a shiver run down my spine, Lena thought as she tried to ignore the tingle still dancing along her long curved backbone, I guess I need even more than *that menagerie* scratched.

When she felt she could hold her head up, she leaned back against the driver's broad headrest with her hands braced firmly on the wheel, but she still couldn't completely catch her breath or forget the feel of a summer wind quick with life down her back.

She tried to take another deep steadying breath and instead felt a shudder travel through her body, rattling her entire being and leaving her fingers and toes tingling.

"Woooo," she said.

She looked in the rearview mirror and saw that her big brown eyes were even wider than usual staring back at her. She truly looked like the "old pop-eyed fool" that her younger brother, Edward, had always claimed she was. Lena didn't wear much makeup, just a good rich moisturizer, some color on her cheeks, and some dark brown liner above the lashes on her bottom eyelids. Other than her favorite copper- or wine-colored lipsticks, that was all she had ever used unless it was a formal occasion. But now it seemed all the color, including the earthy red highlights she had applied that morning along her cheekbones, had been drained from her face.

"Good God, I need some of that heavy full-stage makeup that Yvette used to wear," Lena said, speaking of the muscular transvestite from her childhood who frequented her father's bar. As she examined her face in the mirror, she brushed her thick eyebrows up with her fingers, dabbing her brow and slender throat with a white Kleenex from the hidden compartment next to the driver's seat. The cleft at the base of her throat was glistening with sweat, like the pearls of her necklace.

She kicked off her new beige and white gingham linen mules and curled and uncurled her toes inside her fresh pair of gartered stockings and that made her feel a bit better after a while. She had gone barefoot a great deal as a child. Taking off her shoes always made her feel better.

She looked at herself in the mirror again and blinked because for a second she thought she was seeing double. When she opened her eyes and looked again she saw only one image in the mirror. She could have sworn she saw another face, wide, open, almost familiar and unthreatening, beside hers in the reflection. But no matter how friendly it appeared, it still was an image that had no business next to hers in the mirror.

Right then she willed herself to look away, to breathe a little more comfortably and to forget the extra face in the mirror. She knew of bright ambitious black women in their thirties who had died slumped across their desks, their terminals or personal computer keyboards, dead of heart attacks, from work and stress. Her two brothers, Raymond and Edward, the only brothers she had in the world, had died before their fortieth birthdays of heart attacks.

At forty-five, Lena did not want to become a statistic or the main character of a cautionary tale told at professional meetings and family reunions:

"Uh-huh, she just worked and worried herself to death!"

"I just need to slow down here, that's all," Lena reassured herself out loud to steady her nerves. "I just need to slow down."

She blew one more time and reached over to pick up her thin, long, quilted Bottega purse from where it had tumbled onto the floor next to the cellular car phone, carefully avoiding her own gaze in the mirror. The small gold snap had opened and spilled her sterling-silver lipstick case, one of her mother's ribbed Cartier fountain pens and her tiny cassette recorder. She retrieved everything and opened the silver tube of lipstick. Lena tried to outline her full lips without a mirror, but her hand still quivered a bit, so she stopped.

Don't want to end up looking like a clown, she said to herself with a dry laugh as she leaned forward bravely toward the mirror.

An approaching car honked a friendly greeting to her and although she couldn't begin to figure out who it was, she honked back to let him or her know she was okay.

"Lord knows, I don't feel like dealing with a bunch of people stopping by the side of the road to worry about me," she said aloud.

But the contact with another living person—even just the honk of a horn—did help to ground her. She took a deep breath, and looking around, noticed that she was near the home of a little girl who was her classmate in grammar school. Or rather, she was near the site where the house once stood. The Big Flood of '94 that had swept through the center of the state and swelled the Ocawatchee River over its bank the previous spring had washed away the frail-looking house.

Lena had heard Mrs. Hartwick, the first-grade teacher who took over when Sister Ann suddenly disappeared from the school, call the child "Little Lost World" under her breath one day. And the image had stuck with Lena.

The memory of Little Lost World, the little golden-brown girl with the sad face and the nearly sandy hair, made Lena feel the burden of sadness in that child's face. Lena promptly blessed the child and her long-gone home.

"Poor Little Lost World's house, I hope she made it," Lena sighed.

Lena could not remember when she had first started blessing people's houses, imparting brief benediction or healing or praise or tears on the inhabitants—past and current—of each domicile. A stranger's house got the same quick intense blessing that her grandmother's best friend Miss Zimmie's house got.

"That's Gloria's first husband's mother's house. Wonder if she's still alive and doing well?"

"Randy's wife's new family got a nice deal on that three-bedroom ranch house. Hope they can keep up the payments."

"Miss Roberta's children certainly are keeping their mother's house up nicely."

"That little rickety house over there by the box factory sure looks cold, I hope the folks inside aren't freezing."

Most folks would have said, "Good God, what an exhausting thing to do, blessing this one, blessing that one." But actually, it was just the opposite. Lena felt rejuvenated by the holy habit. As she sensed the blessing go out of her body, she felt the power of the blessing reenter it. If she started out from her house out by the river in a bad mood, sleepy, dispirited or weary, overcome by her duties, by the time she reached her destination, she was the Lena that everyone knew, loved and counted on. She knew none of her people liked to see her with even a pensive look on her face.

"Lena, what you got to be all frowned up about?" they'd want to know. "Shoot, if I had *yo'* hand, I'd throw mine in!"

So the blessings turned out to be blessings for everyone. Lena was like that, had always been. The blessings just flowed out from her. She was a blessing to her family, to her friends, to Mulberry.

But for a number of years now, Lena had begun to feel an anger at her blessedness. Once when she was complaining to her best friend, Sister, about all the things she had to accomplish before the end of the year, Sister had said serenely, in that oracle-from-the-mount voice, "Oh, Lena, your only problem is you just have an abundance of blessings."

It had made Lena mad as hell. She imagined Sister sitting there with her legs crossed, dressed in some ritualistic robe, dispensing what she thought was her very own bayou brand of wisdom.

Lena had to keep herself from going right through those telephone wires and confronting her dear friend full flush in her face with the strength of her anger. But as soon as she took a second or two to think about what Sister had said, she realized that maybe it was true. Maybe she did just have an abundance of blessings.

It was only later that night, as she lay alone naked in her bed, that she had begun to muse on her condition and get mad all over again.

Just walking through her house in the morning reminded her of how blessed she should feel, how blessed everyone told her she was, how much of a blessing she was to everyone. But lately, she found that she needed daily reminding that she was.

It was a shock to think that now—in her mid-forties—she questioned what she had been told and believed, what had given her her identity, her entire life: that as the baby of her family, she was a lucky little girl.

This morning, after the strange shiver down her back and her near brush with death, she felt guilty that she had almost forgotten Little Lost World and her little former house. So she blessed it again quickly, turned on the ignition with a roar, and pulling out into the deserted highway, whizzed on along the Ocawatchee River toward downtown, picking up speed as she went.

She touched a button on the dash, and the window silently dropped. With a more familiar breeze blowing on her face and through her braids, she realized how much better she felt. The blood no longer raging through her veins, throbbing in her temples; "You stupid fucking bitch" no longer ringing in her head, making her feel bad and unloved. After realizing that, she couldn't stop herself from "blessing" everything she came across.

She cut through Pleasant Hill for a while, drove past her parents' house—closed up, deserted and, the neighborhood children said, haunted—and her first housing project across the street, then pointed the low sleek nose of her Mercedes up Forest Avenue. Even at this early hour, it seemed that the few people out and about seemed to know Lena and her car.

If it had been a couple of hours later, children heading to school would have waved and hollered, "Hey, Miss McPherson! Hey, Lena! Hey, Lena! Hey, Miss Mac! Look, there's Lena, hey, Lena!"

Those who had been warned to be respectful of adults yelled, "Hey, Miss Lena!" But they all knew her and screamed the same thing.

"Hey, Miss Lena, give us a ride in that car they only got one of! Yeah, give us a ride! Give us a ride."

But Lena would just smile, wave and honk her horn two times to let them know she saw them. "Bless their hearts," she'd say softly. She knew better than to stop and try to pile two or three of the children into her snug car because immediately twenty or thirty of their pals would magically appear for their rides, too. And Lena just didn't have that kind of time.

The children had gotten their attraction to and love for Lena honestly. Their mothers and fathers, aunts and uncles, play mamas and grandparents, felt the same way about her.

Even at this hour, early-rising folks like herself—bus drivers, workers at the box factory, maids, grandmothers and people out scouting from bed to bed—coming out their front doors, sweeping off their front walks, getting in cars for work, opening up corner stores and beauty shops, hurrying to the corner bus stop, all called to her, too, as she passed through.

"Hey, Lena, give me a call." "Hey, Miss McPherson, my cousin need a house." "Hey, Lena, I need you to take care a' that *thang* for me!"

She honked back at them, sending out blessings, and cut back to the highway by the river. As she relaxed a bit, feeling the real power of her blessings, she began handling the chic little car as if it were an extension of her own shapely body.

She thought briefly of swinging back toward the top of Pleasant Hill by jumping on a little-used leg of the expressway and going by St. Martin de Porres, her parish school and church, for early morning Mass and communion with some of the nuns and old-time Catholics. But she caught a glance at the digital clock on the dashboard and saw it was too early for 7:30 Mass.

"I guess the church and I are both blessed enough," she said out loud. She shook her braids—trying to ignore the still-tingling feeling down her back and in her crotch—straightened her shoulders, and continued on downtown just as the sun was peeking over the town's horizon.

2

MULBERRY

By the time Lena backed her trim little car into the space
marked BLUE BIRD CAFE AND GRILL—OWNER in the lot behind
the corner of Broadway and Cherry, the sun was beginning to flood
the cloudless sky with shafts of color, and she was finally breathing
normally. She had just about convinced herself that nothing had
really happened earlier that morning back on U.S. 90 along the river
other than some careless driving.

"I just gotta watch myself," Lena said softly as she swung her big
shapely legs out of the car and stood straightening the narrow tan
leather belt on the waistband of her short skirt. She settled the belt on
her long waist just above her hipbones and adjusted her sweater on
her gently sloping shoulders.

Standing next to her car, Lena looked like an unlikely survivor of
what her family had called "the War of Destruction of Downtown
Mulberry." The phrase had been repeated so many times around her
parents' house and downtown at The Place that her father had estab-
lished fifty years before that now Lena could almost see those words

written as clearly as if they had been printed in her junior high school history book.

The corner building that housed the family's juke joint and liquor store looked like a lonely survivor itself. It was the only structure left standing in the entire square block.

At the intersection of Broadway and Cherry Street, the old downtown district Lena McPherson once knew looked as if it had taken a direct hit from a passing tornado. A few business establishments, including Lena's bank and a government office building, still survived and functioned on the periphery of the old section. But few structures were left standing in the area that had once been the bustling center of Mulberry, Georgia, and the very heart of black folks' community in the small town since its establishment two hundred years before.

One block over, the town's original shopping district was just a square block of gutted pathetic-looking department, specialty and notions stores with boarded-up display windows and broken windows on the top floors.

The old Woolworth's was probably the saddest sight for Lena. Some of the red in the original sign had been eaten away with time, pollution, rain, wind and an occasional hailstorm. But mostly, the paint had fallen away from neglect. The building that had housed what Lena thought was the most important store downtown was now just an empty rattrap with rough wooden floors. Where else could you purchase a bobbin for a Singer sewing machine, a pair of lace-trimmed white cotton anklets, one goldfish and a slice of homemade coconut layer cake all in the same spot?

But long before the store closed for good, Lena had watched the quality just go downhill through economic, cultural and societal shifts. During the 1960s when separate eating sections for white and black were outlawed, the store tore down the little counter with twelve stools in back, put in a new toy section in its place, and enlarged the white section with more booths and counter space.

The food in the integrated lunch bar never did taste as good as the turkey and dressing and the ham-salad club sandwiches and the four-layer chocolate cake and the special cake made with alternating tiers of yellow cake, lemon-cheese icing and fluffy egg white frosting—just like her mama made—served in the colored section. Even the potato chips didn't seem as greasy and crunchy in the new black and white section. The eight- and sixteen-ounce glasses stacked in simple pyramids at the end of the counter didn't sparkle the same. The baked hen and corn bread dressing was never as moist. And the integrated counter's coconut layer cake had a funny little undertaste.

Lena was only one among many in town who mourned the passing of the colored lunch counter as well as the food at Woolworth's downtown.

Her father, Jonah, the consummate businessman, saw the efficacy of consolidating duplicate store sections. But he, too, mourned the changes. He was used to sending around to the five-and-ten-cent store late some afternoons to see what kinds of vegetables they had. The two waitresses, who also cooked there, took delight in sending Jonah his favorites—rutabagas, okra and tomatoes, corn and chicken and dumplings. Nellie didn't care for chicken and dumplings, so she rarely cooked them.

"Wife won't even make him chicken and dumplings," one waitress would mutter to the other as she dished up heaping portions of the rich doughy concoction to send around the corner and down Cherry Street to The Place. She knew that because Jonah had told them so one day as he had breezed through the store taking the shortcut to the alley down the steps behind the colored lunch counter. "You know, Nellie won't make me chicken and dumplings like ya'll make," he called out as he spied the dish bubbling in a pot. "She doesn't care for them."

The other waitress would suck her teeth, remembering how dapper and handsome he had looked in a sheer white short-sleeved shirt and roomy linen slacks, and put an extra piece of corn bread in the white paper bag intended for Jonah. "And you know he give her everything she want. Nellie always has thought she was cute."

"A man like Jonah!" the first said indignantly.

Many folks who had worked near downtown and only had fifteen minutes for their lunch break would order their lunch one day ahead so when they sat down at the counter and picked up their forks, their plates would be set before them ready for them to dig in.

Woolworth's was just one store closing downtown that broke Mulberry's heart. Fragrance-scented Davison's, where her mother had bought her Hanes stockings by the box and the Vanity Fair slips and bras and panties that Lena had worn as a teenager and took away to college, was just a shell with nothing inside but dust and trash and the occasional remains of a squatting runaway. The new store out at the Mulberry Mall didn't even have the same name.

Burton-Smith was another one. Lena's grandmama had insisted that the small millinery store had the widest and most grand selection of cloth and notions in the whole area. Women making their weekly pilgrimage each Saturday to the store's sewing department would dive into the bolts of cloth and skeins of yarn and spools of cotton and silk thread.

People talked about the store as if it were a person.

"Well, I mo' go down to Burton-Smith to see what *he* got."

But that was all gone now, too.

Some folks in town felt that way about the whole area. Downtown gone. The expressway cutting through the heart of the city. The outskirts of town turning into office strips and manufacturing complexes. At least, the new construction brought a level of prosperity to folks Lena knew: Houses were bought, businesses were started, offspring were sent to college, second cars were purchased. But she could see no good godly reason for the changes in downtown.

She stood in the empty parking lot behind her place of business for a moment with her butt resting against the side of the car. She was surprised that she was still a little weak in the knees from her incident in the car.

Instead of going straight into the back door, Lena took her regular longer route down the alley where Mr. Brown's service station stood, around the corner and up Broadway, blessing empty spots where much of her Mulberry history had occurred. She blessed Miss Emily and the peanut shop. She smiled and remembered all the old and young heads she had seen sitting up in Stanley's Barber Shop talking trash and playing checkers while Mr. Stanley slowly and painstakingly swept the linoleum floor repeatedly of short black prickly hairs.

Her high-heeled Chanel mules made a *clack-clack* sound on the smooth concrete of the wide country-town sidewalk. The sound seemed to echo up and down the empty street. It reverberated past where the old Greyhound bus station—immortalized in a local blues singer's lyrics, "I'm washing dishes in the bus station cafe now, but I won't be washing for long"—had stood, smelling of two-day-old traveling people with their bag lunches of fried chicken and pound cake and bananas crowded into the waiting room of the bus station. The sound of her heels echoed past the site of the historic Burghart Theatre, where Bessie Smith had performed in the late twenties; past where women, legendary "Broadway Jessies" in tight skirts, the scent of cheap perfume emanating from their pulse points, had lolled in the lobby of the barely respectable Cornet Hotel on the corner of the alley.

To many folks, Lena McPherson *was* Mulberry.

Walking up the street by herself, Lena evoked the swing and feel of decades of her people in Mulberry. It was a shame that no one was around to appreciate how good she looked striding up Broadway.

Lena's looks laughed in the face of her forty-five years. It was not so much that she looked young for her years, which she did, for which she could thank her father's melanin-rich chocolate-brown genes, as it was that she looked like herself, just as she always did. Barely changed from the time she walked Broadway as a girl dressed in her blue and white Blessed Martin de Porres Catholic School uniform.

Lena had grown taller than people in town had expected. Her mother had teased her daughter all the time when they were standing together, "Shoot, Lena, I could eat peas off your head." But she couldn't. Nellie only came up to about Lena's earlobe. Lena had shot up over Nellie, who wasn't very tall at all, in her teen years to nearly five foot seven inches and stayed there the rest of her life.

She wasn't what one would call thin or slender. She had full high breasts, a small delicate-looking waist and a slender trunk like her mother, so she appeared willowy. Yet she had inherited her father's family's round low butt and big shapely legs.

"Look at her, Nellie," Grandmama would say as they both pinned half-finished tailored Sunday suits and wide-skirt party dresses on Lena's teenaged body, "she look smaller in clothes than she do buck naked. She got one of those deceptive bodies like your people."

And Nellie, pins in her mouth, hands on her hips, would have to nod her agreement.

Lena's clothes, now made by all the top designers—Versace, Lagerfeld, Lauren, Robertson, Mizrahi, Karan—seemed to just barely graze her body as if she had just finished spinning around.

That made her look young, too.

Gloria, The Place's manager, would look at Lena some mornings striding in dressed in the short white suit with colored bows all over it that Patrick Kelly had made for her when he was still a struggling designer in Atlanta, and just chuckle with admiration and envy. "Girl, you know you lucky. You got the best traits from *both* sides of your family!"

Precious, Lena's rotund personal assistant at the Candace office, would watch her boss slip out the back door of the realty office complex—her breasts and butt bouncing *just a bit* with every step she took—and just sigh. All Precious could do was wordlessly bite into another tasteless rice cake and go back to work choking back hopelessness.

Walking up Cherry Street, Lena looked like Mulberry from a few decades before: healthy, a little country, bursting to grow, mysterious, comfortable, familiar, prosperous, old-fashioned yet current.

Unemployed, unattached men, some of them fairly young, drifting through the old center of downtown Mulberry on a bus or a freight train would spy Lena striding into The Place and stop to yell, "Hey, baby, you got a nice ass to be almost a *redbone!*"

Lena wasn't a redbone. But she did have a lot of red in her skin. Folks down at The Place would put her "somewhere between teasing tan and pecan tan." And that was just about right.

Her brothers had teased her at puberty that she looked like a lowercase *s* from the side when her preteen breast and hips and ass had begun to develop. Thirty years later, she was still shaped like an *s* but now she was a capital *S*.

Lena had a sly look about her sometimes. Around the eyes. Not a mean, manipulating, calculating look. Rather a mischievous, chuckling, sparkling, I-know-a-secret kind of look. She had had it all her life. Her laughter, a deep, knowing, throaty chuckle, went with it. Although most people could not quite describe that look or the laugh, not exactly, almost all of them felt they liked the look of it on Lena's face and the sound of her small-town southern voice. And they felt some connection to her because of it. Nothing they could put into words or wanted to. They just felt it.

"Well," people in Mulberry said decades after her birth, "you know Lena was born with a caul over her face. And you know what that little piece of skin mean. But our girl ain't just lucky and pretty 'cause she was born with a veil. She special."

"Yeah, you ought to get her to rub that no-luck rabbit's foot for you, Jerome."

That sly look was partly what made old winos like Yakkity-Yak and Black as a Skillet continue to think Lena was special until the day they died. It was what attracted sinners and saints to her equally. It was what made children trail behind her in department stores just knowing good things would follow.

For decades, folk sitting out in front of shops and businesses and bars and restaurants all up and down Broadway and Cherry had shouted their intimate acknowledgment of her parentage and birth.

"Hey, there, Lena. There's my girl! There's that special girl! Come here, Lena, I bet you can give me a good number to play."

Lena always thought they didn't know the half of it. Sometimes she could even close her eyes when it did not frighten her too much and envision her own birth scene at St. Luke's Hospital.

Dr. Williams at Nellie's feet, old Nurse Bloom next to him, the other young nurses standing around them, looking like they had seen a ghost.

Lena had indeed come into the world looking like a spirit with a caul—a colorless piece of fetal membrane—stretched over her face. The attending physician and the midwife-nurse seemed touched by the rare birth. Everyone there did.

Even the youngest nurse's aide in the tiny black hospital knew *something* about a child born with a caul over her face. In her head, Lena could see the young medical assistant leaning over her hospital crib and cooing, "Ooo, little baby born with the veil over your face, you *are* lucky like everybody say. I saw your daddy's big old Cadillac outside. And you know you gon' be happy 'cause you can see the future and have spirits to guide you. And they say you gon' even be able to see and hear people's thoughts.

"Um, you *are* a lucky little baby girl," the nurse's aide had said, shaking her head in envy.

Lena had heard the same thing all her life. These shouts greeted her each time she came downtown to her father's whiskey store and juke joint or to view the features at the Burghart with her brothers or go shopping with her mama.

"Hey, little girl, I know who your daddy is. You Jonah's daughter. The one born with the veil over her face. You Jonah's child, all right. Look at ya. Look like your daddy spit you out. Makes you wonder if Nellie had anything to do with it, don't it?"

Now, other than in folks' stories and in photographs lining the walls of her office downtown and at home, the phantoms of all those people, sounds and smells were just about all that was left.

Save the sound of the heels of Lena's mules on the sidewalk, the only thing stirring on the once-busy corner now was the idling green and cream city bus that sat at the intersection spewing out diesel fumes as the driver waited for his scheduled time of departure. Coming from the now-deserted downtown area this early in the morning, the uniformed driver had a glazed look in his eyes and no passengers.

"Um, um, um," Lena said aloud to herself as she turned the corner onto Cherry Street and took out the gold ring of twenty or more keys from her purse, "downtown Mulberry, a ghost town."

She said it, the pronouncement on her hometown, in the same way that she reminded herself from time to time, "Um, um, um, Mama and Daddy and 'em dead."

From the front, the liquor store and the bar and grill that comprised The Place sat side by side in the two-story brick building. But actually the small square whiskey store fit into the missing corner of the larger L-shaped juke joint. Although folks called the entire building The Place, they were usually only referring to the bar and grill. A wall of colored windows separated the liquor store from the grill side.

Thick black lettering on a white background on a sign hanging over the entrance to both establishments read:

BLUE BIRD CAFE
GRILL and LIQUOR STORE

Lena walked past the entrance to the juke joint and stopped in front of the liquor store. Through the plate-glass door, she could just make out the outline of the handsome portrait of her parents, with the brass engraving underneath, "Jonah and Eleanor McPherson, The Founders." She had hung the portrait above the shelves on the liquor store side of The Place in an antique picture frame her mother's friend Carrie Sawyer had given her.

Everyone in Mulberry knew Lena's mother as "Nellie," but for the formal portrait Lena thought the "Eleanor" was proper. She did hear Cliona from Yamacraw shout the first time she read the brass plate, "Lord, they 'un hung some picture of Jonah in this place with some 'oman name of Eleanor!!"

Cliona was outraged, outspoken and ready to go to the management about it. The management came to her. Lena had rushed over just in time to avert a full-fledged hissy fit to explain that "Nellie" was a derivative of "Eleanor" and that the painting was indeed a picture of her mother.

It had also been Cliona from Yamacraw who had inquired, "Which one of them girls named 'Candace' down at that reality company? Shoulda' named it 'Lena.' "

In the portrait, her mother sat in a high-back embroidered chair dressed in a rather low-cut soft green dress with her russet hair pushed back from her small narrow face. Her father, Jonah, stood beside her casually decked out in an open-necked shirt and a dark jacket and light-colored loose pants. His dark handsome features, the grace in his hands, the slouch of his shoulders all mirroring Duke Ellington in his heyday. Like many black men of his era, Jonah had crafted his image after that of an icon of his time—his style, his mannerisms, his dress, his hip talk. Lena had noticed how many of her contemporaries' fathers had the same Ellington look. How they shook their heads on their necks when they thought they were cute. How they rolled imaginary balls of lint between their thumbs and forefingers when they talked importantly.

The thought of those two handsome healthy people gone, burned to nothing in the holocaust of a plane crash, began to sadden her so that she turned quickly to the front door of the juke joint. She needed a quick shot of assurance that some things on this earth remained the same.

But as soon as she had turned, she stopped at the entrance to The Place, sensing something awry. Seeing the empty spot on the sidewalk in front of The Place, Lena realized that she missed the covey of seven or eight of her "children"—teenaged boys and girls, the first ones to show up in the morning, gofers who hung around off and on all day and throughout the night waiting for a chore or an opportunity or a friend to appear. Lena's "children" were the next generation of her mother's "boys."

When Nellie had opened up and run The Place during Lena's

childhood, her mother had always referred to her helpers as her "boys." Short Arm and Yakkity-Yak and Dear One and Rat-Face from Tybee and Shine. Some of them, old men now, were still around, happy and willing to do anything for Lena as long as they were able.

Lena's children were male and female. They had names like Sharee and Jamal and Shan-tay and Javante and Chiquita, names they were given at birth, but just as many had names like Nellie's boys: Def D and Boom-Boom and Fish and Junebug.

Throwaways, runaways, forgotten children of foster care and no care with eyes so old they might have seen the pyramids built. They were all just trying to catch a break. Lena would say that very thing at Jaycees meetings and civic luncheons and fund-raising dinners and anywhere else she thought it could help.

"If these kids could just catch a break . . ." she would lobby. But Lena was about the only break they caught.

They stood outside the door every morning but Sunday waiting for a safe haven to open up for them and hoping to see their benefactor.

In the seventies, they had greeted her with:

"Morning, Miss McPherson, Good morning, Miss Mac. Morning, Miss Lena. Looking good this morning as usual. *Looking good?* Shit. Shake it but don't break it. Morning, Lena, you looking good right along." In the nineties with:

"What it is, Miss Lady? Miss Mac, how's it hanging?" "Humph, Miss Mac got back!" "Ooooo, Miss Mac, let me borrow that suit." "Looking good there, Lena." And "Damn, girl!"

Sometimes one of them—usually little Chiquita—would sing a few stanzas of Salt 'n' Pepa's "Big Shot."

The feeling over the years, however, was the same. Even with all their bravado, they couldn't completely hide it. The need and loneliness and yearning would be so thick in the air some mornings, Lena felt she could barely move through it as she walked. It was all the young people—flashy-raggedy, mascara-dirty, fake-tough rusty hands and elbows and necks—could do to keep from running up to Lena and snuggling their heads of braids, fades, waves, shags, extensions and curls up under her arms and breasts and chin as if she were their mother. And some cold winter mornings when there was ice at the edge of the Ocawatchee and in shallow ditches in low-lying neighborhoods like East Mulberry, it was all Lena—forty-five years old and childless—could do, too, to keep from calling them to her to cuddle up under the warmth and comfort of her luxurious fake fur or her shawl-collared black cashmere coat and suckle a little love.

She settled for planting a kiss on an occasional forehead, matching a young person every now and then with a good new home somewhere in the state, nearly single-handedly supporting any cause connected with the young folks and the homeless, and offering her little flock of street urchins hot drinks, juice, carbohydrates and fruit in the morning at the front of The Place. By the time regular customers began showing up, the morning refueling would be over and her children would have hit the street again.

Lena would see them throughout the day as she went about her business all over and around Mulberry. Their starter jackets ripped from a tussle, their gray sweatpants wet and muddy in the seat, their Nike Light Up the Night sneakers blinking red from behind in only one shoe. BLINK, blank, BLINK, blank, BLINK, blank. Like one hand clapping in the growing dark.

Lena blessed her children's spot on the bare pavement and went on into her place.

3

DANCING

"**S**omething's up," Lena said quietly to herself, still standing at the door of The Place. She sounded like her best friend Sister when she entered any unfamiliar situation. She'd grab hold of Lena's arm and say, "Something's up. Hold on a minute." Then Sister would scan the scene and try to figure out just what was a bit out of kilter before they entered.

Lena paused inside the glass plate door just long enough to sniff for the stale beer odor mingled with cigarette and cigar smoke that always lingered in the juke-joint air. She had loved that scent ever since she was a child opening up the downtown liquor store and grill on Saturdays with her mother. And Lena still loved it. It smelled unhealthy to most folks, but it reminded Lena of a party.

Lena didn't smoke cigarettes. Her realty office complex was smoke-free *and* perfume-free. The charter that she and her original twelve employees drew up stipulated that. Everyone agreed that, even with the plant-filled atrium, there were too many women in the enclosed space to have conflicting scents. And she had suggested making

The Place smoke-free, too. But even the nonsmokers hadn't had much enthusiasm for the plan.

But this morning Lena had to take two or three deep deep breaths before she could detect a whiff of the customary juke-joint air.

"Something's up," she said again.

She stopped at the door and called out, "Mr. Jackson! Mr. Jackson! It's me. Lena." There was no reply, and Lena went on in, locking the clear double plate-glass door behind her.

Before turning the last bedroom light out and climbing into bed the night before, she had put on her tortoiseshell reading glasses and pressed the blinking button on the black phone at her bedside to check the messages that came in while she was on another line. She had recognized the brusque voice of Mr. Jackson, who was leading the crew investigating the walls of The Place for termite damage. And it was a good thing, too, because he didn't bother to identify himself.

"Lena, meet me down at The Place at seven before we get started tomorrow morning. Got something right interesting to show you."

Lena had never heard anything approaching excitement in the voice of the no-nonsense contractor, the father of one of her high school classmates. But the tone in this message made Lena almost eager to get down to the juke joint and liquor store the next morning.

The Place had been closed for nearly a week for repairs from possible termite damage from the big flood the year before. And Lena was beginning to lose her patience with the work that was appearing to drag on.

Inside the dark juke joint, everything seemed strange and dead. No music playing. No smells from the grill. And she could barely make out shapes. Nearly everything in the place was covered with drop cloths or sheets of thick clear plastic. Things looked unfamiliar draped in ghostly garb. She could see the long L-shaped bar that ran along two walls of the place, the walls farthest from the door, and the door at the back of The Place that was a true high-security risk because it offered quick escape for quick-fingered thieves. But that was about all she could see distinctly.

The weak morning light was trying to stream through the tops of the plate-glass windows above the mural of what downtown Mulberry used to look like at that very spot. The unpainted sections allowed the customers to see either blue sky or black. The Place was the kind of bar where people didn't want to know whether it was day or night outside. And Lena had wearied of the calls *she* received all through the day and night from spouses, bosses and family complaining, "Miss McPherson, you keeping my man/woman/aunt/brother/daddy/husband down at that place way past dark. He/she starting to miss work!"

Lena thought so many times, Like I'm physically down there barring the plate-glass doors of The Place with my body, keeping somebody in there.

She didn't have to. Nobody ever wanted to leave The Place at the end of a day, except the folks who worked there. And sometimes *they* sat down at one or two in the morning, put their feet up for the first time that day and had a beer themselves before they cleaned up, closed up and headed home.

The Place had never been closed for an entire week, she didn't think. And her customers—some of whom called her "*Lil* Boss Lady" in deference to her mother—had moved from mere complaints to almost real threats.

Old men flagged her car down on street corners and insisted she pull over.

"Lena, baby, I don't like it atall. Ain't even got nowhere to go no mo'. If you don't get that stuff finished up down there at The Place," they'd say as they leaned down into her car, bringing with them the smell of old man, "I just may go on and do that work myself!"

Each time, she had to remind the complainant and herself how lucky they all were to have discovered the seminal termite damage before the creatures could do any real damage. Just about everyone in Mulberry who owned a structure of any kind had been on the lookout for termites after the previous year's flood had engulfed so much of the town. Health officials had warned that the floodwaters from the

Ocawatchee River had not finished their destruction even after they had receded but had left much of the soaked Middle Georgia town susceptible to the wood-loving creatures' appetite. And although no one liked to think about it, the termites were breeding and flourishing just as all other life in Mulberry.

Closing the juke joint for even a couple of days seemed to take a big chunk out of some folks' lives.

The big greasy-looking stainless-steel restaurant stove and grill behind the bar near the front door was clean and cold, a rare condition, under the sheets of thick plastic. Even the big gray smoke hood over the stove had been cleaned and draped in plastic. On a normal morning, Lena thought, the stove would have been red-hot by now with ham and bacon and sausage sizzling, a giant pot of grits bubbling, bags of white and whole-wheat bread and stacks of trays of cozy brown eggs in cartons waiting for their orders. Lena's stomach growled a bit in response to the thought and realized, looking down at the large square face of her wristwatch, that it was 6:45 A.M., past time for her breakfast. She felt around in her quilted purse until she found her tiny microcassette tape recorder and spoke to her assistant, Precious.

"Presh, call Miss Louise in East Mulberry and let her know I'm okay. She'll worry 'cause I missed breakfast. If you talk to her after noon, tell her I had a big lunch. Make up a menu heavy on vegetables if she asks."

Lena dropped the recorder back in her purse, then snapped her fingers and retrieved the machine.

"And will someone please call Mr. Pete's son in Pleasant Hill and find out what 'thang' I'm supposed to be taking care of for him?"

Lena snapped her purse shut and looked back at the empty stove. She missed seeing Miss Chevron, the cook, standing over the smoking grill, a bandana tied over her graying head, sweating and wiping it away with the red-and-white-checkered dish towel thrown over her shoulder.

At each stool at the counter, Lena saw the image of a different old customer of The Place. It seemed that some of them, like Peanut and Yakkity-Yak and Red, had sat there so long their afterimage still remained. She could almost touch their backs like taps for the draft beer as she passed their designated seats.

Lena couldn't see them, but she knew the tall beer taps had been drained and cleaned before being covered. The workers had left the neon signs hanging on the walls uncovered, but Lena didn't bother to try to turn them on. Most of them were new promotions like green and pink palm trees for some tropical wine cooler, but Lena had made sure that there were also a few older signs for Bluebird grapefruit juice and Pabst Blue Ribbon beer. Some no longer lit up when they were plugged in. She knew there was no electricity in the outlets against that side and back wall. But she knew there would be juice for the jukebox.

When she could finally make out the rounded top of the jukebox draped in a spectral white painter's drop cloth, she went for it as if it were a long-lost friend. She didn't like seeing her family business shrouded like this.

She hadn't been inside The Place herself in more than a week. Gloria, the manager, was overseeing the renovation work there and didn't like folks hovering over her workers any more than Lena did when she was trying to get something done. So Lena had made a point of staying away. Anyway, she had more than enough to keep her hopping without this responsibility, too.

As Lena moved slowly toward the jukebox, her eyes adjusted bit by bit to the darkness. With each careful step, she could feel the grains of dust and dirt and crumbled Sheetrock crunch under her feet like spilled grains of sugar. It set her teeth on edge.

God only knows what the new black and gray tile I just put in after the flood looks like now, she thought. The workers had stacked some lumber and equipment in rows, making aisles and a working space in the middle of The Place.

She threw her thin purse strap over her shoulder, flung the cover off the jukebox like a magician and stood there a moment letting the dust settle. She had to admire the old retooled nickelodeon she had finally bought, instead of leasing, for The Place. It made her smile just to run her fingers over the red square buttons and the selections printed under the clear plastic next to them. The buttons felt a little greasy. When she touched one of them, she thought she could feel the pressure of every thumb and forefinger that had ever pressed that particular key.

Lena even had songs on the jukebox that everyone acknowledged and respected as hers, just as they had with her mother. Everybody at The Place seemed to have his or her own personal song. Nellie's song had been "Please Come Home for Christmas." Lena's song changed all the time. Folks let her get away with that.

"Aw, Negro, that ain't your song. 'Lonely Teardrops' is yo' song, fool!"

"Well, maybe I changed my song."

"You can't just up and do that whenever you feel like it. Then it don't make no difference."

"Well, Lena do it all the time."

"We ain't talking 'bout Lena McPherson, we talking 'bout yo' black ass!"

When Lena stooped down and pushed the plug into the socket in the wall, the red and blue lights blinked on, the two separate stacks of records and CDs swiveled around and the music began to play.

The crimson and blue and pink lights from the machine played in dark corners of The Place and danced with the dust beams floating in the growing morning sun. It began to really look like a party in there.

Lena prided herself on having one of the best jukebox selections in Middle Georgia. She had even tracked down "Hotter than That" by Louis Armstrong, "Match Box Blues" by "Blind" Lemon Jefferson and some classic excerpts from Moms Mabley party albums on there, too, that made folks say, "Sh, sh, sh, quiet. Listen to this. Listen to this."

The last laughter from a Redd Foxx album was winding down and then "Bring It on Home to Me" began to play, filling the large

L-shaped room and the liquor store next door with the sweet familiar sounds of Sam Cooke.

"Um, what do you know?" Lena said. "My song."

> *If you ever change your mind*
> *About leaving me, leaving me behind*
> *Bring it to me*
> *Bring your sweet loving*
> *Bring it on home to me.*

The familiar music made The Place feel a bit more like its old self.

Lena smiled and began to sway by herself, doing the Stroll, to the thirty-year-old music right there on The Place's postage-stamp-sized dance floor.

> *I give you jewelry, money, too*
> *But that ain't all, ain't all I'll do for you*
> *Ooooo, bring it to me*
> *Bring your sweet loving*
> *Bring it on home to me*
> *Yeah. Yeah.*

It was her song!

Feeling bold, she spun around smartly as if to face her partner. Ever since the near collision that morning, she had felt a little tipsy, a tad reckless, as if she had a buzz on. She wasn't a good dancer. Never had been. Her lack of coordination had been a curse from the age of thirteen. Whenever she had passed the wide floor-length mirror in the upstairs hall at her parents' home, she could see the reflection of her teenaged self and her Blessed Martin de Porres eighth-grade friends Gwen, Brenda, Marilyn, Carroll, Dorothy and Wanda before all of them except Gwen ceased speaking to her—trying again and again to teach her the latest dance steps before the next party.

"Lena, on your right foot, on your right foot!"

The thought of her teenaged friends evoked the scent of Noxema and Gwen's White Gardenia perfume, and Lena thought she smelled it there in The Place until she realized it wasn't a sweet scent she smelled at all. It was something else. This morning there was something more than the usual smell of old beer and cigarettes in the air.

Damn, Lena said to herself, this day is turning out to be just full of surprises, twists and turns. Even though the unexpected had caused such havoc in her life, she couldn't help feeling a little thrill at the prospect of something new.

This spring morning there was a human scent mingled among the regular juke-joint odor, musky and strong but not unpleasant, like a sweaty man or an animal passing through the woods. She stopped dancing in her high-heeled mule tracks and stood dead still for a few seconds. She lifted her face and sniffed the air a couple of times like the deer that forded the river and came crashing through the woods that surrounded her house.

Lena sniffed again. It smelled like a man. A man who had been doing heavy work. Well, at least that proves they been doing work in here, Lena thought.

Then she went back to her dancing. It never crossed her mind how strange she might look dancing with herself at daybreak on the darkened, cluttered floor of The Place. She had done and seen and heard and said strange things all her life. Folks in Mulberry had always let her get away with strangeness.

As she swayed to the music, her eyes closed, her head thrown to the side the way dancers at The Place had held their heads for decades, she caught herself smiling. The new scent put her in the mind of the breeze on her neck. And she finally admitted to herself that the whiff of wind playing at her neck made her feel coquettish and whorish.

The feeling reminded her of Gloria back when she was a young barmaid. She'd tell Lena, home from college, "I'm a little piece of leather, but I'm well put together." Gloria always smelled of perspiration and perfume with a mole courtesy of Mabelline to the right of her nose.

"Sorry to be so late, sugar," she would say hurriedly to Lena and The Place in general as she tied a big stiff white butcher's apron over her purple minidress. "But I couldn't find no clean panties this morning. Spent too much time looking for some 'cause I just knew I had to have a clean pair somewhere. But I couldn't even find no emergency ones with holes in 'em or nothing. So I came on out without wearing none."

She would pause to slip a sliver of Juicy Fruit between her painted purple-red lips and walk up to the counter and her day's first customer. Reaching for the order pad she had hung on her apron sash, she would look over her bare shoulder at Lena and confide: "Been feeling right whorish all morning."

Lena had on a pair of silk tap panties trimmed in ecru lace but that's how the scent in the juke joint this morning made her feel . . . "right whorish."

Too bad I don't feel this way more often, she noted, and chuckling at the thought, spun herself lightly on the tiny uncluttered dance floor.

Lena felt at home there in what had once been the center of her family's universe in the small town of Mulberry. For nearly half a century, someone named McPherson had gotten up with all the other early-rising working people in Mulberry and come downtown to open up The Place. For the majority of those years, it had been Lena's mother, Nellie, who had arisen, prepared breakfast with Grandmama, gotten her children off to school and opened up each morning. Now, Lena didn't have a family to care for, but with all of her other businesses and holdings, she rarely showed up at the juke joint and liquor store more than two or three times a week.

There didn't seem to be enough hours in her lifetime—let alone in a day—to accomplish what was set before her.

She had been an early riser since she was in high school. Then it was ghosts and nightmares and witches riding her that kept her from sleeping soundly through the night. Now she got to bed late, too, so she had taught herself how to *use* her time. For more than two decades, she had been getting up before dawn to walk around her house and get started on her day. Lena had responsibilities.

There were things to do: Make phone calls to older folks who didn't sleep much either. Send flowers or fruit or money for a sick customer or celebrating child or an ambitious elementary school teacher. In addition to advice and succor, she gave tangible gifts to those she loved and felt responsible for—a box of steaks, a set of tires, rent money.

Lena often saw trouble coming on the horizon and just knew that in a few days she would probably be faced with a "regular" in dire need of immediate healing or help. And she knew that when it came, the problem would arise at the worst possible time. So she had gotten in the habit of warding off those offenses with some preemptive strike that settled things down for a while: an unexpected Honey Baked ham, or a gift certificate from a store out at the Mulberry Mall, or a check to someone's grandchild, or a new book of fiction for a discouraged young writer. Nothing big or flashy or spectacular.

Old women all over Mulberry bragged about the seventy-fifth birthday or the golden anniversary (even though their spouses were long dead) remembrance and call they had gotten from Lena McPherson.

"And it wasn't no *dry card, neither*," the old folks would say as they waved the accompanying check or gift certificate around under the noses of their neighbors.

Sister was the first one to call the practice "hush mouth." But Lena had taken the expression on as her own. Several times a month, about once a week, she would sit down to her desk at her own house and do her hush-mouth duties. Ordering items on the phone from catalogs, writing what she considered little pieces of checks that she knew might save someone's life, calling florists and tracking down economy sizes of obscure curative lotions, ointments and plasters that her older friends and customers swore by.

Whenever Sister was running around her home in New Orleans doing a million things at once, taking care of this son or that son while functioning as the sole caregiver to her aging mother-in-law even though her husband had brothers and sisters right in the city, making sure her entire household ran smoothly while preparing for her thrice-weekly lectures as well as the anthropology majors' trip, she would compare herself to her busy, joy-giving, gift-giving friend.

"Girl, I'm so tired. I had to 'pull a Lena' yesterday," she'd tell her secretary as she dragged into her office just before an early morning class.

Even on nights—and there were plenty of them—when Lena was too tired to even plunge into the invigorating cool waves of her indoor swimming pool, or too behind in her paperwork to sit in her sauna and relax, she always found the energy and the time to go through her phone messages and see if anyone really needed her that night.

Most of the folks calling were people she had known all her life. There were no other folks on earth—now that her family was gone—that she cared more about.

"Lena McPherson? Shoot, I couldn'a made it lots of times if it hadn'a been for her."

"Hell, me and my family wouldn't have no roof over our heads if it wasn't for Lena McPherson."

"Lord, I couldn'a got my mama buried proper if it wasn't for Lena."

"Shoot, Lena McPherson the hand I fan with."

She was beginning to feel about the same way her ousted customers did. She was missing the familiar smells, the sweet sweet sweet sexiness of an old R&B tune like "At Last" sung by Etta James on the jukebox, the loud sudden raucousness of a tipsy couple's laughter.

Lena had no sooner thought of the song than the jukebox made a whirring noise and Etta James began singing.

At last, my love has come along
My lonely days are over
And life is like a song . . .

Umm, Lena said to herself, now, *that's* my song for real!

Dancing by herself through the makeshift aisles of the deserted Place reminded her of all that—the music, the laughter, the flirting and fighting, the love, the comfort, the sanctuary—all that The Place offered. And she determined again to tell Mr. Jackson that very morning that he and his crew needed to get cracking on this job and get out of there so she and Gloria could get The Place back open.

As she danced her way along the grill's bar through the stacks of lumber and copper wiring, on to and through the piles of dusty, moldy Sheetrock, Lena tried to ignore the increasingly strong musky odor and the breeze on her neck inside the building where there was no source for a breeze.

This was shaping up to be the best time and the most relaxation she had had in a long time. Lena found so few places and opportunities to enjoy herself.

First thing that morning, she had seen a cat's eye in the drain of her big shower wink, wink, winking at her, and had wondered just what the upcoming day held. This kind of thing happened all the time to Lena. An image—like the blinking cat's eye—that wouldn't go away, a flash of a memory, a lingering question from a dream, the image of a face in a cloud that looked familiar. Over the years, she had learned to control these images that had once controlled her by just rubbing her hand over her face and her braids and brushing it all away. Or at least most of it. But she couldn't do that this morning.

As she continued to dance herself around the uncluttered spot in the middle of the bar, she felt almost caught up in a whirlwind. As she continued to spin, she felt herself growing dizzy. Not from the twirling of her lone slow dance, but from the musky scent in the air.

As she danced, dipping and swaying to the words, "For you are mine, at last," on the nickelodeon, the scent grew stronger and stronger and more distinctive.

"That smells like a man's underarms," Lena said dreamily to herself.

Then she laughed to herself.

"Now, that smells like a man's crotch," she said as she took another step and dip in her dance and another deep breath of the scent.

"That's how he would smell behind his ears," she concluded after stopping in midstep to sniff the air again.

Now the scent seemed to be wafting from a definite direction. Lena barely opened her dreamy eyes as she danced, gently, sensuously swaying her hips and shoulders to the music, down a path through tables, chairs, the mess of construction, smelling her way as she nearly sashayed toward the back wall.

She could barely make it out, but there seemed to be a red-and-white-checkered tablecloth stretched across a section of the wall. She danced toward it.

Still swaying to the music—"At Last" playing again because she wanted it to—she pulled the cloth down, stirring up clouds of dust and wood shavings, and exposed a huge gaping hole in the wall. She was so content at that moment, enjoying her dance so much, that at first she wasn't really disturbed by the unexpected excavation Mr. Jackson and his crew seemed to be doing. But as soon as she saw what was behind the makeshift curtain and the wide jagged opening, about five by five feet, in the back wall of her establishment, a building she felt she knew inside out, she understood perfectly why Mr. Jackson had summoned her downtown at practically dawn and why his voice on her answering machine had had an eerie edge to it. The music was still playing on the nickelodeon, but she stopped dancing. Her purse slipped from her shoulder and landed on the floor with a tiny dusty *thump*. She just let it lie there in the dust.

She blinked a couple of times to make sure her eyes weren't playing tricks on her. Lena had thought there was only a crawl space with room for storage behind that back wall. But she could see she had been mistaken.

Right there beyond the broken plaster and board wall, near where the extra ice machine usually stood, was a room she had never seen before, furnished with a wooden table, chair and footstool.

"So this is where the smells were coming from," Lena said aloud to herself. "But where did this secret *room* come from?" she wondered as she stepped over the threshold and into what felt like the looking glass.

4

SECRET

Lena stood perfectly still for a few moments, letting the secret space surround her. It seemed almost to embrace her.

Actually, the room really didn't look secret. It didn't look as if it had a thing to hide. The light and air made it seem open and accessible. As Lena stepped entirely into the room, she could almost hear it speak. It had a deep friendly voice.

"I been here all the time. Where you been?"

It had an almost teasing, laughing tone. "Huh, where you been?"

No, Lena said to herself as she turned around slowly, taking in the brick and wooden walls, this place doesn't feel secret, just undiscovered and private. Even Lena, who prided herself on her inquisitiveness and who was acknowledged by all in the small town as one of the most inquisitive women anyone knew, even Lena hesitated a moment, then decided out of respect not to read when she noticed the elegant cursive marks on the yellowed sheet of crisp-looking onionskin paper lying catercorner to the edge on the sturdy wooden table.

"This is private," she said out loud, sounding like her grandmother, as she patted the fragile paper gently with the flat of her hand and left it alone. But she could not resist picking up the feather quill pen lying next to a clear blue bottle of blue-black ink and examining it before putting it back exactly as she had found it.

Strong morning light was coming in from somewhere. Lena tilted her head back and studied the ceiling, but she couldn't find the direct source of light. It seemed to bounce back and forth off one wall then the other, practically flooding the high narrow space with sunlight.

On the far wall of the room was rough exposed brick, but built into the structure was a clever lever and a cantilever supporting a window that opened and shut automatically, allowing fresh air into the room at regular intervals. It was almost like a fan set on low. After just a few minutes of examination, Lena had to smile at the ingenious design.

"Well, Lord," Lena said in admiration. "Would you look at that?"

The first time Lena, still a little thing, had exclaimed, "Well, Lord," her mother had looked as if she had just seen a ghost. She brought her pretty manicured hand spread out against her décolletage and sucked in her breath sharply. Nellie had not heard the exclamation since her father-in-law had died some ten years before.

Looking at her strange little daughter, Nellie recalled how the older man always began each task—whether helping a friend to change a tire or dressing for a friend's funeral, whether standing to wash his hands for dinner or going to the state offices in Atlanta about his taxes—with the call, as if he were setting out on an adventure. "Well, Lord" was a prayer of resignation and supplication, an incantation spoken to ask for strength.

"Well, Lord." The old man had always said it with feeling and irony and resignation.

Lena's grandfather had died the year before Lena was born, and when "Well, Lord" came out of Lena's face, Nellie felt a chill in her bones and rubbed her hands over her arms to smooth away the chill bumps.

"Lena, where you get that expression from?" Nellie had asked, not sure she really wanted to know. She had meant to keep her voice casual as she asked, but she couldn't pull it off. It came out sounding like the most important question she had asked since her second son's birth and she had asked, "Is the baby all right?"

"From Granddaddy Walter," Lena said, before she could pull the words back in her mouth. She was always answering questions honestly before she realized her answer had unsettled some adult.

So Lena didn't use the expression as freely as her father's father had. She reserved it for truly special, wondrous, momentous situations.

Gazing up in the newly discovered room behind the wall of The Place, she said it again.

"Well, Lord?" This time with a bit of a question in her voice.

First, she stood in the path of the fresh air drifting down from above. She stepped a few feet to the side like a girl dancing in a recital—"Step together and you lean to the side"—and could still feel the air. Then suddenly she again smelled the familiar aroma of man like a breath of fresh air.

Because of what she and Sister called her "curse," it had been a long time since Lena had smelled a man so intimately. Her curse was not her monthly menses. At forty-five, Lena knew she would soon be seeing her periods wane, then disappear altogether. Lena's curse was being able to gaze into another's soul.

From the first time she ever tried to make love when she was a senior at Xavier University with a grad student friend of Sister's, she had been cursed with a vision of her lover's past. Just when they got past the kissing stage and had moved to the caressing stage, even before they got completely undressed, Lena would have to call a halt and stop the graphic pictures in her head. It was never anything like murder or assault on another human being, although she did see one man go into her purse when she was in the bathroom. But the pictures she saw were enough to cause coitus interruptus.

"Who wants to screw someone who kicked his dog that morning?" Lena asked Sister on the phone after another failed attempt.

No matter who her man of the moment was, just at the point of sexual play and intimacy in their relationship, the powers of her birth caul would kick in and she could suddenly *see*. She could see in the way old folks meant when one would look at her as a child, point a bony finger and say, "Listen, this child can see a heap a' things."

Surrounded by shafts of sunlight and the masculine odors in the secret room, Lena smiled and almost felt herself settle into the feeling of safety and repose that suffused the area. When she heard the board creak behind her, she didn't even jump. She just put the quill she had found on the table down and turned to greet Mr. Jackson with questions about the newly discovered space. But instead of the countenance of the grizzled construction boss behind her, Lena saw stars.

She should have been forewarned. But Lena had put so much out of her mind about how things were when ghosts and demons and voices and visions visited her whenever they pleased that she hadn't seen the warning signs.

Over the years, she had taught herself to ignore the signs of ghosts as well as the actual apparitions. She had just made herself go headlong on into any situation, knowing that she would be safe.

The one time that her grandmother's ghost had come back to her—on the night of the old lady's funeral—she had assured Lena it was going to be okay. Lena still thanked God—particularly in her prayers at night and in the morning—for having the mother wit to cling to her grandmama's promise of safety when that poor old Nurse Bloom had sent her on such a chase of spirits and chants and witch-hunts in the middle of the night.

"Bless their hearts," Lena prayed softly to herself every night on her knees by the side of her bed for Nurse Bloom and her grandmother—the senile old woman who had tried to protect her at birth and the sharp old woman who had tried to protect her all her life.

Signs of the spirit world were not on Lena's mind this morning.

Later, when she tried to recall what had occurred with her in the secret room, it seemed she had seen the odd-looking stick of wood when she entered the place. As she had all morning, Lena felt more than she saw. She *had* noticed the board barely hanging by one nail from a low beam—rough and unpainted—out of the corner of her eye just as she entered the room, but it hadn't appeared menacing. It was just a plank of wood.

She didn't know if she had been whacked in the head with the two-by-four or if she had turned and foolishly walked into the beam and whacked herself in the left temple. She didn't plan to tell anybody, but the blow felt more like a metaphysical blow than a physical one. Lena could not tell if she had been really hit or not.

The force of the strike was so sharp and personal that, even though she could sense the pain in her head, Lena felt her spirit had been assaulted more than her body. It made Lena feel that she had been slapped in the face. Not that Lena knew firsthand what it felt like to be smacked in the face with the open palm of someone's hand. But she did know the cumulative effect of a slap.

For decades, it seemed, Lena had seen the women with their maid's uniforms on or their red McDonald's uniforms or their pin-striped business suits purchased at Rubinstein's out at the mall standing on corners waiting for rides or slipping into the seats of their own cars parked outside garden apartments. Women with black eyes and swollen faces still having to get up and go to work in the morning. Some tried to hide their injuries when they spied her looking at them. Others stood stolidly and returned the gaze. Lena blessed each one she saw.

"Um, um, um," she'd intone to the interior of her snazzy little car as she drove through the streets of Mulberry scouting property and business opportunities, "having to go to work with a black eye."

Lena remembered one Saturday when she was home from college and somebody in The Place was talking about some woman who had come in the night before with a big knot on the side of her head, right above the bone over her eyebrow. Another customer sat there with a big eggplant-purple bruise down the side of *her* face, running along the length of her right arm and leg and, everyone assumed, along her body, too, under her clothes. To the folks there, it looked as if she had been slammed against a wall, hard. She sat there and talked about the woman from the night before as if no one could see her own battle scars and as if she didn't see them either.

Lena noticed everyone looking at the bruised, scarred woman sideways out of the corners of their eyes, embarrassed for her. Finally, Gloria couldn't stand it any longer.

"I'll tell you one thing," Gloria had said from where she was leaning against the edge of the counter dressed in her traditional summer uniform of panties, a purple elastic bandeau-type bra and her white starched apron. "A slap *will* clear your damn head.

"You know, at first, it really hurts, stings, you know, but after a second or so, you begin to realize that the actual strike cleared your head. And you find yourself thinking clearer than you ever thought before.

"Now, the next slap let you know you truly getting your ass beat."

Gloria stopped talking for a bit and went over to one of the sinks under the counter at the front of the establishment.

She stood there awhile, everyone in the place hanging onto her every word. The small trim woman with the curves of a beauty queen always had been able to command attention. It was one of the things that attracted Lena to her as a manager. Gloria had said many times, "Lena, all you got to do is put one powerful black woman in a room, a room full of anything—white women, white men, black and white women, black and white men, even Indians, I guess—and before you know it, she'll be at the center of things. She'll be running the whole shebang. That's one reason they don't like us."

Gloria continued after a while as she stood there dipping a big terry-cloth rag in and out of the hot sudsy water. "Yeah, that second lick is what should let you know what's what. *But* if you can get out of there before that second one, if you act before it's that third and fourth and fifth one, you'll see that that first one cleared your head right up so you can see to take care a' yourself.

"Yeah," she said as she came back with the steaming soapy white towel and wiped the space in front of the bruised, battered woman, "a slap in the face will clear your damn head if you pay attention to it."

Gloria's talk had worked as well as a slap for these women. Before anyone knew it, Gloria and a few of the regulars and then even more women began meeting between 6:30 and 7:00 A.M. weekdays for coffee and talk. The talk ranged from how it used to be back in the country, to their children, to what kind of birth control most of them used, to serious emergency help for someone's friend who had run from her house the night before with just her underwear on her back.

Whenever Lena ran into the group in the morning, she always remembered what had started it all.

"A slap will clear your damn head!"

"Damn, that slap didn't just clear my head. That coulda killed me," she said aloud to the new secret room just before she lost consciousness and fell to the floor, raising dust all around her in a shaft of morning sunlight.

5
HOSPITAL

Although he was driving the lead vehicle taking Lena home, Mr. Jackson was not pleased at all with the way things had gone.

First, Lena wouldn't let him call the paramedics to come to The Place and take a look at her. "That bump on the head or whatever you got deserves to be looked at properly, Lena," he had told her.

"I'm really okay, Mr. Jackson," Lena said over and over as the distressed man—still robust in his seventies—lifted her effortlessly from the dusty floor of the room and set her gently on the lone straight-back wooden chair. But he wasn't listening to her.

"Oh, my God, I done messed around and let this girl get beat up and mugged in her own place. They gonna have my hide for this! Now, why I have her come down here by herself in the dark?" he berated himself as he brushed her off and delicately rearranged her disheveled burnished braids with two fingers.

Her head did ache a bit, but Lena kept insisting she was all right, showing him her unopened purse he had picked up off the floor on the other side of the wall, opening it and pulling out her brown leather wallet, her small collapsible phone and key ring; stretching her arms out to show him there was no evidence of bodily harm—no cuts, bruises or abrasions—pushing her braids out of her face, lifting them from her neck to prove there was no blood, reassuring him of her safety and health.

"Lena, you were laid out on this floor when I come in!" Mr. Jackson argued. Lena watched him stand there tossing his age-softened plaid wool jockey's cap from one hand to another. She was grateful for the ingenious contraption that allowed fresh air to flow into the room. As long as she continued to take deep breaths, she kept feeling stronger and stronger. And she needed her strength because she had no intention of letting Mr. Jackson make a big deal about this little scrape. Besides, she could barely concentrate on her health because the breeze that had only fondled her before was now enveloping her in its gusts. She just hoped nothing happened while the building contractor was there.

"Mr. Jackson, I think I must have just tripped over the entrance or something. I fell, but I didn't hurt myself or anything," she continued as she looked down really examining herself for the first time since she came to, with Mr. Jackson lifting her off the floor of the secret room. She had a small run in one of her pale stockings that looked like a sexy sheer seam up the back of her right leg. But other than being a bit dusty, that was all. Sister would have said bluntly, "Serves you right for trying to show off those legs with those short skirts."

Lena looked up at the worried man and smiled her most persuasive smile. But then he insisted that she at least go by the emergency room of the Mulberry Medical Center just a few blocks away. The smile faded, and she balked again, but he would not be moved.

When they got to the parking lot behind The Place, Mr. Jackson had asked if it was okay to let one of his men follow them in her car. She saw the man, a boy practically, tall and lanky, running his hand tenderly along the lines of her sleek one-of-a-kind Mercedes as she gave over her car keys. Um, Lena thought, now the inside of my car is going to smell like a strange man.

The contractor led her to the passenger's side of his big white Ford truck and gave her an arm up into the cab.

It's a good thing it's not an emergency, Lena thought as Mr. Jackson pulled slowly out of the parking lot into the alley, taking special care not to hit the curb at Cherry Street and possibly jar his passenger any further, then crept along the nearly deserted street like an old lady.

Once at the busy city hospital, after a couple of hours, he almost started a fight in the waiting room. Lena was still lying fully clothed on a cot in an examining area of the emergency room, but she heard him raising his voice outside her room.

"What you mean no *evidence* of a contusion or concussion? The girl was hit in the head. I tell you, a loose board was hanging right over her head when I found her laying out on the floor," Mr. Jackson insisted.

"There's got to be at least a bump on her head or some dizziness or something on one of those head scans ya'll do," he continued over the calm explanation of the attending physician. "And you gon' just stand there and let her walk out of here when she just might fall over and *die* at any moment?"

The physician raised his voice at that and Lena finally remembered she had talked with this young doctor and his wife after Mass one Sunday at St. Martin de Porres.

"Now, Mr. Jackson, don't be having folks in town thinking I ain't taking care of Lena McPherson," the young E.R. physician said uneasily. He had meant it to sound like a joke, but the northern boy had gone to medical school in Birmingham and knew enough about small southern towns to know not to mess with a leading and beloved citizen.

Lena lay back on the cot and wished she could still go to St. Luke's Hospital, where she was born. She had never been in any hospital overnight since then. Never in for a baby's birth. Or a broken bone. Or to have her tonsils taken out. Or for an emergency D&C. She was in and out of hospitals all the time visiting this one and that one, but she had never had to stay there herself.

She closed her eyes and pictured the little one-story building with the simple professional black and white sign out front stating: ST. LUKE'S HOSPITAL. Then, in smaller letters: Front Entrance. The rear entrance had nearly been obscured by the mass of pink and white and red roses growing in back. She could see the faces of the nurses and orderlies, dressed in starched white cotton, scurrying around silently, trying to keep up the high standard of the founder and owner, Dr. William A. Williams.

But in the little town's rush to be a part of the world back in the sixties and seventies, Mulberry—in the name of revitalization, growth and urban renewal—had allowed and encouraged wholesale razing of neighborhoods and streets and historically significant buildings, as if the tiny burg had a real urban section to renew. And the private hospital that had served Mulberry's black community for more than half a century was torn down like a pile of trash to make way for a little-used urban playground. At the last minute, there was talk of a protest and the town officials moved up the scheduled demolition in response to the rumors. Lena's gardener, Mr. Renfroe, and his crew barely got to the site in time to save the roses.

All Mr. Jackson's fussing had accomplished was to keep Lena at the city hospital all day and into the evening having a battery of tests run on her to prove she had not sustained trauma to the head.

By the time Lena just insisted that they find something wrong with her or let her go, the hospital staff was as ready for her to depart as she was to leave. They had taken her purse and her little black cellular phone away from her at the start of her visit. But they gladly returned both to her a couple of hours later. All morning long, the nurses had been kept busy bringing phones to Lena or calling her to the phone because "they say it's vitally important," the women and one male nurse intoned flatly for the twentieth time. Precious and some of her office and department managers—Wanda, Brenda, Carroll, Marilyn—slipped in and out all day with papers resting on leather attaché cases with "LLL" marking the spots for Lena to sign.

"Here, Miss McPherson, put your magic on this for me."

"Here, Lena, sign off on this, and we'll be through."

"Here, Miss Mac, I replaced the tape in your recorder."

Lena kept smiling and shrugging and saying resignedly to the hospital staff, "Business."

In the final analysis, the doctors couldn't tell her any more than she had known that morning: Her cholesterol count was high, not over 200, but high. Her pressure was slightly elevated. And she needed to find a stress reliever in her life. But she was in pretty good shape for a woman her age and was basically healthy as a horse.

The young doctor told her, "Ms. McPherson, we did an EKG, ran CAT scan, did X-ray and blood work and rushed it all through. But didn't find a thing."

So the young nervous doctor gave Lena a shot for the pain she still felt in her head and sent her home with some pills, a low-fat, low-cholesterol diet guide, and an admonition to be watchful for signs of dizziness, headaches or blurred vision.

She wasn't a bit surprised to find Mr. Jackson still waiting for her outside the doctor's office. He didn't even ask Lena if she needed a ride. He just guided her to his truck and cranked up the engine.

But instead of driving straight out Riverside Drive toward Lena's house, the unsettled man turned back toward downtown and headed for Pleasant Hill. Lena just looked at the determined man behind the wheel. Now, Mr. Jackson knows good and damn well I don't live at Mama and Daddy's house, Lena thought. But she felt a little woozy, and she was just too weary to correct him.

"By rights, I ain't got no business taking you home, Lena. You need to stay in that hospital overnight," Mr. Jackson said, oblivious to his mistake as he drove toward the big three-story red brick house trimmed in dark green paint on Forest Avenue. Mr. Jackson called the color "country green." It reminded him of when he was a boy and city folks painted their porches that hue. He had painted many a porch in that color himself when he was making his way up in the business.

As Mr. Jackson drove down Forest Avenue, he suddenly slammed on the brakes, throwing Lena against her seat belt.

"Damn," he said as both of them watched a line of snapping turtles, slow and heavy with eggs nearly two months earlier than normal, making their way across the road from the stream in the direction of the river.

"Umph, never seen so many turtles and other water creatures in my life," Mr. Jackson said as he brought the car back on his side of the road and turned into the long drive leading to her family's large brick house. "You hit a couple of those bad boys on the road going 'bout fifty or sixty and you can kiss your sweet behind good-bye."

Lena raised her head a bit as the truck shimmied on the road and thought, Well, damn, it looks like *something* is determined to get me today.

She shook her head gently a couple of times like one of her horses to clear her thoughts. The medication they had given her at the hospital had finally kicked in, taking the edge off the strange pain in her head. She didn't even want to think it for fear that Mr. Jackson might hear her thoughts and take her back to the hospital, but Lena knew he was right. She *had* been hit with something back at The Place that morning.

When Mr. Jackson pulled up to the end of the driveway of her parents' deserted home, Lena just rested her head back on the truck's seat and did not make a move.

She didn't really ever want to go back inside the house on Forest Avenue. Indeed, it was her childhood home. Her mother and father's only home. The house that they had run together with her loving bossy grandmother. The house she left and returned to briefly before, during and directly after her college days.

The house held many of her memories of being loved and spoiled and catered to and protected and babied. The only problem for Lena was that the big old brick house on Forest Avenue also held most of

her memories of being tormented and bedeviled, stalked and terrorized, manipulated and confused. The elegant old house haunted her
with those memories whenever she entered. Lena agreed with the
children of Pleasant Hill and most of the rest of Mulberry. The house
was haunted.

Lena had done everything she could from what she had heard and
read to calm the spirits of her family's house: burning candles, splashing holy water around, burying one of her braids in the backyard near
the stream. Nothing worked.

She knew that part of the problem was hers. Not only had Nellie
thrown Lena's caul tea out, but her birth caul had not been saved or
preserved with any kind of respect, either. She knew that because her
grandmama's ghost had told her so on the night of her funeral the
only time she had ever come back to her.

Her grandmama's ghost had made her put on her slippers first, and
taking her outside in the night, had pointed to the very spot behind
the house down by the little stream that ran into the woods where
Nellie, in disgust and ignorance, had burned the dried skin from her
daughter's birth.

"Your caul is gone forever," Grandmama's ghost had lamented the
loss of Lena's treasure. But Lena had not seen it as a loss. Now she
could hardly bear to look down toward the stream and woods behind
her family house.

She would have sold the house and property in a minute if the
town had let her. But she couldn't bear the thought of being questioned about her actions every time she showed her face.

"So you *sold* your mama and daddy's house to *strangers!??!*" she
could just hear people inquiring over and over.

"Shoot, if it wasn't for Mama and Daddy, I don't think I'd ever go
back into that house," she'd told Sister one day over the phone.

But she had to fight like a madwoman ten years before to keep
townspeople from assuming she was moving back there when Jonah
and Nellie were killed in the crash of *Miss Lizzie,* their twin-engine
Beechcraft.

They flew around so much. Jonah, proud of his pilot's wings and of Nellie's acuity in learning to fly, and navigate, too, would jump in that plane and fly off at the drop of a hat. He had taken to flying in the same way he had embraced railroad travel. They flew to Washington, D.C., for the weekend. They flew to Atlanta for dinner at Jonah's favorite restaurant. They flew to the Georgia coast for fresh seafood. They flew to the Florida Keys to watch the sun set into the waters of the Gulf. They flew to Miami to take a three-day cruise to the Bahamas. They even flew to Las Vegas and came back richer.

Jonah—still handsome and charming, his dark brown skin unlined, his thick black hair graying at the temples along with his bushy mustache, his black eyes still dancing—had, as people in Mulberry said, "come in."

"Well, it look like Nellie hung in there long enough with Jonah 'til he stop running around all over Mulberry with other women and come on in," one woman would shout to another as they sat under beauty shop hair dryers.

"Yeah, and the two of them actually seem to be enjoying theyselves," the other would add. "I know I wouldn't be getting in no little plane like that at the drop of a hat. I guess you have to live with a man that long before you can trust him with your very life like that."

In the same way that people in Mulberry had said all his life, "Jonah know he love a train," they later said, "Jonah know he love him a plane."

Years before their death, Frank Petersen, Lena's friend and confidant who had worked as a houseman for Jonah and Nellie and then in Lena's own home until he weakened and died, had predicted their demise. He would say to the room in general from time to time, as he moved around the house on Forest Avenue or her house out by the river, cleaning and washing and sweeping with his brown felt hat pulled down on his head, "They probably gon' die in that plane."

The one time Lena heard him mutter this as she raced around looking for the white silk scarves Jonah and Nellie liked to wear when they flew, she had to restrain herself from hitting the grizzled old man.

"Don't ever say that again, Frank Petersen," she practically hissed at him, and stormed off to wish her parents clear skies. His feelings were hurt for a while, and he left the house early that day without saying good-bye to Lena, which was unusual. But Lena couldn't help herself. Hearing her friend pronounce her parents dead from a flaming crash, their bodies fused with bent, twisted shards of metal and melted scraps of plastic scattered among a stand of scorched and toppled pine and palm trees, made her face her own visions.

Lena hadn't told anyone. Not Gloria, not Sister, not Frank Petersen. No one. But years before her father even bought a plane, she herself had seen her parents' demise in the fiery crash along the coast of Florida in the fall of 1985. It left her with one of the biggest dilemmas of her life. Did she trust her own visions or not?

No, Lena thought, I don't *ever* have to go back in that house.

And she turned to the distracted nervous man holding the truck door open for her and told him so.

"Mr. Jackson," she said wearily but evenly, "you know I don't live here. No one lives here. Take me *home!*"

6
HOME

Lena felt better the moment Mr. Jackson hit his blinking signal and turned into the dirt road leading onto her own property. With the window on her side of the truck's cab down, she could feel the familiar breeze from the river. She felt on safe ground.

She had to chuckle to herself at the way Mr. Jackson had reacted when she turned him around on Forest Avenue.

He had looked at Lena as if she were speaking Martian.

She had repeated it. "I don't live here, Mr. Jackson. No one lives here."

Lena thought that for a minute, Mr. Jackson looked as if someone had hit him in the head. "Wha'? What you say, Lena?"

"I live out by the river, Mr. Jackson. This was my parents' home."

"Way out there in the country?" he had asked gruffly, trying to recover as he threw the truck in reverse and motioned for his man to follow him back out to the Forest Avenue entrance. "You gon' be by yourself?"

"Oh, no, James Petersen, Frank Petersen's brother, is always out there at the gatehouse," Lena rushed to say of the man who now took care of her and her house. But she thought, Now, why the hell do I have to go around making everybody else feel comfortable about me going to my own house?

When she passed the small cottage that belonged to her houseman, she envied him for a moment. She knew he was sitting in there, his feet up on an ottoman, his duties done for the day, his dinner eaten, his next day loosely planned, and open on the table beside him, a new mystery Lena's favorite bookseller had sent.

This time of night sometimes, it felt as if Lena's day were just beginning. She knew as soon as she got rid of Mr. Jackson, she had calls to answer and bridges to cross before she slept.

She rubbed her hand over her forehead wearily at the thought and was grateful when she realized that the gesture quieted the man sitting beside her. She certainly didn't feel like talking and entertaining Mr. Jackson and, besides, that breeze was in the cab of the truck now and was caressing her head and forehead. She was too tired to fight it anymore. All she wanted to do was lean back and let it stroke her. And that's exactly what she did all the way out to her house by the river.

Lena had named her estate "You Belong." It was how the land made her feel. In all on both sides of the river, she owned a hundred acres. She had purchased the first eighty acres when she turned thirty. The next year, as a gift to his future grandchildren, Jonah bought the ten acres on either side of her when he heard they were for sale.

The house was built only about fifty yards from the river at its closest point, but the way the buildings were situated on a shoulder of land nuzzling into the water, the river ran on three sides of her property.

She had also built a pier and deck at the end of a natural path in the woods that extended over the river. She did not own a boat, but she agreed to the architect's idea to include the dock.

Even though Lena's house was much too sprawling and grand to be called a cabin, that's how Lena always thought of it: her own private cabin in the woods. The way she referred to it, folks who didn't know her thought that it *was* a cabin. "My place out in the woods. Out by the river," she'd say casually.

She never intended for it to be so big. But she just kept adding all the luxuries, accoutrements and special features that she had ever wanted. She knew she had to have an automatic clothes rack that spun the selections in front of where she stood. Lena loved to stroll through her closet, walk past her mother's beautiful things—tailored suits, sexy sleeveless dresses, cashmere jackets—past her own designer originals that Yvonne in Atlanta and Yvette in Chicago, twins from Mulberry, sent for her selection, past her racks of shoes, past Miss Christine's vintage tailored suits and sheer silk blouses.

Then Jonah had come through and insisted, "Lena, you in the liquor business. You *ought* to have a wine cellar." Then Nellie had put in, "Oh, baby, steam would be so good for your skin."

Then everybody in Mulberry who heard Lena McPherson was building her own house out by the river got into the act.

The best black masons, bricklayers, carpenters and plumbers in the area assumed they would be called into service. It took a great deal of smoothing over to hire the ones she wanted and not crush the others.

Folks would call her and her parents all the time with suggestions. Even Mr. Holbry, one of Jonah's business competitors and staunch enemies, to hear them tell it, couldn't stand holding on to the information he had just to spite his rival. So he called Lena late one night at her house with the phone number of a man in South Georgia who had gotten his hands on some twenty-four-inch-wide oak flooring— enough for three large rooms—that had been salvaged years before from an old plantation house leveled by a tornado down by Thomasville.

"These some beautiful wood panels, Lena," Mr. Holbry said over the phone, almost in a whisper as if not to let anyone, especially Jonah, know what he was doing. "A few of 'em got nicks and burn marks, but that just give 'em age and c'arcture. They been sanded lightly and varnished 'bout four times already. You know the mens that made this flooring, had to be black mens, slaves, was some kind of artists. The man that got this wood—now, you call right after we hang up . . . if you interested. This man say each plank a' wood fit together with the next so smoothly that it's a pure-T joy just to work with 'em."

Mr. Holbry had hung up the phone right proud of himself. But he never took Lena up on her invitations for him and his wife to come out for a drink and to see the floors in the living room, Lena's bedroom and her office until after Jonah died.

"This ain't hardly no *cabin*, Lena," Mr. Holbry said as he and his wife walked out on her deck with Baccarat wineglasses in their hands. He shook his head in admiration of the house's mitered corners.

The landscaping and construction took more than a year. It was spring when she finally moved in. It wasn't a two-story house, but it might as well have been. The ceilings were so high, another floor could have easily fit above. In the back of her mind, Lena optimistically thought, if my family expands, we can build a loft up there for the children.

Building her house at thirty-two, Lena felt sure she had childbearing years ahead. Children, a mate, a family that would fill the house. She never envisioned the future without a family. It was one of the reasons she prayed never to be blessed with a calling to be a nun.

The dwelling *did* have many of the elements and feeling of a cabin. The house was made of Georgia pine and white oak logs with hard-to-find cypress logs for the decks and trim. All of it was cinched together with sturdy homespun-looking notches and wooden nails by local master carpenters and builders.

There were hardly any paintings hanging on the beautifully finished walls. Instead, Lena was drawn to textile art—fabrics, hemp, woods, metal, rock—things that had texture that she could see *and* feel.

All through her big wooden house, dramatic mud cloth from West Africa hung within reaching distance of a muted Cherokee Indian blanket from northeast Georgia and next to a delicately stitched old circle quilt Miss Zimmie, who had grown up in South Mulberry, had made for her own marriage bed.

In the main Great Jonah Room, she had hung Native American brown and orange and gray and green blankets and rugs high on the walls among the rafters. They were made by Seminoles in North Florida and by Cherokee Indians before and after they were forced to leave their homeland and make a death march west to Oklahoma. Some were so fragile, delicate and aged that she had them hanging under glass. Some were modern works she had bought in the last five years from a Native American community down by Wrightsville.

Her treasured African and Caribbean pieces were the same. Ancient and modern hung in community on the walls of Lena's home. A two-hundred-year-old flat basket woven and used by African slaves on the Georgia coast to fan the chaff from the rice they grew made a perfect companion to the fanned basket from Sierra Leone, used for the same purpose, and the straw tray woven the year before by a black woman artist who had moved to a farm outside of Mulberry. Sister, in her travels around the world, prided herself on instinctively knowing just the piece Lena would love as a gift.

In Kenya, Sister had bartered for the mud cloth that was now hanging over Lena's dining room table. She had also introduced Lena to the yellow, blue, black and white works of Ndebele women from southern Africa.

Nellie had given Lena everything out of her grandmama's old room on Forest Avenue: a daguerreotype of another era complete with four-poster bed, red chifforobe and an heirloom dresser, where only Lena, the baby of the family, was always welcomed. Lena had dispersed her grandmother's treasures—right down to her old chenille robes and shirtwaist dresses hanging in the chifforobe—throughout her own house so wherever she moved, she was reminded of the old lady.

It all worked beautifully together—the textiles, the wood, the glass, the sunlight, the woods, the river.

On one wall of the Great Jonah Room, Lena had hung a huge framed photograph of her paternal grandparents hanging merrily from the Silver Crescent caboose, Granddaddy Walter's snap brim set at a cocky angle with one arm around his bride's tiny waist. The picture had been enlarged from a daguerreotype taken on their wedding trip to New Orleans. Whenever Lena looked at the picture, she recalled her grandmama saying, "One reason Walter look so pleased is we setting off on a adventure."

The ceilings of nearly all the rooms had intricate patterns of the same sturdy pine beams that held the house together, even the pool room, the bedroom and master bath, which had glass ceilings or skylights.

Mr. Buck had laid the red clay tiles in the kitchen to echo the naturally geometric pattern in the ceiling where Lena had hung her complete set of Calphalon cookware from long black antique iron hooks.

Although the house was centrally heated—even the sturdy stable had heating vents for her horses—there were fireplaces in practically every room. Huge sturdy fireplaces that were big enough to walk into and so exquisitely constructed that they were works of art rivaling the ones hanging in the rafters and on the walls.

Mr. Buck, the artisan who had laid each stone himself, combined local and North Georgia river stones and mortar to create pieces of massive sculpture in the Great Jonah Room, in her office, in her bedroom suite, in the extra bedroom and in the sewing room. From the outside, there were only two huge chimneys rising from the sprawling log frame.

"Um, nice *big* rooms!" Mr. Buck had boomed as he first inspected the blueprints for the house and rotated the thick smelly cigar stump in his mouth evenly.

The mantelpiece for each fireplace was made from a single white Georgia pine tree that Mr. Buck had let Lena help fell right on her property and replace with a tiny pine seedling. Varnished pine French doors made from the same Georgia pine logs topped by more windows off every room allowed air and sunlight in everywhere.

The two main fireplaces, huge hulking creatures of stone and mortar, were like people sitting in Lena's house. One sat in the northwest end of the house facing the Great Jonah Room on one side and Lena's workroom on the other side. The other fireplace, as big as its sister in the opposite wing, faced Lena's bedroom on one side and her unused sewing room on the other.

The cypress deck wrapped around the bedroom on the east to an enclosed porch on the south side that overlooked a crook in the river.

The stables and barn, nestled among pine oak and pecan trees to house her three horses—Baby, Goldie and Keba—looked as if they had been standing there for decades. The strong but weathered wood the builders used to assemble the multi-area structure on a new sturdier frame had been brought from farmland Lena had bought outside of Wrightsville. Lena had bought the property just for the barn and stables. The old farmhouse that had at one time stood nearby had burned to the ground years before and the family didn't have the heart even to inspect the site, let alone try to build a replacement for their homeplace. Until Lena drove by one day on one of her countryside real estate explorations and spied the barn and stables surrounded by what seemed like a mile of weathered wooden slotted fencing, the property had stood vacant for years. A month after Lena purchased it, a rich deposit of kaolin chalk was discovered underground.

As sprawling as the estate was with its stables, barn and outbuildings at one end—a good hundred yards away from the house so no smell invaded her living quarters—an indoor swimming pool in the middle and an enclosed screen porch and a glass-enclosed atrium off her bedroom suite at the other end, Lena's home was surprisingly unpretentious. It carried its size and accoutrements with such grace and naturalness that few people ever said she was putting on airs.

How could they? Few people had ever seen the whole place inside. It never dawned on Lena to offer guests tours of her home, her own private home, even though most visitors were aching for a deeper look into Lena McPherson's world. It seemed to her it had taken nearly a lifetime to find a refuge of some peace and privacy. She couldn't imagine throwing her private abode open to the Mulberry public, her public, the way she had done with her very life.

Folks she had known all her life. Folks she had sold homes to all over Mulberry who had insisted that Lena see each and every inch of their new abodes waited and waited for the invitation—formal or impromptu—to view Lena's new quarters. But they waited in vain.

Her house and property out by the river were hers.

For a brief time when Lena lived in a number of houses all over Mulberry that she redid and then sold for a tidy profit, she was never able to fully make any of them—the Victorian three-story prize with a stand of ginger lily and climbing white roses out front that had been the home of her piano teacher, Mrs. Frazier, behind her school in Pleasant Hill; the little cottage in East Mulberry with a tiny bathroom with fifty candleholders around the tub—her own, the way the house out by the river was. Her true home was located, designed, built and decorated especially for her. Lena wanted it to be a combination of a ranch and a woodsy lodge.

It was set smack in the middle of a huge stand of woods that looked untouched since the time that only Cherokee and Seminole Indians marched through single file on their way down from the Smoky Mountains to ceremonial mounds east of Mulberry. The surveying and landscaping crew cut one long winding road into the heart of the property from the main highway to get Lena the best site for her home and still leave most of the big and valued trees—like the grove of rare golden Japanese rain trees that had seeded themselves over a half acre—and vegetation undisturbed. The comfortable rutted dirt road twisted and turned all kinds of ways just to avoid a beautiful old magnolia. And it swerved and detoured to bypass other stretches of land—like the bog where ice-blue irises and wild orange gladioli grew in natural ovals—that the surveying crew knew were especially prized by the nature-loving landowner.

The site she decided on for her house and other structures was on a shoulder of land that somehow extended into the bend of the river so that she had water on the east and west sides of her home. And it was high dry land, too. That was how she was able to have a wine cellar so near the river.

Her bedroom suite, the pool room, the dining room and the wrap-around deck with the enclosed porch off her bedroom faced the river on the east. Her office, the sewing room and the greenhouse faced the river on the west through a long wooden screened porch. The main Great Jonah Room, now filled with hickory tables and oak bookcases that ran the width of the house, faced both ways.

For more than a month, Lena had walked and driven around the property with Renfroe, the gardener, and the architect—a tall sturdy dark woman from North Carolina—to see where the sun set among the trees in the summer, spring, autumn and winter.

Long before they laid the foundation for the sprawling house, Lena knew how the dappled sunlight would look at daybreak from plush damask love seats by the bay window in her bedroom.

And she knew the lay of her land—land she had found herself just driving around one day in late summer—and how the view and the sunrise would change over the passing of the seasons.

In the spring, she knew she would be able to sit at the computer in her work space, with French doors thrown open, and smell the tangle of wisteria vines that covered and, Mr. Renfroe warned her, threatened to kill two tall pines sticking out of a grove of cypress trees.

She knew that from her kitchen window, she could pause in the late autumn and watch the low golden light glance off the rustling leaves on the tops of the hundred-year-old pecan trees on the other side of the well-worn bridle path that would weave along the river and throughout her property. In the dead of winter, she knew she could stand and warm herself by the fireplace in her bedroom and see the cold wind coming off the Ocawatchee and chilling the blooming tea olive bushes on her land on the other shore.

Nature had already done so much. Blessing the bucolic site, She had placed sweet fragile-looking dogwood trees with white blossoms throughout the woods and all around the planned site of her house; scattered mounds of vivid pink, crimson, violet, rose and vermilion wild azaleas and wild hydrangeas at the base of tall Georgia pines; seeded wild cherry trees in a clearing where the blossoms could be easily seen from three directions; planted tall hedges of wild-species roses and Indian hawthorn in sunlit spots; strung vines of yellow jasmine all up and through the oaks and pines and rhododendrons like garland on a Christmas tree; blew ageratum on the wind from the south to brighten a cove, loblollies and magnolias springing up out of the ground tall and displaying their nearly obscenely fragrant white blossoms. At first, Lena and Mr. Renfroe felt they were gilding the lily by adding their own landscaping ideas. But they could not help joining in. They just took their cues from Mother Nature and continued her theme.

In open spaces on high ground, they planted peach trees and plum trees and pear trees and pomegranate trees, dotting the grassy rises. Mr. Renfroe gave her a few ground rules about planting fruit trees— distance apart, soil requirements, sun required—and then turned her loose to decide where to plant things. He only had to come back and rearrange a few of her choices and she could see right away they were the best decisions. Mr. Renfroe knew his horticulture.

Between her house and the stables, a cluster of pecan trees, ten years old when she built the house, grew thirty feet into the air. A tangle of lavender wisteria had overtaken one side of the stable. In the spring, the scent of the flowers in the air made it impossible to smell the horses' manure.

The stable with its brick flooring and wood and steel paddocks was erected at the edge of a winding road at the northern side of the house. Goldie was a magnificent golden palomino that only Lena and the best riders could handle. Keba was a dark red chestnut mare whose coat looked like Lena's hair in the sun when she washed her braids and stood outside to let them dry. Baby, a black filly, was truly the baby, the last animal she added to her family, expecting and getting most of the attention from Lena and the stable hands. She was not as large in stature as her "sisters," Goldie and Keba, but she was strong and frisky and adventurous, sometimes too much so. With Lena on her back, Baby would take on any obstacle they faced in their rides: ford rushing creeks, plunge down treacherous ravines, strain up fierce inclines.

When Lena drove her burnished Mercedes into her compound in the evenings, the three steeds would gallop along the corral's wooden fence with her car, their big heads and hers thrown back in an arc, all their tresses—her braided hair and their free manes—blowing in the river-cooled wind. Their spirits seemed to ride each other.

Just at the turn where the wild grapevines grew, throwing tight sweet purple and green scuppernongs at her feet, the horses would veer off to the right, and she would take the road to the left. They would meet again at the exercise rink near the barn.

Nearby, there was a sprawling weeping willow tree. She had seen it in the spring down by the river about to be washed into the still-rushing waters as the Big Flood of '94 receded. She was able to get a few of her mother's boys from down at The Place—one with a truck and hoisting equipment—to come out and save the tree for replanting.

Just that week in April, Lena had noticed that the big graceful tree was putting out lime-green leaves all along its slender tendrils, turning the very air around it verdant. It had seemed to happen overnight.

Lena missed so much in the passing parade of life. She would look up one day and the trees on her property were just putting out baby buds. Then, she would look up in what seemed like the next week and the same trees would be dropping their brown and gold and orange leaves.

"Good God, don't time fly," she would say as she zipped along to another meeting or house closing or banker's appointment, sounding like her own grandmother.

Deeper in the woods in the opposite direction from the river, Lena and Mr. Renfroe even found two mulberry trees growing in a clearing. One was a weeping mulberry that formed a houselike canopy over the two of them that reminded Lena of the chinaberry tree house that she and her first childhood friend, Sarah, shared on Forest Avenue. The gardener said the trees were at least two hundred years old. He was as pleased as Lena was to find them there.

"You got a good-luck piece a' land here, Lena," Mr. Renfroe told her with pride as if she had personally cultivated every stick on the place.

And he was right, too. To be so close to the river, the surveyors found that Lena's land was on extraordinarily high ground. When the big floods of '94 had come, no one could hardly believe that Lena wasn't washed away out there by the river. But she wasn't. Even the wooden bridge on her land that spanned the river where it narrowed before rushing into town was not washed away by the deluge. Her wine cellar wasn't even flooded.

From the beginning, Lena felt it was a blessed place. From the moment she stepped foot on the property, she felt she belonged there.

On her first trip to Mulberry after Lena started building her new house, Sister declared the property out by the river an "ecotone."

"See how the river meets the land meets the air meets the woods?" Sister asked as they walked the land for the first time, explaining the meaning of the term. "It's an ecotone, the overlapping of all these environments. It's the best place for life to form. You know, like the Garden of Eden, the Tigris and Euphrates, the Nile Valley.

"Good spiritual place, girl. And you a Scorpio. The river, a swimming pool, little streams. More water. Good place, girlfriend." And she poured a warm libation of valerian tea from her paper cup right there on the ground to sanctify the spot.

Lena felt safe and protected on her own land. It was hers. It felt like hallowed ground.

Sister had told her, "Some folks think hallowed ground is where some powerful somebody is buried, but it's not. Actually, hallowed ground is where some powerful somebody *live!*"

In the spirit of women and water and life, Lena had named her swimming pool "Rachel's Waters" in honor of the ghost of a gentle slave she had once seen on a Georgia beach. Lena was seven when she wandered away from her brothers on a family vacation and discovered a thin, dark, damp apparition sitting on a whitened beached log, not far from the rice plantation she had fled, smelling like the very ocean itself. Rachel the ghost sat at the spot where she had drowned herself.

Rachel had explained, "This is where I wanted to be, this is where I *choose* to be. This is where I is."

Lena tried her best now to forget the ghosts, gentle and scary, that had haunted her childhood. But Rachel—a woman who chose to kill herself in the waters of the Atlantic Ocean rather than submit to slavery—was one she wanted to remember.

It was on her property that Lena was at last able to make peace with the woods, any woods. Even though she did not know she was doing it, when she was a teenager, she had spent many a night sleepwalking in the stand of pines and oaks and magnolias and dogwoods that grew on the other side of the stream behind her parents' house on Forest Avenue. Then one night she had actually awakened in the middle of the woods in her soaking cotton nightgown with her back propped up against the rough bark of a sycamore tree, lost and confused and scared.

For most of her life after that, she could not bear to go into any verdant patch of earth or wooded area except for her grandmother's garden. Just the sight of a tree's bark up close could sometimes terrify her. If she accidentally brushed against a decorative rubber tree in someone's office or a big ficus tree in the Mulberry Mall, she would have to keep herself from crying out at the psychic pain of the touch.

But as soon as she laid eyes on the thick undeveloped land out by the river, she began to make peace with the woods. There was something of the sacred in the woods on her land. She felt it from the beginning. From there, it seemed an effortless step for her to learn truly to love the woods.

Lena had bought the land with her own money, money she had

earned herself, something she didn't get much credit for because everyone in Mulberry knew that everything Lena touched turned to gold. She was just a damn smart and lucky child.

Jonah would brag to his friends around the poker table that Lena wasn't allowed to gamble with him.

"Shit," he'd say, throwing his handsome head over his shoulder, "my baby could pee in a Coke bottle swinging from a chinaberry tree on a windy day. She's the luckiest Negro I ever seen in my life!" He tried to feign objective wonder, but all the men and the one woman at the table knew he was just eat up with pride over his wheelin', dealin', chip-off-the-ol'-block, look-like-he-coulda-spit-her-out, moneymaking daughter.

Her father was only briefly disappointed that she didn't take the land that he had given her across the street from his own home on Forest Avenue and build her own home there. Nellie told him it was an "unreasonable idea."

Later, she had just shaken her head and muttered, "Goodness gracious, men can be such fools! Why in the world would Lena want to live right across the street from us? Like we some of those old-timey people who have to live all on the same little patch. Like Lena says, 'We're living in a *global* village now.' "

Lena's plan to tear down the rickety old shotgun houses barely still standing there and to build single-dwelling low-to-moderate-income housing (a project she had begun planning as an economics assignment in college) in their place did little to assuage his hurt feelings. But when the moderate-income houses were snapped up in a more than break-even deal and the news of the project began spreading— first through local media, then a piece on CBS *Sunday Morning*— Jonah wouldn't stop bragging about "my baby girl out 'changing the world around her,' as they said on CNN. And making a profit in the bargain."

Even Nellie had to laugh and say, "Now, you *know* that's Jonah's child!"

Lena had to admit she reveled in all the attention the project brought. She couldn't help herself, she was the baby of the family. She loved attention.

But what really lifted her heart was the sight of a little dark brown girl with braids and beads in her hair playing under the huge mansion of the chinaberry tree next to her new house in Lena's project. The little girl, Teesha, was in college in Atlanta now, but she was still one of the children Lena thought about when she honked her horn each time she drove by the houses.

As the motorcade of Mr. Jackson's truck and her little car following passed a low open field of sprouting Indian paintbrush and rudbeckia, she was gladdened again to be nearing her own home. The contractor's man stayed outside with her car, but Mr. Jackson insisted on escorting her in.

The last thing Mr. Jackson said as he reluctantly rose from his comfortable seat in the Georgia pine-walled Great Jonah Room was, "Now, you promise to lie down and call down to the gatehouse or call me if you don't feel so good. Now, you promise?"

Lena nodded her head solemnly with as sincere a look as she could fake on her face.

"I *am* a little tired, Mr. Jackson. I think I'll just wait 'til tomorrow to handle anything. I'm just going to stretch out and go to sleep. The doctor gave me some medication. I'll take it and go to sleep."

"Okay," Mr. Jackson agreed as he headed down the hall next to the wall of bricks of colored glass she had salvaged from one of the nightclubs her father had secretly owned in the fifties and eventually torn down for the property. Lena could tell the contractor was slowing down and reconsidering his exit when he reached the end of the hall. But she patted him on his broad back and ushered him on out the side door leading to the side driveway and walked him to his truck.

Lena remembered to say, "You'll have to bring your grandson out to ride again sometime soon," as Mr. Jackson and his man pulled away around the stables and on out the road back to Mulberry.

Lena almost wiped her forehead and went, "Whew!" as she watched Mr. Jackson's truck's rear lights disappear down the dirt driveway that was more like a rutted country road with tufts of grass growing merrily down the center. The night was cool but not chilly; and the full moon flooded the land with golden-orange light right down to the river.

Lena was exhausted, but she could not resist walking along the fence by the road a bit where wild honeysuckle and Carolina jasmine tumbled along the fence posts. The evening breeze blew a bit, bringing the scent of the wisteria growing on the side of the barn along with the sweaty scent of her horses—all bedded down for the night—with it. She was relieved at first when the wind ruffling her skirt and zipping through the braids of her hair just felt like the evening breeze. Then, as she leaned her back among the pink and white and purple trumpets of blossoms in the fence, she wrinkled her nose prettily in disappointment the way her mother had when she realized that the night air held no scent of a man, just that of honeysuckle and the nearby river's waters.

She found herself wistful, missing something she felt she had never fully grasped, as if it were vapor in her hands. When she spied first one, then three and then five or six lightning bugs in deep woods across the road, she had to smile in childhood memory of collecting the bugs at dusk, of putting them onto her ears for earrings that glowed in the dark.

But her tranquillity was short-lived. By the time she had gone back inside and just thought about turning off the outside lights and locking up, she saw a new set of headlights heading down her road.

She knew it had to be a stranger because everyone who had made the trip before knew enough to slow down when they turned onto her bumpy little road.

One of the main reasons she found any peace and solitude in her home space was its distance from town. She got some satisfaction from knowing what folks in Mulberry said about her house and property.

"Uhhh, Lord ham mercy, Lena live *waaaayyyyy* out there by the river, don't ya, Lena?"

"Oh, don't go visiting *her* anytime near sunset 'cause you sho' gon' get caught out there where there ain't even no streetlights or street signs atall! Shoot, ain't no streets!"

"Let me tell you, Lena McPherson live in the country! She sho' nuff live in the country!"

The drive did indeed discourage some folks. But not all.

"Now, how Cliona from Yamacraw get a ride all the way out here at night?" Lena wondered aloud as she looked out the long wall of wavy glass that exposed the back of the house to sunlight. Cliona stood at Lena's door under a yellowish floodlight trying to sneak a peek inside the house. She was dressed fairly sanely this evening, not like "a patient from the crazy house at Milledgeville," as Grandmama would say. Someone had even thrown an old heavy tweed coat around her bent shoulders against the dampness of the night air.

God, I hope that old lady ain't out trying to drive again, Lena thought as she unlatched the door and, fixing a smile on her face, ushered Cliona from Yamacraw into the hallway.

"Miss Cliona, I can't believe you found time to come way out here to visit me this late. Come on in. You by yourself?"

Lena didn't make any comment on it, but she noticed that the old lady was clutching a small Listerine bottle full of clear greenish water in her wrinkled hand like an old girlfriend as if Lena didn't have the whole Ocawatchee River of Cleer Flo' rushing by her house right outside.

7

GIRLFRIEND

It seemed sometimes that Lena had a glut of girlfriends. Everyone in Mulberry claimed to be Lena's friend. She was godmother to so many children that at some point she finally had to call a moratorium. The christening, birthday and graduation presents were no problem. It was the drain of remembering all those events and dispensing all that love as her godmother, Miss Rita, had done for her.

Lena had cosigned so many business loans for women around Mulberry to start their own enterprises—catering, sewing Afrocentric clothes for children, designing greeting cards, baking and selling real tea cakes and opening day-care and geriatric centers—that she had her own loan officer at the bank who dropped whatever she was doing whenever Lena walked in the door of the beautiful old bank building. The vast majority of the businesses had done very well.

Over the years, she had employed and mentored a dozen or so of the same women who as eighth-grade girls had refused to speak a word to her for nearly five years of school. Now each one swore that she had been a closer friend and classmate to Lena than the next. Sometimes they even believed themselves that they had always loved Lena, and she had always loved them. That they had always been her friend, and she had always been theirs. That they had always been close. As Lois now said, "Since we were schoolgirls, we've always just *clung* to one another."

Sometimes Lena had to laugh right in their faces. The women didn't even care. They were just glad that Lena's good nature had enabled her to laugh about it.

Lena knew as well as they did that the women, now in their forties, some of them grandmothers, remembered all too well their treatment of her in school when they found her just too strange, too much for them. They remembered one day when they all decided to stop speaking to her for the next five years at Martin de Porres School. In fact, each one of Lena's "friends" had a special, particular memory of that cold ostracism that would come flooding back to her every once in a while. Lena got sick of seeing the look in their eyes as these same wicked scenarios played in their minds. So, she tried to treat them all with the love and sweetness of a truly dear old friend to help them all forget.

Their private demons from the past bounced up from the dead whenever Lena gave them the day off for their birthdays, sent get-well cards to their grandmothers, paid for retreats to mountain resorts and seaside spas for them all. Whenever she did anything nice and unexpected for them, they remembered their unkindness to her, their meanness, their un-Christian behavior as girls. They felt they had to take her forgiveness, her kindness for granted or they wouldn't be able to live with themselves.

Lena could hardly be blamed herself for wanting to forget what it was like to be hated. It was hard enough to live with herself and all her own ghostly baggage as it was without the memory of their hatefulness, too.

It had started at about age thirteen and went right on through adulthood until Lena returned from college. Of course, Sister had lightened the hateful load somewhat by bullying the girls at Xavier into at least pretending not to be so hostile. The force of Sister's personality made them give in and soften toward Lena.

Then, when she returned to Mulberry from college and claimed what everyone in town knew to be her birthright, things seemed to change. Even though she attended parochial school all her life, former public school children who had been lukewarm toward Lena now remembered her as a star and model pupil and their best little playmate. True former classmates, like Wanda and Brenda, who had systematically disdained and ignored Lena all through their teens, girls who had refused to speak her name as they sat in the same classroom at Martin de Porres, implored her to be the godmother to their babies.

Marilyn, one of Lena's main pubescent torturers and now one of Lena's highest-earning Realtors, a member of the Millionaire Club every year since 1988, bragged one afternoon to her mother-in-law, "You know, Lena was one of my *best* childhood friends." Lena had come by to drop off a mohair baby's blanket for Marilyn's newest arrival. Marilyn couldn't seem to stop gently patting the fluffy white yarn of the blanket against her throat and then rubbing the downy material against her baby girl's fat smooth cheek. In between, the new mother would smile up at "Auntie Lena" as if she *had* actually loved and cherished her all her life, since they were "childhood friends."

"Lena, I'm surprised you still speaking to those you-know-whats," Sister said when Lena passed along news of her colleagues and their families.

"Shoot," Lena would say with a shrug, sounding for all the world like one of her old lady friends, "life is too short, Sister, for that shit. It's a vapor, girl, gone just that quickly, that easily. And all that stuff you hold on to just weighs you down in this world. In the next one, too, I guess."

Lena never could hold a grudge. She had so much. And so many of the women had worked a long time with hardly any material reward. Lena believed in being supportive.

She even drove forty miles outside of Mulberry just to see her gynecologist, Dr. Sharon, because they were in college together. Dr.

Sharon, like all her friends and colleagues now, had *warm memories* of their salad days.

Some of the women Lena befriended were divorced or widowed. Some were single like herself. Most had left Mulberry about the time Lena came back. But over the next twenty years or so, most of them had come straggling back home.

"Yeah, ain't no place like Mulberry," she had heard her father's and her own customers declare for no particular reason but the joy of home.

Carroll was the last of Lena's former classmates to return to Mulberry.

"Girl," Wanda had told her over the Candace WATS line, "I don't know why you're still out there in L.A. scuffling and working and living from cutoff notice to cutoff notice when you could be home with a *good life* working with us and Lena. Shit, girl, what you trying to prove? You ain't got nothing holding you out there, do you?"

Carroll had been thinking about home for nearly twenty years. She thought about it one more night, then called Wanda back with one last doubt. Carroll just couldn't believe that Lena was really hiring her former tormentors.

"Don't be no fool, girl, come on home. You know Lena McPherson ain't holding no grudge. Shit, what she got to be mad about? Hell, she *got everything*."

"Yeah," Carroll said suspiciously. "And she willing to share it with *us*?"

So Carroll came on home, too, with lovely tales of how she and Lena had spent *hours* on the phone during their years in high school at Blessed Martin de Porres. She came home, also, to a position at Candace Realty, Motto: "We got on different colors, but we all look good."

But she kept asking her friend Wanda, "Didn't Lena used to be lighter-complected than she is now?"

Lena seldom remembered much of the pain and cruelty inflicted on her by the girls she grew up with in Mulberry. Sister, however, knew Lena had been scarred by the girls' rejection of her. Sister continued to marvel at the fact that Lena seemed so free of venom and fantasies of revenge, but she knew that her friend had put a great deal out of her mind just to be able to function normally in the world.

Lena forgave her newly discovered "childhood friends." She prayed for them and did her best to help them.

Even though she had scores of women who counted themselves her *best* friend, she really didn't have a friend in town among her contemporaries whom she could call with a little quick girlfriend talk.

"Hey, girl, I know you cooking dinner, but let me tell you this right quick."

She had not had time to foster those kinds of relationships with anyone other than Sister and her one true childhood friend, Gwen. And Gwen had disappeared years before into a commune in Northern California to write a book. Lena had found so little time for long chatty lunches and dinners over outrageously fattening food and too much champagne or Saturday afternoon shopping sprees through the Mulberry Mall.

Yet Lena never did feel she was totally alone. Her grandmother's ghost had promised her that much when the old lady came back to Lena the night of her funeral.

"You ain't never alone, baby," Grandmama had said, giving Lena the mantra that carried her through college, soured relationships, the deaths of her mother and father, her brothers and Frank Petersen. "You ain't never alone, baby."

And she wasn't. Even in her dreams, she was reassured that there were loving spirits all around her. Her favorite dream was a recurring one in which she felt enveloped in the love of the spirits she called her "Grandies."

The women were dressed in beautiful gauze, chiffon-like gowns of every color imaginable from the palest mint-green pastel to deepest, richest maroon. In her dream, Lena recalled thinking: Each one of these women is my Grandy. Each one is for me. Each one loves me. The women in Lena's dream—some live, some dead—were her maternal grandmother, Lena Marie, whom she had never met; her grandmama; her kindergarten teacher, Miss Russell; Miss Zimmie; the slave ghost Rachel. There, too, were the other women around Mulberry whom she had loved and cherished, Miss Onnie, Miss Annie Mae, Miss Eula, Miss Joanne, Miss Pansy. Then, there were the faces of women she did not recognize even though she saw the love they held for her.

The dream women, her Grandies, would pass her around from one pair of soft sweet-smelling arms to another as if she were still a baby. They would kiss and coo over her, nuzzle her and whisper soft wordless sounds of safety and love. One of them, either Grandmama or some famous woman like Zora Neale Hurston, would take Lena in her hands and ever so gently place her at their feet to sleep snuggly in the sea of their beautiful ethereal skirt tails. Then, they would all lean back, her grandmama at the head of the sorority, and smile.

In life, Lena's grandmama didn't have enough friends her own age around to have a proper quilting circle, but Grandmama had exchanged scraps of material with her younger friend Miss Zimmie, who had especially deft hands. With both Grandmama and Nellie sewing so much for themselves and Lena, there were always piles of beautiful material—maroon and black and royal-blue velveteen from Lena's Sunday dresses, cotton and wool plaids in bright primary colors from her play dresses and pastel linen from her parade of Easter outfits—neatly folded and stored in Davison's department store bags in the sewing room closet downstairs. Grandmama would give the material to anyone who asked. But she kept a special dress box on the overhead shelf with the very best swatches of material for Miss Zimmie.

Now, when Lena went to visit Miss Zimmie—the closest thing she had to a grandmother of her own—she always worked her way back to the old woman's bedroom to see the quilts she had hanging over a frame with pieces of Lena's past expertly stitched in.

A swatch of green embroidered *peau de soie* from her first dance dress, a strip of velvet from a Christmas program dress, a piece of black silk from her first evening dress, a square of electric-blue mohair fabric from a Sunday suit.

Lena tried to visit Miss Zimmie's when she thought she might catch the beautiful old woman, her dark gray-streaked hair up in a soft pompadour, at her machine or tatting her ever-present lap sewing. Even though she liked to say, "The old gray mare . . . ," Miss Zimmie still had good vision, and it allowed her to read and sew well into her eighty-ninth year of life. She had even needlepointed pillows for Lena and herself that proclaimed, "I EARNED IT."

"No, no, thank you. I can make it by myself. I'm an independent old lady," she would declare in a firm pleasant voice as Lena and anybody else in the trim spotless house raced to move chairs and boxes and flowerpots and door edges and anything else out of the independent old lady's way.

Miss Zimmie had flowers in her garden even in the dead of winter. If she had a winter yen for the summer yellow of sunflowers, she'd just go right out and purchase the tall showy flowers in plastic and stick them in her yard. She didn't have a yard full of plastic. Miss Zimmie was too organic for that. But she told Lena she had lived too long to deny herself the pleasure of a sunflower or a rose just because they weren't currently blooming.

Lena went to her grandmother's friend for wisdom as well as succor.

"I don't worry about what I can't remember anymore," Miss Zimmie had told Lena on her eighty-fifth birthday. " 'Cause some things I don't want to remember. Truly. I thought about it and realized there were all kinds of things that I have no desire whatsoever to ever recall again. Some things, Lena, you supposed to forget."

It was advice Lena took to heart in dealing with her childhood friends.

She forgot their past nastiness, and she prayed for them and their families.

It wasn't difficult for Lena to do. She and her former classmates from Martin de Porres did share certain experiences and passages in their lives whether they were speaking to each other at the time or not. They had all been together when the unthinkable happened. As hard as it was for her non-Catholic friends to believe and even more difficult for her Catholic friends to fathom, Lena and her old friends had witnessed their classmate Jessie Mae slap a nun.

Lena was in the eighth grade, one day in late April just before the first procession of the year honoring the Blessed Virgin, when her teacher, Sister Gem of the Sea, went too far. Looking right at Jessie Mae, the sister said, "I want you girls to bring in your white dresses for the procession this week for me to see. Everyone's mother can't be counted on to dress you all like virgins in Mary-like dresses."

Jessie Mae, a big girl for her age—almost as tall as the teacher—had had all the insults she and her family could take. She leapt up in the woman's face and cursed Sister Gem of the Sea out for everything she could think of. In her mother's name, Jessie Mae called the holy woman everything but a child of God.

Then, frustrated by the nun's response of a cold, placid blue-eyed stare, Jessie Mae did the unthinkable.

"You old dried-up heifer," the girl shouted, and slapped the nun full in the face.

The other eighth graders let out a collective gasp.

The solid flat sound of the lick rang out as clearly as the principal's school bell on the top floors of the school building alerting everyone on the second and third levels that something momentous was in progress.

The nun was stunned for only a moment. With the imprint of Jessie Mae's hand on her face as clear as if it were painted there with Mercurochrome, she lost her cold facade. Drawing back her arm past her shoulder, Sister Gem of the Sea brought her opened hand around in a smooth perfect arc and returned the slap. It nearly knocked the big teenager off her feet.

Then it was as if someone had announced, "Come out fighting at the sound of the bell!" Jessie Mae pounced for the nun's stiff white wimpled throat with both hands outstretched. The nun jumped alert, put her hands up and bent her knees slightly in a pugnacious pose. They collided amid a swarm of slaps, punches and clenches.

"Nun fight! Nun fight!" the incredulous students in the room shouted, jumping from their seats and surging forward. Some of them hopped up on desk seats and desk tops—a transgression against the cardinal rule: "Treat everything in this school as if it were your own"—for a better view. It was better than a Saturday afternoon matinee at the Burghart Theatre.

The eighth graders cheered and whooped as the nun and the girl fell to the floor in the front of the classroom and rolled around on the cool tile, scratching and clawing and digging and biting at each other. The students' screams rose to a higher pitch.

And when the two women—for that is what the fight had made of them: equals, both women now—were pulled apart, the nun's veil was on the rough wooden school floor, exposing the woman's closely cropped reddish gray hair, and Jessie Mae was on her way out the school door.

It always made Lena chuckle to think that her best friend in the world was a woman whom she called "Sister." Just calling her name made Lena think of the nuns, the Sisters of the Blessed Sacrament, who had taught her.

Lena sometimes felt like a nun herself. Going around doing good works, not having sex regularly, living alone. The only difference was she didn't live in a stark cell with only a cot and a kneeler in it. Her comfort and clothes were the only things that set her apart from the white women in black who had taught her.

Sister had thought the same thing many times. Lena was like the novices who took on the vows of poverty, chastity and obedience.

"The only vow my girl doesn't adhere to is *poverty!*"

Hell, I might as well be a nun, Lena would say to herself. Then, she'd get a little frightened. Even at her age, she didn't want to tempt

God at all into giving her a vocation to the convent. She had read of women in their later years joining some cloistered order, living in quiet serenity in some mountain convent like St. Theresa.

At eleven, twelve and thirteen, she had knelt in the pews of Blessed Martin de Porres Catholic Church and prayed that she would not be found worthy to be called to the convent. The Sisters of the Blessed Sacrament had told them all that a vocation, a calling to the priesthood or religious order, was so strong, so God-sent, so nerve-rattling, that it could not be ignored or denied.

Then, they pulled out the story of St. Augustine, with Monica, his mother, praying for his conversion night and day. They pointed to Mary Magdalene as another example of God not letting up 'til He got what He wanted.

"The Hound of Heaven will hunt you down until you are His!!!" Sister Louis Marie would boom until Lena wanted to squeeze her developing preteen body under her desk.

The nuns were bound and determined to get somebody from the parish to take on the habit, say the vows, make the commitment, tote one up for their team. But they had yet to make a score. It had gotten to the point that the nuns scolded the girls in eighth grade and higher when they talked of college plans or marriage. "And no one wants to become a bride of Christ? Girls, show a little parish spirit!!" the sisters would say as if they were world-weary mothers saying to their unmarried daughters, "Just show a little ankle!"

But Lena felt a nun was just a woman with more restrictions.

She liked the idea of a sisterhood, of a woman's world. She just didn't like the restraints. And without thinking about the mechanics of her plan, she had, over nearly three decades, done something about it.

Lena's sphere now was a world in which the women still did the majority of the work, but there was a major difference. Unlike the world Lena saw around her when she was growing up—a world in which her grandmother sewed nearly all her clothes as a matter of fact and a matter of love, where Nellie rose early to open her husband's

business because he had been out carousing all night, where nuns ran
the parish school, convent, church and rectory as well as outreach
programs under the direction of the priest—hers was a world in which
the women received credit and payment for their work. Lena saw to
that.

It was what made Cliona from Yamacraw feel perfectly comfortable arriving unannounced at Lena's front door out by the river after
dark like one of her girlfriends.

8

DUTIES

Lena didn't think Cliona from Yamacraw would ever leave. Cliona kept looking at the big pendulum clock on the sideboard that Lena had taken from the dining room mantelpiece in the house on Forest Avenue and saying, "Lord, Lena, let me get on out of here tonight and let you get some rest. An old lady like me don't need much sleep. But you practically still growing. You need your rest." But she didn't budge from her soft leather perch on one of the turquoise love seats by the window overlooking the deck, and the Ocawatchee beyond. The small Listerine bottle of Clear Flow sat self-importantly on the table in front of her.

Lena had made the mistake of offering the old woman a cold Coca-Cola when she first came in.

"I'll take a caffeine-free Coke, if you got one," Cliona had said as she dropped her tweed wrap from her shoulders and got comfortable while Lena headed for the kitchen. "You know caffeine messes with my medication."

Then, Cliona from Yamacraw sat there, and she nursed that Coca-Cola and she nursed that Coca-Cola until Lena thought she would just stand up in her own living room and scream. As she sat there serenely smiling at the older woman, it seemed that a million ideas, projects, errands and duties raced through her mind. God, the whole day in the hospital put me so behind, she thought. Just how am I going to catch up with today's business and be ready to start again tomorrow morning?

There was the closing on two houses that she had missed. She knew the families—both first-time buyers—had been disappointed that she had not been there personally to witness the signing of the papers with them. I'll send them both a nice small fruit tree—maybe peach or pomegranate—to go in their new yards, she thought, making a note to Renfroe on the scratch pad in her head. There was the industrial property she needed to take a look at in the next county before it went to another buyer.

There was a farm in Macon County Lena had heard was just about to be bought out from under some people who knew some people who had relatives who still came into The Place from the country every other Saturday. They had told her about it. So I need to get on down there, she thought, grateful that Precious called her appointments each morning to confirm or cancel.

And now that she thought about it, no one ever told her what "thang" Mr. Pete's son had wanted from her. Maybe, Precious took care of that, Lena thought. Mr. Pete had been such a good friend and poker buddy of her father's that she did not feel right saying no to his son.

She felt the same way about Cliona from Yamacraw. Lena knew the old woman had some kind of reason for being out and about after dark and the last thing she wanted to do was offend an old customer. Even one whom her mother had always referred to as "that crazy woman from Yamacraw."

"Yeah," Cliona was saying when Lena drifted back into the conversation, "me and your mama was real tight. I thought highly of Nellie, and I know she thought the same of me."

"Um," Lena said with a nostalgic little smile. But she thought, If this woman doesn't get out of here soon, *I'm* gon' be the crazy woman from Mulberry.

All Lena wanted to do was strip out of her dusty-feeling, slightly soiled clothes—clothes that had been in a near collision, a mugging of sorts, a stay at the county hospital, and now a visit from Cliona from Yamacraw. She wanted to pull off her hose and underwear and dive naked into her deep blue indoor pool.

Lena loved to walk around her house naked. Raised in a household with two brothers and no sisters, Lena had not known the freedom of being completely nude whenever she felt like it until she had moved into her own house. At the end of a long day, shucking off her fancy duds, walking barefoot and buck naked from the bathroom to the bedroom to pick up a book, from the bedroom to the kitchen to get a donut or piece of fruit or square of buttered egg bread, then back to the great room with pear juice or butter dripping down her chin. Lena thought it felt like heaven. Walking around naked in her own house made her feel as she did after receiving Holy Communion at St. Martin de Porres. That's how she felt: natural and at peace.

And her isolated location in the heavily wooded area by the river gave her the privacy to walk around naked and feel safe and at peace. Maybe once or twice, Frank Petersen or his brother, James, after he had taken Frank Petersen's job, had walked into the house and come upon her nude.

It had never concerned Frank Petersen one way or another.

"Shoot, I practically seen you grow up, Lena-Wena," he had said with a toss of his nappy grizzled head. "Besides, I done seen some of the prettiest women in the world naked. Seen Josephine Baker, 'La Bakir'—that's what we fighting boys used to call her over in Paris, France. Yeah, seen La Bakir wearing nothing but her smile. Not even a bunch o' bananas.

"So, you ain't got nothing to be hiding or trying to cover up or shield from *my* eyes. I done seen it *all* over there in Paris, France, Lena-Wena."

But his brother James had not been to Paris, France, and seen it all. Actually, neither had Frank Petersen. He had only told Lena that when she was a little girl believing everything that came out of his mouth. And he had wanted it so much—to go to France, to drink red wine found in the cellar of a chateau, to serve proudly in World War II in the 135th Artillery—he believed it himself. Frank, the elder brother, liked to think of himself as the kind of man who *would* have gone to France if he had gotten the chance. And from what Lena knew to be true, he had been around in this country.

Frank Petersen played delightful ragtime on the piano. He knew how to set a formal table for a dinner party using all the pieces of the silverware her grandmother, mother and she kept in blue velvet-lined boxes. He had loved a big old fat woman named Bessie Mountain who jilted him and used him and left the county with what money he scraped together for her. He was ashamed of what happened between him and Bessie Mountain but not that he had loved her.

James, on the other hand, didn't move out of the Stamps, Arkansas, house he was born in until he traveled to Mulberry on the Greyhound bus to take over his brother's position with Lena when Frank died. And James was in his fifties then.

He had promised Frank years before when the older man admitted to himself that he was mortal and would wear out that he would come see about Lena if she needed it.

"James," Frank Petersen had written in his final letter to his baby brother, "Lena ain't got nobody."

Frank, an ailing septuagenarian, had told Lena about the letter he had written his brother so she wouldn't be surprised when he showed up with his hat and his bags. Frank Petersen had always been a good brother. James would say, "Frank been good as a daddy to me all my life." So, James didn't hesitate to promise.

James admired his older brother and in some ways tried to emulate him, but Lena walking around naked in the house like it was the most natural thing in the world to do was beyond his tolerance.

"Good God, Lena, go put on some clothes! Suppose you had some chirren running around here. For God's sake!"

James would be really offended for a good while. He'd rush from the room, his eyes averted, walking just heavily enough to let Lena know that he wasn't playing, he was truly annoyed, truly offended by her behavior.

When Lena thought about James, she made herself not think about his brother, Frank.

Frank Petersen—he had admonished the world, "My name is Frank Petersen, and you spell Petersen with an e"—had been such a part of Lena's life so fully and so comfortingly for so long that she had to work at not seeing James as only a reflection of his brother. The brothers were so like each other in looks and mannerisms that it was hard to believe that they had lived such different lives apart from each other.

While Frank Petersen, an old beat-up brown felt hat set at a jaunty tilt on his regal graying head, had been the quintessential bon vivant, his younger brother, James, who refused to wear a cap of any kind, was the quintessential homebody.

James had only shown up in Mulberry seven years before—a blink of an eye in the time continuum of a small town like Mulberry, even a small town that was part of the region that had attracted international and national factories and headquarters recently.

James favored his older brother in stature and grace, but they really didn't look like each other. Frank Petersen had had the rich brown lined skin the color of snuff juice. His brother, James, was lighter brown with softer graying hair.

They both stood about six feet tall. And they held their shoulders erect with an innate grace and elegance. But they were so different.

His brother called him "James" like Lena did. But she noticed that when anyone came through town who knew the family back in Arkansas, they referred to her houseman as "Jame" without the s.

"Lord," one tall, heavy, loud, gatemouth woman from near his little town kept saying as she walked parts of Lena's property, "what *Jame* 'un fallen into here in *this honeypot*!!!!???"

That kind of talk embarrassed James Petersen. He had almost wanted to apologize for his friend. Mostly, he didn't want Lena thinking that he was thinking of her as some kind of "honeypot." He worked for his wages and more. He knew how valuable his labor and presence were in her life. He had viewed it secondhand for years through Frank's job.

But he was quieter, less assuming, than his brother, Frank Petersen.

So, James said the same thing to his visitor as he did to anyone who commented in any way on his job, his home, his paycheck, his reading material, his stature in Lena's household . . . his business, period.

"I'm quite comfortable with my situation."

That's all he said: "I'm quite comfortable with my situation."

James Petersen did seem happy and content living in the gatehouse, which was about a fourth of a mile along the long winding dirt road from Lena's house. She had built it for Frank Petersen. So there were certain unalterable specifications. The small house, made entirely of local stone and mortar, had to be at least four hundred yards from the main house and buildings because Frank Petersen had insisted on his privacy and own space.

"Every time I look up, I don't want to be seeing you and your house, Lena-Wena," he had told her as they sat in the breakfast room of her parents' home at the long shiny table that now sat in her house poring over the plans.

"I understand that, Frank Petersen," Lena had shot back defensively, because she was sort of looking forward to having him for a neighbor. "I'm sho' not moving all the way out there to be up under somebody all the time. I want my privacy and my quiet, too. I certainly plan to respect yours."

She stopped and sniffed as she smoothed out the blueprints.

"I'm not going to be all up in your face, you know. Have I ever gotten in your business before?" she asked a bit indignantly.

She had gone too far. Even Nellie, who was cutting out the pattern for a little striped linen shorts set for one of Sister's twin boys, had to join Frank Petersen when he started laughing.

"Has she ever gotten in my *bizness befo'*????" Frank Petersen had nearly screamed, choking with laughter as he stood up and, taking the papers from the table, went to the bank of windows in the dining room as if for better light.

Nellie was still chuckling to herself as she tried to steady the long sharp tailor's scissors along the dotted line.

When Frank Petersen caught her eye over his blueprints, Nellie couldn't hold it in any longer. And she, too, burst out laughing.

"Baby, you do a lot of things," her mother managed to say through chuckles, "but staying out of people's business is definitely not one of them."

Nellie may have laughed at Lena's comment, but she was deadly serious when she warned her baby girl to ease up on herself. "Lena, baby, you cannot dance on every set," Nellie would tell her over and over as she saw the toll life in Mulberry was taking on her daughter.

Nellie still gloried in Lena's new beautiful house, she still joined her husband in bragging about Lena's business acumen, she still let the women at church go on and on about Lena's accomplishments and sweet temperament, but she also knew that Lena didn't sleep well at night. Nellie knew that Lena did want children. And she knew that Lena was as high-strung as she herself had been as a young woman.

So, Nellie had been happy and grateful for every single person who did something for her child.

James Petersen, who kept her household running so smoothly, made it possible for Lena to lead the kind of life that she did. She and Sister had both finally admitted what they had disdained in white women's intimate conversations with black women: how close they were now or had been as children with their housekeepers. How they *loved* the black woman who had all but raised them. How they still kept in touch with her. How they paid her insurance premiums. How their mothers didn't care about them *half* as much as their maids. How she was the most important person in their lives and how they couldn't have made it without her.

Lena and Sister finally had to admit that they, too, loved their housekeepers. "Oh, but it's different from the white girls who declare and swear that their housekeepers are their best friends," Sister insisted. "It's not like we're saying that or anything."

Lena thought for a bit, rolling her brown eyes slowly as she pondered what her friend had just said.

"Well, actually, Sister, it is just like that. How do you usually start your mornings? Who do you have a second leisurely, friendly cup of coffee with?"

"Oh, but we don't . . ."

"Yes, we do."

"Yeah, but we don't . . ."

"Sister, you just said yourself that you look forward to talking with Mrs. Allen more than your mama."

"Shit, you right. We do sound like them, don't we?"

"Well, for God's sake, girl, don't make it sound so bad."

"*Make it sound bad??!!*" Sister nearly sputtered. "We're talking whitegirlstalking'bouttheirmaidshere."

"No, we not," Lena corrected her. "We talking 'bout blackgirls-talking'bouttheirmaidshere."

And they both had to laugh at themselves, their lives and their sister girls.

"Well, I don't care really how it sounds. I loved Frank Petersen all the years he was with us. And now I love James Petersen. I mean, Sister, he makes my life wonderful. He makes sure I have clean drawers and nightgowns and jeans without thinking about it. I come home from work for a break in the evening and go out to cut some fresh flowers for the dining room table and sit down and eat a homemade meal with fresh vegetables from some old lady's garden and herbs from mine.

"And James Petersen makes that all possible. Shoot, Sister, you said the same thing when you had some help right after the twins were born. How you didn't know how you were going to part with Mrs. Thompson. Was that her name?"

Sister smiled wistfully just thinking of the efficient woman who made her able to be a mother to her two youngest—twin boys—when she was too tired to lift either of them to her breast.

"Yeah, Mrs. Thompson did save my life," Sister said with fondness. Then, as if answering Lena's question, she added, "I don't know *where* that old woman is now. Things just got busy after I didn't need her anymore, and she drifted away. Or I guess we did."

They were both quiet for a while. Lena tried not to make her silence chiding. But her silence, like everything about Lena, was too strong. Sister heard just what she was thinking and was hurt.

"Well, dammit, Lena," Sister said, trying to hide her defensiveness, "everybody ain't like you."

It was true. Lena kept up with everybody. "Well, you never know how long you gonna have somebody," she would say as she urged a patron to go on and call his great-aunt in Alabama, his only living relative, before she passed away or got too old to know who he was.

She never had to press too hard with anyone to take her advice; too many had seen their friends stretched across the bar at The Place mourning without relief after ignoring one of Lena's warnings that "You know, time is short."

She had sat by Frank Petersen's bed, too, when he died. She had wanted to move him up to her house so he wouldn't be alone. He had dismissed so many people from the Round the Clock Health Services, Lena had to apologize and move on to another service.

No one could do anything to suit him, but Frank Petersen wasn't interested in relocating.

"So, now you gonna try to move me out of my own house?" he asked weakly from his big easy chair set up by the window overlooking the river and a field where the horses romped. Lena was immediately sorry she had suggested it.

"I'm not trying to move you out, Frank Petersen," Lena said as she tried to put another blanket around his legs, resting her hands briefly but firmly on his bony knees. She touched him as often as she could without him starting to notice. Each time her hand made contact with his skin, his hair, his nails, his frame, she tried as hard as she could to put the magic on him and cure his illness. It wasn't easy. Frank Petersen didn't encourage much touching. Never had. It was a habit he had fostered when he first started working at the McPherson house on Forest Avenue when Lena was seven.

He didn't want any misunderstandings with the family and especially with Lena about touching. No matter how much Lena loved Frank Petersen and how much he doted on her, he didn't want any misunderstandings.

So, even when he was old, sick and dying, Lena knew she had to be careful that the times she pressed her hands to his skin, his hair, his nails, his frame, that the touch felt casual, familial. The way it always had.

"I just thought you'd like some more company. That's all," Lena continued, trying to speak breezily.

"Company?" Frank said derisively. "What company? You ain't never home as it is."

"Well, I plan to start doing more of my work right around here," she said, picking up things around the room and putting them down. She had never been nervous around Frank Petersen a day in her life. Not even when he showed up the first evening at her parents' house in Pleasant Hill with a case of Coca-Colas from The Place and began washing the dinner dishes because her mother needed some help.

Frank Petersen had stayed on working four or five days a week for a bit more than thirty years to take care of the house on Forest Avenue, washing dishes, taking down drapes for cleaning, changing bed linen and mopping floors for the McPhersons until Lena built her own house.

In Lena's mind, there was nothing odd about a man taking care of her household. Other than her mother and grandmother, that's all she had ever known.

There was something about one woman taking care of another woman's household, her duties, the washing of her drawers, that stood in the way of Lena being able to live freely. She couldn't say why she wasn't a bit disturbed by the idea of Frank Petersen washing and hanging and folding her intimate apparel and cleaning up after her and her family all those years or of James, for all practical purposes a stranger to Lena when he came, picking up his brother's duties as if he had been doing them all his life.

Frank Petersen had made sure before she noticed the deterioration in his health that she would be the executrix of his estate, such as it was. He had just wanted her to know his life.

When Frank Petersen's health began to fail seriously, she had tried to hire one of the women she had known for years down at The Place to take over his duties. But the business relationship, begun in friendship and cordiality, always ended in hurt feelings and animosity. Lena just wanted her house cleaned, her windows scrubbed, her bathroom smelling like eucalyptus oil, the fruit and vegetable drawer in her refrigerator clean enough to eat out of because late at night when she came home tired and weary, she sometimes did. And she was happy to pay more than most schoolteachers made. But try as she did, over and over, she couldn't find a black female housekeeper who gave *her* any respect in her own house. She tried to hire customers from The Place. It didn't work. She tried to hire daughters and cousins and nieces and daughters-in-law of her patrons and friends. It didn't work. She even tried to hire anonymous women from employment services. And that didn't work either.

They left trash, big actual chunks of trash—bottle caps and the dead leaves of plants and dust bunnies—in the corners of her house.

They cleaned the bathroom and left fingerprints on the mirror and globs of toothpaste dried to the sink basin and hair in the tub. They let mildew grow in the grout of her steam room even after she impressed upon them how special the room was to her. The final straw was a short dark woman, the niece of a trusted customer, who left a sopping-wet cleaning rag draped across the keys of her computer, the computer that held every bit of business she conducted.

The wet towel on her computer was like a sharp pair of scissors left in a child's crib. Lena couldn't even bear to think about it and its implications.

Even black women who loved Lena couldn't bring themselves to clean her house. Even the cleaning crew who kept her offices spotless swore they just didn't know how to clean her house.

"Lord have mercy," Sister said from her spotless home in a suburb east of New Orleans. "Grown black women claiming they don't know how to clean a house. Shit, you could get Diahann Carroll to come in there with her heels and diamonds and flawless complexion and perfectly coiffed hair and she'd know enough not to sweep dirt in corners."

It was Frank Petersen who finally called an end to the foolishness. Lena didn't know when he did it or where he got the strength to pick up the phone and call his brother, but he did. He called James Petersen and said, "Brother, it's time you came this way."

James packed up his few clothes, his favorite books and a couple of unopened jigsaw puzzles in his cousin's large suitcase and a dusty old steamer trunk he found back in a closet and left Arkansas that very day.

The sucking sound Cliona from Yamacraw was making with her drink brought Lena back to her big sitting room.

Finally, Cliona drained her glass and rattled the ice cubes a bit. Lena stopped herself just in time from saying, "Can I get you another, Miss Cliona?" There seemed nothing left for Cliona from Yamacraw to do but finally complete her mission.

"Now, I heard 'bout your little accident," the old woman said.

Lena thought, Good God, if this ain't the smallest town when it comes to news. I don't know why we bother with radio and TV.

"Oh, Miss Cliona, I'm okay. I didn't have any accident."

"Yeah?" Cliona replied. "That ain't what I heard. I heard you took a pretty bad lick to the head."

"Oh, that was Mr. Jackson's talk, you know the contractor doing the work down at The Place," Lena said easily. "I just tripped and fell. He was just being overly cautious."

"Um-huh," Cliona said suspiciously. Then she caught herself and said, "Oh, Lena, baby, I didn't mean no harm." And she smiled, her false teeth—teeth Lena had paid for—big in her mouth. The last thing she wanted to do was call Lena, whom she had always thought of as her special little girl, a liar. Lena leaned forward a little toward the old woman and smiled back. So Cliona from Yamacraw just kept going.

"Well, I brought you some of this fresh Cleer Flo' water. Collected it late last night right when it started. Powerful. Now, you take this water and . . ."

Cliona stopped and, covering her mouth with her wrinkled hand, began to laugh.

"Listen to me," the old woman chuckled. " 'Bout to go and tell you, a child born with a veil over her face, what to do with this Cleer Flo'."

Lena just smiled politely.

"Thank you, Miss Cliona," Lena said as she stood, took the bottle from the woman and reached down to hug her neck. Cliona from Yamacraw smelled faintly of the sweet scent of Dixie peach snuff.

The scent made Lena even more gentle in helping Cliona from Yamacraw on with her coat and ushering her out the door to the late-model van where a young cousin of the old woman's waited with the motor running and the radio blasting. He turned the radio down and reached over to open the car door for his elderly cousin.

It was only after Lena had settled Cliona from Yamacraw in the front passenger's seat that she remembered why people said Cliona was a hard person to take leave of.

"Okay, now, Lena, baby, bye, now, sugar. See you later, sugar pie. Bye, now, baby. See you later, Lena, baby. Ha! See you later, tell you straighter, you know that one, Lena? Huh, Lena? Baby, you know that one? Well, I guess we going now, see you later, now, Lena, baby, sugar dumpling pie. Bye, baby. Bye, Lena. Bye, sugar. Bye, baby. Bye, Lena. Bye."

Lena could hear her all the way down the road throwing adieus out the window as they drove off. She stood under the two-hundred-year-old pecan trees by the side of the driveway and chuckled at the good-byes in the night. Then she wearily headed for her house.

9

RITES

I'm gonna have to get something nice for Miss Cliona, Lena thought as she locked up the back door and began unbuttoning the tiny pearl buttons down the back of her creamy sweater. The gesture of putting her hands down her back reminded her of the little incident in her car that morning, but she just closed her eyes briefly and shook her braids around her neck to clear her head of the memory and the questions. The tips of her braids slipped down her sweater and brushed across the tender spot on her back and sent a shiver down her spine.

"Oh, quit!" she said in exasperation as she headed back down what she called "the Glass Hall." Practically everything in Lena's house had a name. Lena pretended she had forgotten all about the ghosts and such in her early life, but she had created reminders all over her house.

When folks teased her about the practice, Lena just laughed her rich throaty chuckle and said, "I name it and I claim it." And she'd throw her head over her left shoulder the way her father did and laugh again.

That attitude was the reason she named the portentous overbearing overwhelming main room in her house "the Great Jonah Room" after her father. The sewing room was Grandmama's. The big sunny kitchen was Nellie's. Sometimes, she could hardly bear to go in there and warm up her food, it recalled such poignant memories of her mother. Her swimming pool was Rachel's Waters. The stable and other outdoor buildings were named for her wild brothers, Raymond and Edward, because they had as boys loved so to rip and run and explore outside. And although he had died a teetotaler the year before she was born, Lena named the wine cellar after Granddaddy Walter.

All named for dead people and ghosts. Her family and loved ones were only alive in names of rooms and swimming pools and barns on her property.

She came back into the Great Jonah Room and went right to where she and Cliona had sat. Lena agreed with her mother's assessment of Cliona from Yamacraw's general sanity. But she picked up the bottle of river water in the Listerine mouthwash bottle, opened the black plastic cap and poured a few drops into the cup of her hand. Then, she held her head back, dipping her braids to the middle of her back, and splashed the cool clear water on her forehead like a rite of baptism.

Her head had stopped hurting, but talking with Mr. Jackson *and* Cliona from Yamacraw for the previous three hours had blown her pleasant woozy high from the shot in the hospital. Lena found her purse on the floor by the sofa and, with some ginger ale she poured over ice at the rolltop desk she used as a bar, took two of the yellow and orange capsules the young doctor at the hospital had given her in case she had any pain or trouble sleeping.

As she continued undressing, she sighed heavily, happy to be home. She kicked off her mules under the low table sculptured from a huge slab of live oak tree trunk in front of one of the aqua leather sofas. Her feet still ached a bit even out of her high-heeled shoes. Some nights, when she took her shoes off, she felt like Pearl Bailey and wanted to exclaim, "Lord, these mules of mine are killing me! My feet! My feet!"

Dropping her sweater on the back of a high-back cane rocker, she walked to the oversized French doors overlooking the deck, her yard beyond and the river beyond that and threw them open. Many nights she slept with the alarm system off so she could leave the French doors on that side of the house open and feel the night air and the breeze from the river.

The railings around the edges of the sprawling winding cypress deck that wrapped around the house and a huge nearby oak tree were a mass of tiny white flowers and dark shiny cupped leaves that exuded a heavy exotically sweet smell all the way over to where Lena stood inside the door. The scent of the jasmine drew her to the door and outside.

She was surprised at the changes out there. It seemed that in the week since Sister had come through on her way to a year's sabbatical in Sierra Leone and they had been out on the deck, vines and trees and plants on her property had exploded with color, scent and life. Azalea bushes that were mere shrubbery the week before were now mountains of white and pink and red blossoms. The weeping willows and weeping mulberry trees had been mere reeds blowing in the March wind. Now they were all—fifteen of them along the river-banks—shimmering with the verdant haze of new growth.

Among the willows and mulberry and the azaleas and tangles of wisteria, a powwow of lightning bugs seemed to be assembling. Lena didn't know when she had seen so many among her woods.

"It's so early in the year, not even early summer, for them to be around," she said as she stood there watching the fairy show the insects were putting on in the woods.

She had to chuckle as her gaze landed on the remnants of the ceremony she and Sister had performed out on the deck—"It's best if it takes place outside," Sister had said—in the light of the new moon.

"Lena, you *are* a little foolish fool," she said to herself gently.

It had been a ceremony to summon up a man for Lena, a wonderful man, a sexy man, a wise man, a generous-spirited man, a smart man, a funny man, a loyal man, *her* man.

All week, she had felt a little silly telling James Petersen not to disturb the site, but Sister had warned her not to move any of the elements of the ceremony ("Even if it rains") or the rites would be void or the results turned inside out. James had silently shook his head, chuckled and said, "Okay."

The half-burned candles; the silver and black snakeskin that was a twenty-five-year-old gift from her brother Edward, who was obsessed with reptiles; the vial of salt; the pictures of saints; the water from Florida. All the elements were still there.

They had both been a bit tipsy from the home brew Sister had smuggled in from her last trip to Guadeloupe. "Girl, as long as I have a piece of your hair or one of your fingernail clippings and your picture with me in the bag," she would tell Lena all the time after some trip in which she had safely and easily brought back contraband, "I can get anything I want through any customs in the world. They just wave me on through."

She had warned Lena, "This stuff is strong, yeah. This stuff don't play," when she set the tall recycled rum bottle on the deep long picnic table that had once sat in Lena's family's breakfast room. But they poured themselves a couple of fingers of the smooth strong brew into two crystal goblets. And while they stood and sampled from the pots of delicious food on the stove, they kept sipping.

"Shoot, Lena, I remember the kind of stuff you used to do down home at school and the dreams and night visions you told me about before we went to see Aunt Delphie in Vieux Carré," Sister had said as she drew bottles rolled in brown paper with red twine twisted around them from a croaker sack in her carry-on bag she had placed on the breakfast room table. Then she brought out different-colored candles—white for peace, pink for love, red for winning. "And I know the rituals and stuff. So I don't see any reason why the two of us together can't call up just about anything we want."

Thinking back on that strange night, Lena muttered to herself,

"And we were just high and tipsy and silly enough to think we could do it, too."

They had even smoked a couple of joints Sister had been reckless enough to bring back from Jamaica or some island the month before.

As they moved around Lena's house and deck, giggling and bumping into each other and giggling some more, Lena heard Sister muttering and chanting all kinds of things in preparation for the ritual.

"Shoot," Sister said under her breath, "I just can't go out the country and leave my girl with nobody to watch over and protect her. Lord, I hope this does some good. Oshun, Our Mother, help us."

Even as tipsy as they both were, Lena knew that the ritual she recalled hadn't been completely authentic, couldn't have been. Halfway through the ceremony, Sister admitted she had forgotten the exact words to say and could not read her own writing, so she winged it. Lena remembered seeing her hesitate over whether to light the pink candle or the white candle first.

Then, she sucked her teeth and pulled a crystal vial from her bag. She uncorked the top and stuck her index finger in.

"Stick out your tongue," Sister had instructed Lena, and placed a dab of salt on the tip. She dipped the same finger in the small crystal box and placed a dot of the salt on her own tongue and swallowed.

"That's so we speak the truth in what we ask for and in what we truly want," she explained as she recorked the vial and placed it on the altar they had constructed there on the deck.

"You know, Lena, you need some more lights leading to your altars outside. With all these trees growing like something in a myth, it seems to be getting darker and darker out here."

Then Sister struck a big wooden kitchen match from the matchbox Lena handed her and lit another pink candle.

"I don't know why we never did this before," Lena said as she walked around the large guest room on the west side of her house where Sister was staying. The furniture in the room was Nellie's original angular blond guest-bedroom furniture that was all the vogue in the fifties. It had been in the attic on Forest Avenue for two decades when Nellie had given it to Lena for her guest room. And now it was back in style.

Sister had just chuckled when she saw Lena's room in its original state. "Miss Nellie was nothing if not current." She remembered the stylish woman she had first seen standing on the railroad station platform in Mulberry at Easter break her freshman year at Xavier. Lena's mother had looked fresh from the streets of New York or Paris in her cool, stylish, sleeveless seersucker dress in green and white puckered stripes and her high-heeled leather mules and a straw bag. Sister had always wanted a mother like Nellie. Her own mother, a stolid Louisiana bayou woman with all kinds of people in her background, was more a country woman, good, loving, true. But not a modern, slim, beautiful woman who was comfortable on the streets of the city. Sister's mother didn't even like to come to New Orleans, practically a stone's throw across the river from her country home, because its pace was too fast, its sights too varied.

Even now, with Nellie dead and her own mother still living three doors down from her to be a doting, comfortable grandmother to her own three boys, Sister felt a twinge of guilt over her secret wish to have a mother like Lena's.

But then, Sister had a number of secret wishes.

"Shoot, Lena, even though I *really want* to call you up a man, I have to keep myself from being so jealous of my students and single folks and you sometimes when I think you can go out and date . . ."

"Date?" Lena asked slyly.

"Or whatever it is you young single people call it now," Sister answered with a smile. "Whoever you want. It's not that I want anyone else. Douglas is a good man and God knows we've been through things together, weathered so much. But sometimes I would gladly give over my eldest child just to be able to smell another man.

"Sometimes I catch a ride with one of my single students just so I can sit in his car a few minutes and smell his smell, a new one, a different one, one that I don't know inside and out. Shoot, I can tell you right now what Douglas smell like at any given time. Ask me!!"

"Well," Lena said, "I *have* smelled my share and I guess yours, too, and knowing, being able to recall one man's scent sounds pretty good to me."

Lena had dated *and smelled* her share of men. But it never went anywhere. For her, it was difficult getting past the first-time attempt at lovemaking.

As long as the relationship remained this side of intimacy, everything was fine. Lena would sense a stray thought sometimes or an embarrassing moment, but rarely would she feel some man's ugly secret until they were nearly in the throes of passion. It was only when they touched each other intimately or kissed deeply that the man's thoughts and past came seeping out for Lena to hear and see right there as he inched his hand up the darker skin of her inner thigh. She would steel her hand right on the buckle of his pants or the flap of his zipper, trying to forge on, to concentrate on the act.

It got to the point that before each date or setup Lena had she would first pray, "Dear Lord, don't let me see so early." But it was always the same. She would see early enough to stop herself from being able to have a fulfilling sexual encounter.

She had grabbed up her clothes and purse and shoes so many times and rushed for the nearest exit while her date lay on the sofa or the floor or the bed of his place and wonder what the hell just happened. The same scene had happened so often in her twenties and even into her thirties that she had just finally given up on getting past some kissing and fondling and stroking. It was finally too frustrating for her.

When a man told her, "Well, Lena, I don't know what I did wrong, but give me another chance," she wanted to yell at him, "Go! You got diamonds in your back. You look better going than coming to me!" the way Frank Petersen had said under his breath when Lena's grandmama had flounced out of the house on Forest Avenue when Lena was little because Grandmama claimed she could smell "that stinking wino's nasty cigarette smoke."

Even Frank Petersen finally had stopped making fun of Lena's gentlemen callers because he came to fear that he was somehow impeding her progress as wife and mother.

"Good God from Gulfport, Lena, that Negro sho' got a big head. If his head was a hog's head, I'd work a whole year for it!" Frank Petersen would say as he came into the house after passing one of Lena's friends on the way out. But a few years before he died, he started keeping his opinions and critiques to himself. Then he progressed to, "Well, Lena, that one wasn't so bad, was he?"

If Frank Petersen hadn't died of liver failure when he did, Lena was sure he would have eventually started placing ads in the personals for her:

"Rich, good-looking, healthy woman looking for a man!"

If Sister's ceremony to conjure her up a man worked, she wouldn't need an ad.

"When was the last time we did this?" Sister asked as she proudly unwrapped a dried two-prong root and propped it up against the red plaid cloth it had come in.

"Not since college," Lena answered. And then spying the root. "Ooo, Adam and Eve root?"

"Uh-huh," Sister said casually. "I even got an Adam and Eve *and* the Children root at home. But I figured we'd just work on you and him for now."

"You sound so sure of yourself, Sister," Lena said.

"Well, girlfriend, I feel that way. I brought all this medicine with me, and I haven't talked to you about anything like this having to do with you in twenty years. And here you are agreeing to do the ceremony. It feels right.

"All you need is to just have your cat scratched," her friend continued. She said it matter-of-factly, not as a joke or anything lighthearted, just as one solution to the problem. Lena noted it was the solution of a woman who had been married to the same virile man for twenty-something years.

But Lena took her friend's comment seriously anyway.

She watched Sister continue to take items out of her croaker sack.

They were things that Sister had from a ceremony she had attended at the International Yoruba Festival the year before in Cuba. Sister was so pleased she had had the presence of mind while there to go to some highly recommended botanicals to purchase herbs and roots and seeds for ritual and for planting. It felt good helping Lena. Sister knew how many folks Lena helped, herself included.

On Lena's land, the gardener had planted a number of herbs—skullcap and tilo and valerian. Other than the mild teas Lena sometimes prepared for her older friends who had problems with their nerves or slices of valerian root she dried for them to place in their pillows, she used most of the plants in flower arrangements.

"Umm," Sister had said, picking up her ancient-looking canvas bag and searching through it again. "I thought I had a picture of Mary Magdalene in here. She'd help us with the love thing. You do want love, too, don't you?" Sister asked Lena as if she were her hairdresser asking if she wanted her ends clipped with that shampoo.

Lena had chuckled a little grunt and said, "Sure."

"Yeah," Sister agreed, going back to her bag one more time to look for the saint's picture, "that's what you really need, yeah?"

"Uh-huh," Lena said vaguely. She was trying to remember where she had recently seen a picture of Mary Magdalene in her house. But after the rum and a couple of tokes on the joint Sister had rolled, Lena was having difficulty recalling anything.

"Bring a Bible while you in there, Lena," Sister had called.

"Okay. You need any more candles?" Lena had replied.

"Nope, we got enough," Sister had called back.

Lena walked unsteadily back inside to the wall of recessed bookcases in the great room and pulled down a volume, then she paused a moment at the rows of candles—votive, tapers, tall fat scented ones—she kept on the table and sideboard and in the rolltop desk and all around her house that she was always too tired to light at night.

Seeing the candles again now as she walked back into the house through the white French doors of the pool room and continued undressing, she wondered what she could have been thinking, lighting candles and praying out on the deck with Sister.

She and Sister *had* completed the ceremony that night a week before, but much of the rest of the evening was a blur.

"Calling me up a man, indeed!" she said aloud, and sucked her teeth.

Her temples still throbbed, and she knew a swim would help to clear her head.

Wiggling out of her short champagne silk slip and tap panties and popping open her satin bra, she headed for the deep end of the pool. She had left the doors to the deck open and was surprised that the scent of the jasmine permeated all the way to the far wall, where it even overwhelmed the fresh clean smell of eucalyptus oil coming from the cedar-lined sauna. Dropping the underwear on a long white and blue linen chaise longue, Lena stood naked in her beautiful sprawling house next to Rachel's Waters and listened to the silence of her life.

10

MAGIC

ena didn't like for it to be too quiet out at her house. When it got too quiet, especially in the pool room, she heard things.

Quite often, while she was swimming, what she heard were voices. If she didn't have her music blaring all over the house as she swam her laps alone late at night or very early in the morning, she often could hear the muted sounds of conversation. Most times she could just make out the sounds and the rhythms of dialogue, but not the exact words. Sometimes she could hear what sounded like crowds of people conversing, shouting, arguing, murmuring. Other times she could distinguish only two voices speaking, clearly conversing with one another. Sometimes there was even laughter.

The sounds unnerved her yet helped her fight loneliness in the big house by herself.

She preferred swimming at night, with all the aqua lights in the pool extinguished and the water temperature on the cool side. Then, with the glass ceiling overhead and the tall cathedral windows looking out on the forest and river, Lena felt as if she were truly swimming outside under the stars, but in comfort and safety.

Lena did not think that much about her personal safety. She did not seem to have to. She tried not to do anything truly foolish like make her own night deposits or carry a lot of cash or credit cards around with her or carry a gun the way her father had. And she let it be known that she didn't.

Folks would just suck their teeth at her in real frustration when she didn't *ever have* more than three or four dollars in her fine leather purse to purchase a case of Girl Scout cookies from somebody's cute little industrious granddaughter who had set up her sales operation at a busy bus stop at the end of the day.

"Got all the money in the world and ain't even got twenty dollars in her pocketbook!" even children would say under their breath. "Grandmama say she ought to have enough money on her to choke a horse!"

They would whisper. But Lena could always hear them. And she just laughed.

She usually didn't need any money inside the Mulberry city limits. Lena had *accounts* all over town, just like her daddy. She had heard him use his accounts all her life.

"Yeah, man, put that on my account."

"Just put that aside for me. I'll pay for it later."

"Woman, I ain't got no money on me. Just put it on my account."

If anyone demurred, Lena remembered, her father would reply, really puzzled, astonished.

"Well, then open me up one. Open me up an account! God knows I'm good for it."

Jonah prided himself on having accounts with everybody: merchants, friends, customers, clients, poker buddies, debtors. Long after the time when any business establishment other than a bar would let customers keep a running tab, Jonah had them running all over town.

He enjoyed the idea that his word was worth money all on its own. Lena had inherited the practice from her father the same way she had inherited The Place, not only by legal means but also by proclamation.

"Who else they gon' leave The Place to except Lena?" Gloria had told the staff there. One or two of them tried to pull the loyal manager into gossip about Lena and her holdings.

"Shoot, she ain't just the only surviving heir. She the best businesswoman or businessman in this town. I know lots a' folks who wish they *could leave* their family businesses in Lena McPherson's hands," Gloria said, ending the loose talk. "Shit, she the hand *all us* fan with! She deserve everything she got!"

And Lena did have a lot.

At the end of each day, when James Petersen finished his house-keeping duties at Lena's house and headed down the road to his own, he went through his checklist before leaving.

1. Outside lights on
2. Bedroom, kitchen lights on
3. Jacuzzi temperature set at 108F
4. Pool temperature set at 70F
5. Food in refrigerator, microwavable dishes on counter
6. Music playing
7. Alarm system charged and on

So everything was all set for Lena when she had walked in.

She hardly got *any* exercise anymore. She just didn't have time anymore for the things she loved to do. She rarely had time to put on her tight brown riding pants with the suede inseam and her shiny chocolate riding boots and head off on Baby or Goldie through the bridle paths that wove over her property. She stopped once in a while on her way in or out to give Mr. Renfroe or one of his assistants a hand in the garden. Then, she would look at her watch and have to move on.

Swimming twenty laps every other night or so was the only physical activity she clung to in the midst of her buying and selling and renting and investing and making money and doing for others.

Some nights when she couldn't sleep, she'd get up, feeling alone and lonely, and swim until she was worn out, then try again to go to sleep. She was a good strong swimmer. She had learned at college. Pulling her thick long bushy hair back in a fat, barely controlled ponytail for an entire school year, she had become one of the strongest swimmers in her P.E. class. She had wanted to learn to swim ever since seeing Rachel, the kindly ghost of a slave on the Georgia beach who had chosen drowning over bondage. She prayed for the repose of Rachel's soul along with her parents' and brothers' every night. But Lena did not think of Rachel's act as a damning one of despair. Rather one of belief.

As a girl, Lena could not learn to swim at home. The idea of Lena getting her thick, nappy, barely controllable hair wet every day of the summer at the public pool for black folks had been beyond the comprehension of her family and the endurance of her mother, who had the actual combing job. So Lena just bided her time and waited until she was away from Nellie and home. She had learned to swim, named her pool in honor of Rachel, and some nights, felt it had been *her* salvation.

This night she dove into the water at the deep end of the Olympic-sized pool without making a splash. Splitting the dark water with her scythe of a body felt almost as good as the cool river water of Cleer Flo' she had just splashed on her forehead. But as soon as she cut through the surface, she let out a cry that sent a stream of bubbles floating to the surface from her mouth. She dove into the pool expecting the usual brisk cool water but instead the water was warm, soothing, not steamy, but hotter than body temperature. The warm water was a surprise, but a pleasant one: comforting and inviting like the waters of a womb. Lena barely kept the pool heated. She liked the stimulation of swimming in the cool water, then stepping over into the heated bubbling waters of the Jacuzzi.

It took a while for Lena to collect her wits about her in the unusually warm water.

"I can't believe James Petersen didn't check the water before he left," Lena said out loud to the empty room. "I guess the thermostat is broken. Come to think of it, he didn't leave any music playing, either."

She could hear the faint cooing of the mourning doves that often roosted in the eaves of the glass roof. It called attention to the room's silence. She swam along the edge of the pool until she came to a small table jutting out over the water. There were two lounge chairs set up nearby. One thick fluffy white terry towel was thrown over the back of one chair and another towel was folded at the end of the table. A blue-and-white-striped terry-cloth robe was draped across the arm of the other chair.

Lena dried her hands and picked up the remote control on the table extending over the pool. In the lonely tired state she was in, she knew what she wanted to hear. She didn't hesitate but pressed the remote control for the compact disc turntable in the wall of the pool room and then hit the advance button.

Carla Thomas began singing she was so lonesome she could cry. And Lena sang along with her. But then Carla moved on to sing about a diamond ring, and Lena lost interest. Marriage was not her desire, love was.

Lena swam twenty-five laps in the warm water, then floated on the surface of the water, looking up at the moon and stars through the glass ceiling.

Um, she thought, looking at the clear view she had of the stars in the heavens, I need to buy me a telescope.

The exercise had worked her body and left her feeling good and tired. She always tried to find time for her swim, but even with her own pool in her own house, she often couldn't fit it into her hectic schedule. Lena so often felt that putting her foot out of bed in the morning was the first and last conscious decision she made every day. After that act, caught up in her duties, she felt as if she were being carried like a leaf on the surface of the rushing Ocawatchee River.

Sighing, she lay back against the side of the pool and listened to the music.

After a while, Lena began to sing in sync with Dinah Washington:

*"And if it's not asking too much
Please, send me someone to love."*

"God, I wish I *had* somebody," she said out loud to the empty pool room. Her words, spoken softly, echoed in the cavernous room.

It was only lately that she had begun to believe that she had made a major mistake by not gritting her teeth, ignoring the pictures in her mind and getting pregnant by one of the best of the lot of men she had been attracted to over the years. She didn't know where the years had gone.

How could she be forty-five, she thought, and not have accumulated more in the way of family—real family—blood family? No mother, no father, no brothers, no sisters, no babies. Lena was so tired of loneliness.

She felt like a statistic, Category: African American woman, fortyish without a man, a child or hope. She knew that somewhere there was a printed form that offered that choice with a neat box next to it to check off.

She was so deeply lonely, she thought again, this time more than a prayer, more than a plaint, it was a surrender.

"God, I wish I *had* somebody," she said again.

Suddenly, she felt something brush against her thigh. It felt like a large fish swimming around her legs.

She had never truly *felt* anything like this in her pool before.

Lena had all kinds of inflatable animals and toys floating in her pool for company that brushed up against her all the time as she swam. Some were the size of a bed pillow. Others were almost as big as she. She was used to the feel of plastic or vinyl things touching her thighs as she cut through the water or as she floated on the usually cool surface.

She had, in fact, sensed another presence in the pool with her on a number of occasions. It had not happened often, but she remembered each instance as if it were a family reunion. A few times she was sure her grandmother was swimming past her in the cool water, brushing past her favorite granddaughter, leaving her spirit in the wake she made. At those few times, Lena was overwhelmed by the sense of peace she felt throughout the water.

Then, one time, she just knew that it was her father Jonah, an excellent swimmer, who was swimming in the waters of her pool with her. She never sensed her mother or brothers as she swam there. Nellie had always feared water. She never went wading in any pool or ocean or river or stream. When Lena as a child fell into the creek behind their house, her mother had screamed of having to "rescue my child" from the tiny rivulets of the gentle stream. She raged if anyone turned the hose on her.

"You little foolish fools," she'd scream in her special "I'm completely sick of you children" voice as she covered her head and ran for cover.

Lena didn't think the spirits of her brothers—strong swimmers, too—had ever shown up in the waters of her pool. She figured their ghosts would probably be swimming around at their favorite swimming hole, Pate's Rock, in the woods behind her childhood home.

So, this time, she stopped, took a breath and controlled her urge to jump out of the pool in one leap. But she swam rapidly over to the light controls at the edge of the pool and turned on the switch that flooded the aqua bottom of the pool with light.

Lena looked around her nude body in the blue water searching for what she had felt brushing against her legs. But all she saw were some familiar toys floating on the surface. And the spot that had been touched on her body was still tingling.

"Good God," Lena said aloud. This encounter in the pool, she knew instinctively, was different. This thing that had brushed against her leg had the feel of life, of skin, almost of blood coursing through veins. Almost.

She felt for a moment as she had as a child when she had "put the magic" on something. It was a family joke that was taken seriously. Her mother, her father, her brothers, her grandmother had all seen it with their own eyes. Lena had been able to "put the magic" on things.

She could fix a broken milk shake blender or get the family car to start in the morning when Nellie would be rushing to drop her children off at school before heading downtown to open up The Place or even take the lines out of the television screen when the family was trying to get a channel from Atlanta. She could do it just by touching the thing.

Lena felt as if she had just put the magic on something in the warm water enveloping her in the pool. Had charged something. Had fixed something. Had invited something. Had healed something. And as she treaded water naked beside the bank of lighting and security controls, she wondered what that something was.

She was trying to decide whether or not to convince herself it was nothing when she felt the touch again, this time down the front of her body and between her legs.

For a second, she thought she saw a quick flash of light like a spark on one of the flat Ocawatchee River rocks embedded around the sides of her pool. Then she felt it again, this soft seductive swirl around her legs like a waterspout, and she was reminded of the wind on her neck.

This sensation was a great deal more insistent than the breeze that had been teasing her all week. It was a lot more determined than even the breeze down her back that morning on the highway. This thing in the pool with her was not playing! She felt herself pressed to the side of the pool with *something* beginning to separate the folds of her vagina.

"Stop!! Stop!!" Lena heard herself saying, flailing her arms in the warm water. "Just what the hell is going on? No! Stop!"

This time she *did* jump out of the pool, her heart beating fast. And just as suddenly, the feeling was gone, leaving her chilly, breathless, excited and naked by the side of her heated pool.

11

SMOKE

The last time Lena had had such a vivid experience with visions and spirits and feelings and voices, she was still in college.

For Lena, college was to be liberation. By the time she was a senior in high school, she just knew that all her daily terrors—the sleepwalking, the childhood memories of ghosts, her skewered premonitions, the hatred the girls at school still harbored toward her, the fear that just about anybody could be a ghost—were connected with the town of Mulberry and her close familiar home and community.

Her Grandmama's ghost had told Lena to find out something about herself and the caul and her powers before it was too late.

But she hadn't.

She procrastinated and vacillated and waited to get in touch with Nurse Bloom, who had witnessed her birth and knew all about what she called "special little baby girls born with a caul." She kept right on avoiding any contact with St. Luke's Hospital and the possibility of running into the old nurse right through her teens.

She had never felt so torn. She kept putting off and putting off going to the old nurse the way her grandmother's ghost had instructed her in order to gain some bit of insight into her specialness. It frightened her more than the visions she saw, more than the voices she heard, to even think about discovering more about herself.

And by the time she got up the nerve, when she was seventeen, to go seek out the old nurse and midwife who had assisted at her birth and tried to protect her, it was too late. Nurse Bloom, suffering from early senility, just smiled when Lena came into her room. The old woman did not even know who she was.

If I can just get away from this town, she had thought over and over, as she set the table in the dining room for herself and her parents, as she sat in Mother Josepha's homeroom class at Martin de Porres, as she talked on the phone with her one remaining true loyal friend, Gwen.

Lena figured her best route of exit was going away to college. Early in her senior year in high school after she had accepted the fact that Nurse Bloom couldn't help her, she sent for brochures for Howard University in Washington, D.C. The brochures had pictures of intelligent-looking, happy black students dressed in plaid Villager skirts and chinos walking the campus with armloads of books and pads. She brought home pamphlets for large universities in western states like California and New Mexico filled with pictures of white students and an occasional Spanish-looking person that her parents hardly scanned. Lena even sent away for information on Columbia University in New York City. But when Lena asked Nellie to read the slick folder with the photograph of its urban campus on the cover, her mother just looked at her as if she had suggested something as ridiculous as bringing home some boy and losing her virginity on the living room sofa. It was a struggle to get her parents even to listen to the idea of Lena leaving the state, let alone the region, for college.

She became desperate. She didn't know how long she would be able to keep her escalating strange behavior a secret from her family. She didn't know how often she was walking in her sleep now. Once or twice every few weeks, she would wake to find the bottoms of her feet black and her pajamas ripped, wet and dirty. But as far as she could tell, since the night she had awakened in the woods, she was the only one in the house who knew about it. And she was sure that if her parents knew she was as likely to be out roaming Pleasant Hill and the nearby woods at night as she was to be in her pretty eyelet-covered bed, they would just use it as a reason to keep her close to home. "For your own safety, baby," she knew they would say.

All along, Lena had planned on Xavier University because she knew she would have the support of the nuns at Martin de Porres for a Catholic institution. And in her mind, New Orleans—three states over—was just far enough away for safety.

As soon as Lena was accepted there, she began keeping a road map she got from Mr. Brown's filling station downtown under her bed. At night before saying her prayers and falling into a troubled sleep, with the joints of her finger, she would count off the miles that she hoped she would put between herself and her craziness the following fall.

As the weeks passed, Lena was surprised at how few problems she encountered trying to get away from home. Somebody must finally be looking out for me, she thought, like Grandmama promised.

When Nellie and Jonah drove her through the streets of Mulberry to the railroad station downtown on a September evening, Lena's heart raced all the way there. She kept expecting something like a huge monster to rise up out of the road in front of her mother's white Pontiac Bonneville with black leather top to bar her way on her final leg of departure. But none arose.

Lena was so excited about finally leaving home, getting far away, that at first she didn't even notice all the people standing on the station platform when she and her parents climbed out of the stairwell into the evening air. Her brother Raymond was there from Texas with his new wife, Jackie. He grabbed her hair as she went by the way he did when they were children and messed up her careful hairdo.

Frank Petersen stood down the platform leaning nonchalantly

against a steel post with a Pall Mall dangling from his mouth. When she had seen him at the house the day before, his only parting advice had been, "Take up French, Lena-Wena."

Gloria had worn the short purple dress that was Lena's favorite. She made Lena take the twenty-dollar bill she pressed into the girl's hand. Then she kissed her, leaving a big slash of lipstick on Lena's cheek. Seymour/Yvette even flitted through the station briefly to drop a small red Christmas candle in Lena's Aigner leather purse and to remind her, "All right, girlchild, don't let me hear 'bout you being the candle, the wick and the flame, too, for some man down there in New Orleans." Then he shook his Diana Ross wig and floated down the metal steps lightly as if he weighed 95 pounds not 195.

Her mother had been so proud of how beautiful and stylish Lena looked in her forest-green light wool suit—"Perfect for traveling," Nellie had said to the smiling saleswoman who happily toted up the mountain of purchases the two McPherson women had made that day. Lena thought the same thing about Nellie as she watched her mother through the train window standing on the station platform dressed in a soft gray turtleneck sweater, straight camel skirt with a kick pleat in the back and high-heeled black kid pumps. Nellie had felt like crying as soon as the train pulled into the station and the thought of the distance the smoking monster would put between her and her baby girl—"I don't care if you get to be eighty-five years old, you'll still be my baby," she had told Lena every year of her life on her birthday in November. Nellie stood on the platform, her brown eyes softly pink around the rims, her tinted auburn hair glistening like copper in the setting sunlight, biting her bottom lip to keep back the flow of tears and looking like a heartbroken heroine in a paperback novel. She had been able to keep her tears in check fairly well until Lena had hugged her good-bye on the train and whispered in her ear, "This my mama right here." Then Nellie had cried like a baby as she answered, "This my baby right here."

Jonah, finally getting thick around the waist from a lifetime of good food, stood next to her, his arm draped around his wife's shoulders. He was as pleased that Lena was traveling by train as he was of her college aspirations. Lena watched him from her car window as he walked up and down the platform proudly telling every porter, waiter and lineman—all of whom had known his father, Walter, when he had worked in the train yards—"Seeing my baby off to college, that's what I'm doing here!"

Lena almost weakened and started to call to the conductor to "Hold it!" when she looked out the train window at the intimate circle of loving faces of her friends and family on the platform. It made her laugh in surprise.

"I've got friends," she said to herself softly as if she had never thought of it before. "People here who love me. Why am I going so far away? I may have come through twelve years of Martin de Porres with only Gwen speaking to me, but look at these folks who love me."

Yet at 5:10 P.M., just as the conductor yelled, "All aboard!" she remembered the sleepwalking in the woods and the horrible visions in her dreams of people with their throats slit from ear to ear and corpses clawing their way up her bed sheets from the bottom of her bed. So she just smiled back at the faces outside the window and waved good-bye as the Silver Crescent creaked into slow motion and pulled out of the station.

Out of the corner of her eye, for just a second, she thought she saw two giant cats jump from the station onto the moving train. But when she leaned forward and looked again, she realized with a chuckle that it was just the conductor in his navy-blue suit, waving all clear to the engineer.

As soon as the figures on the platform were out of sight, Lena said, "Well, Lord," went to her Pullman compartment and changed into a pair of jeans and a sweater she had packed in her carry-on luggage. For the first time since she was seven, she was embarking on an adventure of her own making. At seventeen, she felt free and unencumbered, the way she had when she had traveled to the beach with her family with her hair in a hundred braids.

By the time the Silver Crescent rolled into New Orleans, its last stop, twelve hours after departing Mulberry, Lena had stopped looking around every corner and intently into the face of every stranger she saw. She had seen a man on her way to the dining car who was dressed in what looked like clothes from the last century, but she just kept on walking and didn't look into his face. She had met two other Georgia girls headed for Xavier. They *looked* normal and the last thing Lena wanted was solitude on that train, so she invited them into her compartment for the remainder of the trip. She felt safer in the company of two or more people.

The three girls disembarked at their destination in a swirl of makeup cases and Samsonite luggage and skirt tails, because the Catholic university didn't allow its female students to wear slacks everyday, only on Saturdays. They didn't have to search for a taxi. The school had sent a big yellow school bus painted white with a nun at the wheel to transport and protect its students.

However, Lena found the nuns' protection only extended so far. Her first night in her new dormitory room, she woke up half the floor with her screaming and pleas for someone to save her from the ghosts and creatures that attacked her. She tried to reassure the girls who shook her awake that the cafeteria food must have given her a rare nightmare. But the very next night the same scene from a horror movie: bloodcurdling screams in the middle of the night in a women's dormitory. The terrors continued for three more nights in a row, with Lena screaming she was being pulled down a hole by her feet and couldn't breathe. Her dorm mates' concern turned to irritation and fear.

Lena's assigned roommate, a big girl, at first so pleased to have a roommate as pretty as Lena with six Samsonite suitcases and a steamer trunk full of stylish clothes, soon regretted ever leaving her tiny town in Texas for a school in the big city. Lena's wild screams and thrashing about in her sleep scared the girl to death. By the end of the week, Lena's roommate had packed up her few belongings in her cardboard-thin suitcases and moved out of the room without asking the dorm mother's permission.

It didn't take long for word to spread throughout the dormitory that Lena was strange. No one said anything to the dorm mother, a graduate student from Nigeria who was still learning about black folks in the American South, but the residents traded stories among themselves. One coed swore that on her way to the bathroom in the middle of the night, she had looked out the window and seen Lena walking across the green in the middle of the campus not wearing a stitch of clothes. At the first dorm meeting, another quietly repeated the story that Lena actually chanted some strange voodoo curse in her sleep. She swore she heard it one night when she listened through the door with a plastic glass to her ear.

Before Freshman Week was out and the upper classes were settled in for the semester, Lena was alone again just as she had been through all of her high school years in Mulberry: no friends, and folks fearing and shunning her. But in New Orleans, she didn't even have her one friend, Gwen. *She* was on the other side of the continent at Berkeley.

Lena tried her best to sound upbeat when she called Nellie and Jonah on the hall phone outside her room. But the first time they asked her if she liked her new roommate, Lena burst into tears. Nellie was ready to get in her black and white Bonneville and drive down there to New Orleans to get her baby, but Jonah joked her out of it.

"Now, we 'un babied Lena for almost eighteen years, you can't expect her to just grow up overnight just because she's away from home. She's just homesick now. She may have a few tough days getting used to school and a new town and all. But she'll be okay. She's smart and tough just like her daddy."

At least there was one thing Lena was used to: being alone. And she was totally alone amid the sea of freshmen until one evening during her second week in college when there was a rap on her dormitory room door.

"Come in," she hollered, a little afraid to offer entry to God knew what.

The door swung open slowly, revealing a girl whom Lena knew lived on the floor above hers. Lena had seen her standing on the landing of the stairs in short flowered baby-doll pajamas and fuzzy slippers.

"My name is Marian," said the tall young girl with a figure like an hourglass and the first natural hairdo Lena had ever seen close up in person. "But you can just call me 'Sister.' Everybody does."

Her hair—black, thick and nappy—stood about an inch and a half from her head and was so perfectly trimmed it looked sculpted. Her skin was smooth and clear, except for a small pimple on her cheek. Folks at The Place would have described her as "a good-looking dark-skinned colored girl," but Lena knew right away that Sister was one of a kind, hard to pin down with a phrase.

She came in the room and plopped down on the vacant bed like an old friend. She was only a smidgeon taller than Lena, but Sister had a lankiness about her that made her seem taller. She put Lena in the mind of an old friend. Her familiarity made Lena want to smile. She just sat there and stared.

"I guess you know what they saying about you, yeah," this girl called "Sister" said without the least bit of self-consciousness as she rose and began examining the bottles and jars on Lena's scuffed dormitory dresser.

Lena pretended not to know what her visitor was talking about. But Sister paid her charade no mind.

"They're saying you some kind of witch." The way Sister said it, it sounded like the most normal thing possible for one teenager to say to another. She picked up an atomizer of Shalimar, sniffed the cap, then sprayed a spritz of the perfume down her breasts. She dropped her chin to her chest suddenly and took a deep breath. "They saying that's why you had all those curly-headed boys around you at the Freshman Dance."

Lena thought the girl's tone was serious yet playful, so she didn't feel the least bit offended by her charge of black magic.

"Now, me," Sister continued, "I don't care for curly-headed boys. I figured out a while back that curly-headed ones think they cuter than you and on top of that they can't even kiss and stuff because they always worried about how their hair is looking. But that's what these half-Creole girls think, that you some kind of witch 'cause you had all them boys they want."

"That's what you think, too?" Lena asked as she pulled her knees up to her chin inside her new long green cotton robe and closed the Gwendolyn Brooks novel she was reading.

"I don't know. Thought I'd come down and see for myself," Sister answered as she moved on to Lena's long wooden jewelry box and held up every pair of gold earrings she found to her pierced ears and checked herself out in the mirror. The only jewelry Sister wore was a long string of purple and pink pop beads that she had wrapped a few times around her neck.

"Aren't you afraid like the other girls?" Lena asked. It was beginning to feel like a game of Twenty Questions.

"Shoot, girl, where I come from a witch ain't nothing but another person, probably your grandma or your cousin or somebody."

"Where's that?" Lena asked, truly interested in this new young woman who seemed fascinated rather than repelled by her.

"Where's what?" Sister asked, still looking in the mirror over the dresser as she held a pearl on a thin gold chain up to her throat.

"Where you're from," Lena answered.

"Right down here," Sister answered, and walked over to Lena's closet and peeked inside. "Good God, girl! Look at all these clothes in here! All these yours?"

"Uh-huh," Lena answered. "Where's right here?"

"Right here, outside of New Orleans, in Algiers Parish," Sister said as she pulled the string switching the closet light on and stepped inside with widened eyes. She pronounced New Orleans "New Or-*leans.*" "They make you stay on campus your first year even if you live right here in the city. Nuns! That's why I'm here.

"Shoot, I wish you were a little bit taller," Sister said with disappointed lines creasing her forehead as she held one dress after another up to her chest and looked in the door mirror. "What size shoe you wear?"

"Eight, triple A."

"That's more like it, yeah," Sister said with more enthusiasm as she eyed the pairs of shoes hanging in two plastic caddies on the wall.

Then, she sat down on the floor and examined every pair without saying another word, just sighs of appreciation at every pair of shoes Lena owned—the cute black and taupe and red leather flats; brown-black and oxblood loafers; the small heels in neutrals and colors; high-heeled ostrich skin pumps and suede pumps, and boots both for weather and fashion. When Sister was finished, she stood with her hands on her hips, her elbows akimbo, and stared at Lena with a smile playing around her face.

"Well, Lena, what should I tell the girls upstairs about you?" she asked. Then, she added, wrinkling up her face and making her voice rise into a cracking little falsetto, "Are you a *good* witch or a *bad* witch?"

The fact that the other girls in the dorm thought that she was a witch at all hurt Lena's feelings. It felt like more of what she had been suffering through at school ever since she was thirteen. But Lena couldn't help herself, she had to giggle at Sister's imitation of good witch Glenda.

The sound of her own laughter surprised her. It was the first time she had really laughed since she arrived in New Orleans. To laugh, and to laugh with Sister, a friend, after such a hard dry spell was so sweet. It was like eating her mama's fresh orange and coconut ambrosia at Christmastime, or like being let in on a joke at The Place.

Lena didn't do any more studying that night. She and Sister spent the evening getting acquainted, with Lena doing most of the talking about her family and Sister trying on nearly all of Lena's clothes. By the time Sister asked Lena directly about the screams everyone heard coming from her room at night, Lena didn't even feel self-conscious about talking about her recent nightmares. But she kept the facts of her birth to herself.

In one night, Sister had learned more about Lena's private life than most anyone else knew. But when Sister went back upstairs to

her own room, she refused to answer even one inquiry that her roommate had about the witch on the floor below.

The next morning, Sister met Lena coming out of the bathroom
with her plastic bucket of toiletries in her hand and a towel wrapped
around her and tucked in under her arm. Sister was already dressed.
She wore the new plaid pleated skirt she had casually taken upstairs
from Lena's closet, which looked like a miniskirt on the taller, larger
girl. She also had on Lena's new orange cotton sweater.

"Get dressed," Sister commanded, "we got somewhere to go.
They're expecting us."

"But I have a class in fifteen minutes," Lena had protested.

"Look, Lena, this is more important than some class. Get dressed.
If we hurry we can catch the next No. 18 in time to transfer to the
Elysian Fields bus going toward the French Quarter. We call it 'Vieux
Carré.' "

As they rode toward Canal Street in the sultry bayou heat of early
fall, both of them dressed in Lena's new clothes, Sister explained her
theory.

"You know what I think? I think that the reason you're having
these bad nights is the witches are riding you, that's all. And I *know*
somebody who can fix that!"

Sister sounded so upbeat and sure of herself that Lena felt a little
less strange sitting on a bus going she didn't know where in an unfamiliar city with a new friend beside her. She nodded her head dumbly
and thought about how Grandmama used to say that the witches rode
her at night, dancing on her chest and sucking her breath, voice and
will away.

Sister kept right on talking.

"Her name is Aunt Delphie. At least, that's what I call her. My
family's known her forever, my great-great-great-grandmother knew
her grandmother in olden times and before, I guess. But you should
call her Madame Delphie, okay?"

Lena nodded again and noted that Sister pronounced the name
like a French girl. *Madame Delphie.* Sister chattered all the way across

town, pointing out historical and personal spots of interest like a tour guide, hardly leaving room for Lena to speak.

"Over there is where my first boyfriend lived in the Ninth Ward. That little park over there is where I lost my virginity. I went to a high school dance once down there. There's Madame Leveau's house. That's the back side of Jackson Square. Maybe later on, we'll ride on down and get some beignets and some chicory coffee at Café du Monde."

They got off the bus near Canal Street downtown and walked over three blocks to Dumaine Street, then down to Rampart. Lena was certain that Sister was going to lead her deep into the Old Quarter, down narrow back alleys, through wrought-iron fences and maybe up a winding back staircase or a wide fan one like in *A Streetcar Named Desire*. But when they got halfway down the block on Rampart, on the edge of the Quarter, Sister stopped and pulled Lena up two steps leading to the door of a small wooden shotgun house that looked like all the others on the street.

A short squat Creole-looking woman with soft golden skin and thin, greasy, crinkly black hair answered Sister's knock eating a dry soda cracker. She squinted in the daylight at Sister and led the two girls inside to the long dark narrow hallway without saying a word. Sister took Lena's arm again and pulled her down next to her on a bare deacon's bench as the woman disappeared through a curtained doorway off the hall. When Lena leaned over to whisper a question in Sister's ear, her friend just shook her head and put her finger to her lips as if they were sitting in church during Mass.

The light in the hall was so weak that Lena found her eyes pulling, making it hard to see anything clearly. But the darkness seemed to heighten her other senses. There was a smell in the close air that she thought she had smelled somewhere before, but she couldn't place it exactly. At first, she thought it smelled like food cooking or burning. Then, she decided that the odor was too pungent to be anything to eat, even in spicy New Orleans. It smelled more like someone who had been working in the sun. Lena longed to lean over and ask Sister if she knew what the scent was. But her friend was sitting next to her so stonily that Lena didn't dare disturb her again.

To Lena, it felt as if they sat there in silence for half an hour, but after about ten minutes, the short Creole woman returned and held the door to the front room open for them. Sister rose with a polite smile and pushed Lena ahead of her into the room. Then, Sister closed the door behind them and stood by the entrance with her hand on Lena's shoulder. Lena reached for Sister's hand in the darkened room, but her friend just squeezed and patted her shoulder and pushed her forward a few steps.

It took a couple of seconds for Lena's eyes to adjust to the darkness. Her heart did not stop pounding the whole time she was in there. Heavy dark material was stretched across the four windows on two sides of the room that blocked out all the natural light. The only other light in the room came from two candles burning on a low table placed against the wall opposite the door. As far as Lena could see, other than two straight-back wooden chairs, the room was bare of furniture.

From her right, a voice seemed to come out of the darkness. "You, child, the one born with a veil, come here."

Sister came forward a half-step and said, "No, Aunt Delphie, Lena wasn't born with a caul, she . . ."

But Lena interrupted her, "Yes, I was."

Sister looked at her friend with surprise and respect and stepped back against the door. Even the woman sitting across the candles and charms from her seemed interested. Sister was impressed. And frightened.

"Come here, child," Aunt Delphie repeated impatiently. Lena moved in the direction of the woman's voice.

In the darkened room, it was difficult for Lena to get a good look at Aunt Delphie. All she could make out was a seated figure in a light-colored flowing garment. What she felt pushing through her veins, pumped by her heart, was not fear, but excitement. Lena knew that her mother would have laughed out loud at Madame Delphie and the trappings of mysticism in the room, but in her heart, Lena felt a connection to the woman that was nearly religious.

Lena moved toward the woman gratefully, as if she were going toward her grandmother. Just as she got in range of seeing the woman's face in the candlelight, Madame Delphie held up her hand to stop her advance. Lena could see the woman's eyes fly open and her back stiffen against the spine of the chair she was sitting in. She looked over her shoulder just in time to see Sister step back a bit in shock at Madame Delphie's reaction to her friend.

The woman took a deep breath that seemed to steady her a bit and motioned again for Lena to approach her.

She reached over and pulled the other straight-back chair closer to her side. Then, she motioned for Lena to take a seat there.

When Lena did, Madame Delphie didn't waste a minute.

"Child," she said right away, "so many spirits are trying to get to you. It's been that way all your life, hasn't it?" the woman asked.

Lena didn't know if she was supposed to speak or not, so she just nodded her head dumbly.

"I know Sister brought you here, but she does not know how deep it is, does she?" Lena could barely hear her whispery questions. But the woman lowered her voice just a tad and leaned closer to Lena.

Madame Delphie smelled like incense, but not the kind Father O'Donnell had used in the Eucharist Adoration and Benediction after Mass when she was a child that made her sick to her stomach. The woman had a sweet spicy smell that made Lena smile.

Lena looked around one time to make sure Sister wasn't within hearing range.

Then, she replied, "No, uh-uh, Sister doesn't have any idea. She just thinks the witches are riding me, giving me nightmares."

Madame Delphie could not help herself, she had to give a little chuckle through her nose and toss her head, tied up in a red and white and orange scarf, at that understatement.

"Sister, she a good friend, yeah. Don't let her go."

"I won't," Lena promised solemnly.

"Now, as for you, I know she brought you here for me to fix you. But you know I cannot do that," Madame Delphie said with some regret, but with respect, Lena noticed, as if she were talking to a peer.

Lena didn't know when she would get another chance like this, so she screwed up her courage and asked, "Why not? Why can't you fix me?"

"Well, for one thing, I don't have your birth caul. You don't either, do you?"

"Uh-uh, Grandmama's ghost told me Mama burned it."

And Madame Delphie shuddered in just the way the ghost of her grandmother had the night of her funeral when she had come back to see Lena.

"Well, I still could not do that much even if we did possess the skin without some more information.

"And the one, the woman, who oversaw your birth. She is no help? Oh, never mind. I see. Nurse Flowers . . ."

"Nurse Bloom," Lena corrected timidly.

"Nurse Flower. Nurse Bloom. Either way she gone a little out of her head, eh? She no help, no."

And they both sat there like two old women commiserating over the senility of a once-reliable friend.

"Well, I can't fix you. But I can take you a step closer maybe," Madame Delphie said.

Knowing how her family felt about education and how her mother felt about the supernatural and such, Lena couldn't believe that she was sitting in a strange house on the edge of the French Quarter talking to an even stranger woman about spirits when she should have been sitting in biology class. But she still couldn't shake the feeling that what she was doing was right.

"Go to the altar," Madame Delphie directed.

Lena did as she was told.

"Take the white candle laying there in the middle."

Lena picked up the candle with a trembling hand and, with the short slender taper clutched in her hot, sweaty palm, came back to stand in front of the woman.

Madame Delphie asked, "If I tell you this candle can help you, can help straighten what has been crossed, would you believe in its power?"

Lena looked down at the candle in her hand and thought a moment.

"My mother calls it old-fashioned foolishness," Lena said. It was the first thing that came to her mind. Then, she giggled nervously because she was embarrassed that it had just popped out.

"I did not ask you what your mother believe," the woman fairly roared, causing Lena to stifle her giggle immediately. Now, she was just nervous. "I ask if *you believe.*"

Lena paused awhile thinking of her dead Grandmama and her belief in signs and how she had died the night the screech owl flew down the chimney and into the house on Forest Avenue. She thought of all the visions and voices and touches.

"Take your time, girl. It is an important question, yes," Madame Delphie said solemnly. "Do you believe?"

Lena opened her mouth a couple of times to reply, but no sound came out. Inside her, it felt as if a storm were brewing.

The simple question had thrown her into such a state of confusion that she was actually dizzy. Without thinking, she brought her empty hand up to her face and rubbed her temple to try and settle her thoughts. All her life, Lena had tried the best she could to handle her visions and powers. She had tried living with them, ignoring them, renaming them crazy. She had gone to the church for help. She had left home. She had even tried putting the magic on herself.

Each time, she had believed with all her might that her remedies would work. They never had. And now she found herself once more in the same predicament: with only one friend to her name and everyone else calling her a witch. How can I dare believe? she wondered.

But even as she had these doubts, other feelings flooded into her soul with such a rush that they seemed to wash away her doubts and fears. She stood alone near the middle of the nearly bare room, but she felt as if she were being tugged—one arm east, the other west—between two giant hands.

Then, a voice right at her ear seemed to whisper to her, "Believe!"

Lena glanced around at Sister a few feet away, who quickly looked to the bare wooden floor. It had not been Sister who spoke, blowing in her ear with the word, the injunction: "Believe!"

Lena took a deep breath and answered.

"Yes, Madame Delphie. I believe." And she felt a tingle all over.

"Humph, I know you do. Take this candle and light it before you go to sleep. And make sure you are alone. Sister!" she shouted at the girl standing by the door. "See Marie on your way out."

Then, Madame Delphie rose, and Lena saw that she was not a large woman as she had thought at first, but a small stout one about her grandmother's size. Madame Delphie began moving across the room toward a dark curtain hanging across a doorway, but when she passed Lena, who was unable to move, the little woman reached over and touched the girl's shoulder tenderly. The touch was like a shot of electricity that set Lena trembling all over. Then, Madame Delphie moved on behind the curtain.

Lena sat on the hall bench a minute or two, while Sister talked with Madame Delphie's assistant at the end of the hall. But when the two girls emerged back into the sunlight, Lena realized that her knees were still shaking. She had to lean against the peeling wall of the house to steady herself.

"Aunt Delphie's something else, yeah?" Sister said with a smile as she watched Lena try to gather herself.

Lena just nodded her head, dumbly. It felt as if it weighed a hundred pounds.

When her legs settled down and her voice came back, Lena reached into her shoulder bag and asked Sister, "Did you have to pay something?"

"Don't worry about it," Sister said as if she had just bought her friend a Coca-Cola. "My treat." They headed back up the street toward the bus stop.

Sister wouldn't let Lena ask any questions about Madame Delphie and what the candle meant.

"I was told you need all of your strength and attention for tonight when you light the candle and sleep," Sister told her as they rode on the bus back to campus. "Aunt Delphie's assistant told me you shouldn't talk much, to eat lightly—no beignets—and rest, but don't sleep 'til nightfall."

"But what's the candle going to do?" Lena had to ask something.

"Lena, I'm the one who took you to Aunt Delphie. I take my duty very serious, yeah. So please don't keep asking me questions when I'm supposed to keep you quiet, okay?"

Lena didn't know how she was going to make it until dark. She had so many questions, she thought she would crack open if she didn't get some answers. But Sister had turned so solemn about her duty, Lena felt she had to respect it.

By the time the sun began dropping to the earth, edging toward first dark in the muggy New Orleans heat, Lena was so jumpy, she knew she would never be able to fall asleep at all that night, let alone at such an early hour. But Sister moved around Lena's dorm room with such assurance, sticking the white candle into a small green bud vase, placing a book of matches from the cigarette machine in the basement next to it, and pulling down the shades at the windows, that Lena made an effort to lean on the feeling of near confidence she had felt when she told Madame Delphie she believed. Lena felt this time she might at last find safety with Madame Delphie's methods.

It was akin to the feeling she remembered having when her grandmama would say to her, "Don't worry, baby, Grandma ain't gonna let nothing happen to her little puppy."

Although her first inclination was to grab onto Sister and beg her not to leave, she let go of the fear and told Sister, "Good-bye."

"Good-bye?" Sister laughed from the doorway. "Where you think you going? Good night, girl, I'll see you in the morning." Then, she shut the door firmly on her way out.

To Lena, the closing of the light wooden door sounded like a prison cell door slamming shut on a lifer. Just to make sure she could get out, she got up from her seat on the edge of her bed and opened and closed the door several times. Then, before she could lose her nerve, she went right to the white candle on her tall dresser, lit it and slipped under the covers of the bed in her pink bra and panties.

With the covers pulled up to her chin, she watched the candle flame reflected in the dresser mirror. The flame burned low and steady for a couple of seconds, then grew tall and flickering. Lena didn't take her eyes off the flame and when it started emitting a light gray stream of feathery smoke, it occurred to her for the first time that falling asleep with a candle burning was a fire hazard, especially in the old wooden barracks-like dormitory.

Maybe I should try to stay awake and watch the candle so there won't be an accident, she thought, keeping her gaze on the taper that now was spewing billows of the gray smoke. She was so mesmerized by the yellow flame, she didn't even notice how much smoke had filled the small plainly decorated room.

She was beginning to find it difficult to breathe and the smoke had distorted or cloaked everything that was familiar to Lena. She heard a noise like a book falling to the floor over in a corner she could no longer see. She pretended to ignore the sound, repeated again and again, but it got louder and louder until it sounded like a freight train headed straight for her narrow twin bed.

Lena was too frightened to move and when the train sound had rumbled through, right past her bed, it left a room full of voices in its wake. Now she had no intention of moving. Every direction seemed to hold myriad voices and the outlines of human beings.

Now the smoke was so thick she could barely breathe.

"Ghosts!" Lena said aloud, and immediately felt herself being pulled in all directions. "Oh, God, I'm going to die!"

And as she gasped for breath, the life actually began leaving her body. She could see bits of herself floating up into the smoke. She could feel herself becoming less and less real. And she began to cry.

Then:

BAM-BAM-BAM!!

The sudden knock on the door—hard enough to push the unlocked door ajar—stopped everything that was going on in Lena's dorm room.

"Emergency dorm meeting. Five minutes. In the main parlor." The hall resident's voice cut through the smoke in the room, then moved on down the hall to the next room.

BAM-BAM-BAM!!!

"Emergency dorm meeting. Five minutes. In the main parlor."

Lena looked around and was stunned to find her room as it had been an hour before. But she felt as if she had just gotten a whipping: hurt, weary and defeated. She got out of bed, grabbed her fleecy robe and staggered up the one flight to Sister's room, entered without knocking and fell across her narrow twin bed.

She didn't look to see if anyone else was in the room. She didn't wait for Sister to ask any questions. She just started talking.

"Sister, I am *never* gonna do that again. I don't care what anybody says."

"Um, it was a bad one, huh?" Sister asked sympathetically without need of a blow-by-blow explanation.

"A bad one?" Lena almost had to laugh. "I guess you could say that. A bad one? Sister, I almost just died in there."

"I don't know, Lena, maybe you ought to . . ."

"I know what I *ought* to do, Sister. I ought to just forget all this. Lighting candles. Seeing ghosts. Shoot, I almost suffocated in there with all that smoke. I'm going to stop being a part of it."

"I don't want to talk about this again, okay?"

"Lena, I think this might be more . . ."

"I'm serious. I don't ever want to speak about it or acknowledge all this veil stuff anymore."

"Lena, maybe it's not for us to . . ."

"I can't take all this, Sister. I got to turn it loose. I'm almost eighteen years old now. And I'm making this decision for myself."

Lena paused and looked Sister dead in the eye.

"Listen to me, Sister, when that woman, when Madame Delphie, said 'Believe!' I did. For that moment, I let go and for the first time in my life, I think, really believed all the stuff I been seeing and hearing and folks been saying about me all my life. For just that moment. And then later, Sister, up here in my room, I swear to you, believing and lighting that candle and sitting in my bed hearing voices and seeing things, I could feel myself being sucked up by, I don't know, some other world or something. I could just feel myself losing myself bit by bit, like molecule by molecule, and not just my body but my soul, too."

Lena stopped and gulped air trying to catch her breath.

"Oh, Sister, I'm not ever gonna do *that* again. Not ever. It wasn't just the spirits that came with that candle and me believing. That *was scary*. But it was mostly that feeling that I belonged over there with them."

And Lena stopped as she shivered a bit inside her soft pink robe. Then she continued.

"And I think if I stop taking it so seriously, things will just settle down."

Sister just sighed and clucked her tongue in disbelief. "Well, Lena . . ."

"No, Sister," Lena said, speaking quickly. "Let's collect the other paraphernalia from Madame Delphie's assistant and take it out to the Dumpster tonight.

"I really think I been taking this stuff too seriously. Just 'cause I have a few nightmares and I walk in my sleep. Lots of people do that.

"So, I'll just deal with it like everybody else. And things will just settle down."

Sister didn't say anything because she knew Lena needed a friend right then to be on her side. But she didn't believe for a minute that things would ever settle down for Lena.

In the nearly thirty years since, Sister had spent many nights keeping her husband Douglas awake with her restlessness over Lena wandering the world pretending not to be special, a child of the veil. Her birth velum burned by her own mother in the trash. No one to watch over her because the unsettled spirits scared the protective ones away.

She knew that over the years, Lena had just ignored sounds, looked the other way when she thought she saw something other-worldly. Didn't answer when some mist seemed to call her name.

And from her experience and her mother's and her grandmother's and her great-grandmother's experience, Sister knew it was going to all catch up with Lena one day.

12

VAPOR

When Lena awoke the next morning, she was amazed that she felt rested. After her scare in the pool the night before, it surprised her that the witches had not ridden her all night.

It crossed her mind as she sat up on her white piqué-trimmed sheets that what she recalled of the night before had, indeed, been a dream. With the sun peeking in through the skylight over her head, she remembered clearly that her heart had been racing wildly when she jumped out of the water. She did not see anything swimming around in the water, but she decided not to get back in there. Instead, she had cut out the lights and slipped into bed without even saying her prayers.

In the light of day, she felt safe and brave.

"I can't believe it actually felt like somebody was really in there with me," she said aloud as she draped the white piqué robe at the foot of her bed around her shoulders and headed for her bathroom. She was going to say, "Felt like ghosts brushing up against me," but she did not want to invoke the spirit of the little girl she had spent her senior year at Martin de Porres avoiding. At the beginning of that year, a little girl from the kindergarten class had walked up to her at recess and with a very serious face said, "My name is Sonia. Are you named Lena?"

Lena had smiled, putting down her Coke, and nodded.

"What can I do for you?"

The little girl, dressed like Lena in a tiny blue plaid skirt and white blouse, glanced to her left, then glanced to her right, then over her little Peter Pan collar. With a curl of her finger, she motioned for Lena to stoop down to her level.

When Lena, puzzled, bent down, Sonia had said, "Ghosts be brushing up against me. They be brushing up against you, too?"

The only other child in her small parochial school who had also been born with a caul was seeking a kindred spirit. But Lena had left little Sonia standing there and had avoided her until graduation.

Now she wished she had Sonia's phone number. Lena knew the little girl would know how it had felt in the pool the night before. As if ghosts were brushing up against her.

As she did each morning when the sun streamed through the overhead skylight as she brushed her teeth, Lena had to stop and admire her bathroom. It demanded attention. It was more a suite than a room. The huge walk-in shower stood like a solid entity from the middle of the room to the wall. Lena reached in and turned on the hot water.

The inside of the large white-tiled stall was interspersed with hand-painted blue and green tiles Mr. Crockett, the plumber and tile man, had made himself. He had blushed at Lena's idea to extend the length of the shower to the outer wall and make the entire wall glass so she could enjoy the stand of birch gum and junipers outside while she showered. The magnolias were about to burst open with luscious openly seductive white blooms and the birch gum, tall and healthy, spoke of good luck to Lena.

Mr. Crockett wanted to tell someone other than his wife, "Man, Lena McPherson got a shower you can see right into from outside!"

What he didn't even tell his wife was that the glass wall of the shower faced a nearly impenetrable wall of birch, and a voyeur would have to get in there, then climb some fairly tall pines to see inside.

She rarely used it, but she also had one of the most beautiful bathtubs in the state. Mr. Renfroe's cousin in Madison knew about the find of stone in North Georgia. "New quarry, old marble," is all the old gardener said to explain the expense of digging, carving and shipping the tub to Mulberry that he had okayed.

The owner of the quarry accompanied the tub to Lena's new front door. The stonemason, back in North Georgia, kept telling his wife, "It was a colored girl!" until she had to tell him to "shut up about that colored girl!"

As the shower stall steamed up, she hit the button for the first CD on the stereo controls over the sink. Salt 'n' Pepa with their girl Spinderella was one of her favorite choices to get her going in the morning.

"Oo, baby, baby. Ba, baby, baby, baby," Lena sang along, grinding naked in the wide lighted mirror in the bathroom with her burnished braids pulled up on top of her head in imitation of "her girls" on their latest video.

Lena washed her face with a soft loofah that Nellie had grown herself when she read that the gourd's soft skeleton sloughed away old dead skin and age. Nellie had grown so many that even now, ten years after her death, Lena still had enough—dried, seeded, bleached and hanging from the rafters in the barn—to last her the rest of her life. And that was after she had given one to every woman she knew.

The women didn't use the loofahs, but Lena felt she had done her part. They didn't think she could, but Lena could hear the women tell each other, "Yeah, but she don't tell folks she got a sauna and swimming pool out there in her house by the river, too, along with that loofah thing!"

The women could talk all they wanted. Lena was not about to share her few private retreats. She had a steam room, too, in her bathroom and whether or not the women in town knew about it, she cherished it as much as she did her shower.

It had been specially designed and built just the way she wanted it. Mr. Crockett had just shaken his head at Lena's luxuries. The triangular steam room was built into one corner of the cavernous bathroom with two long white tile seats forming a comfortable "V." The third wall and door to the room was made of frosted glass that let in just enough light to keep claustrophobia from settling in on Lena in there.

As she rinsed her face with handful after handful of tepid water running to her faucets from the deep well dug into the aquifer under her land, she could hear "Sexy Noises"—her favorite dancing-in-the-shower music—flooding the room with percussion. She lifted her head above the sink and grabbed a thick white hand towel from the heated rack to her right to pat her face dry. Her mother had taught her never to rub her skin dry after bathing no matter how invigorating it felt. Even when she was a little thing, no more than three or four, her mother would lift her from the tub in the upstairs bathroom on Forest Avenue, set her down on the thick bath mat and gently instruct her in the proper way to dry soft, delicate female McPherson skin.

"See, baby, just take the towel and pat, pat, pat *all* over. Pat, pat, pat. Uh-uh, don't rub like that, like your brothers or your daddy. They boys. But I always want you to treat your skin gently, okay? You gonna do that for Mama, baby?" In Lena's head, her mother continued to talk in the soft sweet tones she reserved for her only baby girl. "Take care of that pretty skin God gave you. They can call it McPherson skin if they want to, but you get it from my side of the family, too."

Lena could only safely think of Nellie's maternal instructions for a few seconds. If she lingered any longer in her childhood, she knew she would soon be recalling other less sweet memories.

"Oh, shoot," she said under her breath, a little shudder running up her back.

Lena thought she had caught a glimpse of a figure standing behind her in the mirror.

She had to make herself turn and look directly into the spot where the figure had stood. It was empty.

"Well, damn!" she said.

She did not want to give in to this vague presence, these ephemeral eyes that seemed to peep out at her from all kinds of places. Lena had never been completely comfortable with mirrors. Since she was a toddler, she had lived in fear that anytime she looked in a mirror, the glass would throw back more than just her reflection.

But Lena had gotten over many of her fears. And now she stood her ground and looked herself dead in the eye in the mirror over the bathroom sink.

"You gon' have to get a grip, girl. We ain't going back to that! I just can't live like that again." It was hardly living. Ghosts showing up whenever they felt like it.

"I thought I was gonna lose my mind."

Along with the sensation in the pool the night before, this fleeting figure in her mirror was really giving her pause. She continued to give herself a good talking to.

"I'm a big old rusty woman now. I'm not a baby scared by ghosts in the night. I live way out here by myself. I'm not afraid of the dark. A glimpse of something out the corner of my eye is not going to send me into a hizzy fit. It's not!"

I wish I had a mama or grand I could trust to hear my sadness and not get upset, she thought. I'd tell them just how hard it's been. But she knew from experience whenever she shared her sorrow and pain, her fear and terror, with anyone other than Sister, the word spread so quickly through town and around that she had to do extra duty to calm the city down. She knew no one had ever *intended* to betray her confidence. But her sadness, it seemed, was just too heavy a burden for anyone to bear alone and before Lena's confidante knew it, word was out.

Others seemed to just make jest of anything she worried about, belittling the problem. "Aw, Lena McPherson, get out a' here. If I had all your money, I wouldn't have a care in the world. Just like you."

"Lonely? Hell, you get first crack at every man in town."

"Yeah, I wish I could sit out by the river by myself without all these little crumb-crushers climbing all over me."

Lena finally took the advice of Miss Annie Mae, whom Lena had discovered rocking and moaning on her porch one afternoon as Lena made her rounds.

"Miss Annie Mae, tell me," Lena implored her, used to making everything right. "What's wrong?"

Miss Annie Mae looked up with bleary, cloudy eyes and half smiled at Lena.

"Baby," the old lady said, "I'll just tell my troubles to the Lord."

That's what Lena did now, especially with Sister away in West Africa. She just told her troubles to the Lord.

Right then she said a quick little personal prayer.

And she did feel a bit more confident as she stepped in the shower, glancing boldly into the full-length mirror by the steam room door as she did. She stood inside the stall and listened to the thump of "Sexy Noises." Even in the early morning light, Lena could see the outline of some of her favorite juniper trees outside the glass shower wall.

"Aren't you afraid ghosts will be looking in at you while you're naked?" Sister had teased uneasily about the legendary spirit-haunted trees.

The water from the shower massage reminded her of the unusually warm water in the pool the night before. Lena didn't even have to aim the spray of the revolving shower head at her body to recall the sensation from the night before of air filling her, tickling her clitoris and lifting her hips into the air.

I'll have to tell someone to take a look at that thermostat, she thought. I've never had my pool that hot.

Suddenly, an unexpected sound cut through the shower spray and the seductive music.

"Ahem."

Lena stopped shampooing her pubic hair with a soapy white

shower mitt and playing with the shower massage she held in her hand. She stood stock-still with the spray from the shower head pelting her in the chest and listened.

"Is there someone out there?" she called over the sound of the shower's water. She hit a button on the tile wall with one soapy hand and "Sexy Noises" ceased. She listened.

She heard it again. "Ahem."

"My God," Lena gasped as she grabbed at the loose shower massage that was splashing water all around and trying to regain her footing. "Who is that? Who is that??"

Again, all she heard was, "Ahem."

"Who is that? James Petersen, is that you?"

She knew it couldn't be James Petersen, since he tried at all costs to avoid her whenever she might be walking around nude. There was no way he was wandering into her bathroom while the shower was running.

"Who is that? Who the hell is that?" Lena was insistent now. She looked around the shower stall for something, some weapon, with which to defend herself. All she had was a loofah on a light balsa stick; some pink and purple plastic bottles of herbal soap, shampoo and conditioner; a small plastic hippopotamus in a hat and a tutu that one of her godchildren had given her, and a short-bristle back brush and a tiny wooden nail brush. There was a huge maidenhair fern growing over the top of the shower stall. But it was no good to her as a weapon. The stiff brush was the heaviest thing in there, so she grasped it. It was a puny defense, but Lena didn't have much experience defending herself. She usually didn't have to. She thought briefly of the shotgun Jonah had bought for her and taught her to use. But she did not know *where* that was.

"I'm not in this house all by myself," Lena shouted toward the shower door, her voice cracking and giving away her fear and deception.

There was a split second's pause. Then came back the reply.

"Lena, it's me. Herman."

Lena was truly speechless. She thought, Now, who the hell is Herman? He said his name as if he were identifying himself for some official position.

"It's just me," the intruder said, "Herman."

He had a real country-sounding voice that had an unfamiliar, foreign taste to it, a little flat on some syllables and words, but somehow smooth.

He pronounced "Herman" as if it were "Hur-mon" with the emphasis on the first syllable. She almost didn't know what he was saying at first. She appreciated his repeating it.

"It's me, Lena. Herman."

She opened her mouth to say something but nothing came out. She was thinking, Herman? *Herman?*

Lena started to open her mouth to scream, but she smacked her lips and felt the Sahara Desert in there. So instead she turned the shower's spigot toward C and filled her dry mouth with cool water. It didn't help. She still could not find a voice to speak. She did not know what to say if she could. But she did like the sound of this Herman's voice.

"Lena, I'm a spirit," Herman said.

Oh, God, she thought. It's the ghosts and stuff. It's starting again. Herman kept right on talking.

"Lena, I come 'cause you called me."

Lena started to say, "Oh, you must be mistaken. I most certainly didn't invite or call you in here," as she stood on the other side of the shower door with her large white wash mitt in front of her vagina. But she heard herself sounding like somebody from Milledgeville, if the state still kept the insane in institutions there. Yet, she did not know what else to do.

Her heart was racing and so was her mind. A man, a spirit come here to my bathroom??!!! she thought.

"You called me here, Lena. I couldn'a come if you hadn'a called me up," explained the voice on the other side of the door. "I sho' looks forward to meetin' ya."

The invitation for Lena to step outside hung in the air like steam. Then, there was silence again.

The image of calling up a ghost reminded Lena of her friend. "God, I wish Sister was handy," she muttered to herself inside the steamy shower stall. "*She* might be able to handle something like this!"

But the very thought of her can-do friend seemed to make her brave.

Lena couldn't help herself, she was intrigued. She cleared her throat.

"Hope I ain't being a foolish fool here," she said softly as if Sister were right there to stop her if she were.

Her heart was still thumping in her chest like the machines at the paper plant, but she dropped her "weapon" on one of the shower seats and moved toward the door. Lena had yet to utter a complete sentence to this "Herman" outside. She couldn't believe she was doing this, but she opened the shower door a crack, just wide enough for her to reach her hand out and grab the big white Turkish towel hanging on a hoop nearby. It felt a little like sticking her hand into a dark hole at the fun house of an amusement park—frightening and exciting.

Okay, she thought, making a deal with herself, if nothing grabs my hand and pulls me out, then I'll know it'll be safe to proceed.

Snatching the towel inside the stall without looking out the door, Lena breathed a shaky sigh of relief. But she also felt a thrill of exhilaration. She had to stop for a second or two to catch her breath. Then, she tried to wrap the fluffy white towel in the least seductive fashion she could. It did not work. No matter how she threw and wrapped and twisted and tucked the towel, she managed to look cute. So, she covered herself as decently as possible, shook her long heavy wet braids free of excess water and took a deep breath.

She had not heard a sound from the other side of the door since she had snatched the towel inside. But she sensed that "Herman," or rather "Hur-mon," was still there.

She felt some trepidation. But surprisingly, she was not scared.

She thought back to meetings she had had with other ghosts when she was younger. How her heart had raced, how the hair on her arms had stood on end, how sometimes she had felt dizzy at the sight of a headless body or huge animal or a mist or vapor covering and smothering everything in its sphere. But this time she was different. Lena felt just a little anxious, like before a blind date.

Her mother would have warned, "Curiosity killed the cat, Lena. Watch yourself." Nellie and Grandmama had always told her she was too curious for her own good. But now she didn't care about taking any solid advice from ghostly relatives. She *had* to see what this Herman looked like.

Under her breath, she muttered, "Well, Lord," sounding like her dead Granddaddy Walter before he embarked on an adventure.

She opened the shower door all the way, letting out a puff of steam, and stepped out. Lena was surprised the door didn't make a creaking noise like in a haunted house when she closed it. But she steeled herself anyway for what she was about to see. She didn't even flinch when she turned and saw him.

13

HERMAN

Herman had a noble face.

Lena loved his face immediately.

It was a face that she had seen in the arrangement of leaves on a tree in the woods, a shape that was there in the sunlight, then gone in the shade. It was a face that she had seen in the clouds. It was a face that showed innate gentleness.

It was a face, she realized suddenly, that she had seen in her dreams.

His face was broad but not round. His cheekbones were high and wide and seemed to stretch his sweet dark skin so tightly across his visage that Lena could not imagine him ever aging. It was difficult to think of anything old or aging or dying while looking into his face. As a child, Lena had heard her mother often exclaim, "Lord ham mercy, Lena, every sin that woman ever committed was written on her face this morning." Looking at Herman made Lena think, Every kindness this man has ever committed is written on *his* face this morning.

Lena thought, Um, he's the picture of health.

On his right temple, half-hidden in the thick edges of the thicket of his longish hair, was a faint scar shaped like a half-moon. Lena was shocked at herself, but she had to restrain her hand from reaching up and caressing it.

His eyes were black, as dark as midnight down by the river with no lights on. But they sparkled like something in a fairy tale. His brows and lashes were thick and just as ebony as his eyes. His eyebrows looked as if someone had wet a thumb with spit and smoothed the short hairs down. But his eyelashes were curly and unruly.

He had a good head of hair, coal black, like his eyes. And his eyes and hair seemed to have life in them. He had long bushy nappy hair, like a lion's mane around his broad face. It was not in dreads, but it was thick enough to be. His short bushy mustache made him look daring, dashing, adventurous.

Lena thought his mouth below his bushy mustache appeared made to sing songs. She did not know why she thought that, but she did. And his lips looked so soft they made her lick her own lips.

His nose was what her Grandmama called a "proud African" nose.

A tall drink of water, Lena thought as she watched him stand there in her bathroom on her fluffy white looped rug, leaning back on the counter behind him while standing back in his legs like a sexy woman, his muscular arms crossed over his barrel chest to let her take in all of him. Or what there was of him. Although he stood a full six feet tall in full color with poetically beautiful tensed shoulders and slightly bowed legs, he was nearly transparent, translucent. Almost a vapor. Lena could just barely see the counter and bottles and towels and his dusty black hat through him. The steam wafting from the shower stall hung in the air around him, almost seemed to be a part of him.

Even as a vapor, he was himself. There. Set. Herman. Himself.

He gave new meaning to the phrase "ghost of a man."

He was the most solid ghost of a man she had ever seen. He had the kind of shoulders Lena liked: broad, solid but not thick and overly muscular. His thighs, Lena's favorite part of a man, were long, lean, sinewy, and strong.

He looked to Lena to be about thirty-five years old or so. But with his flawless bittersweet-chocolate skin, Lena thought, there's no telling how old he is.

He reminded Lena of pictures in biographies of old-timey black men like farmers and blacksmiths and coopers and cowboys standing in front of their fragile-looking wooden country homes or beside their horses.

He was wearing simple brightly colored clothing: a light green cotton long-sleeved shirt with the cuffs rolled up over his arms to the bulge right above the elbow. And even with his big shirt tucked neatly into his pants, Lena could see he had a nice flat hard stomach. His pants were heavy cotton dark nondescript work pants, but they didn't look like any work pants Lena had ever seen. They looked like they might have been handmade, but Lena thought, Now, who in the world makes their own work clothes?

He was a man who looked good in his pants. He had narrow hips like many country boys Lena had seen down at The Place—lanky with a little huskiness thrown in to let you know he was used to doing a good day's work—and a real nice behind she could see from the side that was not too high or too low. Nice.

On his feet, big feet, Lena noted, he wore heavy boots, well-worn, but beautifully made of black leather with square heels and stirrup marks on the instep. They looked to Lena as if they had weathered many a trip.

She tried to picture him in some Gucci loafers and no socks, a loosely constructed linen suit, black Ray-Bans. But even when she squinted, she could not get him out of his original clothes in her mind's eye. He seemed to *belong* in them.

The dusty black weather-beaten hat on the vanity behind him looked like it belonged to him, too. It was used, serviceable and a little sexy.

She was thinking how sexy he was, when he spoke, startling her.

"Mo'nin', Lena. How do ya do?" he asked politely, formally, and sort of tipped his head toward her.

He was smiling so broadly, Lena had to admire his strong small white teeth. She smiled back.

He took this as encouragement and began his introductions again. "I'm Herman. I'm here 'cause you called me up."

His insistence that she was responsible was really puzzling her.

"I'm a spirit, Lena. Been one fo' most a hundred years. But you called me here and made me real. You did that. And here I am."

She still stood speechless, but she thought, You certainly *are here.*

As if to put a real punctuation mark at the end of that sentence, Herman stretched out his nearly transparent arm to her, and Lena watched in amazement as the limb began to materialize before her. As in an anatomy class, she saw the marrow and the bone form—she could see how his wrists' sockets fit together, how his elbow worked, how his fingers flexed—the tissue and muscle and cartilage cover that, the blood and tissue around and through and over that. Then, the beautiful dark brown skin, callused and cut and burned and scarred in places, over that. Then, a few curly dark hairs appeared on his knuckles and above his wristbone.

Before the sweet brown skin appeared over his beautifully symmetrical skeleton as his entire body began to materialize, she saw his heart beating in his chest, the blood rushing in one side, pumping out the other. She saw his lungs appear and fill with air. She witnessed his skull forming—he even had what her grandmother had called a "sense knot" on the back of his skull—over his brain.

"Jesus, Mary and Joseph," Lena intoned like a nun as she watched, transfixed and naked, except for a towel.

Watching the creation, the transformation, Lena thought, There ought to be music. Creation music. And right away, the wind outside began rustling the trees and the heavy metal wind chimes hanging in the enclosed porch leading to the deck outside the French doors of Lena's bedroom.

She was too charmed by the beauty of the metamorphosis to be frightened by its macabre aspects. She was too charmed by this spirit of a man, this "Herman."

He became more and more real, more and more solid, more and more firm, more and more precise, more and more tangible right there before her eyes, as if fed by her seeing him.

In a matter of seconds, she could no longer see right through him at all. He was truly there.

He sighed one time, then he spoke, repeating his declaration in an ever stronger, more forceful voice.

"I'm Herman. I'm here 'cause you called me up. I sho' 'nuff wanted to come. But I wouldn't be here if you didn'a called me here. Period."

Then, he reached over and casually took her hand lightly in his new one. Lena could feel the blood coursing through the veins of his elegantly formed wrist, could actually feel his pulse. And she felt a tingle that traveled from her fingers all the way up her shoulder to her chest. There, it made her heart flutter a bit. The feeling was so thrilling, she had to catch her breath. He then escorted her as naturally as anything through the bedroom to the deck as she clutched her towel to her naked body.

She did not hesitate a moment but trailed behind him silently. She hardly noticed where they were headed because she could not take her eyes off the strong concave spot at the small of his back. Even beneath his shirt, it appeared sculptured.

Outside on the wide, deep sycamore deck, more wind chimes played along with the orchestral sounds of the Ocawatchee rushing by. Lena smiled at the beauty of the natural music.

Herman led her to the cushions in a teak swing hanging from long ropes connected to a high beam over the deck and they sat. He continued to hold onto her hand. Not against her will yet securely. She thought she could actually feel him become human.

With his unencumbered hand, he pointed to the remnants of Lena and Sister's man-summoning ceremony.

"This when it happened, Lena. You called me up."

It took a second for Lena to realize what Herman meant.

"You trying to tell me it worked?!" she shouted, catching her breath. "That the two of us, half-drunk, performed a ceremony that called forth a man!!? The ceremony called you up?!" Lena asked incredulously.

Herman just laughed. Not a foolish or a derisive laugh, just a truly tickled one.

"All this little stuff," he said, smiling and pointing to the ashes and candles and pictures. "The power ain't in this. These thangs just to show that you *willin'*. Willin' to do the ceremony. Willin' to go to the trouble to get the pink candle. It show you believe.

"But yo' 'ceremony' didn't call me up, Lena. *You* called me up. It was *you*, Lena. *You* invited me in. That's all it took. An invitation from you."

Lena turned away to try to hide her smile. This ghost, this Herman, pronounced the word "invitation" as if it were "imitation." He said it a bit like folks she remembered from her childhood at The Place, like her elderly gardener still pronounced it.

The pronunciations sounded so dear to Lena's ears. It was not so much that this Herman mispronounced some words as it was that he stamped them with the imprint of his own style of speech. This Herman *claimed* his words!

Lena felt in her bones he was coming to claim her, too.

When she didn't say anything, Herman continued. "I been watchin' you fo' decades, Lena."

Lena pulled her hand away from the ghost's at the disquieting thought of being secretly watched. Even if it was by a ghost. She could see by his face that the gesture hurt his heart, but she felt exposed and vulnerable at this news.

He seemed to twitch a bit and added quickly, "Nothin' improper. Nothin' I don't think you would think improper, anyway." Herman put his newly formed elbows on his newly formed knees and leaned forward with a serious look on his face. And she pulled her towel a bit tighter around her.

"Lena, it wan't like that," he said softly. "Shoot, spirits been watchin' you since ya been born."

"I wasn't *at* yo' birth, Lena. But I sho' did hear 'bout it," Herman said.

"What do you mean, you *heard* about it?" Lena wanted to know. She could not believe that the Mulberry gossip mill extended even into the beyond.

"Oh, we spirits communicate wid each other more than we talk to ya'll," Herman replied matter-of-factly. "And yo' birth gave us a lot to talk about. It was almost like it shook the whole afterlife world.

"I was on my way back hereabouts to Mulberry to see what the to-do was all about when yo' mama poured out that caul tea in that green vase a' flowers and yo' protection from mean spirits along wid it. There was noise and disturbance in my world like I had never heard when that happen. Lena, it was like all heaven and hell had been let loose. Oh, the howls and screams and shrieks and yells and lamentations that went up that day. Oh, Lena, even I was a little disquieted by it all.

"Word got 'round 'bout yo' mama throwin' out that precious caul tea about as quick as word of yo' birth. Shoot, Lena, from what I hear, yo' birth, now, *that* was som'um," he said as if he had been conversing with her all his life. Then, he chuckled. "*Almost* as impressive as yo' *ritual* the other night."

Lena could not seem to help herself. No matter how many times she silently warned herself to keep alert while sitting nearly naked with this strange man on her deserted deck, she kept getting more and more comfortable with him.

"You were around when I was born *and* last week when Sister was here?" she asked.

In reply, he closed his dark eyes and began to imitate the sounds perfectly that she and her friend had made as Sister had invoked the spirits to arise with a love for Lena.

Maybe, he *was* there, she thought.

"Lena, I *was there*," he said. "There was a wanin' moon that night and when ya'll lit the white candles, a big old cloud passed over it."

Lena felt a little chill on her bare shoulders and realized the sun overhead had gone behind a cloud.

"I heard ya'll both. From the first word you uttered, Lena, I knew it was me you was callin' up. I didn't even have to fight nobody else off to get t' ya this time."

Lena would have been embarrassed for anyone to know it, but she felt a little swell of pride at the idea of this good-looking, kindhearted spirit fighting to get to her.

"Shoot, Lena," he said, seeming to read her mind again, "I'd fight the very devil fo' *you*."

Lena had to bite her bottom lip to combat the hot rush that flooded her entire naked body. Herman kept on talking.

"And when Sister was finished chantin' what she had learned from Madame Delphie, you, Lena, you was sayin', 'Jesus, Jesus, Jesus, Jesus, Jesus, Jesus, Jesus, Jesus, Jesus.' "

Lena looked at him with her mouth hanging open.

"See," he said triumphantly, "I told ya I was there.

"But that's all mumbo jumbo if you don't truly open yo' heart to belief and, Lena, whether you know it or not, you did indeed open yo' heart to me 'cause we sittin' here talkin' to each other."

She recalled her prayer from the night before. But all she said was, "Um."

"Mostly, Lena, I wanted you to see me in the full light a' day. So you could see clearly.

"You had a night to think on it. And I had a eternity to toss and turn thinkin' I done misread yo' invitation."

He paused.

"Lena, I don't care how good it feel now that we laughin' and talkin' and all. Now's the time I want to get this straight. I been wantin' you a long time, Lena. But I don't want you gettin' the wrong idea. I want us both to understand right now that I wouldn't never come up inside a' you like I did last night in yo' pool ifn you hadn'a asked me in. I wouldn'a done that. I don't do that. I ain't that kinda man. I wa'n't alive, and I ain't that kinda man dead. You hear me, Lena?"

She started to nod yes.

"I sho' didn't mean to scare you or force you. By the way you was actin' in yo' car and dancin' yesterday down at that place a' yo's, I was sho' you saw me or felt me there. You looked right at me and cussed."

"Give me a minute here," Lena was finally able to say.

"Lena, I know the difference 'tween 'quit' and 'no.' I do. And I swear to God, all I heard was 'Quit.' "

"Just give me a minute here," Lena said again. She felt she needed to slow things down a bit. She was falling so easily into conversation with this full-bodied spirit that it scared her a bit. She had hardly spoken since he had shown his face. And she was having trouble believing that this ghost was truly real.

"To tell you the truth, Lena, I'm havin' some trouble believin' I'm here myself," Herman said, reading her mind again.

"I been floatin' 'round these parts a long time, 'cause this the last place I lived. Middle Georgia, South Georgia and North Flor'da. This used to be my old stompin' grounds. And, too, this spot a' earth meant som'um to me. But like *this? Flesh and blood! Bone and muscle!*

"Naw, Lena, I just been kinda floatin' 'round from what seem like place to place.

"Sometimes it feel like I been in the belly a' the whale fo' just three days and three nights. Then, again, like now, it seem like I been waitin' a eternity.

"To be honest wid you, Lena—and I don't ever plan to be nothin' else but—even though I been hangin' 'round Georgia and Flor'da, mostly, I don't know *exactly* where I been these last hundred years 'cause I ain't been in yo' world or the next."

"The last one hundred years?" Lena wasn't sure if she had heard correctly.

"Well, this here nineteen hundred and ninety-five, ain't it?" he asked.

"Um-huh, April second . . . or third . . . or fourth." Lena couldn't believe that with Herman sitting so near she could not even remember the correct date.

"Yeah, that's when I passed. The first week of April in eighteen hundred and ninety-five. Kicked in the head by a mule."

Herman turned his head to Lena to show her the half-moon scar on his right temple. It made her gasp. And Herman sort of reached his hand out to comfort her. He merely brushed her bare shoulder above where she had the towel tucked around her, and she felt better right away. The touch, electric and warm, felt like a blessing. It left her arm tingling.

"Oh, it was my fault, really, Lena," he said reassuringly. "My mind was somewhere else, som'um I was workin' on, probably, can't remember what it was to save my life. But I know I was distracted. And I came up on the mule from the back too fast, sudden-like.

"I shoulda knowed better, Lena, but, like I say, my mind was somewhere else. He just r'ared up and kicked back on me with both hind legs, and I was dead 'fo' I hit the ground."

Lena found herself growing sad at the picture Herman painted. Herman lying on the ground, blood gushing from his wound, his brain kicked into stillness. And he rushed to make it better for her.

"I wouldn'a been no good fo' anybody if I had 'a survived, Lena," he said with a self-effacing grin and a shake of his generous-sized head.

Lena did not think that was a bit funny, but she had to smile at this man making fun of his own death to try to make her feel better. Then, she chuckled at the thought of Herman, this handsome husky black man from another century, not being good for anything.

"I'm good fo' you, Lena, baby, I'm yo' man. You called me here. You called me up just as good. I'm yo' man."

Lena liked the sound of that. She had never had anyone refer to himself as her man.

"In the car the other mornin' by the river, last night in the pool, I just got too close," Herman continued. "But I tell you. Next time, *you* decide when we get that close again, all right?"

His suggestion made all the difference in the world to Lena's comfort.

Lena stared at him as the pieces fell into place.

"Herman," she said, using his name for the first time. "You were the breeze. You were the face in the mirror in the car. You were the smell at The Place."

Herman smiled and nodded. And Lena suddenly felt she was talking with a trusted friend, not a strange ghost.

They sat on the deck—she still wrapped in her big fluffy towel, her wet braids hanging to her shoulders and dripping down her bare back in the morning air—and talked.

"There was just always som'um 'bout you, Lena, that seemed to draw me to you when you seemed to need some he'p or some guidance or some protectin' a little. I'd be right there beside you in Middle Georgia. Then, the next thang I know, I'd be off somewheres else, down deep in Flor'da or over in the panhandle where we went scoutin' for oysters and such.

"You know, it ain't easy fo' a spirit, even one still caught 'tween this world and that, to just move around anywhere he please. Yo' spirit is just so tied to some places and sometimes to people.

"That's what happened wid you. I'd see you as a little thang bein' pulled over alive into a world of dead folks by another pretty little girl, and I can't help but tickle her feets so she let you go. Then, the next thang I know I'm down in the bogs of the Okefenokee Swamps. Next time I see you, Lena, you a big girl layin' out in the woods behind yo' house at night. Scared as you can be. And rightfully so, too. There was all kinda thangs out in that night wid you. It was like watchin' a baby rabbit 'bout to be set upon by a wildcat."

"In the woods? Was I about sixteen or so?" Lena asked, remembering her nights of sleepwalking as a teenager and the terror of waking one night alone and lost in the woods dressed only in her nightgown.

"I don't know how old 'xactly you was, Lena, but you looked to be 'bout a girl in her teen years. I didn't know what to do 'bout you. Lena, you was surrounded by all kinds a' spirits. So I just girded my guts the way my pa had taught me as a boy and strode right into that scene.

"Well, I musta been more powerful than I thought or I was just doin' what I was supposed to do, 'cause them spirits scattered. They just broke in a million pieces, it seem like, and scattered."

Lena, sitting on the edge of her chair, listened as if she were five and her grandmother were telling one of the ghost stories that Nellie thought were too graphic for the children. Especially for Lena, whom her mother had marked in the womb as high-strung.

"Then, there was the time I saw you on the train. You was goin' to college, I think. You didn't even know how surrounded you was with spirits ready to do you harm. I was real glad when you made it through that. Then, later in yo' dormitory room, I think you saw the spirits then, didn't you?"

Mostly, Lena just nodded or shook her head in response to what sounded like rhetorical questions. Every once in a while, she would think, I'm sitting here on my deck talking to a ghost in broad daylight. But for the most part she did not give her behavior a thought. Herman enthralled her.

Lena was learning more about life, death and herself in one conversation with Herman than she had learned in her whole life of struggling and bumping around trying to find things out.

She had not felt this relaxed with anyone since she first encountered Sister almost thirty years before.

Herman told her all kinds of things about spirits.

"Ghosts can only terrorize folks who *allow* theyselves to be terrorized," he told her.

"It's easier fo' spirits like me to come back to this world 'cause I ain't completely crossed over yet.

"I gi' you my word that you the first livin' human who been able to draw me completely back into the world. I'd stop by a campsite and try to eat a piece of fried fish or tripe or som'um good I couldn't resist. But mostly I just been wanderin' and watchin' and observin'. Content to do it. There's so much to see and appreciate in yo' life. Somehow, we can't seem to get the knack a' that while we still here livin'."

Herman tried in different ways to explain to Lena about the state he had been in since his accidental death in 1895. But in the final analysis, he had to admit, "Lena, I don't rightly know why I'm still out here like this. All I know fo' certain is that with each tick of yo' clock, with each passin' of each one of yo' years, I seem to get stronger and stronger. I feel I must feel less dead right now than just about anybody around, 'live or dead."

He paused and looked Lena dead in her eyes.

"And now, Lena, I know why I'm here. 'Cause *you* want me here. Period."

Lena could not help herself. She believed him.

She believed she had invited Herman in, and she was beginning to feel it was the best decision she had ever made.

14
CATCH-UP

When Lena heard James Petersen noisily coming into the back door for the day, she jumped like a cat.

"My goodness, what time is it?" she exclaimed, trying to gather both her towel and wits about her.

Herman tilted his head back and looked up at the sun.

"Oh, it's 'bout 'leven-thirty or noon," he said as if he were checking a clock.

"Noon??!!" Lena shouted.

"Uh-huh," Herman answered. Lena could have sworn she saw him smile.

"Noon??!! You mean to tell me I been sitting here talking to you all morning?"

Herman just nodded his head.

"Noon???!! I can't believe this," she screamed and, wrapping her towel more securely, hurried inside.

She could hear James Petersen coming through the house toward her suite.

"First, I waste all that time in the hospital yesterday and now all this morning *with a ghost,*" Lena muttered to herself and Herman as she headed for the bathroom, tucking her big Turkish towel in above her breasts.

"I do apologize, Lena," he said lightly, following her. He said it sincerely, but Lena couldn't help but feel he was almost teasing her. Then, he dropped all teasing tones.

"I'm especially sorry for that business yesterday mornin' down at yo' juke downtown."

Lena spun around in her tracks. She turned and looked directly into the calm deep face of the ghost leaning on the jamb of her bedroom door.

"Of course," she said. She had sensed the connection earlier. "That was *your* room!"

But Herman didn't have a chance to reply.

James Petersen was standing at the bedroom door calling to Lena through the open door to the bathroom.

"Lena, you still here?" he asked, surprise on the verge of concern in his voice. "Everybody was worried 'bout you. They just called me to check. How come you didn't tell me you had a accident yesterday?"

He did not wait for her to respond.

"You call in sick?" James Petersen asked, averting his eyes as he almost caught sight of Lena in the bathroom mirror unwrapping the big white towel from her body and then, suddenly, rewrapping it outside the shower.

"Sick?" Lena could not get herself together enough to answer sensibly. "Sick?" she repeated dumbly while she watched Herman starting to fade over by the door to the bedroom. She could almost see through him the way she had when he had first appeared. But she could still see him. James Petersen did not seem to see Herman at all.

"Good God, Lena, you got thirty-six messages on your machine," James Petersen shouted right through Herman as he glanced over at the machine next to the bed he was stripping of linen. "Didn't you hear it ringing? Oh, look, the ring is turned to 'off.' "

James Petersen was surprised. "You do that?" he asked as he balled up the linen and tossed it onto a chair.

Lena answered vaguely, "Oh, right. The phone. The answering machine, James Petersen." But she was still watching the spot where Herman stood.

"I guess those pain pills they gave me at the hospital made me oversleep," she called to her houseman in the next room. Herman had all but disappeared now.

Lena had only rushed from the deck into the bathroom through the bedroom, but she felt that she was running in circles as she hurried into her dressing room through the second bathroom door. She could not bring herself to walk through the vapor of Herman that still lingered in the doorway between the bath and the bedroom.

She grabbed a red Versace suit with a short tight skirt from the rack, threw open a couple of drawers and boxes, snatched some silky red and black underwear and sheer hose out and headed back to the bathroom, dropping her towel on the floor as she slipped into the shower again. She felt clammy all over.

"No telling how many meetings and appointments I've missed already," she muttered as she soaped her loofah mitt in the steamy shower and quickly scrubbed her body.

The spot on her bare shoulder where Herman—she said the name out loud but in a whisper just to see what happened and the door to the shower rattled a bit, making Lena jump and giggle—had briefly touched her in conversation was still tingling a bit, and she barely washed it.

Herman had faded from sight by the time she hurried out of the shower. But his old hat was still resting on the vanity of the sink as if it belonged there. She looked around for James Petersen, then she reached out and touched the battered hat. It seemed to shimmer a bit where it sat. Then, slowly, right before Lena's eyes, it disappeared.

She stood a moment in the middle of the huge bathroom and stared at the spot where the hat had rested, thinking about her morning visit from Herman.

"Uh, uh, uh, a spirit, a ghost, come to be my man," Lena said aloud as she finished drying off and reached for the bottle of lotion on the counter. She had to laugh.

"Now, what else was I expecting?" she asked herself with a dry chuckle.

She slipped into her red outfit and, flipping open her cellular phone on the way out the door past James Petersen, called Precious to say she was on her way into town.

When she slid behind the wheel of her car, she expected the interior to smell like The Place the day before. She was disappointed that it did not. She looked several times in the mirror as she pulled out onto her road, hoping to catch a glimpse of a ghost there. But there was none.

Lord help me, she thought, I think I miss him already.

Out on U.S. 90, Lena had meant to gun the motor and fly into town. Instead, she found herself cruising along at the speed limit while singing softly to herself,

> *"Looking everywhere*
> *Haven't found him yet*
> *He's the big affair*
> *I cannot forget*
> *Only man I ever think of with regret."*

All day long, she tried to play catch-up. Rushing into meetings breathlessly to be greeted with puzzled disapproving faces. Getting someone else to collect and deliver the cakes for the raffle at the church even though the nuns and ladies who provided the baked goodies all said how surprised they were and how disappointed the children were that she didn't come herself.

Through it all, she went about the day singing the same tune under her breath the way she, as a child, had heard Dinah Washington purr it on her parents' old 78 rpm records.

"There's a somebody I'm longing to see
I hope that he turns out to be
Someone who'll watch over me."

She sang it in her off-key fashion with such quiet contentment that the women at her realty office got a little miffed that Lena was not a bit more contrite about throwing a monkey wrench in their well-ordered schedule two days in a row. All day at the hospital and she wasn't even sick, they thought. Then, a whole morning of scheduling wasted. And at the end of the week, too.

The women—for only women worked at Candace and Lena never had to face even a mention of sexual discrimination—moved around the bright and airy office complex behind Lena and looked at each other out of the sides of their faces. Wanda, Brenda, Carroll, Deborah, Caryl, Dorothy and Lois—friends of a sort since elementary school—knew Lena was usually sensitive about her nonsinging voice. Now, the women noted silently and with raised eyebrows, here she was singing out loud as she signed contracts or headed out the door to show a special client a property. Then, here she would come back in singing the same tune. And she didn't sound too bad, either.

Just more of Lena's luck, they thought.

Her employees all knew she was born with a veil over her face, and although they appreciated working in the caul's lucky aura, they did tire of Lena McPherson always getting first pick of anything new or nice or eligible in town, or in the state, for that matter. She seemed to meet the new men in town in just the same way she was always the first to sport the newest fashions. She looked good in the clothes, but the affairs seemed to die abirthing.

"Hell, it never work out, do it?" local women from Savannah to Atlanta asked each other over the phone. The newly divorced president of the nearest agricultural college—"Man still husky in his fifties!"—a few years before was the last straw.

Her former grammar school classmates, returned to Mulberry and the South from Southern California and upstate New York and Minneapolis with ended marriages and nearly grown children in tow, would hardly be able to keep from cutting their eyes at her in Mass. "She didn't even hardly mess over that last one. That college president. Didn't hardly even mess over him."

"Well, it still ain't right that she just *automatically* get the new men 'cause she got the prettiest clothes in town. Shoot! I do very well, thank you, for a schoolteacher. And I could stand to meet a man myself."

After Lena's last dating fiasco, Toya, an office assistant, met her boss at the espresso machine and laughed, "Oh, Miss McPherson, you probably gon' end up marrying the *garbageman*!"

The married women in town were the worst.

"Lord, ham mercy, all these young single women here," her married sisters would proclaim at parties where she was one of the "young single women there."

"Lord, let me get my *husband* and go home. Let me get my *husband* from up in through here with all these young single women with no children and no responsibilities and go home."

If Sister were present, she would always lean over to Lena and say, *"Please*, take your *husband* and get away from here. Please! Get him off my bra strap."

Lena had learned a thing or two in being a pretty single woman for more than two decades. She had learned to say "No!!!" whenever the husband of one of her colleagues or clients asked her, "Lena, want to know a secret?"

When Lena had first hurried in that afternoon, flushed and radiant in her fire-engine-red suit and red patent-leather Gucci mules, she had muttered something about an emergency at home that kept her all morning, but that did little to placate her people. They took into consideration that she had spent all the day before in the hospital. But that was yesterday and folks had *business* they wanted to conduct.

Some, like the receptionist, Mrs. Jeffries, who had known Lena practically all her life, were genuinely concerned.

"Good God, Lena, where you been?!! We didn't know what had

happened to you. Mr. Jackson called three or four times. Come here, baby, you got a piece of thread on that pretty suit. Why, Lena, we thought you was *dead* out there by the river."

Lena just gave her a quick hug and a quick apology. "I'm so sorry to have worried you all." Then, she moved on.

"Well, we called you four or five times," Wanda said as she gathered papers into her briefcase and popped the screen off on her computer. But all Lena offered in explanation was an absentminded "Uh-huh," because her mind was on Herman, wondering if he would be at home when she got there.

Precious gave Lena the names and numbers of missed appointments who would not be placated by a call from a personal assistant.

"Mr. Potter at the bank said he didn't think you had ever missed an appointment. Mr. Jackson finally came by this morning just after you called. He said he was 'bout to head out toward your house if he didn't get an answer. And Miss Louise won't believe me when I tell her you had vegetables for lunch. She wants to talk with *you*."

When Precious had finished her litany of guilt, she stopped and looked at Lena intently.

"Can I do something else for you, Miss McPherson?" she asked as she poured her boss a crystal goblet of mineral water and brought it to her desk.

When Lena smiled her thanks and shook her head, Precious leaned down and really looked at Lena.

"Really, Miss Mac, are you okay? You look kind of funny."

Lena just laughed and waved Precious on back to her work. "Oh, I'm fine," she assured her.

Lena *felt* kind of funny. Although her attention was now on her myriad duties and responsibilities—juggling real estate, personal, community and business concerns the way she always did—her real focus was out at her house: the ghost of a man with whom she had spent the morning.

In just a matter of a few hours, Herman had made Lena feel as if she truly had always had someone watching over her. She felt as if throughout her life, he had taken her firmly and gently by her shoulders between his two strong hands and turned her out of harm's way.

It seemed Herman had been watching over her all her life, all day and all night.

> I'm a little lamb who's lost in the wood
> I know I could always be good
> To one who'll watch over me.

It had made Lena feel safe and protected to hear Herman tell that morning of times he had seen her in trouble and tried to help. Of times he had tried to veer her away from some scary, frightful ghost. Of times he had even wrestled like Jacob with the angel to keep some angry lonely vindictive spirit from overwhelming her. The images began to soften her memories of those terrorizing times.

Then it came to her.

Herman was her guardian angel!

Lena immediately thought of Sister Gemma in fourth grade who had instructed all the students at Blessed Martin de Porres Elementary to leave a little room on the edge of their seats for their guardian angels to sit.

"Now, he's with you all the time and it's only right to think of him," Sister said, for the guardian angel was always a "him." Years later, Lena was still angry with herself for not having questioned the automatic male gender of all guardian angels. "So, just scoot over a bit when you sit at your desk or in the pew in church. Even if it's not a Catholic church," the chunky Irish nun assured the Protestant children in the class.

"You see, you don't even have to be baptized into the *one true church* to have a guiding spirit. No, you don't. God gives one to each and every soul He creates. Catholic and Protestant. Jew and Gentile. Isn't our Lord generous?"

Lena had to chuckle at the memory now. She certainly felt blessed with the Lord's generosity in sending Herman to watch over her. She even looked over her shoulder every now and then to see if he was standing there the way he had stood in her bathroom that morning.

She handled her duties, made apologies, smoothed ruffled feathers, soothed concerned townspeople. But the whole day, she was thinking about this solid corporeal ghost she had last seen disappearing in her bathroom.

"A ghost!" she would say softly to herself. Her mind landed briefly on Rachel.

Umm, she thought suddenly, I wonder if Rachel knows Herman. Maybe, she had something to do with his coming here, she speculated.

Then, she thought, If he died a hundred years ago, maybe he was a slave, too, like Rachel! It was a sobering thought. But to Lena, Herman did not look any older than thirty or so. She assumed that spirits did not continue to age after death.

She continued to calculate in her head as she sat at the big flat teak table she used as a desk and returned missed phone calls, if he died in 1895, then slavery still existed when he was born.

Maybe, he looks younger than he is, she thought.

What she really wanted to do she could not: reach for the phone and call Sister with the news of this new man in her life.

She chuckled to herself recalling the Mae West line: "It's not the man in your life. It's the life in your man."

From his smile alone it appeared to Lena that this man, though dead, had plenty of life in him.

"Herman."

She said it softly as she sat at her desk, the telephone poised in her hand. She felt a little tingle run through her body.

"Herman."

She said it again, the way he pronounced it, "Hur-mon," a little louder this time, and felt a smile spread all over her face.

15

STARS

It was dark, and a big old full moon was shining in the blue-black velvet sky dotted with what looked like every star in the galaxy by the time Lena got her business day about straight and headed back to her home out by the river.

She and Precious were the last ones to leave the Candace offices. But even after a long day, Lena wasn't a bit weary. She was so excited she could hardly keep still.

"I wonder, will he be there? I wonder if James Petersen saw him. I wonder how he's going to come and go? I wonder where he'll sleep . . . I wonder . . ."

She laughed at herself because she didn't even feel like a little foolish fool.

For nearly her entire life, and especially since she had met Madame Delphie in New Orleans, she had felt in danger of being enveloped, eaten up, consumed by that other ghostly world that she knew existed. Now here she was driving as fast as she could to embrace just that world.

By the time she hit U.S. 90 along the Ocawatchee, she could feel her heart pounding as if she were sixteen and going on her first date. She was gunning the motor at 85 mph, fast even for her. But she was excited.

Her stomach felt as if it were full of butterflies. And her entire body felt flushed as if she had driven into a wall of fire. She dropped a window and let the cool spring evening air into the car. The night air felt chilly on her skin, but she was still hot.

Her heart had not settled down since she heard the first "Ahem" outside her shower that morning. It was still beating wildly in her chest, and she unfastened the shiny top button on the jacket of her suit to give her heart a little more room.

Lena hit the CD selector and smiled when Billie Holiday's voice joined the sound of the night wind whistling through the automobile.

> You're my thrill, you do something to me
> You send chills right through me
> When I look at you, I can't keep still
> You're . . . my . . . thrill.

When she crossed the wooden bridge spanning the Ocawatchee on her dirt road, she felt for a moment that someone had arranged a greeting party for her. All over the surface of the river, flowing clear and pristine in the darkness, lightning bugs—thousands of them, it appeared to Lena—floating in droves, signaled their welcome to her in green fluorescent flashes.

BLINK-BLINK, BLINK-BLINK, BLINK-BLINK.

There were so many fireflies that it was difficult to see the reflection of the sorrel moon on the clear glassy surface of the river. It seemed there were hundreds more than the night before when she had first noticed them.

And there was music in the air. So many animal noises that the racket drowned out Lady Day. Tree toads, said to be in danger of extinction worldwide and a harbinger of the end of life, seemed to be having a noisy convention on Lena's land, all singing alto. Frogs on the banks of the river added their bass with deep throaty roars. Cicadas, awake after a seven-year slumber, sang their sopranos and falsettos on cue. Other crickets and creatures of the night joined their chorus to the symphony already being played.

Altogether, they sounded like a true symphony. The din grew louder and louder as she neared her house. Night birds hooted and screeched. A family of bobwhites began calling to each other—"Bob-white! Bob-white! Bob-white!" A lone loon put in her crazy-sounding laugh.

And Lena had to laugh, too.

The symphony was turning into more of a shivaree.

The fireflies, flying low right along with her car, frolicked in the air, lighting the way along with the Mercedes' headlights cutting through the tunnel of darkness formed by the overhanging oaks and pines along a stretch on her road.

She honked her horn *beep-beep-bee-beep-beep* when she drove down her winding road past James Petersen's house to let him know she was home and everything was okay with her. But when she pulled up in the driveway between the house and the stables and parked the car, she questioned whether she was in the right place. She recalled from her childhood that ghosts could do just about anything they wanted, unfettered by the laws of gravity and time and matter as mere mortals were.

I wonder if Herman created some kind of lovely ghostly mansion on this spot while I was gone, she thought. Then, she smiled at the thought of his name. Herman.

There were no lights on outside and a strange new light seemed to be burning inside at each and every window and glass door of the place. Lena was sure that some of the lightning bugs must have gotten inside. Every window in her big log lodge seemed filled with soft golden natural-looking light, welcoming her home.

She tried to be cool, but she found herself flying from the car along the stone alee of roses and mantles of bridal veil hanging overhead in pots and annuals flower beds bordered by crossties up to the back door of her house where the southern jasmine was thinking about budding. Soft light was shining from that entrance, too.

Herman met her at the door looking as real and solid as he had that morning, sporting a warm shy smile. Lena thought, This man is light itself. He's what's shining in my house.

"Good ee-bah-ning, Lena. I lit some tallows fo' you," he said, holding the door wide open, in a casual yet grand gesture.

Lena stood there a moment, gazing at this big good-looking old-timey man standing in her back doorway, welcoming her home. Other than Frank Petersen or his brother, James, it had been years since anyone was there to greet her when she returned home at the end of the day.

"Um," Lena said to herself. "So, this is what it feels like to have family again." She smiled and entered, feeling the depth and passion of his welcome warm her as if he had indeed lit a "tallow" deep in her belly.

Herman took a step back in his big soft black leather boots—a graceful step, Lena noticed—to let her in, and Lena let out a little gasp, "Oooo." All along one wall of the Glass Hall and into what she could see of the rest of her house was aglow with what looked like a hundred burning candles.

He must have lit every candle in the house, even the birthday candles, she thought, enchanted by the look of her cabin completely illuminated by the flickering light.

"I used all I could find. What ya think?" Herman asked, closing the door behind them. Lena could hear a taste of uncertainty in his voice, and it moved her. He really cares what I think of what he's done, she thought.

"It's just beautiful," she said sincerely.

"I care 'bout everythang got to do wi' you, Lena. Like I tole ya this mo'nin', I'm yo' man. I loves you already. You just got t' decide if you my woman. That's all."

"That's all?" she asked, smiling. She could hardly believe how much fun she was having just messing with this man.

"That's all," he said, smiling back at her.

Lena dropped her purse on top of a heavy flowered silk throw with bronze-colored fringe on the back of the sofa and walked through the rest of the house on the deck side. There were burning candles leading all the way through the pool room into her bedroom suite at the other end of the house. Out on the deck, Herman had lit tall fat candles inside hurricane globes that had not been lit since her last weak attempt at a dinner party more than a year before.

He had even lit some of the candles left over from the man-calling ceremony.

"I didn't think you'd mind me ligh'in' up all yo' candles." He paused and smiled. "Even them *ceremonial* ones. I don't think you gon' have much more use fo' *them*."

He came up behind her and stood looking over her shoulder at all he had done. Lena could feel his breath on her neck, and she had to step away quickly to catch *her* breath.

"Mind?" Lena said, walking on through the house and rubbing the tingling spot on the back of her neck. "Everything looks wonderful."

Her house always looked ready for company. James Petersen saw to that. But tonight the house *felt* cozy, too.

Lena had seen his old black hat hanging on her grandmother's antique mirrored coatrack by the back door when she had first come in. So, she figured, he planned to stay awhile.

Herman had laid and lit a good-sized fire in the cavernous fireplace in the main room. As Lena walked by, the heat felt good against her legs. The country smell and the pop and sizzle of seasoned split oak wood filled the house to the rafters. Clever Mr. Buck had vented all her fireplaces so the heat and smell blew into the house and didn't go up and out the chimney with the smoke. She noticed Herman had carefully replaced the huge leaf-embossed screen so no sparks from the pinecones he had also thrown in there could pop out and burn her as she passed.

Herman had also laid a smaller fire in her bedroom hearth against the cool of the spring night air.

She stepped out on the deck in her bare stocking feet just in time to catch something in the sky that looked like a spark from the fire. "Oh, my God, it looks like a comet," she whispered in awe as the shooting star arced across the sky.

"You had any sup'er this ee-bah-ning, Lena?" Herman asked as if he asked her that every night.

She jumped a little at the sound of his voice. I got to get used to *that*, she thought.

"Uh-uh. Not yet. I usually get something before I go to bed."

"Well, there's a whole heap a' cooked groceries in there in yo' kitchen. And it look good, too. I waited fo' ya."

When Lena walked into the kitchen ahead of Herman, she saw that he had already started heating up the food in her favorite heavy gray pots on the stove. It smelled good.

"I usually just stick the food in the microwave," she said, lifting lids and stirring the big pot of black-eyed peas, turning the gas flame down a bit.

"I looked at that box," Herman answered her about the microwave oven. "Real interestin'. Right clever. But it ain't the same as heatin' it up on the stove over fire, is it?"

He came over to stand by Lena and eyed the food hungrily. She turned with a big silver serving spoon in her hand and lifted it to Herman's lips to let him taste. He closed his eyes and took the whole spoon in his mouth.

"Ummm-mmmmmmmm-uh," he said as he slowly chewed and swallowed. Then, he sighed.

Lena smiled at Herman's appreciative yummy sounds. Her intimate gesture of feeding him from the silver spoon had even taken her a little bit by surprise. But his grunts and purrs made it seem so natural, just the way it should have felt.

"That sho' taste good, Lena. You eat like this every day?"

"Uh-huh," she replied. "I call them my CARE package meals."

The town women and the one man who prepared the CARE meals did care for her.

Most of the food she had consumed in the last ten years had been cooked by the loving hands of Mulberry women, and one man who died the year before of AIDS. They felt it was their lifelong duty to feed Lena after her entire family was dead. Like mourners come to a never-ending wake, the steady stream of food continued into her house out by the river this tenth year after the double memorial services had been performed.

Old women who knew her, knew her daddy, knew her mama, knew her grandmama, knew her daddy's family, knew her mama's family, ever went to The Place, whose husband or man ever went to The Place regularly, or were the recipients of the family love or largesse continued each week to send Lena food.

Delicious food, hot-right-from-the-oven food.

Fried chicken, with thick light brown crunchy gravy. Chicken-fried steak with darker brown gravy. Pork neckbones and spaghetti simmered in tomatoes and onions and bell pepper. Pork roast, standing rib roast and pot roast. Roast hen, turkey, duck and chicken. Chicken and dumplings.

Pots of collard greens from somebody's garden kept Lena regular for a week. Pole beans with little new potatoes and onions cut in quarters the way her father had liked them. Squash casserole, baked macaroni and cheese and candied yams. Pickled beets and peaches and bread-and-butter pickles.

They sent turkey and dressing and rice and gravy that didn't taste like Sunday dinner but tasted more like Thanksgiving or Christmas.

And the desserts! The desserts! The women and Cecil sent red velvet cakes, chocolate layer cakes, lemon-cheese cakes, coconut cakes, German chocolate cakes, lemon pound cakes, applesauce cakes. They sent banana pudding and bread pudding with raisins, pineapple chunks and peach slices. They sent peach and blackberry cobblers; icebox pies and coconut cream pies and lemon meringue pies. If they had their way, Lena would have weighed three hundred pounds.

"Lots of it gets taken out to the homeless shelter or one of the soup kitchens in town where 'my children'—some young people in town—eat some meals. James Petersen takes it for me usually in the afternoon before I get home or the next morning."

"Then, why don't the ladies just take the food to the soup kitchen d'rectly?" Herman asked.

Lena just chuckled at the idea of trying to explain the machinations of her and her folks. "You *are* new around here, aren't you?"

And he chuckled because *he, too,* knew how good it made him feel to do something for Lena.

Herman began humming to himself as he moved around the kitchen getting out of Lena's way, watching where she kept bowls and plates and utensils. Hearing the tune, Lena reached over without even thinking and turned on the controls for the music system. Nat King Cole singing "Mona Lisa" filled the cabin.

Herman was not really in the way. It felt good to Lena to have him in there. She even pretended she couldn't reach a big serving bowl and a crystal flower vase in the cabinets over the soapstone sink and needed his long arms to get them down for her.

"Oh, happy to he'p ya," he said, and leapt sprightly to retrieve the desired items.

Lena could see he wasn't comfortable standing around doing nothing. So, she asked him to get the pails of cut flowers inside the door on the west-side screened porch.

She never even considered that Herman might not know his way around her house.

He came back bearing two deep tin flower pails of daffodils, delphiniums, jonquils, dogwood limbs, twirls of wisteria blooms and even some early roses and sprouting grapevines.

"Lena, this part a' yo' magic?" he asked.

She smiled at Herman's handsome face framed by the beautiful spring blooms.

"No, that's Mr. Renfroe, the gardener's magic. He cuts flowers from all over the property whenever he works, either in the morning or the evening when the stems are nice and stiff, he says."

Lena came over to the pails and began choosing big tall flowers to put into the vase she had filled with sugar-sweetened tepid water. Herman watched her as if she were creating life with the pink, yellow and purple blossoms.

"He takes most of the flowers in to the nursing home in town or by Miss Onnie's house or Miss Pansy's or Miss Emma Floyd's, they can't get out and garden anymore. And on the weekend, either I take some or he takes some by St. Martin de Porres for Mass.

"But regardless, he always leaves some pretty ones for me on the side porch out of the sun. I used to have a house full of orchids. A man from North Carolina delivered them. But even with the greenhouse, I couldn't find enough time to keep them going."

With a grunt, she picked up the enormous arrangement she had put together and headed for the Great Jonah Room. Herman followed her wordlessly.

"If I don't have time to arrange them, James Petersen puts them out for me. He's pretty good at it," she said, placing the huge arrangement on a long narrow wooden table behind one of her copper-colored leather sofas facing the fireplace, then standing back to see how it looked there.

"Oh, I'm sorry, Lena," Herman said, bringing his hand to his broad brown brow, still mesmerized by her flower arranging, "I shoulda he'ped you wi' that. But I swear, you looked so pretty 'rrangin' them flowers there that I couldn't think or move fo' a minute."

Lena just smiled and went back to the kitchen to clip and arrange the other flowers. She tried and tried to set her face in an experienced "I've heard that shit before" mold, but she couldn't stop smiling and blushing a pretty hot color.

"You look like a flower yo'self in that red outfit, Lena." He walked in behind her and took down a large blue pottery vase from the open-faced cupboards and handed it to her.

"Pretty vase. Look like som'um my Indian people made."

"It's Seminole," Lena explained, taking it from him and filling it for the first time with water.

Herman just smiled and said, "I thought so. Seminoles some a' the folks I grew up with."

Lena turned the tap off.

"You grew up with Indians?" she asked. "You weren't on a plantation, you weren't a slave?"

She had not meant to blurt out the question, but it had been on her mind.

"Naw, Lena, my peoples wasn't slaves," Herman said. He stopped, lifted his strong chin a bit and studied Lena's face as he continued, "My pa and my ma took off from slavery."

Lena held her breath as Herman paused again. Then, he spoke.

"My peoples was Maroons!"

"Maroons!!?" Lena asked.

"Yeah, baby. My folks run off from the plantation they was at in South Georgia, place named Cypress Oaks, long 'fore I was born. Mama was pretty heavy wid my oldest sister when they took off into the night. We'd sit 'round the fire at night in the woods in Flor'da, and they usta tell us children about that night and the plans they made fo' the run fo' freedom.

"How they prepared, keepin' some a' they little vittles saved back. Who they told the truth on the place and who they had to lie to till the moment they left. Who they left behind. How it hurt that they couldn't take everybody. How everybody wouldn'a wanted to go, to take the chance, if they could have. How good and scary it felt to leave, to just set foot off the place."

"You mean to tell me ya'll were Maroons in Florida?" Lena felt as if she had stepped into a history lesson.

"Well, when my folks run off they headed south 'cause they'd been listenin' and payin' 'ttention. And they knew how close Spanish terr'tory was. Soon after they took off, my pa and my ma, they met up with a band of Indians, Seminole is what they was. Huh, honest people.

"Did you know Seminole mean 'runaway,' Lena?" he asked.

"Anyway, they had had some experience with runaways from other plantations, and they welcome my family. Ma had her first child right there on the Seminole settlement."

"So, you weren't born in Georgia?" Lena asked as if she had just met Herman at a cocktail party.

"Naw, Lena, I was born in Flor'da, not here in Georgia, but I ain't got no sand 'tween my toes. I got pine needles and cypress beads. We lived in a settlement in the nawth part of Flor'da in the swamps. Ain't nothin' but a made-up line separate 'em—Flor'da and Georgia.

"Then, after the war and ema'cipation, I traveled on back up this way, doin' this, doin' that. Kinda settled 'round here in Mulberry."

Herman looked at Lena and smiled. "Sho' am glad I did." Then, he continued.

"Naw, baby, my daddy warn't no slave. My mama neither." Herman paused. "Naw, baby. They was warriors!"

And Lena just nodded her head.

"The Indian tribes 'round down south, you know, they didn't play, neither. Seminoles waged three wars wid this country fo' they freedom. But, Lena, everythang they used in everyday life, they made it pretty. Remind me a' *my people*. Them Indians and us black folks was good to each other. But ya'll don't know nothin' 'bout that, do ya'll?" Herman sounded sadder for humanity than exasperated with local black folks.

She remembered a poem she had written in college during the height of the black awareness movement in the sixties and asked Herman, "Want to hear a poem I wrote in college?"

"Sho'," he said with a surprised smile on his face. "I'd be honored."

Lena put the dish towel on the counter and stood up straight like a schoolgirl in Catholic school.

> "*Grandmama on my Mama's side*
> *Granddaddy on my Daddy's side*

Both said their Grandmamas were longhaired Indians
Lately, no one gives a damn."

"That's a good poem, Lena. You put words up against each other real good."

Lena smiled "thank you" and took a little bow there in her kitchen next to the African violets blooming on the shelf over the sink.

"I wonder how many people think about that? You know, the ties and the connections?" Herman mused.

It sounded like a rhetorical question so Lena did not answer. She kept clipping the ends of the flowers at a forty-five-degree angle and listening to Herman talk. He had a nice voice, strong, unhurried, southern. He talked sort of like Lena Horne, if Lena Horne had bass in her voice.

Lena wondered how long it had been since he had last spoken.

He stopped his talking of the ties between black people and red people to answer her question.

"Lena, I ain't spoke in a hundred years. Ain't had no throat, ain't had no mouth, ain't had no tongue. But I'm happy to say I do now." And he smiled and looked at her so it actually made her blush.

"Why you think that?" he asked. "I'm talkin' too much?"

And she chuckled at his unshielded forthrightness. It spoke of another century, another time when folks didn't spend so much time explaining and dissembling. Lena felt she always had to think twice before she opened her mouth. She thought she was going to like this Herman's frankness.

"Naw, Herman, you're not talking too much at all."

It was the first time she had said his name aloud to him and the sound of it was so intimate, she lowered her eyes and blushed again.

"It's interesting," she reassured him. "You are right. I hardly ever think about Native Americans in a real sense. And I got their stuff all around here.

"Humph, isn't that something?" she said seriously as she gave Herman the big vase of flowers.

"Where to?" he asked, happy to be of help.

"Wherever *you* want them," she said, and immediately felt as if she had just conferred a blessing on Herman because she felt the warm holy feeling flood back over her like the welcome heat from the fire. He smiled and took the flowers to her bedroom and placed them on the linen and mud-cloth-covered table by her bed.

She leaned on the sink and watched Herman stride out of the kitchen. When she remembered that he was hungry, she hurried into the dining room to set the table, throwing one of her mother's damask tablecloths on first. Then, she took down her simple gold-rimmed bone china from one of the white pine hutches in the Great Jonah Room.

Herman stirred the food and heaped it up in big serving bowls, using whatever china struck his fancy. When he put his choices on the table next to hers, it looked like a marriage of opposites. The delicate crème china looked right comfortable with the heavy red vintage mixing bowl full of turnip greens and the big yellow soup tureen from her grandmother's friend Miss Zimmie's kitchen full of lean stew meat and potatoes with carrots and onions. Herman had wrapped corn muffins in a striped dish towel and set them in a basket he had found hanging on the wall.

There were already candles burning everywhere, on the dining room table, on the buffet and on top of the old rolltop desk she used for a small bar. She placed two lit tall green tapers from Christmas in the center of the table. That's when she saw the amaranth-colored hyacinth bloom lying by her plate.

She picked it up and bringing it up to her nose, inhaled deeply.

"Thank you, Herman."

"My pleasure," he said proudly. "Yo' pleasure *is* my pleasure, Lena."

Lena was as pleased as she could be with the situation.

Then, pulling out the dining room chairs her mother and father had occupied, they sat down to eat.

"You want to say grace, Lena?" he asked, stretching his hand out to take hers as if they were in church.

She took hold of his hand, the first time they had touched all night, and felt the rough calluses on his palms and the tips of his fingers.

"You believe, Herman?" she asked.

"Believe?" he said, then laughed. "Shoot, Lena, baby, you can't be dead and not believe in God."

She looked at Herman and smiled at the thought of them sharing faith.

"Well, then, Herman, you go ahead."

Herman bowed his head and closed his coal-black eyes. Then, he lifted his broad head and looked right at Lena, then, he bowed his head again, his thick wild hair framing his sweet dark face like a halo, closed his eyes again and said, "I do thank you, Lord."

He squeezed Lena's hand and then let it go.

As she served up the thick slices of stew meat in gravy, she paused and, looking to Herman, asked, "You eat red meat, Herman?"

Herman just chuckled.

"Lena, you ever had what they calls Apalachicola oysters, shellfish from the long skinny top of Flor'da, the Gulf side?" he asked. "They some little sweet oysters."

"Oh, yeah, Herman. We can get some shipped in. Same day," Lena leapt to suggest.

Herman just smiled.

"Lots a' mens say those little oysters taste like a woman to them. But me, to me they taste like freedom."

"Freedom?!" Lena asked with her own smile at the image of the moist-wet mollusk Herman raised before her.

"When I was growing up in Flor'da, oh, I was 'bout eight the first time the grown folks let me go. They'd round up parties and we'd forage on the coast to harvest us some of those little sweet ones from the waters there. It was only partly dangerous, I guess. We was all dressed alike, our scoutin' party, travelin' the backwoods the mens knew.

"We eat all kinds a' thangs in the woods, Lena. That's why I laughed when you asked me if I eat red meat."

Lena just smiled at the story, remembering how her father, Jonah, had relished good mealtime conversation. Her father had been like Herman: He would eat anything! But she did wonder at how a question about red meat led to a story about eating oysters.

"Funny thang 'bout freedom, baby. It seem to have a lot a' extra arms and limbs to grab hold a' thangs. It ain't always the thangs you want to grab holt of either."

When they finished eating, Herman leaned back in her father's chair at the big dining room table and patted his hard flat stomach and said, "Uh, I feel like a new man!"

Lena saw him reach for her plate and his, but she stopped him.

"That's okay. James Petersen will get those in the morning."

Herman got up in time to pull Lena's chair out for her.

"You want to wait awhile and take a swim, Herman?" she asked, thinking of ways to entertain him.

She walked into the pool room and trailed her hand in the water.

"Water's still warm," she said enticingly. Lena sure did want to see him without any clothes on. He had not left his spot by the fire, so, she came back in and sat on the sofa near the fire, too.

"Maybe later, Lena, but I want to do som'um else right now," he said, standing in front of her. His hips were right about at Lena's eye level, and she kept trying to keep him from seeing her inspecting his old-fashioned buttoned fly.

She held her breath as she waited for him to speak or move.

16
LOVE

Herman stood there before Lena in the middle of her Great Jonah Room a second, turning a bit, his hands hanging comfortably at his side, leaning back in his strong-looking legs, his head tilted to the side like an animal listening.

Lena thought for a second that he was waiting for a signal from the beyond. But he was waiting for the next selection to begin playing on the CD player.

"Good," he said as Duke Ellington and his band began playing "Mood Indigo." "It's a slow tune."

Then, Herman turned to where she was sitting before the fire.

"Come on, Lena, baby." Herman extended his sturdy arm and asked gallantly, sweetly, earnestly, *"Dance wid me!"*

The gesture reminded Lena immediately of every teenaged black boy she had ever seen at a church social, prom, cotillion, sock hop, basement party or sweetshop coolly, serenely sliding across the dance floor headed for her, his next partner. Then, when he got there, not saying a word, not "Wanna dance?" not "Care to?" not "May I have this dance?" not anything. Instead, the young swain would throw his hand palm-up into her lap, look off into the distance as if he didn't care if she accepted or not, and wait for her to take his hand so he could lead her out onto the dance floor for a slow spin.

Lena hesitated a moment as she stared at Herman's hand. It was one thing to dance by herself over the floor of The Place when she thought no one was looking or to dance alone to Salt 'n' Pepa naked in her bathroom mirror. Getting up and dancing with a new man— even if he was a ghost—was a different matter.

"Uh-uh, girl," he said with a serious chuckle. "I done waited a hundred years to dance again! And I get my first dance wid *you* and you sittin' up there sayin', 'No thank you.' Uh-uh. Get up off your pretty butt and dance wi' me. Come on in my arms, Lena, and dance wid me."

He sounded almost as if he were singing to her, serenading her, cajoling her, just tolling her out on the floor. It was so seductive. Each time he said it—"Come on, Lena, baby. Dance wi' me"—it sounded more and more enticing.

Remembering her fiascoes on the dance floor ever since she was thirteen, she still hesitated. She just sat there rubbing her hands together in her lap.

"Aw, Lena, ain't no need to be shame or scared in front a' *me,*" he said, his hand still suspended in the air in front of her. "Anything you do, any way you do it is fine wi' me."

Lena just wanted to grunt and say, "Ummm."

Instead, she rose from the soft leather couch and glided into Herman's open arms, the fire's light dancing in her eyes, placed one bare foot between his long strong legs, slipped her right hand into the space at the base of his neck under the bush of his hair, and lay the top of her head softly against the base of his throat where she could hear his heart beat. *Boom-boomp, boom-boomp, boom-boomp, boom-boomp, boom-boomp, boom-boomp, boom-boomp.*

Lena and Herman discovered immediately that they loved to

slow-dance together. Herman danced an old-fashioned two-step, but he didn't move to the music like a country boy, studied and rehearsed. Herman slow-danced like a block boy, like a juker: slowly, sensuously, casually, unhurried. He curled her all up in his arms and hunched his back over her frame just a little bit so that it looked and felt as if she were inside his body, protected, loved, held. He wrapped his hand around her hand, then tucked both hands in the cocoon between their dancing bodies. He rolled his hips slowly and gently against the top of her pelvis and guided her around the floor.

Lena was able to follow him right away. No awkward movements, no bumping into each other, no stepping on toes, no tripping over feet, no missing the beat.

And he moved unhurried, unhurried.

They danced all over her house, past still-burning, half-burned and burned-out candles on plates and ashtrays and one-of-a-kind glazed bowls, out onto the deck, by the foot of her bed, past the pool, around the messy dining room table, back in front of the fireplace in the Great Jonah Room, then back outside to dance under the stars.

"Look, Lena," he said in her ear, tipping her head back with a gentle touch on her slender chin, "the sky is full a' stars tonight. There's the Drankin' Gourd. There's the Serpent. OOooo. Is that the Crab? There's the Virgin. You don't useshally see her this clear in April."

Lena had never enjoyed a dance so much. She felt lost in the stars and lost track of the time. She felt they must have been dancing for hours. They danced to Nat King Cole. They danced to Otis Redding. They danced to Marvin Gaye. They danced to Prince. They danced to Smokey Robinson. They danced to Earth, Wind and Fire. They danced to Jon Lucien. They danced to Boyz II Men. So, it had to have been a good long time. But Herman danced as if he had all the time in the world.

Humph, I guess he does, Lena thought as she snuggled her cheek into the cave under Herman's jawbone and sighed as she settled into the slow, natural, easy rhythm of his slow drag. She didn't *think* of looking at her watch or her maternal grandmother Lena Marie's pendulum clock.

Lena wanted to whisper into Herman's ear the way she had heard Protestant sisters prompt the preacher straining during an especially moving sermon, "Take your time, now!"

"I thought you wanted me to 'Quit,'" Herman said with a low sexy laugh in Lena's ear, and she joined him in sweet happy harmony. The sound of their laughter together raised such emotions in her that before she knew it, she was weeping, too. Try as she did, she could not remember the last time she had embraced a man and laughed at the same time.

And Herman just continued holding her. Lena could feel his penis growing harder and larger inside his pants and poking against her belly. His erection felt like life to her. And she did not try to avoid its touch when Herman sometimes dipped his pelvis down to catch Lena in the right spot. Then, he'd straighten up and fly right for a while.

Even dancing to Al Green's "Love and Happiness," Herman remained unhurried, rocking Lena back and forth in his arms to the backbeat. They played it over and over. It was becoming *his song*. He especially liked the lyrics "Make you want to do right. Make you want to do wrong." Whenever they got to that part of the song, Herman would turn Lena loose, step back and do a little country-boy clogging step in his big black boots in time with the music as he sang along.

"Make you come home early.
Make you stay out all night long."

Now she could *see* the outline of Herman's hard dick straining against the front of his black work pants.

Lena, smiling and blushing and licking her dry crimson lips with the tip of her tongue, stood in front of the fireplace, barefoot and still dressed in her red business suit, and tapped her foot and bopped her shoulders and head to the beat until he danced back over to her to place his left hand firmly on the small of her back and his right one lightly at the base of her neck. He drew her to him while he played with the small shiny hairs that grew down from the nape of her neck.

"Look a here at her kitchen. My baby, she still got baby hair," he said softly in wonder and amusement, twirling her short hairs around his index finger and humming along with Al on "For the Good Times."

Lena took that opportunity to bury her face deep in his throat and take a deep breath. Herman smelled like topsoil. Not like he had been working in it. Or lying six feet under it. But he smelled to Lena as if he were the dark rich crumbly earth itself outside her door. He smelled like the dirt she ate as a child when her mother wasn't looking. He smelled like the dirt she and her friend Sarah used to make mud pies. He smelled like the dirt in which Mr. Renfroe had just planted the new crepe myrtle trees.

She kept taking deep gulps of his scent and smiling as she was reminded of The Place the day before.

But the air surrounding this smooth, loving apparition was nothing compared to the air that moved in and out of his lungs. It was hypnotic. Each time she felt him breathing on her—her neck, her face, her hair—she fell more deeply and more deeply under his spell.

Their dancing slowed down a bit, and Lena leaned her head back, looking up into Herman's face. His lips were barely an inch away from hers. And she could feel his breath stirring the tiny hairs over her top lip. The hairs from his bushy mustache brushed her face, but he didn't kiss her.

She had to admire his ghostly restraint. She could still feel his erect penis against her stomach.

"I wouldn't push you fo' nothin' in the world, Lena," he said. "This time I'll wait fo' you."

Herman didn't have to wait long. Lena was ready for him.

She reached up, parting her lips slightly and sucking in, pulled

Herman's head down to hers, pressed his mouth to hers, and kissed him. She wanted to watch this beautiful man kissing her back, but she couldn't keep her eyes open.

His mouth was barely moist and tenderly soft on hers. His lips, not quite as full as Lena's, seemed to fit inside the shape of her mouth perfectly. His bushy mustache tickled her own reddish fuzz. She felt his smile on her lips. The heat from his kiss radiated through her body, leaving her flesh hot and sensitive to his touch. When the tips of their tongues touched, Lena felt them both shiver. Her nipples were growing hard and large against the satin of her bra. She could feel his penis tug at his pants. Her vagina seemed to be tugging at her panties, too.

As they rubbed their bodies against each other, Lena felt her clitoris quiver. And she let out a little soft "uhh" from the pit of her soul.

Lena didn't know where they were standing, but she trusted Herman when they both, concentrating on tracing the other's lips with tongues, fell to the big leather sofa in front of the fireplace. One of his strong callused hands reached for the gold buttons of her jacket and the other began traveling under her skirt, up her thigh to the top of her dark gartered stockings, snagging the nylon gently.

Lena was surprised that Herman's clothes—the green shirt, the black pants, the leather belt—were actually real, firm to her touch. When she unbuttoned Herman's shirt, she was half expecting it to just melt away like cotton candy in a hot summer shower, leaving him covered with sticky sugar.

His skin *was* sweet. She couldn't help but lick it when they got each other naked.

And he did look good naked. A life of moving and working and walking, a childhood of growing up in the wilds of North Florida, a life in the last century, had left him with a body taut, toned and strapping. She felt a responsibility to every woman who had ever wanted to make love to such a beautiful black man to run her hands over every millimeter of Herman as she kissed him all over.

"Good God, Lena, I'm already hard enough to plow packed earth," Herman said as she caressed his back and shoulders.

Herman was right. When Lena took Herman's big purplish penis into her hand she felt that it was hard enough to cut through Middle Georgia farmland. It leapt one quick time when she touched it. His pubic hairs were tight and nappy, rolled up into what looked like BBs all over his crotch. Down there, he smelled like the swamps in South Georgia. Lena played with his hairs awhile before moving on.

He was sweet all over, especially his throat and his deep broad chest where a few short black hairs grew inches apart from each other. She kissed each one. And when she finished, Herman kissed her all over—from the palms of her hands to the soles of her feet.

In the midst of their first orgasm together, a core-shaking exquisite orgasm, with Herman inside of her and around her and right beside her coming, too, and watching her at the same time, Lena knew she would remember every detail of this night forever.

All during their lovemaking—from the great room to her bedroom—she saw what was happening between the two of them. Unencumbered by pictures from the past or conversations from the future, she was filled with an intense awareness.

God, it's been years since I had my leg over somebody's shoulder, she thought.

Herman talked all through his lovemaking. "Oh, Lena, you so beautiful. Um-huh, look at my baby's *stuff*!! OOooo, I like the way yo' titties stand out like that. Uh, can I kiss there? You taste good, baby. Oh, Lena, I can't get enough.

"You can't tell me that ain't it!! That gets the butter from the duck!!!"

And he encouraged her to talk back to him.

"Tell me, baby. Tell me how that feel," he exhorted her. "I want to hear ya talk to me, baby. Come on, Lena, baby. Tell it like it is."

But Lena could not seem to form words with Herman under her and above her and inside her and all up through her. Making noises was the best she could do. She could hear her moans and screams and mewls and sobs echoing in the pine rafters of her house along with the scent of oak woodsmoke and love. Lena never knew how much she liked to holler during sex.

"OOOoo, I like when you get up on top of me like that and th'ow yo' body back, Lena, so I can still see yo' honey pot," Herman told her in breathy whispers. "What you like fo' me to do t' you?"

Lena was coming, so all she could do was let out a scream. But she thought, You doing just fine.

And Herman smiled as if he had read her mind.

All through their lovemaking, when he touched her breasts for the first time, tickling, licking and nipping at her hard erect nipples until she came again, he had whispered, "Oohhh, I can't get enough of you."

Lena did not want to break the mood, so, she stifled the questions that bubbled at her lips: "What do you mean, can't get enough?" "Enough what?" "Enough touching me?" "Enough fucking?" "Enough times?"

Herman smiled in her face, slipped his dick inside of her and said, "Enough of you, period."

Lena, who had never been able to get to the point of release with her other would-be lovers, came and came and came in Herman's arms.

As soon as Lena had unbuttoned the flap on his antique pants and freed his tight hard penis to bang against her chest, she thought briefly of trying to search up a condom somewhere in her house. She had not dealt with any other kind of birth control in years. Umm, now, I know I had some Trojans or something around here last time, she had thought, biting her bottom lip and narrowing her eyes in concentration. Now, just where was that? she asked herself. She tried to picture where she had been the last time she was naked and touching another human being. But Herman had slipped down her body and was just starting to kiss her all over with little puffs of breeze colored lime green and ocean blue, and she forgot everything except the fact that she was now making love to a ghost, a man dead a hundred years. And the idea of sexually transmitted diseases floated like a puff of smoke from her mind.

She sat naked astride him in the big suede easy chair the color of the Ocawatchee River when it wasn't Cleer Flo', her bare legs hanging off the arms of the big chair, her braids hanging down her back. In the light of the candles and the glow from the fireplace, Lena saw the sweat form on his beautiful broad brow. She smelled the chemistry of his come mingling with hers. She threw back her head and laughed when she saw that his thick curly eyelashes were sticking to the tops of his sweaty lids just the way hers did when she was a child playing out in the summer heat. Her mother sitting at her sewing machine would ask as Lena came inside, "Come here, baby, let Mama see how hot it is outside." Then, she would check to see if the child's lashes were sticking to her lids and Nellie would call, "Yep, must be mighty hot outside."

It was plenty hot right where Lena and Herman were—on the chair, on the floor, on the sofa, on the bed, on the deck—making love.

There was no way she could forget for long that she was making love to a spirit. One minute, he was as hard and real as the granite of Stone Mountain. She could feel him inside her hard, the veins in his dick throbbing against the walls of her vagina. The next, he was mist, smoke, vapor barely grazing down her breasts, stroking her between her legs, seesawing between the folds of her vagina, easing up her back. Then, he would become a man again.

Lena sighed and shivered a bit at the feel of Herman and the leather sofa on her bare back. She could feel the hairs there sending out little signals of excitement to Herman through the bare leg and shoulder he had resting on the back of the sofa.

As she lay back on the leather cushions, cool against her hot body, he spread her legs, one over the back of the sofa, the other hanging to the floor, then reached down and spread the lips of her vagina. Lena could feel his callused fingers scratch against the sensitive skin of her vulva.

"OOOooo," was all she could say as her body arched, then went limp.

"Oh, 'cuse me, Lena," Herman said with a smile. But he didn't mean it because he then brushed his callused fingers across her tender vulva again. Slowly this time, leading to her clitoris. And he moaned when Lena moaned.

Agile as a boy, he then jumped up on the fat padded arm of the sofa, naked and muscular, and lowered his face into her widespread vagina and traced the folds and flaps and slits of skin and nerve endings with his tongue until she screamed again, squeezing his head between her golden-brown thighs.

Before she could recover, he slipped from the folds of her vagina and crept into every little fold of her skin as a thick, dark gray, smoky mist.

She could feel him in the flap behind her ear. She could feel him in the folds under her full hanging breasts. She could feel him in the folds on the inside of her mouth. She could feel him in the folds of her eyelids. She could feel him in the folds of her knuckles. She could even feel him in the cursed new folds of her behind at the tops of her thighs and between the cheeks of her butt.

Then the smoke, the mist, the vapor that was Herman became a man again.

Herman turned his pretty pink tongue into a long thin soft red spiral that he coiled around the tip of her clitoris, played there awhile, then slowly pulled off as she screamed his name over and over.

"Oh, Herman! Herman! Herman!"

As he altered his consistency shape to please Lena, he continued speaking his passion. Poking Lena with the tip of his penis, he said, "Baby, this one Georgia jumpin' root that's here to please." Then, he changed and modified not just his body shape but also the shape of his penis to accommodate, pleasure, tickle, tease and love his woman Lena. Looking down at Herman's dick, Lena was reminded of different vibrator selections in a small catalog of sexual toys Deborah had passed out at the office. As far as she could remember, Herman covered just about every one in the book.

And these strange metamorphoses of Herman's didn't frighten Lena a bit, no matter how bizarre and fantastic they might have seemed to someone standing out on the deck watching.

For one thing, Lena was on the receiving end of all the changes, and she wasn't about to pretend to complain. I wouldn't *think* of stopping him right 'long through here, she thought, sucking air through her teeth and moaning.

For another, no matter how many changes he went through, he was still Herman to Lena. He was still the tall dark brown man who had been her love and guardian angel before she even knew it.

And Herman was a man of his word. He did nothing without first asking or moaning or groaning, "Okay, Lena?"

"Um-huh," she answered each and every time. Like I'mo say no, she thought as he continued touching her just the way she liked.

Herman went deeper and deeper inside her, touching spots and opening doors to room after room after room that Lena had never opened to anyone. Herman roused emotions she truly had not felt before. And she was grateful then for his sweet permission-asking, "Is that okay, Lena? Uhh, how 'bout that? And that? And that?"

They lay back opposite each other on the big soft couch to catch their breath. Lena did not have to ponder another second. She knew right then she would feel this way about this man the rest of her life.

When she was able to find her voice again, she said, "Herman?"

"Yeah, baby," he answered as he tucked one bare foot under her, threw the other over her and pulled her to him.

"You know, Herman, I think somewhere back there when we were dancing or eating or something, I decided."

"What you decide, baby?"

Lena loved how familiar he had gotten with her so quickly.

"Herman," she said, then paused and smiled. She loved to speak his name. "I decided I *am* your woman."

She had never said those words to a man before. Never. She liked the sound of them so much, she said them again.

"Herman, I *am* your woman. I'm *so glad* you came."

Lena could feel Herman smiling when he kissed her.

He lifted Lena and lay her nude body on top of his nude body—a pretty sight in the fire and candlelight—and held her close.

Slowly, Lena seemed to feel a change in her very blood chemistry. She had the sensation of barely falling—millimeter by millimeter, hardly falling. It felt to Lena as if she were sinking into the very center of the universe, a very warm and welcoming universe.

She began to perceive sparks of life all around her. The universe she was sinking into had a wide and complex life. She felt planets spinning by her in their orbits. She saw galaxies form next to her hips. Shooting stars and comets whizzed by from her vagina toward the top of her head, leaving tails of gold and red down her throat and stars in her eyes.

Herman had eased into her heart so smoothly that before she knew it, he had eased in and taken it over with old-time love.

As they lay in each other's arms all night long, stroking each other, licking, tickling, blowing, fingering, nuzzling, Herman turned to her again and again and declared over and over, "Lena, I am much in love wid you."

Lena—spent, sated and content—dozed on and off throughout the night, smiling through little patches of dreams of floating on blue clouds. But she awoke each time she heard Herman's voice to reply, "Herman, I am much in love with you."

17

BUSINESS

The next morning, when Lena awoke nude with Herman curled up naked in bed next to her, the fire was just dying down in the bedroom hearth. She smiled into his open eyes and said a quick prayer of thanksgiving that the night before had not been a dream. She could not remember the last time she had slept all the way through the night with a man.

She could feel Herman's hard muscular thigh resting against hers, and she noticed his leg hairs were short and wiry.

"Mornin', Lena," he said with a smile.

"Good morning, Herman," she replied. She felt a little shy, a bit abashed at her exuberant lovemaking the night before with a man she had, for all practical purposes, just met. But Herman would not let her be shy or modest. When she smiled back her greeting, she could feel his penis growing against her hip. She rolled over and seemed to sink right into him.

After their lovemaking first thing in the morning, she was tempted to take the phone off the hook and spend the entire day with

Herman. But she remembered the chaos in town the day before when she was merely late, not absent. Besides, Lena was a woman with responsibilities. She had to get up and out and, as her father used to say, "meet her public." She had *business* to take care of.

Lena's magic in the business world was a combination of acumen, luck and just being herself.

She had wanted to explore literature in college, but as a tribute to Jonah, she decided to check out the business department and take a few courses there, too. The very first semester, she discovered she was good at this business business. Commerce, trading, numbers, dealing. Crunching numbers, moving them around, making them work for her. It seemed second nature to Lena.

Her economics professors just laughed and shook their heads at the amount of insight and imagination she brought to the study of business.

Putting together a mock takeover for a final project, Lena would look up at her assigned partner and say, "I can *see it!* Can't you just see it?!"

Her department head was a tough-minded woman who saw Lena, her personal protégée, accomplishing all she had dreamed of doing in the field of economics. The professor could see the two of them sharing the podium as Lena accepted the Nobel Prize in economics. But at the end of her senior year, Jonah, the business world and Mulberry beckoned, and the professor saw her dreams fly off to Georgia.

When Lena returned home, Edward, the younger of her two brothers, had decided to make the Air Force his career. And her other brother, Raymond, did not seem the least bit interested in trying to out-Jonah Jonah in his own town. He had moved to Texas with his new wife Jackie who could not seem to leave her own family.

"Well, Daddy, you always did threaten Edward and Raymond with giving The Place to me," Lena would say when she thought she saw her father down in the mouth because he did not have sons to carry on his business.

Lena didn't have a clue. Jonah was so proud of Lena's business sense that he had to remind himself sometimes that he had had sons, too. He was even proud of her obstinacy in business.

"Caldonia, Caldonia, what make your big head so hard?" Jonah had sung that phrase over and over when she just *wouldn't* follow his advice. Even after Lena had proved time and time again that her business acumen was equal to or better than his, Jonah still sang the song to his smart "hardheaded" daughter.

Among Jonah's friends, especially the men he had been playing poker with since the time Lena was born, his daughter's business acumen was legend. The same men who had raised a glass to Lena's birth had lived to see her buy and resell half the town.

In the midst of any deal, in the heat of bartering, Jonah would throw up both his hands and threaten, "All right, I'm a reasonable man. I'd hate to have to put my daughter on ya."

Sometimes Lena sensed her legend growing in the town without her doing a thing.

Back in the early seventies when she was barely out of college with a fresh Realtor's license, and an idea for her own all-female company named Candace, she was summoned to a house in East Mulberry early one morning. With her permed rust hair in a fluffy pageboy, dressed in her new soft green tweed business suit, Lena had sat at the foot of the deathbed of Miss Roberta, an old woman she barely knew. Miss Roberta had been a domestic all her life, working in hotel housekeeping as well as private homes—"in service"—for the last forty years. The only little break she had given herself was a tall cold beer on Saturdays down at The Place. Miss Roberta had explained very clearly and succinctly from the last bed she would lie in that she needed to talk some business with Lena.

Her family had gathered around her in the sturdy old house with the dusty screened porch in East Mulberry, trying hard to keep life in the woman who kept the life in their family by the sheer force of her own spirit.

Babies cried in the kitchen. Men played cards on the enclosed back porch. Women cooked like it was Sunday and cleaned like it was any other day. Folks had traveled in cars and on buses from as far away as Mississippi to be there for this woman's passing.

Miss Roberta had shooed everyone but her younger sister out of the room with a flicker of her eyelids when Lena arrived with two spiral-cut baked hams, three boxes of jumbo breaded shrimp and two cases of Coca-Colas in the trunk of her new Cutlass convertible. Miss Roberta looked so delicate reclining there, she was nearly translucent. Even so near death, her wrinkled brown skin seemed to glow.

"Lena, you got plenty money," the old lady said in a surprisingly strong voice. "I want to sell you this house. I want to do it right now. And I want my money in hand before darkness fall tonight."

Lena smiled her wide guileless sweet smile while her mind raced with calculations and legalities. Her first instinct was to say, "Do you think this is the right time to be doing this?" but she knew this was likely the *only* time Miss Roberta would get to do this.

But Lena didn't get a chance to respond in any way. Miss Roberta's sister jumped forward from where she was resting against the closed door and spoke sweetly to her big sister.

"Rob, now, I know what this house means to you and the family. Maybe, you should just sleep on this decision a bit more."

Lena was picturing the house from outside and in. It was a one-story wood frame house with two screened cement porches.

"Well, Sis," Miss Roberta said, "you know all the children gon' lose it anyway 'cause I ain't gonna be around to make sure the taxes are paid."

Miss Roberta's sister stopped where she stood and dropped her head a bit. The statement stood in the room like another person. Like a statue of Truth that no one could ignore.

"This way, I can get a good price for it, split the money according to how I want it done and the children end up with something for my efforts."

Her sister thought it over for a moment, patted Miss Roberta's hand and returned to her post at the door with tears in her eyes. Lena felt like crying, too, but instead she thought, How can I help Miss Roberta? She was busy thinking, Cash, cash, cash. How much can I get my hands on tonight? I wonder how much Daddy got stashed away all over Mulberry.

"So, Miss Lena," she said with a teasing tone in her dying voice, as if there had been no break in the conversation. "What we gonna do and when we gonna get to it?"

Lena decided the best tack to take was to act as if she were sitting in her own small office downtown.

"How much you asking, Miss Roberta?" Lena asked.

The dying woman motioned for her sister to come from her sentinel at the door. Miss Roberta had written a number on a crisp piece of yellow lined legal paper that lay folded in half on the bedside table next to a red leather-bound Bible. She handed it to her sister and nodded for her to open and read it. When this was done, she followed her sister's directions, and with a poker face, handed it to Lena.

Lena reached forward and took the yellow paper. Before opening it, she looked to Miss Roberta on the bed and received a slight nod of approval. She had learned that from Jonah.

"Lena, baby, you know how much I like to run things," Jonah had said to her the first year she went away to college. "Everybody is like me. We all want to run things or at least let it appear that way. Business goes much smoother when you in control, but all the other folks think they got some measure of control, too. You know what I mean?"

Lena opened the note, read the number and smiled. Shoot, she thought, I can come up with that much in cash by myself.

The deal was done before the sun set.

Lena had her first property. It grew from there.

"Don't worry 'bout your house. Lena McPherson take care of you." It was said over and over, making Lena richer and richer.

Lena felt as if she were always like Ezekiel, standing in the gap.

She couldn't get over the feeling that she was called to hold the folks in her town, her people, in the cup of her hand, to stand in the gap between them and disaster. Considering the kind of attention she had gotten all her life, she figured she owed people that.

Lena was the executrix of so many people's estates that the probate judge, a white-haired white man named Stanley Booth, finally called her into his chambers.

"Ms. McPherson, now, I know you and I know your daddy, so I don't mean any offense to you. But aren't you in a whole lot of people's inheritances?"

It was true. Lena had been too busy taking care of things to give it a lot of thought, but she was in a whole lot of people's business.

Folks brought her their papers and property, their problems and their perplexities, their hopes and dreams.

"Sell it for me, Lena."

"Don't let our family lose it, Lena."

"Lena, what should I do with the tax refund money?"

And she always seemed to know what to do. At first, just a little twenty-one-year-old cute woman with a degree in economics from a small southern Catholic university not known for its school of business, Lena was afraid to trust her instincts. She had spent most of her life learning over and over that the last thing she could rely on was her skewed instincts. But it seemed in business, she couldn't go wrong following her feelings.

Her grandmother had told her, "Always follow your first mind, Lena."

And her first mind had always told her to give.

She was solace. She was balm. She was love. She was the baby.

Lena didn't like it, but she could feel the presence of death nearby. She didn't even need a sign like a bird in the house or the hooting of an owl during the day. It was almost like a fog or a mist about to settle on a person or a house or an area. Not cold and damp, the way some folks thought. It was just light, dry, wispy and nearly intangible like a vapor.

Lena had felt death around the house as she had sat there dicker-ing with Miss Roberta. In her brief years on this earth, Lena had been present at all kinds of deaths. But it was not something that she would have chosen to do. It was hard on her, these deaths at which she presided.

Shortly after the plane crash, while she was still in deep mourning for her own mother and father, an old classmate from grammar school had called Lena to go with her to *her* mother's hospital room. The older woman had spent her last years in the west wing of Mulberry Acres, a nursing home, away from her own home and her things and her family. Lena's friend didn't say so, but Lena knew she was afraid to face the dying woman alone.

The nurses greeted Lena with quiet smiles and hugs, and her friend *knew* she had done the right thing by asking Lena along.

When the mother heard them come in, she turned her head from the wall to face her daughter. Lena had to steel herself to keep from gasping. It was her own mother Nellie's face she saw, full of pain and forgiveness. Lena could tell it was not Nellie's pain and forgiveness etched on her face but that of the woman who lay there reaching out her hand for her daughter. But Lena, reaching her hand out to her own mother's manicured hand, took the succor the image offered, allowed herself to move into the circle of love and forgiveness that the other two women offered and received.

Lena, who never got to sit by the deathbed of her own mother. Lena, who didn't have bones to bury. Lena, who couldn't for the life of her call up the feeling of her mother's skin where it was beginning to soften along her sharp jawbone. Lena sat by the deathbed of this strange woman who wore the face of her mother, the hands of her mother, the eyes of her mother, and said her own good-byes.

Her friend, grateful for the lead, leaned forward as Nellie's visage slowly faded from the dying woman's face, and Lena stepped away from the bed, back into the shadows. As night fell, Lena saw the woman turn her head to her daughter and smile. In a surprisingly strong voice, she said, "With night there is weeping, but dancing comes with the morning." Then, she turned her head back to the wall and died.

It was the first time for Lena but hardly the last for the sightings. Lena began seeing Nellie all over town. Driving to work, Lena would look in her rearview mirror and see a woman with short red hair in the car behind her, indolently smoking a long cigarette. Lena would almost crash into the oncoming traffic in her amazement. The woman looked exactly like her mother. Lena had thrown the car into Park and turned all the way around to get a better look. Even head-on, face-to-face, the woman was the spit of Nellie!

When the light changed and the Nellie-looking woman and the cars behind her started honking their horns impatiently, Lena still sat and stared over her shoulder at the woman. The more Lena looked, the more she discovered in this woman's face. Lena got out of her car and stood in the street with her eyes squinted up and a hand on her hip, staring at her mother's visage on the face of the woman in the car behind hers. It was her mother's face from ten years earlier.

Lena was so shocked she almost fainted right there beside her little Mercedes in the middle of traffic.

For a while after that, Lena saw her mother's face, no matter how briefly, in every face she came in contact with. It finally made it impossible for her to turn her back on any of her fellow citizens of the world. Haitian orphans—rusty ashen skin bespeaking a life of malnutrition and deprivation—had her mother's face. Women who sat on their front steps or stood over steam tables with their faces bruised and beaten to the color of an eggplant had her mother's face. Winos who offered to do some made-up task in exchange for a drink of liquor had her mother's face. The parishioners who sat next to her in church had her mother's face. Family men looking for housing for their wives and children had her mother's face. Saleswomen and cashiers all had her mother's face. Turning her back on them was turning her back on her mother. And she could not do that.

Even now, years after the phenomenon had subsided, her mother's spirit still asserted itself. Lena would look down at her hands and recall Nellie sitting at her machine in the sewing room when the child had padded in crying from a cut or scratch on her finger. Without hesitation, Nellie had stopped her sewing, dropping the needle, thread and material right where she sat, and gently taken Lena's little injured buttery hand in her smooth reddish brown ones. She would make a sympathetic sound somewhere between "ooohh" and "aaahh" as she examined the wound. Then she'd bring her lips down to Lena's hand and kiss the injured spot, hard enough so Lena felt the magic of the mother's kiss, but not too hard.

Little Lena would be satisfied. Even when she heard her mother mutter wryly to herself, "Ain't no telling where these little hands have been."

Her mother would say the same thing when Lena came to her carrying something for her to taste or smell or rub. Nellie would do the proper thing—taste the drop of nectar from the honeysuckle flower, put the dirty red leaf behind her ear—then she would smile and mutter to herself, "Humph, ain't no telling where this little flower has been."

It was memories like those that steeled Lena for the tasks that seemed naturally somehow to fall to her.

"Oh, Lena, Leroy just passed. Will you please call Mama? She still live down in Swainsboro. Here's a number. Would you please call her and break the news that her baby boy is dead? I just can't do it. And I know how good you are at that kind of thing. Would you do that for me and my family, Lena? I know we haven't talked all that much or know each other that well. But somebody told me you'd help us out. Okay?"

Lena would see her mother's face and hear her mother's voice and have to make the call.

Over the years, she had perfected her technique in taking care of her death duties. She could hear herself on the telephone deftly break-ing the news of death to a family member living up north or to the estranged relative who had not spoken to the deceased in years. Even she was sometimes comforted by the sound of her own voice.

She would begin by making a little Mulberry small talk. Just by listening to her, you'd never know what she was leading up to. Then, she'd talk about life and the inevitability of the cycle of life. How death was a part of that cycle. And on and on, until it was time to let them know about the recent death of Aunt Eula or Uncle Jackson or Lil Bro.

Lena saw the kindness as a tribute to her mother. Nellie had always been the one to dispense care and kisses in her house. Her hysterically funny tirades were followed by voluminous hugs and assurances. Between times of telling them how much they were loved, her mother assured Lena and brothers daily that they were little "fanatical fools," "little motley morons," "a little horse-face heifer," but they were her fools, her morons and her heifer.

While Nellie dispensed love, Jonah lounced out common sense. He was a man who felt he *knew* the meaning of real value in this world.

"Money make iron float." Jonah had said it with a flat, matter-of-fact tone. And he pronounced "iron" as "ine" like it was "line" without the *l*.

Lena felt her responsibility lay somewhere in between kisses and money.

Where Jonah went around collecting money in the mornings, Lena sometimes went about doling it out. Lena went the same route but took a different approach. She could never get him to agree that it was a good idea and a sound business move, even when he saw her largesse come back to her—and quick, too!—more than tenfold. Jonah was serious about his money, *his goddamn money*, to be exact. Just about everyone in Mulberry knew that Jonah McPherson was a man who didn't want to be toyed with when it came to his money.

"Man, don't play with me about *my goddamn money*," Lena had heard him say all her life to his customers, his card-playing buddies and just about anybody he met on the street.

One cold crisp morning when Lena was making the rounds collecting for Jonah while he and Nellie were flying off somewhere, she had an epiphany. Shit, she thought to herself as she tried to gun the motor and drive her new Jaguar out of a near ditch in some part of town where Jonah had a bunch of property and little involvement, what am I doing out here trying to out-Jonah Daddy. Hell, I don't even care about these little collections. They ain't worth the time I spend running these folks down.

By now, she had gotten out of the car and, pulling her mother's antique cashmere wrap coat—a coat similar to the one she had seen the author Zora Neale Hurston wear in photos from the thirties and forties—around her neck and shoulders, walked around the car tipped in the ditch to examine just how deeply entrenched it was. All the time, she kept muttering to herself, "Yeah, if these no-good mother-fuckers would pay their fucking rent on time, I wouldn't have to be here in this ditch in my best, my *best* suede boots, trying to push my new car out of a muddy ditch. God, these no-account, no-rent-paying Negroes!" Her feet were soaked in the wet earth and as soon as she tried to take a step, she slipped in the muck and came crashing down on her behind, sliding down the incline and sending cold water and mud everywhere.

Now, she was really wet, cold and furious.

"These trifling niggers," she hissed aloud. Then, she stopped dead still, the word hanging nastily in the cold air.

She heard herself, felt the bile rising in her throat at the thought of her customers and almost passed out from the force of her ugliness, meanness, stinginess, hatefulness. A word she never used popping out of her mouth like a thoughtless white person.

"Shit, is this what money does to you?" she asked herself as she sat in the muddy ditch. She was so angry with herself for succumbing to the forces of Mammon that she raised her hands out of the mud to the heavens and screamed, "Who gives a damn about *this goddamn money?!!*"

That's when she saw the little boy and girl looking down and laughing at her from the top of the ditch. She took a look at herself and had to laugh, too. She was a funny sight, sitting in the wet ditch like an expensively dressed pig, covered in red mud and slime. Laughing, she splashed the muddy water around her and screamed again, "Who gives a damn about *this goddamn money?!!*"

This time the tiny children clamped their tiny hands to their mouths and squealed at Lena's profanity. The little girl spun around in glee and almost slipped and fell in the ditch, too. And the three of them laughed all the more. Lena suddenly felt light and free sitting in the muddy water. Still laughing with the children, she rolled over and began climbing out of the ditch on all fours to call Mr. Brown's filling station for a tow.

So, Lena didn't get her feet wet anymore—soiling her expensive shoes and despoiling her sweet spirit—going around town collecting money. Instead, she just kept dispensing the money, expecting that it would be repaid one way or another. And it usually was.

After the death of her parents, when Lena was finally able to face the gauntlet of lawyers and accountants awaiting her, she discovered she was the owner of property and businesses and land she didn't even know about. Even she was surprised at the extent of her family's wealth.

That very next Sunday, Lena had sat in a front pew at St. Martin de Porres and heard Matthew 19 read from the altar with authority. "It is easier for a camel to go through the eye of a needle than for a rich man to enter the kingdom of heaven."

The thought sobered her.

It was like hearing the responsorial psalm sung during Mass, "The Lord hears the cry of the poor. Blessed be the Lord."

She wondered, Does that mean He doesn't hear my cries? Is that why He blessed me with so much *stuff* but doesn't seem to hear my cries of loneliness and confusion and weariness. Is it why I have a stunning pink short Chanel suit, a forty-foot indoor swimming pool, and heated stables, but no man, children or joy?

The Scriptures seemed full of references to the difficulty the wealthy of this world faced in reaping the rewards of the next. Even in reading the Beatitudes and the rest of the Sermon on the Mount, some of Lena's favorite verses, she was reminded of her station in life.

"But woe to you rich, for your consolation is now."

She bowed her head and started praying even harder for the souls of her parents, so they, too—though rich—could enter the kingdom of heaven, could find rest.

Lena prayed with fervor for the *repose* of the souls of the dead. She had seen what it was like to wander the earth and the otherworld with no rest. What that ceaseless wandering had done to the souls who had haunted her, moaning and screaming in the night.

When she prayed for the repose of the souls of her dearly departed, she meant it.

"Oh, Jesus, Mary, don't let my mama and daddy and brothers be out there somewhere wandering the earth. Give them rest, Lord. Give them repose."

But regardless of her trepidations about the fate of her wealthy loved ones in the afterlife, on this earthly plane, Lena *made and used* her money. Lena had learned well from Jonah the power of money. And how it can be manipulated in your and your loved ones' favor. She enjoyed her money and the comfort and beauty it could purchase. She wrapped herself in the luxury it could buy sometimes as if it were a cashmere blanket.

Lena wanted to wrap the world, her own little world of Mulberry, in that same soft comfortable blanket.

Lena's generosity. Sister had seen it herself. A woman Lena had gone to grammar school with came by the house while Sister was visiting. Sister saw the check on the kitchen table stuck under a tall pepper mill. It was for five hundred dollars even though Sister heard the woman say as she came in the front door, "I can't tell you how much I appreciate you saving my life like this, Lena. You know I'll pay it back payday. This three hundred dollars is a godsend." Sister wasn't at all surprised at the check or the amount.

Then, as Lena ushered her visitor out the door, Sister saw her press a folded bill into the woman's hand and whisper, "Here, why don't you get yourself a shrimp dinner on the way home."

"You can't always get a check cashed this time of night," Lena said as she came back into the kitchen, "and you cannot face this world on an empty stomach."

Lena's credo was her mama's:

"Mama used to say, 'You can't put a thing in a clinched fist.' " Lena would tell her friend about the philosophy of her own generosity.

But Lena did not give to get. She gave because she saw the need. Talking with Sister over the phone of her futile efforts to get Miss Estelle off the streets of Mulberry with her shopping basket of belongings, Lena would sum it up.

"Life is real and life is earnest, girl."

And for such a spoiled little pretty lucky rich baby girl, Sister would think with a smile, Lena actually understood what she preached.

Lena was just as happy discovering the distributor of some obscure curative lotion that Miss Zimmie swore by as she was when she closed her first million-dollar deal. But doing both for her entire adult life had left her weary.

Although demons and spirits did not still haunt her dreams, other specters did. Sometimes, Lena felt she had just exchanged one type of haunting for another.

Demons of one sort or another came to haunt and worry and plague and menace her. The images of money and responsibility and her people flew and danced and spun around her head into the wee hours. Solving problems in her head, taking care of people before the need arose, paying taxes on time, reminding other people to pay *their* taxes on time, helping to find jobs for folks, matching homes to people, buying and selling property.

Until Herman showed up, Lena had just about accepted that the demons would be there to haunt her forever.

18

LIL SIS

Herman first showed his face in April. By late May, when they could clearly see the Sea Serpent and the Crab in the night sky, he had come up with a hundred ways to call Lena "baby."

Sometimes, he sounded avuncular, like her father's protective old friends and card-playing buddies. Sometimes, he said it like other sexy old men in town who said "baby" like they didn't know they were old. To Lena, the South seemed full of sexy old men, men who reminded her of Ray Charles or Mr. Jerome. Mr. Jerome was a man in his eighties both of whose legs had been amputated twenty years before, and he still made the nurse's aides at the Mulberry Arms Retirement Village giggle whenever they came in and announced "Whirlpool!"

Sometimes, Herman said "baby" briskly, almost business-like. "Hey, baby, hand me that wrench."

Usually, Herman said it as if it were part of her name, "Lena, baby." He said "Lenababy," as if it were one word.

Other times he crooned it, "Le-na, ba-by." Like a four-word song.

And other times it was hardly a word. Rather, a groan. "Oh bbbbbbaaabbbbbbbby."

As far as Lena was concerned, he couldn't say it enough.

It was easier than anyone would have thought for Lena to fall into a relationship with Herman.

They were comfortable with each other from the first night they ate and danced and loved together. She treasured the camaraderie she and Herman shared, their walks and tromps through the woods around her house that evoked childhood and represented the banishment of woodland demons. She felt heart-bursting pride at his mechanical and engineering acumen, as much as he seemed to feel over her special skills. She loved to awake with a wisp of his scent still lingering on the sheet next to her, enough for her to roll over and snuggle into for a few minutes before rising. She loved to do for him and make over him. But the one thing she treasured above all else was their lovemaking.

Lena and Herman fucked until her toes tingled.

Herman discovered that what he couldn't even buy in Middle Georgia in his time, Lena was happy to give and receive. The first time they made love and he kissed and licked her vagina, he just knew he had gone too far. When she returned the favor, he felt he had truly finally died and gone to heaven. Lena learned over and over that this spirit, this ghost, this specter was no ordinary man.

Why, Herman made Lena's pussy *sing*!!

Lena had heard women down at The Place use that expression.

"Girl, I ain't letting that man go *nowhere*! He made my pussy *sing* last night!"

Lena hadn't had all that much experience with sex, but she thought she knew what they meant. After Herman, however, she realized she had not had a clue.

Herman really did make her "stuff"—as he called it—sing. At first, she thought it was Herman down there between her legs singing to himself in exhilaration and ecstasy as he kissed and sucked and tickled and licked and bit and nipped her. She just knew it had to be

Herman down there humming against her clitoris, giving her what he called a "buzz." Then, she realized it wasn't Herman's voice she heard, but one that sounded like her own if she had been able to carry a tune.

Her pussy let out such a beautiful, lilting happy song with no real words that Lena and Herman had to stop what they were doing and just lie back and listen for a while. Lena stretched her arms above her head toward the headboard of the bentwood bed, and Herman just laid his head on Lena's stomach, his thick mat of hair tickling her belly button, and brushed his lips across her pubic hair.

Lena herself couldn't sing a note on command, couldn't carry a tune in a brass bucket. That's what her grandmama would say when she heard the girl trying to sing "Love Child" or some other current hit to herself around the house. She'd say, "Good thing Lena pretty and smart, Nellie. 'Cause she shore couldn't sing for her supper. The girl can't carry a tune in a brass bucket!" Now, that same Lena had a pussy that sang in perfect pitch.

Although the song seemed to float on the air, happy feathery notes that together made a new tune each time her vagina sang, it was not a high-pitched tone. Rather, Lena thought, it sounded low and sexy, like an alto.

Herman just thought it sounded like his woman, Lena. He knew he was the cause of the dulcet tones and was so proud he looked up at Lena and just grinned.

Reaching for each other, Lena and Herman exchanged a hard, deep, urgent, hungry kiss. And their love set "Lil Sis"—as Herman also called it—off again.

Some days the song sounded more like a musical instrument than a voice. Those days it reminded Lena of the sound of a cello. But it was still a voice from deep within her that indeed had been unleashed by Herman.

He didn't even have to be there cheering her on to orgasm for it to happen. All she had to do was think about him to set Lil Sis to singing. And the more she thought of him, the louder and sweeter the music became.

When she went shopping or was standing in an elevator, other people, men especially, surprised her by sidling up and asking, "What's that lovely song you're humming?"

The first time it happened in public, Lena just covered her lips with two fingers and turned red in the face as she thought of Herman and the way he played her like a Stradivarius. She felt that way in his hands, like a masterpiece, a one-of-a-kind treasure that was being cherished.

Lena noticed other folks in the Piggly Wiggly looking around and staring at her with their heads cocked to the side. An old man appeared at her shoulder, his head cocked to the side. "Now, don't tell me. I ain't heard that song you humming in a long time, but I know I know it. Don't tell me. Is it . . . ?" And the old fellow tried and tried to remember, sighed, drawing a blank, and looked to Lena for help.

But the only help she could give the old man trying to name that tune was to hold her knees together and try not to burst into laughter right there in his face. She finally had to leave her half-full shopping basket by the fresh-seafood counter and run out of the supermarket with the music and her laughter trailing behind her.

Until she got the voice under some kind of control where it only sang when she and Herman were alone, she just resigned herself to being embarrassed by the siren's song, even during Mass when her stuff sang along with the choir.

Herman sometimes called her vagina her "box," shortening the McPherson family name "matchbox." He also called the plain brown acoustic guitar that he played in the evenings his "box." She knew the difference, but she pretended she didn't. Both boxes made beautiful music.

"Hey, Lena, baby, hand me ma box," he'd say out on the deck stretched out on a chaise longue by the fireplace. She would get up, ignoring the guitar propped up against her chair, and walk straight over to him.

"Okay," she'd say, "here it is." And she'd stand with her stuff in his face. Boldly.

He would look up and grin, and pulling her down into his lap like his guitar, reach between her legs and strum her instead of his guitar strings.

"Uh, uh, uh, Lena, baby, you gettin' so 'omanish," Herman would say with a deep laugh as her pussy began to fill the outdoors with song.

Lil Sis didn't have a Jessye Norman or Chaka Khan voice. But she could still sound good.

Her matchbox sang all kinds of beautiful love songs. Songs that sounded like Ellington classics, like R&B standards, like Southern Baptist camp-meeting hymns, like Gregorian chant. But as Herman told her one morning when they woke to her music, "Yo' pussy don't sing no blues, do it, Lena, baby?"

Sometimes in her sleep with Herman riding through her dreams, Lil Sis would sing. And often both Lena and Herman would awake in the middle of the night to the music of her vagina just humming away.

Over the summer, Lena got her vagina's voice under control a little bit. She had to. The sound of it singing through the inseam of her cream-colored jodhpurs spooked Baby and Goldie as she and Herman rode the trails and paths of her grounds.

There was something about Lena and Herman getting together that brought out the music in them both.

Herman sometimes called her vagina his "Mulberry bush" and sang to her when they made love.

"Here we go 'round the mulberry bush, the mulberry bush, the mulberry bush. Here we go 'round the mulberry bush so early in the mornin'."

Lena couldn't help but laugh at the childish words in Herman's very grown-up deep voice.

"Here we go 'round the mulberry bush, the mulberry bush, the mulberry bush. Here we go 'round the mulberry bush so early in the mornin'." All she had to do was hear the tune in her head to start grinning.

Lena laughed all the time now, her brown eyes twinkling at Herman's black sparkling ones from across a room. She didn't have to give a thought to keeping a pleasant look on her face at all times and at all costs the way her father had insisted his entire family do when she and her brothers were growing up. At the family dining room table in the middle of a meal, Jonah would feel called to teach his children important lessons of life.

He taught them that the art of making conversation at the dinner table and the skill of keeping a pleasant look on your face were the most crucial lessons in life you could learn. Besides knowing to keep your elbows off the table.

"Mabel, Mabel, big and able, keep your elbows off the table," Jonah or Nellie or somebody enjoying the meal would intone at least once a day. Lena was happiest when she was the one who caught her brothers breaking the rule. She would chant it over and over, dancing and squirming in her chair, getting louder and louder, until her grandmama would lean across the big wide table in her direction as if to pat her on the cheek and say softly, "That's enough, baby. That's getting on Grandmama's nerves."

Lena had always heard from Gloria down at The Place that you were to keep other things off the table, too.

"Don't fuck on the same table you eat off of."

But with Herman, she threw caution to the wind. They made love on the shiny long picnic table in the breakfast room. They merged and loved on the big oval dining room table with the intricately carved base. They enjoyed each other aslant on the shaky drafting table in Lena's workroom. They screwed on the small round kitchen table near the sunny window overlooking the stables and the side garden. They even made love on the redwood picnic table near the deck down by the river. It *was* at night, but Lena did feel risqué making love buck naked in the open since more people than a little used the river during Cleer Flo', boating, even water-skiing some weekends as if it were a northern lake resort.

In the first days after they met, as they drifted on the surface of the swimming pool, Herman pointed to the wooden door with a single window in it and asked her, "What's that?" Lena just smiled and led

Herman to the cedar-lined sauna tucked into the corner of the pool room where they made love until they nearly passed out, surrounded by billows of hot eucalyptus-scented steam, lightly tinted the same green as the woods near the riverbank after a soaking overnight rain. Lena assumed that was Herman's doing. It looked as if he had taken a sharp Crayola forest-green crayon and traced the edges of every object in the sauna.

Lena almost had to give up meetings altogether after Herman learned she was ticklish and that he could become a true spirit and really sneak up on her without her realizing it. "Damn, Lena, you don't use hardly none a' yo' powers."

She feigned mild indignation, but she actually loved feeling the tip of his finger brush across the tip of her nipple as she spoke with some banker about extending a customer's credit. Sometimes he would just slip into her as she told Miss Julia Mae what ingredients to put in a poultice for her frail sunken chest. Suddenly, Lena would feel the tip of his tongue brush the tip of her clitoris and barely be able to keep from shrieking. Lena would come to herself sitting in Miss Julia Mae's chilly dark living room panting and gasping and glowing while the wiry old lady scrambled about trying to fan her and get her a glass of water from the kitchen at the same time.

Lena tried to be stern and irritated, but the sound of Herman's laughter—"Haw, haw, haw"—in her ear made her throw her head back—her cheeks all flushed; her eyes all bright and sparkling—right there in Miss Julia Mae's living room and laugh, too, at her joy.

Herman acted like it was his job to make Lena happy.

He was happy or at peace almost all of the time. It made Lena giggle to see the things that irritated him. He'd cut into a big juicy-looking lemon and discover little pulp inside.

"Shoot, Lena, old thick-skinned lemons. I hate 'em. We need some a' those good old ones we used to pluck from the trees down home in Flor'da. Lena, they was so juicy all you had to do to get the juice was to prick 'em. Didn't even have to cut 'em. The juice would come skeetin' out! That's what we need fo' this lemonade."

He'd continue with the task because Lena would have mentioned wanting some ice-cold lemonade to take down to the river with them. When she protested that the tart-sweet drink was fine, he just frowned his doubt and shook his head slowly. Herman wouldn't be satisfied until they drove around and found a farmer's stand where the vendor had procured some real Florida lemons.

"I want it to be just right fo' you, baby."

And he meant it. He was pleased to please Lena so much and so naturally that she didn't even notice how much he was for *her*, how much she enjoyed the loving attention, how much she had wanted just that kind of open, joyous, generous loving in her life.

Herman seemed finally to be the only one who didn't constantly *want* something from her.

"Don't you ever want anything, Herman?" Lena would ask. "Besides me, that is." And she'd smile, bite her bottom lip with her top front teeth and giggle a deep sexy giggle that rubbed up against the side of Herman's penis.

Herman would wait awhile, long enough for Lena to giggle again so he could feel it, then he'd shrug his heavy shoulders and say, "All I want is to make you happy, sugar. That makes me happy. As far as I'm concerned it makes the whole world happy."

Lena was his whole world. That said of anyone else would have made him sound obsessive or smothering. But Herman was none of that. Lena was the focus of his revived life force, she was the only reason he was still hanging around Mulberry and life, and that was just fine with him. Lena thought he must have left his ego somewhere between this world and the next as he floated around for a hundred years.

She told herself she was just lucky. But Lena had lived her life in an efficiently schizophrenic way, using and enjoying the gifts of the caul, on the one hand, and pretending that there was no such thing on the other. It was why she was able to make love to Herman at night, have coffee with him the next morning, then go off to work as if she had not just kissed a ghost good-bye.

While they read or watched a movie or sat staring into the fire or the night, Herman would reach down and pull Lena's feet onto his lap for a long slow massage for no reason other than he loved her. Lena would just sigh and let Herman do his handwork.

All the while he rubbed, kneaded, caressed and stroked her feet, he cursed and cussed the rows of beautiful high-heeled shoes that Lena couldn't bear to part with.

"Damned high-heeled shoes," he'd mutter once in a while as he massaged in earnest. "Those old pointed-toe high-heel mules you like so much is what did *this,*" he'd say with emphasis as he gently pulled on her toes. "They may make yo' legs look pretty, but I hate them mules, Lena."

He caressed her feet until the beginnings of hammer toes on her right foot had straightened out. With the creamy callused palms of his hands he planed along the inside of her feet above the instep to prevent bunions from forming.

"I ain't gon' have my baby's feets hav'ta go under the knife," he'd mutter to himself.

Sometimes, he would slide the flat of his big hand on up her leg from her instep, over her ankle, past her knee and up the inside of her thigh.

Then, he would touch her all up inside herself.

His touch was one of the first things Lena noticed about Herman. From the first time back in April when they formally met, Lena felt that he wasn't touching her to get her attention or to punctuate a point or for any reason other than to make contact, to feel his skin on her skin. He touched her on her bare shoulder for no reason, just to touch her.

The skin that touched didn't matter as long as it was his skin and hers. He told her, "Lena, I was always able to brush yo' spirit once in a while. Now I'm happy to brush yo' body, too. It's a pure-T pleasure."

It was a pure-T pleasure for her, too.

When Herman came, the whole world seemed to shiver and shift.

Sometimes, just to make her laugh, he would make the earth beneath them move when they came together.

And she *would laugh* and say in answer to his unspoken question, "Yeah, Herman, the earth *did move* for me."

Oh, she loved him so much.

She began to take note of everything he enjoyed.

With a straight face, he would come up to her as she ground strong coffee for him in their kitchen, kiss her on the neck and say, "Lena. Let me take care a' that thang fo' you." Then, forgetting the coffee altogether, he would proceed to "take care a' that thang" for her right there on the kitchen counter.

Herman had to have his coffee in the morning. Lena thought at first it was the caffeine he was craving. But as she watched him watching her each morning measuring the gourmet coffee she had bought especially for him, putting the beans in the small handheld Braun coffee grinder some other man had given her, grinding the dark aromatic beans fine, fine, fine to nearly a powder, she realized he liked the ritual of his woman making him coffee every morning as much as he enjoyed the black strong brew.

What Herman especially liked was watching her. Lena noticed he always appeared when she was washing herself. As she squatted over the bidet, she would feel him materialize on the other side of the white swinging wooden door. She couldn't see him, but she knew he could see her through the door. And she began to like the idea of being watched as much as he enjoyed watching her.

She would see him reach forward and pull open the door with a smile of lust and expectation and excitement playing around under his mustache.

Lena found herself as excited by this turn of events as Herman obviously was. His dick was packing the front of his old-fashioned work pants to bursting.

"Damn, baby," he told her often, "if you don't stop going 'round here so cute, I ain't gonna have no pants left."

Lena would grunt like an old woman surprised at her own still-vibrant sexuality when he talked that way. She reveled in the idea that she was the cause of all his dick-split pants.

Herman loved to watch her slather on the thick white creamy rich lotion she bought from one of her catalog companies. He had even entered one of the bottles of lotion after deciphering the ingredients from the side of the bottle and allowed himself to be rubbed into and absorbed by Lena's skin.

When Lena realized she was slathering Herman all over her still-damp and warm body, she dropped the glass bottle to the floor in ecstasy.

What truly amazed and delighted Lena was Herman seemed to get as much pleasure watching her fully clothed. He would appear in the kitchen and find her standing over the sink eating a piece of juicy melon. When Herman would catch sight of her with the ruby-red juice dribbling out the sides of her mouth and down her lovely planed cheeks, his mind went immediately to the Polaroid camera in the next room. Even with his ghost's mind, Herman could not preserve the essence of what Lena looked like as she leaned over that sink, her breasts resting insouciantly on the soapstone rim of the basin.

It would make him so hot he would come up behind her and ask her to "Please, ma'am" drop her pants. When Lena obliged, dropping the slice of watermelon into the sink at the same time, Herman would drop his own brand new Levi 501s and deftly slip his dick into Lena, who would lean over the rough sink's edge a little bit to make sure she had all of him.

Herman reveled in being a part of Lena's life.

"Who braid yo' hair, Lena?" he asked one day when he saw her examining her hair where new growth had left her braids wobbly at the roots.

"Sister used to. That would be our excuse to get her away from all those men in her life. She would tell Douglas and the boys, 'Lena need her hair done. You know I'm the only one who can do it.' Jesus, before you came, Herman, she was the only family I had. Then, she'd hop on a plane."

But with Sister out of the country and since Herman had appeared, Lena hadn't even given her thick burnished hair a thought. When she was ripping and running with Herman outside—digging and planting in the yard, grooming or feeding the horses, jumping in the Cleer Flo' pond with all her clothes on—Lena just pulled her braids back in a barely controlled ponytail in a gold elastic band. Herman liked her braids like that. He'd walk by her as she studied monthly business records on the computer or as she stood at the sink stringing pole beans the way her father and Herman liked them and pull her hair as he passed.

"Shoot, Lena, this ain't no *ponytail*. This a hoss's tail." And he would give her hair another sweet soft yank.

He came over and examined the roots of her hair along with her.

"I guess it does need braiding again," Lena said wistfully. She missed Sister and didn't look forward to finding a beautician to do it in Mulberry. "Maybe I'll get Chiquita or one of my other children to do it. Young girls with young, nimble fingers are good at braiding."

"Well, my fingers may not be young," he replied, "but *I'll* braid yo' hair fo' ya, Lena. I'd be happy to."

"Herman," she said, surprised and proud. "You know how to braid hair?"

And Herman just nodded his head.

"Damn, Herman, it is the truth, you can do just about *anything*!!"

He smiled and kind of shrugged his strong shoulders as if it were nothing.

"I'll do it fo' you now if you want me to."

Lena hardly let him finish his sentence. She jumped up and headed toward her bedroom in search of the big red comb she used to scratch out Herman's thick head of hair, stopping to lean down to give him a quick kiss on the lips just for being so damn wonderful.

He combed and plaited her hair as if he knew she was tender-headed. But as much pleasure as Herman seemed to take in her long thick braids, Lena knew that the sensation could not possibly compare with the joy and erotic pleasure she got from burying her face in *his* mat of hair. Each time he passed a mirror, he would grab at his hair and say loudly, "I sho' do need a haircut."

The first couple of times he said it, Lena jumped to protest.

"Herman, don't you dare think about cutting your hair! I love the way your hair feels just like it is!"

"Well, if you feels that way," Herman said slowly as he inspected himself in the mirror, playing with her, "I guess I'll just leave it alone."

"I don't know how you could even think of cutting off that old thick motherland hair. Shoot, look at it." Lena would pretend to still be a bit miffed with him for considering such a thing.

"Good thang you stopped me, Lena, baby," he'd continue to tease. "I was 'bout to cut it off right now."

Herman was like that. He wanted to be right now there in Mulberry in 1995 tramping all over her property by the river, discovering all the magic that Lena had made and never known about. This was what was important to him, and he felt himself disappear a bit each time she asked him what was going to become of them.

"Lena, baby," he would say, " 'round the times that the floods come th'ough here last year, I didn't have no idea I would ever have you in this life or the next. I know you only been 'live forty-som'um years, but it feel like I been lovin' ya fo' a hundred. And now I *got* ya. I don't care how many mo' eternities or moments I keep goin'. All I got is right now, sugar. All you got is right now, too. And that's enough fo' me."

Then, he would kiss her or touch her or blow her a kiss that actually landed on her cheek with a *SMAK* sound.

Lena would lie against this large, hard, husky man—her back to his shoulder and side—and feel him breathe as if she were lying against a large animal like an elephant or a rhino. Lena just knew at those times, feeling the strength of his breathing—something he probably just did to make himself comfortable and human-like to her—feeling the strength of his bulk, that Herman could move the world with his shoulders if he cared to.

They tried to act as if they were not already so intimate with each other, but it was useless. Herman already knew Lena much too well to play like he didn't. And Lena, freed from seeing scenes of Herman's life, his good moments and his bad, was making love for the first time in her life with pure abandon. There was no room for pretense in her love for Herman.

When they made love, "merged," Herman called it, he was able to go into her mind in a way he was never able to achieve when they were just talking or holding hands. But the extraordinary thing was that Lena could do the same with Herman. She, too, entered his ghost's mind when he drifted into her subconscious.

It was why every gesture Herman made toward Lena struck her as so intimate, meant just for the two of them.

Looking up at the May night sky full of twinkling stars, Herman would grunt, "Umph."

"What, Herman?" Lena asked, lying beside him in the darkness on the deck outside her bedroom. For weeks after he came, he had gone about the house cutting off lights all the time, muttering, "Lena leave lights burnin' *everywhere*!!"

It wasn't just the waste of electricity and the earth's resources that bothered him. It was the glare in his face at night when he wasn't reading or doing some intricate work. And for the most part, he kept that detailed work for daylight hours.

It was the unnaturalness of all those floodlights outside and all those fluorescent lights and shaded lamps and track lighting. Too much for him. That's what he would say.

"Lena, baby, all this light too much fo' me. Why don't we just let it get dark sometime."

And they did. Lying quietly by an oak fire that Herman had rustled up and Lena had lit when a little cool snap came through in late May or sitting in the comfortable shellacked cypress Adirondack chairs on the deck watching the sun go down and darkness fall.

In mid-summer, Lena and Herman would sit under the dark sky night after night down on the pier on the river, or on the deck outside the pool room, or in the covered swing on the rise of the bluff counting the shooting stars that arched over Mulberry for more than a week in July.

Lena didn't think she had ever seen a shooting star before that year, but with Herman, she saw showers of them night after night.

Looking up at the stars, Herman grunted and said, "You know, I never been to the stars."

Then, he paused and looked over at Lena.

"Wouldn't want t' go now, not w'out you."

Lena reached over and stroked Herman's temple. Then she recited "The Stars":

> "The stars shine over the ocean
> The stars shine over the sea
> The stars look up to the mighty God
> The stars look down on me.

> "The stars will live for a million years
> Yes, a million years and a day
> But only God and I shall live and love
> When the stars have passed away."

"You believe that, Lena?" Herman asked as the last words of the childhood poem evaporated from the air.

"Believe what?"

"That only God and you shall live and love when the stars have passed away?"

She didn't know what to say. It was a poem she had learned for a ladies' day recitation at some Protestant church when she was no more than five, and she hadn't given the words a thought.

"You know it's the truth, don't ya, Lena, baby?" Herman asked soberly as he reached over and gently stroked her face. "Even when the stars have passed away, Lena. You got everythang. You got the keys to the kingdom, baby."

19

LUCKY

Even after Lena's parents were killed instantly in the plane crash. Even after both her brothers died in their thirties. Even after it seemed certain that she would never have a family of her own. Even after losing so much, folks in Mulberry still told each other, assured each other, "Hell, Lena McPherson okay. She *got* everything!"

"They *got everything* already," she had heard relatives and friends say about her family all her life. The McPherson children received the little presents to mark each occasion in their lives: cute cards with dollar bills tucked in them, animal jigsaw puzzles and games for birthdays, and study lamps and dictionaries for graduations. But each purchase was accompanied with the comment "Shoot, them children *got* everything." And usually, someone else would add, "And if they ain't got it, they daddy'll buy it for them."

Then, "Well."

The "Well" said it all: Well, ain't that the way things are? Well, ain't that life. Well, them's that's got . . . Well, ain't life unfair. Well, shit!

And then the little three-dollar gifts—just a "little tokenette of a gift," as Grandmama called them—would be purchased, wrapped and presented along with everybody else's as if nothing had ever been said. Sometimes, as a child and even now, Lena could hear what she called echoes of conversations surrounding the gift she was just receiving in her hands. Before Lena could even say "thank you," she would distinctly hear the gift-giver or the gift-giver's mother or grandmother or husband distinctly say, "Lord knows she don't need this little gift. She *got* everything already. She don't *need* nothing."

The townspeople didn't mean it maliciously or even jealously. For them, it was just a statement of fact. "Them McPhersons, they *got* everything."

As far as everybody in town was concerned, Lena was still a lucky little baby girl born with a veil over her face. When she played the lottery, she won. When she'd play an illegal number at The Place sometimes, it was as easy as playing 222 or 555 or some number that showed up on her car clock. And 222 or 555 or whatever would fall the next day.

She had stopped buying local church tickets for picnic baskets or men's and women's watches or a new Cadillac or a home-baked cake. She always won. She had made enough enemies among the women's auxiliaries of enough churches and sororities, schools and Girl Scout troops to know not to push her luck with them.

Sometimes, Lena would buy a raffle ticket for a television or a VCR when she knew one of her customers was in need of that particular item, and fill in the name and address of that person. They always won.

"What you dream last night, Lena?" folks at The Place had asked her for the first twelve years of her life. Finally, her mother had stepped in.

"Leave my child alone!" Nellie had insisted until folks stopped asking.

But Lena still carried the burden of her birth.

People all over Mulberry had told her so many stories and legends and beliefs about how to protect and aid a child born with a caul over her face that she began to think of herself as an expert apart from her own experiences.

"Now, if the child is born in the spring or summer," Miss Louise told her down at The Place, "then you go out in your garden and dig a hole and plant a piece of the caul over a kernel of corn. And when the corn grow up through the skin and produce, give a ear of it to the child to gnaw. That'll protect 'em from evil spirits just like drinking the caul tea."

"Well, whether it's winter or summer, you know you got to bury the rest of the caul in a glass jar in the yard," someone else would put in.

"Or you can just keep that piece of birth skin clean and safe for the child dried and preserved in a white piece of paper," Miss Emma offered.

Unfortunately for Lena, none of these rituals were performed to protect her. Not all the way through.

But she retained some of her luck. Sister had pointed out, "Good God, Lena, haven't you ever noticed how you always seem to zip through customs? No one ever questions your identification or your personal checks or your credit card. Your hotel reservations are never misplaced, and your luggage is *never lost!* And you got the nerve to *check* your overnight bag!"

Adults had told her all her life how she was just plain born lucky. "Lena, baby, if I had your hand I'd throw mine in," customers at The Place who were shooting kind of bad had told her all her life. "Yeah, baby, I'd throw mine in."

One of the favorite stories told in the McPherson household was of Lena's birth.

"A lucky little baby girl here," Dr. Williams had said within moments of her birth. The doctor—for decades the town's lone black physician who still made house calls well into the 1980s—had a stroke the year before her parents died. And Dr. Williams died the next month.

Mrs. Williams, the doctor's stunning second wife and the auxiliary heartbeat of the old private hospital, was still elegant and vital. She was one of the townswomen who kept giving Lena their beautiful old heirloom gabardine suits and their gossamer-thin silk blouses with fifty pearl buttons down the back. She would swing by the Williamses' beautiful old brick house at the top of Pleasant Hill not far from the hospital site every now and again to show Mrs. Williams how stunning she looked in one of the older woman's elegant hand-me-downs.

"Um, um, um, Lena, you know you can wear a suit." Mrs. Williams would pause and smile. "That's the suit I was wearing the morning you were born, Lena."

Lena heard that all over Mulberry. Sometimes, she told Sister, she felt like the cynosure of a national question like, "Where were you when JFK was shot?" "Where were you when Martin Luther King was slain?"

In Mulberry, it was, "Where were you when Lena McPherson was born?"

It was never asked that way straight out, but it was asked.

Men waiting for their women at the entrance to the Mulberry Mall would watch Lena swing out of her car and stride into the mall with a wave in their direction.

"Hey, Lena, how ya doing? Hey, there, Lena. Morning to you, Little Miss Mac," they'd yell back.

Then,

"How old you think she is?"

"Lena McPherson? Shoot, let's see."

"Lena? She got to be in her forties."

"Yeah, she 'bout in her forties."

" 'Bout? Lena McPherson *well* in her forties. My cousin went to school with one of her older brothers. The first one to pass, I think, Edward. And my cousin two years younger than me. She got to be *well* into her forties."

"Well, now, 'cuse me, but she can't be all *that* old! Yo' name ain't Ray Charles, Negro, you ain't blind! Look at her!"

"Oh, I know exactly how old the girl is. I was playing poker with her daddy the night she was born."

"Aw, man, you didn't play no poker with Jonah McPherson. You know them games was too rich for your blood. You was probably skinning. Playing a game a' Georgia skin."

"Well, I was gambling with Jonah that night. Jackie Robinson had joined the majors a couple a' years before and had just played in the World Series."

"Yeah, that was that year 'cause I remember Jonah let my daddy slide on a gambling bet having to do with Jackie Robinson. And Jonah McPherson didn't never hardly do that."

"Yeah, I remember folks talking 'bout that."

"What? Jackie Robinson?"

"Naw, 'bout Jonah McPherson being so happy with his new baby girl, only one he got, he let some money slide."

"Yeah, like I was saying, that makes Lena forty-four or forty-five, something like that."

"Well, all I know is she ain't no Perdue!"

It was the last pronouncement as the gaggle of men fell into silence again to watch Lena exit the mall and go striding back to her car in a short pink suit trimmed in black cord.

But folks talked about her and her family all the time. What the McPhersons got, what the McPhersons own, what the McPhersons eat, what the McPhersons do. How lucky the McPhersons all were.

To the town, the car Lena drove now was just another example of how lucky she was. It was a Mercedes-Benz SLKII, a sweet little job that was not even on the market yet. It was scheduled for release at the end of '95, but on a business trip to Atlanta, her seat partner on the plane was an Italian man who designed automobiles. "I am Roberto," he said, slipping into the seat next to her and opening his portable computer. "And you are?"

The SLK was his baby, and he was so charmed by Lena that he offered her a test model.

She ended up not even having to pay anything for the privilege of sporting around town in the little copper-colored beauty that no one else could acquire for love, money or influence until the end of the year.

Her children downtown tried to get her to buy a Humvee, or at least a Range Rover, too, for those times she wanted to really take on the elements. But she told them her old green Grand Wagoneer sat in the driveway way too much as it was for her to be going out acquiring another underused vehicle.

"Aw, man!" they would say each time they brought it up. "I thought you was down!"

Folks in Mulberry would just watch her whiz by in the solidly compact prototype two-seater and shake their heads at her luck. One or two old folks even hummed, "Them that's got shall get, them that's not shall lose . . ." with a resigned shake of their heads.

On top of that, so many people in Mulberry knew Lena from her work, from her picture in the paper from time to time, from her one-of-a-kind car, that she didn't even pump her own gas. Some willing man, and once in a while a young woman Lena had seen grow up on the streets of Mulberry, always appeared to pump her gas.

Being lucky or unlucky. It was what everyone she met felt perfectly comfortable proclaiming about Lena.

They continued to proclaim it even after her parents' funeral, a funeral that rivaled the one in *Imitation of Life*, only without the caskets. Folks still said, "That Lena McPherson, now, that's a lucky little girl, that's one lucky woman there."

The day of her parents' funeral, one of the county's black sheriffs, Mr. Longfellow, the man who had made sure Lena passed her first driver's test without any problems, had to mobilize some of his off-duty officers to control the traffic of mourners and rubberneckers. The town's lone newspaper, the *Mulberry Times*, sent out a photographer and probably would have run pictures of the service, too, if someone in the composing room who had gotten out of a scrape thanks to Jonah hadn't destroyed the picture and cutline and substituted an ad.

In the middle of the Catholic Mass for the Dead, someone raised the old southern hymn "That Old Rugged Cross," then "Take My Hand, Precious Lord" (Nellie's favorite), then "Count on Me" and of course, "Jesus, Keep Me Near the Cross." Someone even stood and, sounding like the ghost of Mahalia Jackson, sang, "Soon, we will be done with the troubles of the world, troubles of the world, troubles of the world. Soon we will be done with the troubles of the world. I'm going home to live with God."

So many people stood and raised a prayer for Jonah and Nellie. Old thin women in wheelchairs strained erect. One cherubic-faced young man who had worked his way off and on through Tift Agricultural College down at The Place testified. An old schoolmate of Jonah's said, "I told my bossman, 'I known Jonah all my life. Man, I *gotta* take off and go to this funeral.' " A loud woman in back wouldn't stop screaming every now and then.

One of Jonah's boyhood classmates, a retired minister, stood among the sea of carnations and roses and lilies and gladioli and baby's breath, and warned the entire church, "Don't sit there and weep for Nellie and Jonah like you exempt. Naw, we *all* going home one day! Just like Nellie and Jonah McPherson, we *all* going home one day!"

The little priest was so touched by the Holy Spirit that he stood and testified, too, to the generosity of the deceased toward the school and parish.

There was only one man, an aging local gambler, who took the opportunity of Jonah and Nellie's final service to even a score or two.

"Oh yeah? Well, let me tell you 'bout Jonah McPherson, the dearly departed. He couldn'a *departed* soon enough for me," the heavy-set man about Jonah's age stood up in the middle of the carpeted center aisle of the church and announced. "Everybody in here know what a hard man Jonah McPherson was. Hell, he'd take your last two dollars! He didn't give a damn! Just 'cause a man like to play a little cards, play a little Skin, ain't no cause for somebody with a little money to hold it over his head. To take advantage of him and get that man to sign over his house and property and such to him.

"That's the kinda man Jonah McPherson was!"

Satisfied that he had had his say and delivered his eulogy, the man walked back to his pew and sat down. But the negative testament didn't even begin to break the stride of the funeral. As soon as the disgruntled mourner had sat down, another, more generous griever stood to tell about the time Nellie made it possible for her daughter to stay on in high school without having to clean houses on Saturday.

The service, with its impromptu songs and testimonials, seemed to go on even past Lena's endurance of deathly rituals. And she was so tired from the wake the night before, when it seemed that every man, woman and child in Georgia came through the doors of her parents' house on Forest Avenue to eat, drink, laugh, remember, lie, cry and joke, that she could hardly hold her head up.

"Look at her, poor thing, another Little Lost World," Mrs. Hartwick, St. Martin's former first-grade teacher, said from the door of the basement church as she wiped flour and egg batter off her hands onto her white and pink eyelet-trimmed apron and watched Lena and the other mourners trail downstairs out of church for the meal she and other church women had prepared. "She ain't got no mama or no daddy. Ain't got no sisters or no brothers. Poor Little Lost World."

The women in town took her in totally after that, calling on the phone for nice long talks every week, making sure she was up on Sunday morning in time for Mass, inviting her to every little social occasion in town. Of course, after a while, Lena was listening more to their stories of mourning and grief and need. But she didn't mind. That was the way it usually went.

Before she was seven, she knew that Peanut had contracted TB, lost all his heft and had to go away to the TB home. That was back when he was fat and healthy and women called him "pig meat," one older female customer had told Lena, " 'cause he was young and tender."

Now, he was an old man—skinny as a rail and only as tall as a prepubescent boy—who still came to The Place every single day it was open and who gave Lena a stick of Doublemint gum he purchased there each time he saw her. At age seventy-seven, he lived with the last woman who took him in before he became old and decrepit.

"A mere ghost of a man." Lena had heard that expression all her life. Peanut, so she had overheard over and over at The Place, was a mere ghost of a man after his bout with TB.

He was one of the honorary pallbearers at the funeral. Lena couldn't help herself. Even in the depths of her grief, she thought, I guess an honorary casket is about all little Peanut could help carry anyway.

Lena didn't think it was planned that way, even though Sister swore she could produce research to prove the historical significance of such a ritual, but all of Jonah's former women showed up dressed to kill in various ensembles of widow's weeds. Black lace and black veils and black silk and black voile and lightweight black wool. Their perfume gave the church full of wreaths and wheels and sprays and Bibles some competition.

One hefty woman squeezed in a tight taffeta black sheath broke loose at the door of the church, screaming and yelling and thrashing around.

"I knew you didn't have the strength, Lena, so I did it for you," Sister told her later. "I looked around at that loud-ass screaming woman and the man she came in there with and I gave her a look that said, 'Who the hell are *you*??' "

Then, Sister leaned over and patted Lena's hand as if she had accomplished a great deed of sisterhood for her.

"At least the other ladies had the decency to grieve and weep quietly. Hell, you let 'em sit right up near the front like family." Sister sucked her teeth. "God, the people in this town take you so much for granted."

At the foot of the cement steps out in front of the church, Lena, dressed in one of her mother's black wool suits, had to be reminded by the elegant thin old man from Parkinson's Funeral Home that there would be no ride to the cemetery. No caskets to follow. No dirt to see dug. No hole to look down. No lone rose to be cast on each descending casket. No bodies to bury.

The dead had indeed buried the dead.

Mr. Parkinson would have been the one to take Lena's hand at the funeral and say, "Your mama looks good. Nellie held her color." But he couldn't.

Mr. Parkinson, the elder, had played poker many a night and morning with Jonah and his cronies. Won a pile of money. Lost a pile of money. He felt it was his professional duty to try to console and comfort Lena. He had built a business, a good reputable business, on his professionalism.

Years later, it was the memory of his professionalism at Jonah and Nellie McPherson's funeral service that allowed him to keep his head held high. There was an incident at his establishment. If he had been there, he assured himself, it never would have happened.

A casket was overturned. A body left in the care and security of Parkinson's Funeral Home was desecrated. Customers were upset. Other services were disrupted.

And the gossip. The gossip!!

Mulberry talked about it for months.

A fight! they told one another in coarse places like bars and street corners and over bridge and whist tables. A family argument come to a head! they informed one another as they got their hair washed and clipped and curled. Flipped the woman right out her coffin right down there at Parkinson's Funeral Home! they screamed to each other in Laundromats.

Mr. Parkinson hated that part worse than anything, but it was the part of the story that townspeople loved repeating.

"Woman popped right out of that casket, while the family, the woman's three daughters, rolled around on the floor with the corpse, fighting each other!"

Then, the funeral the next day. All those people, showing up just to look.

Lena leaned toward the natty little funeral director and said, "Mama always used to tell me, 'You can't go to the cemetery with 'em *every time.*'"

Mr. Parkinson, the elder, murmured, "Umm," and nodded appreciatively as he handed Lena back to Sister and the circle of old men and women, her godchildren and the women from Candace that immediately surrounded her and nearly lifted her downstairs to the waiting fried chicken, grits, scrambled eggs, biscuits, juice and coffee Mrs. Hartwick and the other church women had prepared for the mourners.

For months afterward, the entire town mourned with Lena, feeling every one of her grieving pains. They were all prepared to catch her when she finally fell apart. They were fully prepared to do it. They just didn't know how they were going to stand seeing Lena in mourning.

The first day after the funeral that she walked in The Place, Peanut had exclaimed, "Lena, you po' as a snake."

So, she had to buck up right quick, go back to eating regularly and do her mourning where people in town could not see how bad she looked, how bad it did her.

She would have given anything to have a few ashes from her parents' bodies to put in matching elegant urns over the hearth in the Great Jonah Room. She still had the brass urn that had held her Granddaddy Walter's ashes on the mantelpiece in the dining room on Forest Avenue. But after she came back from her first semester of college, she had strewn the ashes herself on the train tracks on Montpelier Avenue right before the seven-ten southbound Silver Crescent headed for New Orleans came through, according to the dead man's last request. Then, she returned the urn to the dining room mantelpiece. And no one at the house on Forest Avenue ever knew.

But by the time she had arrived at her parents' crash site, a heavy rain had rushed through the Florida community and washed away everything but the heaviest pieces of plastic debris. The gray ashes, the bits of charred bone, the scrap of hair still attached to the skin, were all washed away.

No one had the heart to disturb her as she stood in the rain looking like a kindergartner in a yellow mackintosh and tall yellow rubber boots surveying the scene. When Frank Petersen arrived from Mulberry to get her, she looked at him and said, "Frank Petersen, I won't even be able to lay my hand on a tombstone and say, 'This my mama right here.'" And for the first time since she had gotten the news, she fell on the old man weeping.

The only evidence left from the plane crash in which Nellie and Jonah had died was his voice on the air controller's tape informing the small Florida tower that he was having some engine trouble and, not knowing the area well, was looking for assistance in finding a place to make an emergency landing. He didn't even sound nervous to Lena. It was the last communication from the twin-engine plane the couple named *Miss Lizzie* in honor of Lena's grandmama. There was not even a data flight recorder or black box to give some details of the couple's last moments.

Lena usually could feel when death was near. But earlier in the day when she had seen her parents off at the airport, Lena had watched Jonah and Nellie jump into their cute, luxurious Beechcraft at the Mulberry Airport like Sky King and his niece Penny and fly south toward a sunny day in Florida without the least trepidation about her folks' safety on that trip. The mist of death she had felt hovering, she felt, was meant for somebody in another plane, someone outside her blood family. But she was wrong.

"See, Sister, you talk all that caul stuff about seeing the future and powers and everything. But that damn veil ain't never done nothing good for me," Lena cried, weeping on her friend's shoulder the night of the funeral like a disillusioned child.

"Give me my roses while I'm still alive," her mother had said all the time. "I don't need anybody screaming and crying at a funeral when they didn't show me no love in life." And though Lena had pleaded that in lieu of flowers, mourners send contributions to Nellie's and Jonah's favorite charities, the church was flooded with blossoms.

"Give me my roses while I'm still 'live to enjoy them."

It was one of the three phrases that played themselves repeatedly in Lena's mind during the long funeral service and Mass.

Her mother saying, "Give me my roses while I'm still 'live to enjoy them."

Her father saying, "Lena, don't let nobody make a fool out of you in business."

And all of Mulberry saying, "Lena, you know you a lucky little baby girl."

20

CHINABERRY

With Herman around and in love with her, Lena felt for the first time in her adult life that she was truly lucky.

And if Herman's presence on her property was a haunting, then it was the sweetest and gentlest one she had ever experienced.

Most of the ghosts from her past had appeared in terrifying forms: wolves, cats and wild dogs; headless, footless bodies; decaying bodies with heads facing one way, torsos the other; babies who turned into ghouls. They controlled her in her sleep and drew her into dark and dangerous situations to frighten her. They spoke through her mouth, scaring her and getting her into trouble with her friends and teachers. They tried to pull her into their world.

The worst that Herman did was he wouldn't hardly let Lena conduct any business. All through May and past June, after the wisteria had disappeared and the small white flowers on the jasmine vines had taken over, Herman really got in the way of her duties.

It was not that he forbade her to conduct her regular voluminous business dealings. It was just that his "being" got in the way. His laughter got in the way. His invitations to explore her land got in the way. His way of life, so to speak, got in the way. Herman's yearning for Lena got in the way. And Lena's love for Herman got in the way.

The first few days after he appeared, all Lena had to do was think of Herman with his cheekbones like chiseled Georgia granite for him to appear to her.

She would feel the breeze on her neck and then look over to see Herman sitting on the sofa across the room from her. Or she would feel a tickle on the bottom of her bare feet, and he would be lying in bed next to her. Or she'd see a wisp of smoke escape from a late-night fire he had laid and lit for her, and he would be standing there by the fireplace in her bedroom carving the box for a kalemba.

But after a while, Herman did not wait for Lena to evoke him. He'd come sauntering into her bedroom first thing in the morning or be lying next to her when she awoke, watching her, waiting.

Adjusted to living alone, unaccustomed to another body—even a ghostly one—in bed with her, Lena would jump, startled at his presence. But she got used to it.

He didn't seem to need any sleep.

"I don't need no sleep, baby. Other than to run through yo' dreams every now and then so you won't forget 'bout me while you restin'."

"How am I ever gonna forget about you, Herman?" Lena asked sincerely. He was making her so bold.

"I just wanted to hear you say it, Lena, baby."

It still surprised her when she and Herman went out walking on the property and came up on Mr. Renfroe or a stable hand who would look up and wave at her and speak as if she were there all alone.

Herman was so real, so solid, Lena had a hard time believing that other folks could not see him. Could not hear him. Could not feel him.

Those first days, they just walked and talked and explored her property a great deal when she was at home. Right from the beginning, it seemed to Lena that they spent *all* their time together. But they didn't. Lena had too much else to do. She just thought about him all the time. She got up early to spend sunrise and first light with him before going into town and came home as early as she possibly could to end her day with him out on the deck looking at the stars through the telescope she had bought him.

It was amazing to Lena, but things worked out without her hand in it. For the most part, Lena's time with Herman was undisturbed. Her cleaning, stable and yard crews did their jobs while she was at work and only one or two people ever saw her talking to an empty space or riding Baby next to a riderless Goldie.

With James Petersen safely settled down the lane in his own home and the gardening and stable crew finished for the day, Lena and Herman would lie together in the two-person hammock he had found in the barn and strung between two tall pine trees overlooking the river and watch the sun go down. Sometimes, they would lie in perfect silence. Other times, they tripped over each other's words talking so much.

Magic happened all the time when they were out together. If it started to rain while they were out walking down by the river, there would seem to be a bubble around them as they raced back toward the house. One minute it was dry and breezy inside the bubble. The next minute it stopped raining outside and only rained inside the bubble. And they'd arrive home dripping wet and refreshed.

The first time Lena and Herman swam together outside, it was in the waters of Cleer Flo'. They had headed to the river one morning to see what had washed ashore during the stormy night, but when they saw the clear inviting waters rushing past the deck, Herman had suggested, "Let's go for a dip, Lena."

Both strong swimmers, they shed their clothes right there and dove into the green pristine waters of the Ocawatchee squealing like children. The river was full of life. And each time Lena or Herman brushed past a fish or a toad or a tadpole or a crawfish, it sent off electric sparks like an eel, and Lena felt like something from a science-fiction novel.

But Herman did not win Lena over with magic or the manipulation of science. He eased into her heart and took her over with real old-time love and attention.

He slid into her heart so smoothly, so seamlessly, that before she knew it he was truly her man.

Lena didn't know when it actually happened. She knew it didn't really happen overnight, but that was the way it felt. It was just that Herman and the day they had planned or didn't have planned opened up to them like a woodland amusement park each morning. There were horses and a swimming pool and woods to explore. There was a river to fish in and gardens to work. There was a flat-bottom boat to snake up into secluded estuaries. Herman was a lot more seductive than her duties in Mulberry. And Lena just didn't seem to have time for her old routine.

At first, when one of Lena's customers or friends or acquaintances called or showed up at her door needing, practically demanding, some help or intervention, Lena did what she had always done and rose to the occasion. She would rush to the phone or dash out the door with a big pretty peach-colored wool melton shawl trailing behind her and catch a glimpse of Herman out the corner of her eye. He would be stretched out in front of the fireplace with his big sock feet crossed on the table, his drugstore reading glasses low on his nose, a couple of books on the floor, a gooseneck lamp over his shoulder, and she'd immediately regret her decision.

"Shoot," she'd say under her breath as she raced to help the latest caller out of a scrape, "I could be laying up here with Herman." And to make it worse, she would recall the feel of his coarse chest hairs brushing across the tips of her breasts when they made love face-to-face.

So more and more, Lena found herself setting some new previously unheard-of limits. Herman showed up in April and by the end of May, she refused to leave home for any reason before daylight in the morning. By the end of June, she would not let anyone draw her out of the house after dark, "unless it's a dire emergency," she told Herman.

Lena tried her best to stop doing so much of the work herself. She discovered that without her at the helm twenty-four hours a day, her money, holdings and power kept right on working.

She continued her "hush mouth" work because she enjoyed giving. And as Gloria would have said, "Ain't no need to rock the boat right 'long through here." Lena continued signing checks and ordering gifts from catalogs. But more and more, she found herself asking Precious or one of the other assistants at Candace to screen her messages and mail and keep her apprised of important dates and events in the lives of her people.

And she continued sending out blessings to people and households in Mulberry even if she didn't drive past them every day anymore. Lena even heard herself say to a caller, "You know, it's you that your father wants to see at his final moment, not me. He probably doesn't even remember who I am. All you have to do is forgive him and let him forgive you."

Herman would hear her up on the deck talking on the phone.

"Uh-huh, uh-huh, uh-huh. Uh-huh. Of course, I understand how you must feel. Uh-huh. Of course, of course. Uh-huh."

"But I'm still going to have to say I can't do it this time," she persisted, looking out at Herman swinging in the hammock. "I've made another commitment.

"Your father just wants to talk to you. It'll be okay. I'll pray for all ya'll."

Then, she would come outside and slide into her space under Herman's right shoulder.

"You know, Lena, Miss Cora—who taught me to read out the Bible after I was grown—Miss Cora say the Lord don't want no sacrificed victims or no burned offerin's. He want yo' mercy and forgiveness fo' each other and yo' willin'ness to he'p each other out.

"Lena, you he'p a whole heap a' folks out all the time. Doin' all kinds a' thangs. You ain't got to sacrifice *yo'se'f*, too. You ain't *got* to do nothin', baby. We used t' say back in my day, 'All I gotta do is stay black and die.' And that's all *you gotta do*. Stay black and die."

But even when she had done all she could without sacrificing her days and nights to good works, Herman still found her looking off into space with that worried look around her pretty mouth. He'd tell her: "Lena, baby, don't worry 'bout the mule goin' blind. Just hold him in the road." And Lena would have to laugh because she did a lot of worrying about the mule going blind.

He got her laughing most mornings when he awakened her in her bed now that she slept soundly through the night. She could feel the weight of his body on the edge of her wide bentwood handmade bed waken her and she couldn't help it. Before she even opened her eyes in the morning, she would realize Herman was sitting beside her, waiting for her, and she'd awake with a big smile plastered all over her face.

Some mornings, especially as they came up on the nearly hot days of early summer, he woke her with song.

> "Woke up early this mo'nin'
> Sun was shinin' bright
> Told ma wife don't fix me no coffee
> 'Cause I won't be back tonight."

Lena would lie in bed—a luxury she had never allowed herself—and listen to the sound of Herman's rich old-timey-sounding baritone.

Sound like he ought to be singing "Ole Man River," Lena lay in her bed that smelled like her man and thought with a smile. Then, she laughed out loud when Herman launched into the tune from *Show Boat*.

God, he made her happy.

But if she didn't feel like laughing first thing in the morning, he would sense it and respect that feeling, too. On those days, Lena awoke to the sensation of being nuzzled by smoke, by mist.

She didn't dwell on the fact that Herman was a ghost who appeared and disappeared like dew in the morning. He was so full of life, it spilled out all over him and Lena.

"Hey, Lena, come look what I found in the barn!" "Hey, Lena, baby, let's go see if the fish bitin'." "Hey, Lena, hey, Lena, Lena, baby, put on yo' boots and come here a minute."

He called her all the time. And she never tired of hearing him speak her name. "Hey, Lena. Hey, Lena, baby. Hey, Lena, come see this big old blue boulder I found waaaayyy down the riverbank. We can jump in the river off it. Lay on it naked in the sun. Hey, come see. Baby."

"Lena, Lena, hey, Lena, baby," he'd call urgently from out on the deck. And he would point to the sky with wonder at a flock of long-legged wood storks in from the coast. "Look a' *yonder*."

It was difficult for her to talk on the phone, let alone conduct any kind of business in person, with him calling her name all the time. It was just a whisper in her ear, but it was a summons all the same.

His "calls" to her during meetings and visits and errands and conversations roused her to the point where she couldn't do anything but drop what she was doing and answer him.

He was the familiar breeze that intruded on her business. He was the waves of heat that made her fan like one of the ladies at church and made her want to drop her clothes right there in the bank. He was the frog in her throat that prevented her from accepting the Business-person of the Year award held at the new Dupree Hotel.

Some days he'd call her on the phone at the Candace offices. When she placed the phone to her ear, Herman would blow into it, sending a swirl of his breath down the tunnel of her ear canal, leaving her breathless. Sometimes he was the short in the electrical system that plunged the windowless center rooms into darkness and threw out the whole computer system for the week. So *everybody* had to go home.

The few times she tried to ignore the calls and continue with the business at hand, he would start *messing* with her. No one else in the business meeting seemed to notice the gentle breeze that suddenly stirred up one of Lena's giggles. It would lift the braids from her neck ever so slightly and brush across the short curly hairs of her kitchen. It coiled itself around her leg like a vine and spiraled up her leg in tiny teasing tendrils.

She could ignore Herman's calls, but she couldn't ignore his touches.

"Ms. McPherson, am I doing something amusing?" Mr. Potter at the bank asked one morning. It was soon after Herman had arrived, and Lena was squirming and giggling in her seat.

She had meant to regain her composure, sternly rebuke Herman in her head for interrupting a meeting that might lead to a home and good credit for one of her mother's friends' daughter and husband, and return to the meeting to finish up business. But Herman slipped up under her dress and inside her pink-flowered silk panties, making her grab the arms of the big oxblood leather chair and guffaw right out loud in the old banker's face. The sudden laughter sounded like something that Sister used to do in college and still did if something struck her funny enough.

Mr. Potter, whom Lena noticed for the first time had a bald head that was shaped just like an egg, large end up, laughed a little, too, just to make things a bit more comfortable in the glass-enclosed bank office with the understated gray and maroon drapes pulled discreetly around for the private business of finance.

"Oh, I *did* say something amusing, didn't I?" he said.

The breeze wiggled under her deep-rose satin bra that Herman liked so much and pushed one of the wide straps off her shoulder, tickling her there. And the meeting, for all practical purposes, was over. As Gloria used to say when recounting some story of sexual mischief to Lena when she was a girl, "Sugar, church was *out!!!*"

When Lena got to her car, Herman was sitting up in there in the passenger's seat dressed in a new cotton shirt and jeans she had bought for him, right proud of himself. She tried to be furious with him.

"Herman! How could you do that to me in there?" she spoke to what appeared to be the interior of the car even before she looked around to make sure no one was nearby watching.

"Good God, Lena, ain't you *glad* t' be out a' there!??"

"Stop it, now, Herman. You trying to make it seem like you were doing me a favor."

"Wasn't I?"

"No, you were doing yourself a favor. You just want somebody to rip and run with. You just want me to go out playing with you."

"Uh-huh," Herman readily agreed.

"So, you admit you were just looking out for yourself. Not me?"

"It's the same thang, baby."

"Herman, that was an *important meeting!*" Lena knew he had to know what was going on in there.

"You just holdin' up the weight of the world, huh, Lena?" Herman said. "Lena, baby, those people ain't in yo' hands. They in God's hands. And you ain't God."

He didn't say it harshly or even judgmentally. Herman just stated a fact as he saw it. He thought it was something that Lena already knew. But he immediately regretted saying anything.

Lena wanted to be angry to cover her hurt feelings, but when they got to the next corner, she had to slam on the brakes to keep from ramming into the side of another car moving legally into the intersection. Herman didn't miss a beat as Lena was thrown a bit against the steering wheel of the car, straining her seat belt. He reached out his strong solid arm across her breasts, clutched her forearm and held her safe from impact.

"Hold the baby," he said and smiled at her as the car rocked to a standstill. Lena grabbed her chest. And her arm crossed his.

Herman had sounded just like her mother, her father, her grandmother, her brothers and everyone else who had ever loved her all rolled up in one when he said that. When she was little, riding the hump in the middle of the front seat of the green family woodie, her family always made sure that her pretty little face would not ram into the big wide dashboard of the station wagon. Whenever the car came to a sudden stop, somebody in the car would reach across her with a protective arm and flat hand pressed against her tiny chest and say, "Hold the baby."

Herman's gesture evoked all the love and protection she had felt as the baby of the family and reminded her just why she loved this man. She had to struggle to remember just what she had been so furious with him about in the first place. And by the time they got home, she and Herman were laughing and playing together.

As his sabotaging tactics escalated with the coming of summer, Herman felt he had to explain to Lena how he felt.

"Baby, it ain't that I ain't got enough t' do to fill my time while you away. It's just that ya missin' out on so much stuck in those meetin's and speakin' lunches and 'do good' visits of yo's. I want you here wid me. I can't deny that. I can't he'p it."

It wasn't that Herman was always up under her. He had slipped quite happily and unobtrusively into life at her house by the river—at his own pace and seemingly with his own agenda. Sometimes, Lena would have to go look for *him*. She'd find him busy over some project like building a new trellis off the bedroom deck for her Grandmama's moonflowers or repairing a loose board on the deck steps. Or sometimes, he'd be taking a dip in the waters of the Ocawatchee.

"Hey, Lena, baby, you miss me?" He didn't give her a chance to be coy. "Hey, Lena, baby, you miss me?" Just like that. He allowed her little or no guile.

"Yeah, Herman, I missed you," she had to admit, stepping out of her high-heeled shoes into the dirt or the water with Herman.

And he'd smile, satisfied.

She'd often come home and find Herman browsing through her bookcases. He was insatiably curious about some things like the environment, architecture and the human body. Others, such as sports, television or transportation, he could care less about.

Herman would sit for hours staring at the pieces of the toaster or the microwave or her boom box that he had disassembled in his rampant curiosity.

"Now, how this thang work?" Lena would hear him say to himself as she tried to go to sleep on the green-and-white-striped sofa in her office and still remain close to Herman as he explored some appliance.

"You okay over there, Lena?" he'd ask, looking up from his work from time to time.

Electrical advances and laser discs were no reach for him. All Lena did was turn him loose at her computer, and he educated himself about most of the basic scientific advances since his death. He had a quick mind for a man dead a hundred years.

He told Lena he had seen most of these things in his wanderings, but he had seldom had the opportunity to really explore and learn the intricacies and workings of a computer or a silicon chip or a toaster to his satisfaction.

Lena had watched him with sheer wonder and pride. First, he took the front off the computer and, with the half-frame magnifying eyeglasses Lena had bought him from the drugstore resting down low on the bridge of his wide regal nose, examined the inner workings. Lena had heard him say so many times to himself as he hunched over his work, "Lord, if I 'a had just one lens out of these little cheap set of spectacles, I coulda turned the world upside down." And she believed him. He seemed to be able to do just about *anything*.

He let his gaze rest on the circuit board, lifted tiny plastic-covered wires and examined connections. Then, after an hour or so, he picked up a tiny tool from the shammy bag her computer consultant had left there and closed the machine back up. Lena thought he was through, but Herman was just beginning.

"Hey, Lena, you don't mind if I go in fo' a look, do you?" he asked her as he rolled back from the computer table in her new ergonomic work chair.

She was snug on the overstuffed sofa.

Humpph, I don't mind nothing you do, she thought to herself. But she didn't even get a chance to say it before Herman sat up straight in the comfortable chair, closed his eyes and became a mist that entered the computer through the disk slot in the same way that he sometimes became mist and entered her.

Lena was always amazed at the knowledge that he brought from the turn of the century. But then, Herman was an amazing man.

He told her that in life he had been an inventor of sorts. "Now, I ain't no book-educated man. But don't need t' be. I'm that kinda person that been shown a lot in life." Then he paused and added, "In death, too, come t' think of it."

What he mainly invented were tools. Lena smiled so broadly at the information that Herman found himself smiling, too, even though he had no idea why they were amused.

"You *would* invent tools, Herman," Lena said in answer. "Something useful and needed and able to make things easier and faster and better and smoother and fresher and more level. Sometimes, when you touch me, Herman, I feel useful in your hands."

With a smile, he pretended to tip an imaginary hat and bow his head to the side in response to her compliment.

Just watching him handle a simple awl or a small appliance like a coffee grinder, Lena had known that Herman was an inventor.

She had watched him from her bedroom as he discovered a box of Tampax in one of her bathroom drawers. He leaned right there against the counter's edge and read the entire sheet of information and instructions for the superstrength tampon. Then, he took one out of the baby-blue cardboard box and, looking again at the instructions he had laid on the countertop, tore open the thin smoking-paper wrapper and examined the tampon minutely until it was just a fluffy puff of cotton, some thread and strips of white cardboard.

"Umm, right clever," he chuckled and said to himself.

Herman even had a knack for finding and excavating artifacts of tools on her property. Century-old knives—blades made of gray and black stone and flint; handles of creamy-hued animal bone and deer and squirrel skin—fashioned by southeastern Indians. Small intricate red clay pipes made by Africans and African Americans before and after the Civil War to smoke the wild tobacco in the woods during a brief respite. A nearly airtight earthen container of rice with the imprint of the creator's small slender hands inside.

Lena was always amazed at what Herman could find or accomplish in any given stretch of time. He never hurried or fretted over schedules and dates. He managed time the way he talked about it.

"*Time*, baby," he said two or three times a day.

It was Herman's answer to many things.

"*Time*."

He said it with such assurance and peace, sounding like a down-home preacher comforting a grieving widow.

It was his answer to everything she complained about.

"Herman, I don't think these carrot seeds are ever going to sprout."

"Time, baby."

Or,

"If these folks and accountants and everybody don't stop pulling me every which way . . ."

"Time, Lena."

And even when the answer exasperated her, she always found herself later agreeing it was the right answer, the only answer. "Time."

"Now, where did you hear about laser surgery?" Lena had asked one hot day in June as they sat on the cool grass of the riverbank.

"Shoot, baby, where you think I been fo' the last hundred years?" Herman asked back with a laugh.

"Dead!" Lena said with an intentionally dumb wide-eyed expression on her face.

"Well, there's dead and there's *dead*," he said, looking at her over his half-frame eyeglasses.

When Lena paused, pretending to consider what he said, Herman got a bit indignant and asked, "What part a' me *seem dead* to you?"

Lena laughed. "Not one single part," she said as she fell into Herman's lap and seemed to sink right into him as if she were falling back into the waves of the sea or a pile of crisp autumn leaves.

"How old were you when you died, Herman?" Lena had asked in late May as she lay back on the office sofa with his head in her lap.

"I was just a few weeks shy of markin' my fortieth birth date when I died," he answered matter-of-factly.

"Why, Herman, you're not even *forty!?*" Lena squealed. "Lord, my baby's pig meat."

Herman looked at Lena with a sly smile, chuckling at her brazenness and pride, and went back to tinkering with the sauna control box in his hand.

Herman tinkered around Lena's place so much that her household started functioning so much more smoothly, cheaply, efficiently, that even James Petersen took notice. The toilets used less water, the shower and taps, too.

And it wasn't just in the house that Herman made his ghostly presence felt.

Herman showed Lena things on her property. Stones washed down from the mountains by Cleer Flo'. Trees budding out of season. Relics from previous civilizations and peoples. Jewelry made of animal bone and feathers. Unusual markings on Baby's stomach Lena had never noticed before. Gossamer silver snakeskins discarded by growing reptiles. Lena began to walk on the very earth differently.

It amazed her how easily she forgot the busy little town of Mulberry.

When she walked now she felt Herman's arm resting lightly around her shoulders, her shoulder tucked perfectly in his armpit like two pieces of a jigsaw puzzle. She was actually taking time to see, *really see*, the earth she was walking on.

"Ya gotta cherish this piece a' earth we been given, we been born to," Herman said as they walked so far afield on her property that she couldn't even see the tops of her chimneys. "The trick, Lena, baby, is to cherish yo' own little piece of earth, but not to get *tied* to it. 'Cause it ain't nothin' but a piece a' dust, like us, our bodies, that's gon' come and go."

When he found a chinaberry tree on her land, Herman was as excited as if he had created it himself. He came and got her in her home office and brought her right to it.

"You know what we used the root a' the chinaberry tree fo', Lena, don't ya?" he said as he smiled a smile that Lena wanted to just lick off his face. He pretended to wait for her to answer as he kicked at the knot at the trunk of the tree just above the rich dark ground.

"Yeah, they used this root to make a potion to make ya hot. Our folks and the Indians used it in ceremonies and rituals. And other folks just used it.

"Guess *we* can pass on this one, huh, Lena?"

Looking around at a squat prickly bush, he continued the lesson since he had her outside.

"And look a here, Lena. This what we call 'China briar.' My ma usta make a kind a' mush out a' the root. A bread, too. China briar was one of the first thangs I remember ever eatin'."

Herman showed Lena all kinds of things. He explored her hundred acres of property as if it were a tidy little backyard.

While Lena was away at work in town, he uncovered treasures and mysteries that Lena had never even thought about being on her land.

One Sunday morning after they had made love, eaten grits and salmon croquets, made more love, gone swimming and lain on her river deck to dry in the sun, Herman took her for a walk. She had wanted to grab a piece of pie or fruit before they left, but Herman wouldn't let her.

"*I* got som'um sweet fo' you," Herman said, laughing and patting a bulge in his pants pocket.

Lena tramped out in her new heavy Timberland boots just like Herman's and followed him into the woods with a smile on her face. She couldn't get enough of him.

They walked for a good long time along the river to the east of the house. Lena was becoming winded.

"Maybe, we should have ridden the horses, Herman," she said.

"Naw, not this time," he answered over his shoulder.

When he finally slowed down by a big sycamore tree at the edge of the woods, she thought he would take out a tiny copper-colored G-string for her to prance around in. Instead, he pulled out a pair of work gloves and handed them to Lena.

"Here, baby, I don't want ya to get hurt."

Lena thought she could hear someone humming in the distance as he led her deeper into the woods. Then, he held up a bare hand, stopped and pointed up ahead to the biggest circular beehive Lena had ever seen. It hung from the swooping lower limb of a massive live oak tree like mistletoe. Herman smiled at Lena while motioning for her to stand still. Then, he advanced on the golden-colored humming hive.

Herman slipped his bare hand sideways into the bottom of the nest, deliberately, steadily. He only paused a moment with his hand inside the hive, then slowly pulled his hand back out, rotating it slightly to form a cup as it came out. The hive was shaped just like the ones in cartoons she had watched as a child on Saturday mornings in which a hungry old hairy bear would try and try to get that honey. She had imagined that animated honey to be the best, the sweetest, the most golden honey in the universe.

Lena was mesmerized by Herman's performance. It was like a theater piece, silent except for the lazy-sounding buzzing of the bees. Then, Herman drew her into the act. Looking very serious, he lifted his right hand dripping with thick dark honey and flecks of waxy honeycomb up to her lips. She took two of his fingers into her mouth and lifting her chin, sucked the honey off.

It was as sweet as the cartoon honey. The intensity of the sweetness nearly blew the top of her head off when she smacked her lips.

Herman didn't just treat her to honey. He taught her how to survive.

"Here, Lena, tie this cotton kerchief 'round yo' mouth when we out walkin' in the woods," he instructed her, "so yo' breath don't draw those 'squitas and bitin' flies."

And it worked, too. Some days, Lena and Herman looked like

happy bandits loping through the woods or the dirt trails or riding the horses flat out over the rough terrain off the bridle path.

James Petersen back at the house gazing out the kitchen window over the sink would see her head off happily into the woods and chuckle to himself at the sight of Lena outside talking to thin air. "That girl knows she can talk to herself. She got so much on her mind."

Mostly what Lena had on her mind was ways to spend more time with Herman.

One morning Herman woke Lena even earlier than usual. Brushing her face with the breeze of his kisses, he gently roused her.

"Come on, Lena," he urged when she dreamily opened her eyes. "Put on some long pants and boots. Ticks are bad this year. I got som'um t' show you."

Lena sat on the deacon's bench by the door in the Glass Hall and laced up her boots over her pants legs. She was laughing to herself at the many pairs of work boots and outdoor shoes she had acquired since Herman came into her life when he blew in and grabbed her hand. He didn't even bother to ask what she was laughing at.

"Found som'um you might be interested in," he said with a smile playing in his voice, pleased with Lena's cozy joy.

He pulled her down the path to the stables, where he had saddled Goldie and Baby for them to ride. Lena always tried to ride behind Herman so she could watch his shoulders and the small of his back as he rode. Herman—with his near-midnight self—astride Goldie—with her near-sunrise self—was a sight to behold, one that Lena never tired of seeing.

They set off across her property heading south and didn't stop riding fairly hard until they had circled a stand of impenetrable woods and reached a meadow on the other side that looked like something from a fairy tale.

The field was encircled with trailing bramble. Small vines had formed a wall around the dale that was covered with rich juicy-looking spots of amaranth.

Lena could no longer see the river, but she could hear the music of it rushing close by. Pulling Goldie's reins up, Herman sat back proudly in his saddle as Lena took in the expanse of early-bearing blackberries.

Without a word, Herman dismounted, tied his steed to a bush and, reaching into his saddlebag, pulled out two croaker sacks. He handed one to Lena. "We gon' pick *berries*.

"Lena, uh-uh, baby, don't pick that berry. It ain't ripe. Come here. Uh-uh-uh, you mean to tell me I gotta teach her how t' pick blackberries, *too*," he mocked her with a little tug on her hand making the underripe berries in her tin bucket rattle against the sides.

"See this here berry? Now, this un ripe," he said softly, acting as if he were stalking some living, moving, breathing prey. "See how when you look at it, especially in the sun, it almost glisten? And see how plump it is? Plump, plump even before ya touch it. And when you do. OOooo. See, 'bout ready to bust. And when you take it, with these three fingers, and gently tug—lightly now, so you don't break the skin. It's real tender—it oughta come away from the stem easy, real easy like it want to come.

"There," he said happily, sated, holding the glistening berry aloft by the bushes. "And ya got yo' berry."

Then, he reached over and popped the lone fruit into Lena's gaping mouth.

Lena bit down on the juicy nugget, sighed and smiled.

Sister was right, she thought. I do have an abundance of blessings.

21

MINISTRY

Sister always teased Lena that although she owned a liquor store and juke joint, real estate business, and substantial property, what she really did was conduct a "Healing and Miracle Ministry."

Lena was blessed with what folks calling in early on Sunday mornings to the three-hour *Gospel in the Rock* show on Mulberry's WASS radio called "a personal relationship with Jesus Christ."

Although Sister had been raised a cradle Catholic in Louisiana, she was the first person Lena had ever heard discuss her personal relationship with Jesus Christ without sounding like a broadcast from Reverend Ike. It had been Sister who had helped Lena settle her Catholicism firmly on the rock of Black Southern Christianity. In fact, Lena found herself listening to some of those late-night broadcasts when she couldn't sleep and surprised herself by finding solace in the words of an electronic minister.

Sister said that Lena always tried to take the "Jesus Road," that

Lena was "tight with the Lord" though barely within the confines of the Roman Catholic Church.

And even though Lena chuckled at Sister's terminology, she knew it was true that most folks in Mulberry looked to her for just that: healing and miracles. But if it was a ministry, Lena thought, she had been drafted, not gently called.

Most of Lena's adult life, she would try to ignore the voice on her phone or the face at her door, but when she looked around at her sumptuous surroundings, she'd say out loud, "Lord, you make miracles for me, and I won't even do you a favor." Then, Lena would get on up and go see about somebody in the middle of the night or in the middle of her workday.

"Well, here comes Mulberry's own 'Little Flower,' " Father Collins would greet Lena when she came bearing gifts and needed supplies for the parish's school and its children.

Lena did share a number of qualities in common with the Little Flower, the beloved and revered French saint who died at age twenty-four promising that she would spend her time in heaven doing good for those still here on earth. Lena was especially like St. Theresa during Holy Eucharist.

At Mass it seemed to Lena that she always did the same thing. She stood with the congregation and took her place in the procession of communicants leading down the center aisle of St. Martin, waited her turn with her hands folded to step up to the eucharistic minister or priest, smile, hold out her cupped hands in front of her near her face and exclaim "Amen" when she was told, "This is the Body of Christ." Then, she would turn to the left, walk to the minister holding the chalice at the end of the altar, smile, hold out her hands, the right one to cup the cup, the left one to balance the base of the chalice, exclaim "Amen" when she was told, "This is the Blood of Christ."

Then, she would turn and walk back among the scattered procession to her pew to kneel and bow her head to pray. That's what she thought she did each time.

What Lena didn't realize was sometimes instead of saying "Amen" at the altar in response to the "This is the Body of Christ," she said what was truly in her heart. Sometimes her response was, "Well, all right." Sometimes "Yes, it is" or "Well, well, well" like an old woman or "Yes, yes, yes, yes, Lord" or even, "You got that right!"

Even the meanest spirit in the church felt the force of Lena's ecstasy during the Eucharist and was warmed by her sweet spirit. But none of the other parishioners saw what she saw, felt what she felt.

Lena would return to her pew after receiving the Body and Blood of Christ. Then, she would feel herself kneel, bow her head, then begin to rise. Like the Little Flower, Lena could feel herself slowly, steadily, effortlessly rising, rising, rising toward the shiny shellacked wooden beams of the church, rising toward the newly painted white ceiling, rising through the roof like a wisp of smoke through a piece of gauze toward the blue blue Sunday sky.

As she floated among the clouds, she felt enveloped in a cushion of love, like rolling over against her grandmother's soft chest in bed at night. It was one time she was certain, dead certain, there were benevolent spirits who loved and protected her.

Lena had a recurring dream in which all the women who had ever loved her held her and loved her once more. The dream was exactly how she felt during her levitation at church. After she had floated around the heavens for a while, feeling as if she were being passed around from one loving bosom to another, she would feel herself gradually sinking back to earth and her pew at St. Martin de Porres.

Sometimes, the priest would be giving the final blessing to the congregation when she returned to herself. More often, Mass would be over, the priests and servers and ministers clearing the altar or, like the congregation, gone entirely, in their cars driving home or to brunch or an early supper or to watch the game. Lena would be left undisturbed to continue her meditation.

The charismatic group at the church with their Pentecostal fervor and their laying on of hands and their speaking in tongues had quickly tried to claim Lena as one of their own. But Lena was polite yet firm. She didn't fit into any group—charismatic or not.

Although Lena was a respected practicing Catholic, she probably would have been excommunicated if the Pope, whom she believed no more special than Mr. Renfroe, knew what she believed and practiced. While supporting her church and parish, while doing good Christian works throughout Mulberry, while receiving Holy Communion weekly and sometimes daily, outside of church, Lena practiced a mixture of Catholicism, voodoo, hoodoo, New Age mysticism, goddess worship and black Southern Baptist/Protestant/Holiness belief that even Sister found shocking.

She would just as likely consecrate her own hunk of whole wheat French bread and a good bottle of champagne from her wine cellar at altars and grottoes around her house, saying the words "This is my Body, this is my Blood," aloud under the big willow tree as attend the 11:00 A.M. Sunday Mass at St. Martin de Porres dressed in a beautiful raw silk suit, hat and heels. It was all the same to her.

For her, the celebration was just as true. Sometimes, she played music when she conducted her own Mass outdoors, but it didn't seem to matter. The flowers and plants, the bees, birds and bugs all bobbed and danced and bowed in adoration at the Eucharist that Lena performed so sincerely and joyfully. Some mornings, such as Mary Magdalene's feast day, or her grandmother's birthday, Lena could almost smell the scent of frankincense in the fresh air just as it was being lit in the Catholic church in town.

When Lena told Sister she was taking her own consecrated bread to her older Catholic shut-in friends, she heard Sister gasp over the phone.

"Lena, I'm no church theologian, but isn't there a difference in consecrating the Eucharist for yourself 'cause you believe that God gave you and me and anyone who believes the power to turn bread and wine into His own body and blood and actually giving it to someone else as if it came out of a church?"

Lena had accepted Jesus Christ as her personal Lord and Savior, so she felt she had a certain license.

"Shoot, Sister, I been celibate longer than most of the clergy, considering what we're finally coming to believe about so many priests now," Lena said confidently.

No one really should have been surprised by Lena's natural religious fervor. Her mother would not have called herself a religious influence on Lena, but she was. The way Nellie went around the house when her children were younger calling unceasingly on the sacred name of Jesus, it made all the sense in the world that Lena would have been affected.

"Jesus, keep me near the cross," Nellie intoned at the drop of a hat.

Lena *could* pray a good prayer and preach a good sermon. Before Father Collins was severely reprimanded by the bishop of the Savannah diocese, backed up by a letter from His Holy Father himself in Rome, sternly prohibiting women from speaking from the pulpit, Lena and a couple of other women had delivered sermons on Saturday evening and Sunday morning Masses.

Standing at the pulpit those Sundays, Lena had felt she had found her true calling. The words rolled from her tongue like tiny marbles, produced effortlessly in the center of her soul one after another. Her prepared words forgotten in the ecstasy of revelation, she just opened her mouth to the congregation and opened her heart to the inspiration of the Holy Spirit, and a sermon of rebirth and forgiveness flowed from her soul.

"Each one of us made a new man, a new woman, washed in the blood of the Lamb, washed in the waters of the Jordan, washed in the love of our Lord, I am renewed, reborn, a child again. Dead no more, reborn to the spirit. This is what I believe. This is what I testify. In Jesus Christ's name, let us bow our heads and accept His Love."

People in church told her that her sermons were like poetry. And Lena knew in her soul her sermons were good because she loved to pray.

She knew she could pray and that her prayers would be answered.

She had learned the art of prayer from customers at The Place. Old women standing at the door to order a fish sandwich to go because they didn't come into places like The Place would sometimes just break into prayer, as if they were raising a hymn in prayer meeting.

"Lord," they would pray, "thank you for getting me through the night and letting me wake up live this morning. Thank you for not turning my bed into my cooling board. Thank you for not turning my gown into my wrapping cloth."

This part was essential, Lena had surmised over the years, because a good prayer always included those intentions.

There would be prayers for the sick, for the shut-ins, for those bound by drugs and alcohol, for those knowingly living in the state of sin, for fornicators, for those who do not know Jesus Christ, for those who refuse to know Him.

Lena had gained her love for the beauty and wisdom of the Bible from the same people. A few Saturdays of sitting next to Miss Joanna as she ate her scrambled eggs, grits and toast and drank her sweet black coffee and orange juice first thing in the morning down at The Place taught Lena more about the Bible and what it was saying than sixteen years of Catholic school education.

Lena had to shake her head in wonder at the number of biblical scholars she saw in a day going about their lives in their maid and cafeteria worker's uniforms. To say nothing, Lena thought, of the women who should be in pulpits.

During daily Mass, when the priest invited the congregation to offer their own individual intentions aloud, Lena didn't hesitate to pray "for the evil that corrodes our church with more emphasis on gender than on Christian love, let us pray to the Lord."

She had not intended to make such a big deal about women preaching sermons. But there were some things that just didn't seem right and Christian. And Lena always felt it was her place to at least point them out. Simple things, like, if Mary was the Mother of God, then why didn't she get the same rank and adoration as the Father of God. It just didn't seem right.

It was like the way Lena had always felt about her own mother doing so much in the house, in the community and in the family business just to be relegated to someone who "helped Jonah out."

So, just as often as Lena said, "In the name of the Father and of the Son and of the Holy Spirit, Amen," she prayed, "In the name of the Mother and of the Son, Jesus Christ, and of the Holy Spirit, Amen."

She said it just as innocently. She didn't make a big deal of it and try to drown out the person sitting next to her with *her* version. Lena couldn't even pinpoint the exact time when she had started switching back and forth. She just said it because it sounded right to her.

She told Sister, "It just makes sense that if Jesus was conceived in Mary's body and God was the essential father, then Mary with her womb, her egg, sure as shooting was the essential mother."

And in Lena's mind, that made Mary divine, too. Worthy of prayer and adoration.

Lena didn't want to be the one who always was pointing out how the world didn't seem to care a thing about a woman. But in her mind it was the same way the world had taken the pleasure out of things if you thought too much about it. Some of the best-used profanity insulted a woman: son-of-a-bitch, motherfucker, bastard. It wasn't right.

"It seems to me, Sister, that women—Mary, Ruth, Esther, Elizabeth, the women disciples at the foot of the cross—were the only ones in the Bible who were obedient to God," she told her friend one Sunday as they strolled back from her mother's altar where Lena had celebrated Mass. "And they don't get no credit."

The altars and grottoes and retreats Lena had erected around her property emerged from that belief. First, she and Renfroe made a little grotto to Mary, using some medium-sized gray and orange and blue-streaked stones he and his crew had unearthed in their work on her property. Then, she asked Whit, the family's old carpenter, to build a cypress altar to Oshun. It made sense to have a special place for her beside the running waters of the Ocawatchee. Then, while she was out riding her horses, she thought of Yemaya, and she got Renfroe and Whit to help her erect a shrine to her, too. Then, one May 5, Nellie's birthday, she decided to erect an altar to her mother, her grandmama, Mother Hale, Mother Theresa and all mothers.

By midsummer, once Herman arrived, Lena had stopped going to daily Mass at Blessed Martin de Porres altogether. By early fall, she had stopped attending Sunday Mass as religiously as before. From time to time, when she felt especially communal, she would slip on one of her mother's light shifts with a sweater around her shoulders, kiss Herman good-bye, and drive over to Pleasant Hill for Mass on Sunday morning. But usually, Herman and the saints she honored was all the community she needed.

At one altar or another, she celebrated the Eucharist each morning. Alone or surrounded by the spirits of all the loved ones she had lost, she intoned her declaration of faith as she lifted the bread and wine:

"The Body of Christ. Amen. The Blood of Christ. Amen."

22

SOM'UM-
SOM'UM

Lena's grandmama had always said of her husband, Walter, "I could tell that Negro could *really eat* when he poured gravy over all his vegetables!"

That's what Herman did. But even with that clue, Lena was amazed at how much Herman ate. He was a big man, not overly tall and overwhelming, but a good-sized healthy man. Still, the amount of food he consumed was incredible.

He didn't hunker over his plate and wolf his food down. Lena thought he had lovely table manners. He just ate like a man who hadn't had a meal—a good meal—in years. Actually, he hadn't. He said that over the years since his death, he had tried to make himself whole so he could consume some delicacy he had come across in his wanderings, like a nice hot sweet potato warm and gray lying forgotten in some hunter's open-fire ashes. But it never tasted as good as he remembered in life because he could never truly make himself whole. That was until he came to Lena.

Herman ate with gusto, with appreciation, with occasional grunts of pleasure and smacks of his lips. He would bob his head as if he were listening to music even when music wasn't playing. When it was real good, he rocked in his seat.

"Wooo, I'm so hongry, I could eat up salvation and drank Jurdan dry!" he would exclaim as he sat down at the table.

One night in July when they both woke hungry from making love, Lena asked Herman if he had ever eaten potato pancakes in the middle of the night.

"I don't think so, Lena, baby, but I *could* eat a little som'um-som'um," he said as he pulled on the thin cotton drawstring pants Lena had ordered for him.

Over the hot, steaming plate of potato pancakes, thick with chunks of milled potato and white and green onion and lots of cracked black pepper, Herman wiped his greasy lips with a golden linen napkin and said, "Good God, Lena. Baby, now I *know* we meant t' be together. Ain't no way you can cook like this in the middle a' the night, and God didn't intend fo' me t' be yo' man. You my treasure, Lena."

He was as much her treasure as she was his.

They went back to bed smelling like potato pancakes and continued tossing on the big bed, Lena's bites turning into hurried tiny kisses and Herman's tickles drifting into long deep caresses.

Herman kissed her and slowly began to seep into her pores. Lena quivered because she could feel him enter her through her skin and at the same time experienced the sensation of entering Herman through his salty brown, onion-scented skin. When Lena awoke, one of Herman's broad callused artistic hands was resting lightly between her thighs on top of her matchbox and her right hand was lying on his chest covering his left nipple. She could still hear the sound of their laughter in the room. They laughed all the time together, bringing new lines and wrinkles to Lena's pretty, young-looking face.

Gloria was the first one to notice the change when Lena swung through The Place for their monthly meeting in July. "Lena, girl, *who* you fucking? You look great!!"

Gloria suspected for a moment that it was another woman.

Lena *did* look good. She was looking like a woman from a Maya Angelou story. A character from a Toni Morrison novel. A person from an Alice Walker poem.

Lena threw her head back, but with a little lift of her chin that gave the gesture its own unique stamp, shaking the ends of her braids against her shoulder blades, and laughed in a way that made all the women in The Place look at each other and go, "Ummmmm-mmmmmmmm."

"Well, whatever it is, I need to have it stacked up behind my stove like cordwood," another customer, a woman of a certain age, said, shaking her bony shoulders a couple of times at the prospect.

The way Herman enjoyed eating, Lena felt she *should have* cord-wood stacked up in her kitchen.

Cooking turnip greens with their creamy roots and smoked ham hocks for Herman made him as happy as if she had given him a blow job. She reveled in washing the greens not twice, not thrice, but four times before cooking them, ensuring that Herman would not crack down on a piece of grit and spoil the whole experience in the middle of a near-ecstatic moment of gastronomic bliss. It was her pleasure to give the greens an extra dipping in lightly salted cold water.

She put some ham hocks in a little water in a big Calphalon pot with one long cowhorn pepper, and while she washed the tur-nips, the meat cooked and filled the kitchen with an earthy funky scent. When the greens were clean, really clean, she took them over to the big black and white gas stove. She tasted the seasoned water with her finger and savored the slightly salty meaty flavor with an "Umm." She tossed in two medium-sized yellow onions cut in quarters, then added the greens. It seemed she would never get all those greens in that tall gray weathered pot, but she did. And she punched them down with a big fork before throwing in another cowhorn pepper—a red one—covering the pot and turning the flame down to medium.

Whenever she lifted the lid to check on the greens, she'd say the same thing she had heard her mother say a million times. "Lord, greens go away to *nothing*!"

Lena started cooking like her mother, too.

The first time Lena fixed fried corn for Herman—sweet white Silver Queen in the middle of summer—she thought she was gonna have to hose him down.

When he first took a mouthful of the corn, he actually laughed at its deliciousness. "Shoot, Lena, I could eat that every day!"

And Lena smiled at the memory of her father, who truly did love and eat the fried corn that Nellie made every day that it was in season.

But at first, during the last days of spring, they still ate the Mulberry ladies' food as much as hers.

Sister had warned her years before on a swing through Mulberry on her way back from a trip to Haiti that Lena would be making a big mistake if she ever tried to pass off the CARE food package meals as her own and serve it to some man she was interested in.

"Girl, in Haiti, a woman would rather cut out her heart than let another woman even *purchase* the food her man is going to eat let alone *cook it*!!!!!" Sister had informed her as Lena had put bowls of collard greens and rutabagas and perfect tiny corn muffins in the microwave for quick heating.

Lena thought about her friend's comment briefly while she stood by the kitchen window overlooking the stables' tulip and iris bed enveloped in a sheath of sunlight and watched Herman, his wooden stool pulled up to the center island in the kitchen, as he devoured Miss Dorothy Douglass' squash casserole, Miss Mary Davis' crackling bread, Miss Mary Howard's string beans and ham hock, or Miss Doll Odom's chicken and dumplings.

Now, Lena cooked for Herman every chance she got or could steal, day or night. Before he came, Lena had never given a thought to food in the house. But Herman would ask regularly every day, "Lena, what we got in the kitchen to eat? What we got in the larder we can cook?" Some days, he would pretend there was nothing in the kitchen to his tastes. "What ya runnin' here, Lena? A hooch house?" Then, he'd laugh at the plenty in his woman's kitchen.

Herman's determined appetite reminded Lena of what her mother's friend Carrie Sawyer would say when Lena was growing up.

"Nellie, you cannot face this world on a empty stomach," the corpulent woman whose kitchen always smelled like baked goods would say to her friend who came with Lena to visit as she heaped up a pile of collard greens on a beautiful old china plate.

Herman seemed to believe in that. As much as Herman loved to eat, Lena couldn't bear to think of him having faced that otherworld for a hundred years on an empty stomach. The very thought made her get up from wherever she was and go into the kitchen to put a pot of *something* on to cook for Herman.

She started making a grocery list for James Petersen, something she had rarely done before. She had even started stopping by the Kroger or Piggly Wiggly for a fresh fryer or cherries in season that Herman loved.

They didn't always eat heavy. Not every day. Herman may not have had to watch his cholesterol and blood pressure, but Lena was human. She did. So, some days through the summer, for lunch, which Herman called dinner, and for supper, which Lena called dinner, they'd just take their plates out to the garden and pick their meal.

A couple of hands full of tiny Sweet 100s tomatoes, some little baby crookneck squash with the blossom still attached, a couple of green cowhorn peppers for Herman because he liked his stuff hot, tiny immature Yolo Wonders bell peppers that she'd stuffed with whatever kind of cheese they had: Brie, cheddar, Swiss, American.

Some days, they would shuck a few ears of corn right there among the cornstalks and not even make it back to the pot of what Herman called "biling water" he had left on the stove. They would just eat the sweet creamy corn off the cob.

"Good to keep you regular," Herman had informed her.

Sometimes, the two of them caught what they cooked. Herman had shown Lena where a stand of bamboo was taking over a marshy area near an arm of the Ocawatchee that reached into her property. And taking out his new buck knife, he sawed off two long canes for them. They headed down to the river, their cane poles over their shoulders like two children playing hooky to catch some of those fat Cleer Flo' Mulberry mullets that were becoming legendary for their special sweet streaked meat.

They came back with just enough to eat that day—which was four or five good-sized fish considering how much Herman could eat on his own. After they washed and scaled them, Lena made up a batch of hush puppies with lots of chopped onions and fresh-ground white pepper and a little sour grass from the yard and fried them all up. Then, they sat and ate the feast, talking all the time about their fishing exploits.

Herman cleared the table, then snaked up behind her at the sink and nuzzled her neck at the hairline as he slipped his big hands into the front of her shirt and massaged her shoulders and breasts.

"That was some good fish and hush puppies, Lena, good eatin'. I don't know when I *have* enjoyed a meal so." He stopped and kissed the nape of her neck, then continued. "You know, I do 'ppreciate the delicious vittles the ladies prepare, and they good, too. But, Lena, you know, I'm like every other man in the world. I like the way *my 'oman* cook."

Lena had to turn in his arms and give him a kiss, her wet hands soaking the back of his tee-shirt. And before she knew it they were standing there in the kitchen making hard-driving love with Lena's bare butt pressed against the edge of the soapstone counter and Herman's pants down around his knees. When his thrusts lifted her to the top of the counter and she landed with a *plop*, they both chuckled and came.

She became as happy in the kitchen as Herman was making her in all the other rooms of her house.

In the summer, Lena moved around the Mexican-tile floor of her kitchen dressed in shorts, one of Herman's shirts or undershirts and heavy work socks. The shorts made it comfortable when she snuggled under a heavy cotton throw with Herman while she waited for the corn bread to brown.

He liked that outfit as much as he enjoyed her fancy lingerie. But if one of them was frying some fish or a chicken or two or three rabbits in the big black iron skillet on the stove, he insisted she wear the long-sleeved shirt and big linen pants he fetched from a hook in her closet and brought to her.

Herman made cooking for him a pure joy. And his joy soon made Lena's big yellow kitchen a place of beauty and solace. By early July, when the first of the tiny green butter beans that her family had favored so had come in at the farmer's market out by the Mulberry Mall, Lena was cooking up a pot of the sweet green wonders first thing in the morning so she and Herman could have them for lunch when she returned home from her increasingly shorter days at work in Mulberry. Some days, she, like a farm wife, took great pride in boiling up two cups of rice at noon to a fluffy consistency and spooning it into one of her mama's favorite blue and yellow sunflower serving bowls. Then, with the big silver spoon with no slots or holes in it to leak any of the thick pale green juice, she'd heap up serving after serving of the tiny green butter beans over the steaming rice.

The way Herman sat down and enjoyed the dish, Lena began to feel truly sorry for people in life who didn't have someone to cook butter beans and rice for them.

Nellie had told Lena so often that a big part of food preparation—an honored and sacred undertaking in her house—was the presentation, so Lena never forgot to take time to arrange the food fetchingly on Herman's plate.

"Don't think just because you cooked something delicious that your job is over," Nellie had said over and over. "Now, run outside, baby, and get me a few sprigs of your grandmama's parsley and something else that'll look pretty next to the mashed potatoes."

It was her mother's words Lena recalled in the kitchen. It was her father's voice she heard in the dining room when the meal was prepared.

Her entire childhood, Lena had heard a man's voice say, "Children, go wash your hands and come put the ice in the glasses," as a prelude to eating. It was the true signal—like ringing the chimes at the beginning of Mass—that her father was home and the meal could legitimately and rightfully move ahead to consumption.

Herman had brought back that sense of reverence to her dining room table out by the river.

Other than feeble attempts at romantic dinners, no one had sat around her big oak dining room table after she moved to her own house. No one, that is, until Herman brought his big-eating self into her life.

Herman brought a sense of reverence back to her kitchen, too.

He wasn't much of a cook himself. He could "scratch around" okay in the kitchen enough to fill his stomach, "in a fashion," he said. And he *could make* some of the lightest, fluffiest, big old buttermilk biscuits that they sopped for breakfast and snacks, although he'd end up with flour all down his shirt and splashes of buttermilk on his forearms where he had rolled up his sleeves. Herman called the biscuits "catheads" and the molasses he called "mule blood." But really cook?

"Shoot," he said admiringly, "cookin'? Now, that's a *real* skill. That's what you got, baby. Now, you can *really cook*."

It made her proud.

Whenever Lena wanted to tease him about his appetite and her cooking, she'd pat his flat hard stomach or pinch his beautiful black behind, and say, "Herman, don't you think you getting a little thick through the waist? Maybe I need to cut back on the corn. You look almost plump!"

Herman always had a comeback for her:

"I ain't fat," he'd say, "I'm tall. That's all."

It was part of some old song, long forgotten by everyone but Herman.

"I ain't fat, I'm tall. That's all."

23

HAUNTED

"We'll eat as soon as the dressing get done," Lena had heard her mother say hundreds of times when Lena, Edward, Raymond and Jonah would stroll from the living room through the kitchen and back asking if there was something they could do to hurry dinner along.

"We'll eat as soon as the dressing get done," Nellie would say without bothering to look up from the Sunday paper she was reading. The corn bread dressing she made with her own egg bread, Colonial sliced white bread, onions, bell peppers, celery and stock from the cooked hen to keep the dressing moist during baking. Lena pronounced the last two words just as Nellie had, "get 'un."

"Don't look like that dressing gone *ever get 'un*," little Lena would say under her breath to her two brothers. And Lena *knew* how to fix dressing.

"First, you have to make a good-sized pan of corn bread," Nellie had instructed her one Sunday afternoon as she prepared the dressing for dinner. "But this isn't just corn bread. You know that, don't you, baby?"

"Uh-huh," Lena had answered, proud that she knew the difference between regular corn bread—which could be as simple as cornmeal, salt and warm water poured into a hot greasy skillet and fried on both sides in a cake—and what her mother termed "egg bread" that called for buttermilk, cornmeal, flour, eggs, a little sugar, a little salt.

Nellie would, of course, make it without a recipe. Nellie didn't write down any recipes, nor did she follow them. She disdained them.

"Try this, Nellie," Jonah would suggest, handing his wife a recipe he had found in a magazine or on a hotel menu.

She would take it as if it had come from Typhoid Mary. Holding it between her index finger and her thumb, she'd look at the recipe as if it were written in Venusian, and she didn't read the language. Wrinkling up her pretty nose in distaste, Nellie would finally ditch the recipe and prepare the dish using her own instincts.

"Now, I know that lobster thermidor we had in Cincinnati had paprika in it. Hummm. How much?" She'd tinker with it and tinker with it until it tasted better than it had in the restaurant.

"I'm sorry," she would say at the family dinner table in response to the compliments on her dish, "but it's not according to the *recipe*. I'm sorry, I just can't follow a *recipe*."

Then, she'd give a helpless little shrug. What she meant was she *refused* to follow a recipe.

Whenever Lena had asked her mother how to make this or how to make that, the answer always began with, "Give me a moment." Then, she would blow through her clenched teeth and narrow her eyes in concentration as if she had never given the preparation a conscious thought. She'd start with "a handful of this" and "a smidgen of that" and "juuussssssttt a pinch" of the other and Lena would be more lost than found. So, with Nellie gone, Lena just closed her conscious mind's eye and combined what she thought and remembered was correct. And most times, it worked.

One summer Sunday, Lena had prepared the dressing just the way she had seen her mother do countless times, when Herman came into the kitchen, smelling the air and looking at her, then smelling the air again. The golden-brown hen with a red and white dish towel over it sat warm and plump on the butcher-block-topped island with shelves of old blue and cream country crockery below.

Lena didn't even look up from the Sunday crossword puzzle she was doing, but she did smile at her hungry, voracious lover.

"We'll eat as soon as the dressing get 'un," Lena heard her mother's words come from her own mouth. She had never had anyone around her big country kitchen sniffing the air when she made dressing until Herman showed up with his ravenous appetites and love of her cooking.

At the sound of her own voice speaking her mother's words— "We'll eat as soon as the dressing get 'un"—she could for a brief time taste tears in her throat. And for the millionth time in less than half a year, she put her knees to the floor right there and gave thanks that Herman could read her mind and know to walk out on the deck and leave her still for a minute.

If Herman thought too much time had gone by without him tasting his own woman's food, he would ask, "But, Lena, when *you* gon' cook some?" It was all he had to say. Lena was a good cook and proud to cook for him, proud that she could sate his appetite. It gave her prodigious pleasure.

Lena even made a rare trip into town to her mother's pantry off the big kitchen in the Forest Avenue house to get the family's old hand-cranked ice cream churn. The peaches from Fort Valley were about to come in, and they both wanted some homemade peach ice cream. She had a small electric churn from Sweden that she had used once five or six years before to make sorbet when she had attempted a romantic dinner with a newly divorced physician in town. But Herman said he thought the ice cream would taste "off" made in that one.

Lena still remembered the rich creamy dessert her mother had made every week of each summer of their lives thick with peachy threads of fruit swirling throughout. She recalled her brothers fighting over the dasher covered with ice cream, falling down on the floor and rolling around in a double stranglehold while the ice cream melted onto the white china plate. Raymond usually won the fight simply because he truly loved ice cream more than Edward. He also had a good foot and three years on his brother as well.

But even more than the churn, Lena wanted the shiny silver meat grinder that she knew her mother had packed away in the pantry in a compact cardboard box with its attachments and blades wrapped in old newspaper. The day before while she was preparing some oxtails with the abundance of fresh tomatoes, eggplant, string beans and carrots and onions from her and Herman's garden, he mentioned a dish he had not had in a hundred years.

"Brunswick stew, Lena. It was the speshalty of folks 'round here, baby," Herman informed her earnestly, hoping she would take the hint.

Lena made sure it was early on the next sunny day when she drove over to her parents' closed-up house. Unoccupied as it had been the last several years, its few furnishings shrouded in sheets, Lena knew the children in Pleasant Hill were right. Her childhood home on Forest Avenue *was* haunted.

Before she left, Herman had kissed her one good long time on the mouth, then dropped his head and kissed her once more between her breasts. Then, he disappeared off somewhere on the property. He seldom traveled with her. Sometimes, he would appear in the passenger's seat of the car while she drove—she had to get used to *that*—just to tell her something or keep her company or rub her stiff neck. Or he'd only appear long enough to punch up a number on the CD player like "Dedicated to the One I Love," smile at her and disappear again.

There were places that Herman did not seem to *want* to go. It had never occurred to Lena that there were places he *could not go*. At least in his corporeal state.

He went all the way with her to and into Miss Zimmie's house one or two times, and he had even visited his secret room that Mr. Jackson, the contractor, had discovered down at The Place.

After Herman became a part of her life, Lena almost forgot about the discovery. But Mr. Jackson hadn't forgotten. He was down there bright and early the April morning following Lena's incident to check things out by himself.

"Still smell like somebody been screwing in here," he said softly to himself.

It was one of the reasons he nearly panicked when he had found Lena lying on the room's dusty floor, her little short skirt flipped up showing her pretty, expensive-looking underwear, a smudge of dirt on her cheek.

The aging contractor said, "Lord have mercy," every time he thought about it.

He finished the work at The Place in record time after he had left Lena's house that night back in April. He had sealed the rear wall back up and painted over the plaster himself so it looked as if a gaping hole had never disturbed the site. But in the storeroom on the liquor store side of The Place, where Lena had the safe and the private bathroom, the clever contractor had installed a private steel door and a narrow passageway that led to the secret room. And he gave Lena the only key.

He felt it was the least he could do for Lena. She had never mentioned how she had been hurt on his work site. Of course, it got out all over Mulberry, in beauty shops and butcher shops, in barbershops and bakeries, in baby stores and bookstores. How Lena McPherson was "mysteriously injured and possibly assaulted in her own place down on what used to be the corner of Broadway and Cherry. But when they took her to the hospital, they couldn't find nothing."

"You know the girl was born with a caul over her face," people reminded each other. "Yeah, Lena don't talk about it much, but I'm old enough to remember what the old folks used to say 'bout children like Lena born with a veil over their face. You know, seeing ghosts, looking in people's eyes and reading they soul. Riding at night with the witches. Ain't no telling what 'mysteriously' attacked her."

But word of the incident didn't come from Lena McPherson's mouth. Mr. Jackson knew that. And that meant a lot to him. So, the private entrance to the private room was his gift to her.

When he showed it to her, he acted like a young schoolboy, mannish enough to formulate a secret plan and execute it as a surprise gift for her, but too shy to brag about it.

Lena appreciated it more than Mr. Jackson could know. The secret passageway helped her to keep her secret lover to herself. Even though Herman never showed any real interest in the private room, he had gone there with Lena one time in the spring because she was so proud of owning a building where he had lived and worked.

But he had only walked around the edge of the room one time, looked up at the fresh-air system he had designed and smiled to himself, then declared he was ready to go whenever she was.

But other than that, Herman stayed close to home. And even there, Lena discovered, there were places he would just as soon avoid. Her wine cellar was one of them.

Lena didn't have a true basement in her house, but she did indeed have a wine cellar, named for her daddy's daddy. The wine cellar had been a gift from her father, who then commenced to stocking it with the best of Lena's favorite white wines and champagnes and cognac.

"Your daddy, Jonah, had a reputation we got to uphold," one of the liquor distributors would say each November as his man brought in two boxes of a difficult-to-find favorite champagne for her birthday.

It was cool and dark in the brick wine cellar. So, when it first got hot, Lena decided to show it to Herman. Herman drank a good bottle of wine with dinner sometimes if Lena wanted some and on very hot days during the summer, he would throw back an icy beer. But for the most part, Herman didn't seem to care much about drinking alcohol. He was just as happy drinking lemonade or a cold small bottle of Coca-Cola, cases of which Lena now stacked up in her utility room just for him.

But she thought he would like to see the cellar. She was especially proud of its stone walls.

They had sat down there only a little while before Herman started breathing heavily. He didn't like being underground for any length of time. He came right out and told her.

"Lena, baby, I can't stay down here much longer."

And he headed for the stairs.

There were places, too, where Lena just didn't want to go anymore. She still loved The Place and sitting and talking with Gloria once in a while. But Gloria was always so busy, the way Lena had been before Herman came. And she still visited her beautiful old nurturer Miss Zimmie, who never had asked anything of her but her love. Together with Herman, it was enough.

Lena knew where her treasure was buried. That's where her heart was. And Herman was her heart.

She loved him so that when he mentioned the Brunswick stew, she didn't hesitate to brave her childhood haunted house again. For him.

Just entering the fine old two-story brick house on Forest Avenue flooded her with memories and voices and smells and heartache.

It's a shame this big old house is just standing empty, she thought as she stood at the side door with the beveled-glass top looking into the foyer through the interior of the house. She thought sadly of her children downtown with no place safe and warm to go most nights and some days.

As she walked up the short flight of steps on the right leading from the basement hallway to the back of the kitchen and made a sharp turn into the darkened, yeasty-smelling pantry, she felt truly engulfed in the past.

Most of the stacks of shiny cans of food and bottles and jars had long ago been removed from the shelves, drawers and bins of the walk-in pantry and given to folks and organizations who needed them. Only a few huge cans of mandarin oranges in syrup remained.

Lena smiled at the ten-year-old cans of fruit. Her father had bought them from a wholesaler who gave him a good deal. But Jonah had had a hard time finding someone who liked the overly sweet soft canned fruit. The only thing Lena liked about mandarin oranges was their bright Halloween color.

"Um, still can't get rid of those things," she said aloud, and suddenly realized that she was laughing softly to herself. She had trouble recalling when she had last laughed in that house.

There was the bean-shelling party Nellie had lured her to the summer before her mother was killed. Lena had shown up at her mother's dressed for lunch at the Dupree Hotel, but Nellie was wearing a comfortable housecoat and sandals.

Lena just laughed at her mother's trick. The two of them had sat all afternoon in rocking chairs on the screened porch with big paper bags of unshelled baby butter beans between their legs. As they shelled beans like two country women, they laughed and joked, drank sweet lemonade and laughed some more. Then, they pulled out brown leather photo albums and laughed even more at how the family had looked ten, twenty, thirty years before.

Lena felt herself smiling as she scanned the pantry's back shelves. She found the ice cream churn and the stainless-steel meat grinder right away. Someone, her mother probably, had packed the grinder away in what looked like its original heavy-duty cardboard box with all of its parts and attachments. She took the churn and crank out of its box and examined all the parts. It looked as Lena remembered it from childhood. Still shiny in spots.

Looking up at the shelves again, Lena caught sight of the edge of another box peeking out from a corner. She grabbed at the small box on the bare shelf above her. When she did, she heard a stiff scraping noise and about two dozen white four-by-six notecards fluttered out of the toppled tin box to the black-and-white-tiled floor like tiny ghosts.

Lena didn't even jump. The sight of the papers sailing toward her feet warmed her heart. She didn't know why, but she felt as if she had suddenly remembered the face of a loved one.

Without any trepidation, she reached down and collected the cards in a short stack.

On the first card she saw her mother's handwriting, thin, spidery cursive like her spoken language—a combination of southern school-girl grammar and bawdy juke-joint talk—written with one of her vintage fountain pens.

"Recipes!" Lena said, astonished.

In her thin quick hand, Nellie had written BRUNSWICK STEW across the top of the white card that had light blue lines running horizontally over it. She had underlined BRUNSWICK STEW twice, then listed the ingredients:

1 whole hog head
1 3-lb chicken
2 medium cans whole-kernel corn (yellow)
2 cans peas, English
2 large cans tomato juice
1 large onion
1 tablespoon sugar
1 stalk celery
salt & pepper to taste

Then she had written out the instructions:

Take one large hog's head. Scrub it. Remove the hair, eyes and brains. (Set brains aside for breakfast next morning for brains and eggs.)

Put head in large pot along with chicken. Add salt & pepper, onion, celery. Cook until meat of head and chicken is tender. Remove from liquid and save liquid.

Ground meat from chicken & hog head coarsely, add corn, peas, tomato juice, mix well. Cook slowly for about 25 to 30 minutes. You might add stock from the chicken and hog head if mixture seems too dry but not too much.

Add salt and pepper to taste also add sugar. If you like hot stew, while cooking the head and chicken add 5 pods of dried red pepper to the pot.

Reading each line of the recipe brought her mother's voice back stronger and stronger to her.

This, Lena knew, was part of the haunting of the house on Forest Avenue. Dead souls calling out to her from every room, from the linen closets, from the basement, from the pantry. But this voice, her mother's voice in her mother's kitchen, began to hold some comfort for her, not reproach, or loneliness or terror, but comfort.

Lena looked at all the cards again.

She could tell, from the slightly newer, bluer blue ink, her mother had gone back later on and written at the top of each recipe card:

"*Dear Lena.*"

It was a welcomed voice from the grave for Lena.

"*Dear Lena,*" she read to herself, hearing her mother's voice saying the words.

Lena repeated the two words over and over again with all different kinds of inflection and intonation.

"*Dear Lena,*" said with tenderness and love.

"*Dear Lena,*" said with exasperation.

"*Dear Lena,*" said with sternness.

"*Dear Lena,*" said with wisdom and instruction.

"*Dear Lena,*" said with infinite kindness.

"*Dear Lena,*" "*Dear Lena,*" "*Dear Lena.*"

She sat on a huge, restaurant-size can of mandarin oranges and dropped her face onto her bare smooth knees and broke down and wept. Lena felt for the first time in ten years that she indeed had not lost her mother completely.

She looked over at a gallon jug of thick brown Alaga syrup. Jonah bought in bulk until the day he died.

Floating on top of the South Georgia cane and corn syrup was a fuzzy green fungus. She could hear Nellie's voice once more.

"Oh, that old mold is just what my mama used to call 'mother,'" she had explained to a repulsed little Lena. "It won't hurt. Just spoon it off, and the syrup is good as new."

She heard her mother's voice say "mother," and she wept some more.

Lena felt she had found her mother again.

"Dear Lena."

She felt so much better after she had cried. Lena had no idea why she said it, but she whispered, "Oh, Mama, I forgive you. You didn't mean no harm."

She was near shocked to feel a wave of forgiveness for her mother flood her soul and lift a weight off her heart like a beached boat rising in the tide and floating away. Forgiveness for burning Lena's birth caul. Forgiveness for dying and leaving her alone. Forgiveness for not telling her how to be a special little baby girl in this world.

She took a deep breath, wiped away the trail of tears on her face with the flat of her hand and laughed at herself as she squared her shoulders and picked up the tin box and put the recipes inside. She took them out into the light of the kitchen and sat in a shaft of sunlight full of dust beams at the table there and looked over the woods and stream out back and the spot where her grandmama's ghost said her mother had burned her birth caul. She slowly lifted the top of the box and rubbed her thumb along the edges of the stack of cards fitting neatly inside.

She flipped past BRUNSWICK STEW and went on to the next card. Across its top it proclaimed:

"Dear Lena," then,

EGG BREAD, with the ingredients listed below.

And right behind that card in an unusual display of conventional organization, Nellie had placed a white card with the heading CORN BREAD DRESSING FOR TURKEY OR HEN

Nellie's voice rang throughout all the recipes.

On the card for her yellow layer cake, she informed Lena, "Flour three round nine-inch cake pans. You know how to flour a cake pan."

In another recipe, *BISCUIT BREAD*, she wrote, "Now, you know how you've always seen me roll out biscuit dough and cut out biscuits with the cutter. Well, do the same thing, round the whole thing out on the edges and put it in a well-greased skillet to cook slowly and brown on both sides.

"Serve it right away hot with some butter and Alaga."

Lena had forgotten how strong her mother's voice was.

Slowly, bit by bit, her mother came back to Lena in her mind. At first, she remembered Nellie's delicate long throat right in the front where she stroked it from her chin to her chest when she was thinking or ignoring someone and "looking down that long country road" the way she did.

She saw her mother's short slender legs and thin ankles. Then, she remembered her full breasts the way they had looked inside the bodice of a sexy summer sunback dress.

The ideal of "mother" was still Nellie to Lena.

"Lord, I'm worried about my child," Nellie would say regularly to her friends Mary and Carrie. She chided Lena for doing too much, for being there for everybody. And she ain't even got no husband or no babies of her own, Nellie would think.

"Lena, baby, you know nobody's any prouder of you and your accomplishments or what you do for folks than I am. But, Lena, I'm worried about my child."

Lena had just smiled at her mother's reference to her: "my child."

Although all the children in the McPherson family knew they were loved, with Lena it was different. She was the baby of the family. And even when her brothers were alive, Nellie only referred to Lena as "my child." Raymond and Edward weren't even offended by it. They seemed to use the phrase as much as Nellie. Looking up at Lena approaching, Raymond would tell his mother, "Here comes *your* child, Mama."

Lena was her mother's special child, and Nellie *was* worried about her. But then, ever since her only daughter's special birth, Nellie had always felt a bit of unease about Lena's safety and stability and future.

Nellie had just written off most of Lena's strange comments and insights to her being "a high-strung filly" the way Jonah always said.

But even a mother could see that an unusual child like Lena could only do so much. Nellie had given up on trying to talk about it to Jonah. Especially after their sons died so early, Jonah wouldn't believe that Lena couldn't do any and every thing in the world.

But Nellie knew there were limits.

"Lena sho' must be a big help to you now that she 'un got her education and all," a new customer would say to Nellie as she sat at the front of the liquor store watching Lena walking around the other side taking inventory with her new computer.

"A *big help*???" Nellie would retort. "A *big help*? Shoot, Lena the hand I fan with. I don't know what we did before she was here."

Nellie said it all the time. That Lena was the hand her mama fanned with.

Once, Lena had heard a woman down at The Place, she thought it was little skinny Willie Bea, tell her friend next to her at the counter, "You don't understand. You still *have* your mother." Lena had turned away and cried.

But now Lena just smiled to herself at the memory. Although Nellie was dead, Lena knew she still had her. She hadn't for a number of years, but she regained her mother sitting in the house on Forest Avenue reading the recipes Nellie had written down just for her.

She thought of what Herman had told her.

"People got t' love ya in their own way, Lena."

She caressed her haul of cards and said to the empty room, "This my mama right here." She suddenly felt the peace she had felt as a child when her mother would answer, "This my baby right here."

She cried over the recipes one more time, each one with its greeting, *"Dear Lena."* Then, she collected them all along with the ice cream churn, the silver meat grinder and an old gray dishcloth she remembered seeing her mother sling over her shoulder in the kitchen, and left the house happily haunted.

24

HORSE

With Herman around, Lena found happiness everywhere.

She had always wanted to make love in the straw in the loft of her barn.

In the fifteen years she had lived by the river she had planned such liaisons with men who had piqued her interest one way or another. One was a professor of history at Morehouse College she met at an awards luncheon given there for her. He showed up at her house for a casual Sunday brunch dressed in a three-piece suit. And besides the unattractive images of his past that Lena saw flash before her eyes, he seemed intent on remaining fairly well dressed and fully clothed for the entire visit.

She had invited another perfectly good prospect over for a mid-week picnic lunch. But they didn't even make it to the barn, let alone the picnic Lena was anticipating. She had really planned this one. Talking on the phone with Sister, planning the menu, choosing her ensemble for the afternoon: a black cotton sweater over a black lace teddy and wide-legged white silk crepe trousers and white deck shoes.

"You know, something that can go effortlessly from barn to bed," Sister had said on the phone with a laugh.

Lena thought she had made plans for every contingency. She had stashed away toys, some feathers, a big fluffy comforter, Handiwipes, towels, a bottle of her best champagne, two hurricane lanterns for when it got dark (for she hoped to be in there fucking 'til the sun went down), and the green wicker picnic basket filled with strawberries, raspberries, kiwi slices and tiny hors d'oeuvres in a cool pack.

But her date, the owner of a gas station and garage in the next small town, got mad at the very suggestion that they have a picnic in the stables.

"Oh, so it's like that. You gon' ask *me* out here to eat in the barn with the horses and animals." He was really insulted.

Lena had tried a bit to explain, but she got kind of angry herself having to *explain* that she was trying to seduce his black ass. The whole thing ended badly, with him jumping in his souped-up Mustang and roaring off down her dirt road not long after noon, upsetting her horses grazing in the nearest field of clover.

Herman, on the other hand, was proud and honored that Lena wanted him in what he called "varied and divers" places and ways.

It was in the barn that Herman had learned that Lena enjoyed oral sex. Not just getting it—he had learned that the first night he touched her—but giving it, too. He was as pleased as he could be at the discovery.

The first night they made love in the barn, when Lena scooted down to the end of the big striped blanket and began playing with the tip of his penis with the tip of her tongue, Herman had looked down and laughed in genuine surprise and amusement.

"Well, well, well," is what he said as she took his hard brown penis into her mouth, picking a few pieces of straw off first.

"Shucks, Lena, you do *that*?!"

He threw his big head back and chuckled, then moaned in such delight that it spooked the horses beneath them.

"Lena," he said between moaning and sucking his teeth and clutching her braids, "you som'um."

Lena had a generous-sized mouth and Herman's engorged penis, he noticed, fit neatly into her mouth.

"Your pleasure is my pleasure, Herman," Lena said as she let his penis slip from her lips.

Later, as they lay sweaty and sated in the straw, he told her, "Lena, you couldn't even hardly *pay a 'oman* in Middle Georgia to suck yo' dick when I was 'live, and here you are, the one woman in all creation I woulda dreamed of doin' it. And you lookin' forward to it. Lena, you som'um, baby!"

"Do me again, Lena, baby," he had leaned down to her ear and whispered. She reached up and gently pulled his neck and shoulders down for one long embrace and a luscious kiss. Then, feeling as strong as a horse herself, she went back to sucking his dick.

When she and Herman made love there in the stables the first time, Baby, Goldie and Keba below them whinnying from time to time in their freshly cleaned wooden stalls, he teased her by becoming what he was to her at the beginning—a puff of wind.

The first time he came that night, lying beneath her naked body in the fresh-smelling straw, he turned from Herman the man to Herman a swirl of wind that wound up her legs, around her hips, over her clitoris, up into her like a sweet cramp, through her head and enfolded her skull before exploding in a pouf of wind that lifted Lena and all the straw in the place into the air. Lena settled back down in a shower of straw needles and flakes of Herman that landed like manna from heaven and settled on the straw like sweet hoarfrost. Lena just lay back and yelled, "Whoooooaaa," because she felt if she didn't her head might burst open.

As Lena lay there moaning and breathing hard, Herman collected himself back into naked human form, threw his long legs astride her naked hips and slipped quickly—more quickly than he had meant—inside her. As he sucked his breath in and out with each stroke he slid into Lena, he whistled a little impromptu tune that made Lena raise her hips in welcome greeting to each one of his sweet thrusts. As they both came, heaving and bucking against each other, each searching for the other's mouth, they screamed in such release and joy that it really did upset the horses.

It took a while for every living creature and the one dead one in the stables to settle down. And when they did, Lena and Herman lay back in the sweet straw and spent the night sticky and sweaty all curled up together in the hay.

"Oh, Herman," she said as she awoke and stretched the next morning, "I'm so sore. I feel like I been thrown by a horse."

"I always been wild, Lena," Herman said by way of apology. Then, he stretched her out in the hay and massaged all her sore parts.

Over the entrance to Lena's back door was nailed a horseshoe that the first horse she owned, the original Baby, had thrown when she was brought onto the property. The horseshoe had gone flying through the air, missing Lena's right temple by a hair. She had heard it whizzing by her ear. After that, she saw the horseshoe as part of the good luck of the place. Now, Herman seemed a major part of that luck.

He fell right in with the routine of the place with the horses. It had been his idea, in fact, to get Keba impregnated now that he was there to help out.

"Herman, isn't it too risky with Keba way out here? Suppose we can't get in touch with the vet?" Lena had asked anxiously. She hadn't expected to be this nervous, but she had never been through a birth of any kind.

"Just 'bout ten months. Le's see. It's May, no June when she gets wid foal. She'll gi' birth sometime in April. That's just 'bout right," he said. He could see Lena was still unsure.

"It'll be okay, baby. I seen plen'y horses foal. And everythang was just fine. I ain't gon' let nothin' happen if I can he'p it."

"Oh, Herman, I'm worried."

"Have some faith, Lena, baby," Herman said as close to sternly as he ever was with her.

Now, in late summer, Keba was heavy with foal, nearly halfway through her term, moving more slowly but enjoying the careful friskiness. Lena and Herman loved to curry her after she had been out in the fields and to pat her tight rounding belly.

Waking in the night to go to the bathroom, Lena often found that Herman had slipped out of bed and gone down to the stables to check on the expectant mother. His caring for life was so deep, it was palpable.

Lena was surprised that the horses let Herman anywhere near them, let alone on their backs. At least two of their backs. Baby still allowed no one to ride her but Lena. Not even Rick Little, the stable manager, could safely climb on Baby's back. Baby was so spoiled. Herman said so.

"Lena, ya'll done spoiled this hoss so," he declared as he ran the horses around the exercise rink in the corral.

Equestrian organizations all over the South had tried to rope Lena into putting her beautiful estate with the heated stables on their list of party sites during the riding season. Lena just laughed at the overtures and invitations. She didn't have time to spend with people she liked and loved, let alone with strangers.

"I love to ride," she explained to Sister when she gave her friend her first riding lesson. "But I do believe there is something to what they say about horses. Shoot, for me, the horses are better than a whole pack of guard dogs or a bodyguard." The main reason Lena had been drawn to owning horses was their legendary sensitivity to the presence of ghosts.

And it had seemed to work.

"Shoot, it ain't the living *I* got to be worried about," Lena said, bringing up a subject that she had forbade Sister to discuss any further, "it's the dead."

But if horses were true harbingers of spirits nearby, kicking their stalls and neighing wildly, one would never know it by the way those animals seemed to love Herman.

He sat a horse beautifully. Relaxed but regal; in control as Lena imagined Nelson Mandela would ride. And the animals seemed to sense his comfort and look forward to him climbing on their backs.

Sometimes, she and Herman even rode bareback, alone and together. Herman would take Lena's forearm and pull her up onto Goldie's back with him. He'd lift her lightly as if she didn't weigh an ounce. Then, he'd scoot back a bit and settle her in the space over his crotch and pull her back to his chest as Goldie, he and Lena trotted off, her body rolling rhythmically against his with each step the horse took. Riding her land that way, sometimes for miles to the end of her property, in the hollow of her man's body left the front and inseam of her riding britches wet and sticky. Herman would sometimes stop, lift Lena under her arms and turn her around on Goldie's back to face him. Then, they would ride off, her face to his face, her breast to his chest, her matchbox to his dick.

Lena had wanted to buy Herman his own saddle, but he just waved the suggestion away with a quick wide-open gesture toward all the beautiful hand-tooled leather saddles on the walls of the stables.

"Let's use some a' this tack we got," he told her as he took his pick.

"Race ya to the bend in the river," Herman would yell suddenly as they rode, trying to catch Lena unprepared. Then, he would take off racing for the water's edge.

Herman had no interest in automobiles. Lena had asked him a number of times when they were out driving if he wanted to take the wheel, but he declined each time. He had never driven and had no desire to.

Whenever Lena suggested, "Come ride to town with me, Herman," he usually shook his head and pointed toward the stable, then down at his own feet.

"Those hosses out there and these 'hosses' right here all I need," he would tell Lena in all seriousness. After a while, she would suggest car trips just to hear him say it. "These hosses takes me to and fro, Lena, baby. They takes me to and fro."

They both loved caring for the horses, truly caring for them.

As Lena curried the horses, lovingly brushing their silky heavy horsehair free of briars and cucabugs and ticks and clumps of red dirt, she'd think of her own times of being "curried":

Tender-headed Lena sitting between her mama's legs getting her thick heavy coarse hair combed, tears standing in her eyes and her mother's.

Sister scratching out her head and giving her braids all over her head one night while they looked through old photographs.

Falling under the hypnotic spell of Mamie, the magical assistant at Delores' Beauty Parlor, with her head thrown back into the steel shampoo sink.

When Lena got to Baby's strong thin legs, she stopped and smiled.

"Thinking 'bout yo' mama?" Herman asked from the stall next to her.

Herman had a real knack for being able to slip into Lena's head at those times she wouldn't feel violated by the intrusion. But then, Herman had a knack for a lot of things.

In life, he had acquired considerable skill as a blacksmith. On hot days in summer, as he struck and struck and struck the white-hot iron anvil shooting red and golden sparks all around him and into the air at the stable doors, Lena would watch mesmerized.

She had gotten Red, one of her boys from The Place, to scour the countryside to find an authentic smithy's black leather apron for Herman. It was old but still pliable. Lena washed it and cleaned it with love and saddle soap from the supply room. Then, she rubbed it and rubbed it with mink oil until it crushed and recoiled under her hand like her thigh-high leather boots.

While Herman worked over the pounding hot anvil, he wore the apron without a shirt, just the way he knew Lena wanted him to. The sweat beading up on his taut smooth brown skin ran down his chest in rivulets. Lena sat on easy-chair-sized bales of hay and watched Herman work for hours, forgetting any responsibilities she had except to Herman and herself.

The first couple of times she saw him that way, she resisted the temptation to go over to him and touch the tip of her tongue to one drop on his sweaty chest. She wanted to go over and lick his chest and suck his licorice nipples. One day, Herman, who knew what she was thinking all the time, stopped his pounding and called her over to his arms. He enjoyed fulfilling her fantasies.

Shoeing horses seemed to take all day, and Lena was ready for a break long before Herman stopped swinging his hammer onto the anvil. Lying across the bales of fresh hay, Lena began to fall asleep to the rhythm of the hammer.

But she came awake when Herman took Baby's last hoof down from the hoof stand and turned to her.

"Hey, Lena, baby, you got a silk stockin'?" he asked with a smile playing up under his mustache.

"A silk stocking?" Lena was more than intrigued. She could only imagine what Herman's nineteenth-century mind was thinking of doing with one silk stocking and her in the barn. Now, Lena was happy and grateful that none of her plans to fuck other men in the barn had ever come to fruition.

Talking to Herman as they cleaned the barn, lying with him in the sweet hay, she felt like his woman from his time. She felt like the woman in the play *The Drinking Gourd* making secret, intimate plans among the hay of a barn, looking to the night sky, plotting their escape. The only difference: She and Herman would be looking south, not north.

"Uh-huh, yeah. A silk stockin'," he answered, shaking his big handsome head free of sweat as he untied the red cotton kerchief from around his throat to mop his brow. Then, he stood back in his legs like a sexy country woman and stretched.

"If anybody in this here town got a silk stockin', Lena McPherson, it oughta be you!" Herman laughed, pleased with himself for knowing his woman.

"Yeah, I got a silk stocking. Got more than one, as a matter of fact," Lena said. The idea of the silk stocking and the barn was making her hotter and hotter. She felt as if she weren't wearing panties. "What shade stocking you want?"

"Yo' choice, Miss Lena." Herman loved playing with his woman so much he couldn't resist the temptation she always offered.

Back in early summer, when Lena was still going to work three or four days a week, she would walk through the bedroom dressed in thigh-high sheer hose with black lace garters holding them up, a soft satin champagne bra with one wide satin strap hanging down on the vaccination mark on her arm, and champagne-colored silk bikini panties trimmed in the same black lace of the garters barely covering what Herman delighted in calling her "matchbox." She was wearing gold-toned mules and holding her braids up by the back of her hands, checking the gold clasp of her forty-five-inch-long string of pearls from Tiffany looped around her throat twice and hanging to her breasts. Herman couldn't stop himself from chuckling and shaking his head in admiration.

"Damn, Lena, baby, you look like the very Whore a' Babylon in that outfit." He stroked his mustache and rubbed his hairy jaw in the kind of appreciation that made Lena strut through the house.

Now Herman knew what Miss Cora, the pretty little brown woman who had taught him to read from a stolen copy of the Bible more than a hundred years before, was trying to say about the kind of woman who could make a man commit murder. Herman would do anything for this woman, Lena, standing half-naked in front of him. This woman who swathed herself in the most luxurious fabrics and materials Herman had ever seen and wanted to pamper the rest of the world in the same way. She wanted to swaddle the world in bolts and bolts of satin, silk, fine linen, cotton and cashmere. To make it comfortable so everybody could get along, get along with their lives in grace, not scuffling and struggling along. He knew it was Lena's dream. He had seen her dreams, had tried at one time to embed himself in her dreams before he became real to her. He knew her inner thoughts, even the ones hidden from herself.

"The Whore of Babylon, indeed," Lena managed to say in an offended tone before she turned away from Herman, threw back her shoulders and laughed. She *felt* like the Whore of Babylon.

He fully expected her some night to do the Dance of the Seven Veils and take him to a level of pleasure he had not yet experienced in life or death.

Lena knew it was true, she was turning into the kind of woman she had admired and feared since she was five years old. The kind of woman who felt no compunction at all in standing in some public place like The Place or the street corner outside or the Piggly Wiggly supermarket—or in a churchyard cemetery, she imagined, even though Lena had never seen it happen there—and hitting the front of her vagina—*bap, bap, bap*—with the flat of her palm to make a point.

"Girl, let me tell you one thing, this is mine"—*bap, bap, bap*—"and *I'm the one* that decide who it go out with."

Or,

"Yeah, but he ain't had nothing like *this*"—*bap, bap, bap*—"before!"

Lena was turning into the kind of woman who slapped her pussy—*bap! bap! bap!* Like that. Lena had seen women do it. *Bap! bap! bap!* Brazen Broadway Jessies slapping their crotches with the palms of their hands flatly, solidly, so that the gesture actually made a noise—*bap! bap! bap.*

Standing over the hot anvil in the entrance to the barn still sweating from the exertion of shoeing Baby, Herman got mock serious. "May I have the silk stockin', please, ma'am?"

Lena got mock serious right with him.

"Yes, *sir*! You certainly may," she shot back, and hurried off to the house to get the stocking.

She kicked off her muddy boots at the back kitchen door, dropped her soft yellow leather work gloves on top of the shoes and hurried through the house—a house that now smelled like food, candles, flowers, her, Herman and their love. There was also the alive, fresh scent of the river inside the house because all the doors and windows now stood open to the breeze off the Ocawatchee. The air-conditioning had not been on since July.

"I hate that unnatural cold air blowin' on me, Lena," Herman finally admitted when Lena saw him all stoved up with a sweater on inside. "But it make you comf'able. So, I'm all right." He said it seriously.

Lena went right to the controls and with a sharp snap, turned the cold air off for good. Then, she came back, slipped in behind Herman on the sofa, and pulling his broad back into the fork of her legs, she massaged him until he was sweating.

Catching sight of herself in her grandmama's cheval glass, Lena had to laugh at how comfortably Herman had her dressing now: loose soft jeans, one of Herman's undershirts and a white long-sleeved Egyptian cotton shirt she had paid nearly five hundred dollars for.

"Well, at least it holds up well to washing," she had heard James Petersen say one day when he took the shirt out of the dryer after having seen the price tag.

Herman was of the same thrifty mind. "Ain't no need to waste nothin' just 'cause you got so much," Herman said when some of their apparel was ripped from their lovemaking or their adventures in the woods. "Shoot, gimme yo' sewin' basket, Lena, baby," he said, just assuming she had one. "I'll catch up them tears myself. I ain't no fancy sewer like yo' mama or yo' grandmama. But I can fix those few thangs up."

Then, Herman would sit down and sew the ripped shirt or the busted seam or the torn hem. Afterward, Lena would find a shred of cloth or pieces of thread on the arm of the sofa where he had sat and sewn. If they were from his clothes, she always put them away in a small peach and purple and rose trunk-shaped box along with a knot of his nappy hair she had found on his pillowcase.

Lena entered her bedroom and stood in her walk-in closet staring at the bank of built-in drawers and customized racks for the longest time. She didn't move until she heard Herman's voice rising from the barn.

"Lena, what's takin' so long with that silk stockin'?" he wanted to know.

"Here I come," Lena yelled back, but she didn't move. She stood mesmerized by the sight of all the things she owned: dresses, lingerie, slacks, bustiers, boots, scarves, gloves, hats, blouses.

"I ain't gon' never buy these many clothes or this much shit ever again in life," Lena said to the many and varied denizens of her dressing room. Now that she thought about it, she had made all kinds of changes in her dress. She just *couldn't* wear a bra anymore.

"Oh, just let these bad boys flop," she had said in disgust and heat frustration in early summer when it was so hot already in Middle Georgia that she didn't want to wear any clothes at all. And Herman had told her any number of times with sincerity in his voice, "Oh, Lena, baby, I *love* yo' titties just like they are. If they floppin', then I like that."

"Lena!" Herman called again from the stables, concern beginning to show in his voice.

She remembered the silk stocking she had been sent for and hurried back outside with it streaming behind her like Herman's colors.

"Now, the true test of how good a job I did on this here hoss's shoe work is did I finish up the job by filin' down the hoof smooth enough," Herman explained as Lena handed him one long black silk stocking. "When I run this here stockin' over Baby's hoof here," he said, dropping the hosiery over the foot he had lifted to the shoeing stand, "see, it just slide right off."

He was rightfully proud of his work. Lena was, too.

Even Mr. Renfroe and Rick, the lone remaining stable hand, were curious about this mystery man of Lena's who knew how to do everything from shoe horses to repair her computer.

Mr. Renfroe was truly curious to discover if he was truly deserving of Lena. Rick just wanted to meet the man who shod his horses with such care and expertise. The horseman didn't have a silk stocking to slide across the hooves of the animals, but he could see the hooves were as smooth as silk. "I'd like to talk to the man," Rick told Lena.

It made Lena think of the joys of conversation.

"Herman, don't you ever want to talk with someone else besides me?" she had asked him.

Herman stopped sweeping the brick floor of the stables and chuckled, "You mo' than enough, Lena, baby."

Later that night, Lena found reason to question that when she woke with a start.

At first, she thought it was the meteor shower she could still see performing through the skylight over her bed. She and Herman had fallen asleep in each other's arms well after midnight with the sky nearly ablaze with the collapsing stars.

She reached over and felt Herman sitting up in bed with her.

"Som'um spookin' the hosses," was all he said. And Lena felt chills for the first time since Herman arrived.

He got up, put on a loose pair of pants and went outside to investigate. He stayed so long that Lena began to really become worried. Then, she heard his bare feet on the tiles of the pool room next door coming back, and she breathed a sigh of relief. She fully expected him to say as he usually did when she heard some different sound that he would investigate, "It ain't nothin' but spirits in the woods, Lena. That ain't scary. It's just life and death."

But he didn't.

When he returned he was as pale as a ghost under his dark brown skin. He looked slightly disheveled, as if he had been in a fight.

"What was it?" Lena finally asked.

"It was Anna Belle," he said flatly.

"Anna Belle?" Lena asked as she slowly wrapped her fluffy red terry-cloth robe around herself.

"Well, she was in the form of a cat. But it was Anna Belle all right."

"Anna Belle?" Lena asked again, thinking, Who the hell *Anna Belle*? Am I supposed to *know* this *Anna Belle*?

"Shoot," Herman said, trying to hide the fury still in his heart, "Anna Belle the one tried to hit you in the head wid that loose plank the first day you come into my room down at yo' place."

"Anna Belle??!!" Lena asked with the same intonation she had heard women use at The Place since she was four or five years old and started paying attention to the women in her life other than her mother and grandmother.

"Yeah. Down at yo' place. All you felt was the energy and the anger a' the blow. I stopped the lick from actually landin'. That was when I first *knew*, *really knew*, I was gonna be real. When I stopped that blow."

"Anna Belle's blow?" Lena asked evenly.

"Uh-huh. That's who was just spookin' the hosses," he said. Lena could hear him trying his best to sound casual through his rage. She assumed it was rage. Lena had never seen Herman angry before.

"Anna Belle?" she asked again, still trying to comprehend what he was saying.

"Yeah, Anna Belle. I still can't believe she didn't realize everything involved if she had killed you the way she was swingin' that piece a' wood."

"You're telling me some other woman spirit tried to take my head off with a plank of wood . . . ?"

"Uh-huh," Herman said as he carefully peeled an apple he had chosen from the bowl on the bedside table, keeping the shiny red skin in one piece.

"Down at The Place?"

"Uh-huh," Herman said again as he held the apple peel above his head and dropped it on the table in front of him. He looked at Lena and then smiled down at the "L" the curl of apple skin made on the surface of the mudcloth table covering.

"See," he said. "Even the spirits of fruit know you s'posed to be mine."

But Lena didn't want to hear anything about any spirits of any apple peel. She didn't want to hear about any other spirits at all. Lena knew that there were ghosts and hants and spirits in the woods surrounding her house. Right now she wanted to know about this *Anna Belle*.

She had never really considered any woman in Herman's life, alive or dead, who could arouse such passion over him. Lena knew *she* was passionate over him, but some other woman?

She felt jealousy and anger rising in her throat like bile.

"And this woman, this Anna Belle . . ."

"Lena, if I hadn'a reached up and stopped her hand when I did . . . Well, I can't think about it. As it is, she gave you a right big goose egg on yo' forehead. The doctor and hospital machines couldn't see it, but I could. I remember wantin' to kiss it and make it better," he said as he leaned over and kissed her gently on her brow.

But Lena was determined to ask her questions. "I didn't walk into that exposed plank down in your secret room or imagine that I had been hit? And this woman, this Anna Belle, tried to hit me in the head hard enough to kill me!?"

Herman nodded his head silently. Then, he said, "Womens over there talk about how hard it is to find a good man even on the other side."

"And this woman is still around?" Lena asked, looking over her shoulder even though she commanded herself not to. "This woman who tried to kill me???!!" Lena insisted. He cut the peeled apple into quarters and ate them.

He had picked up the bowl of apples that Lena tried to always keep full of fruit for him—scarlet and green and yellow apples, rough-skinned pears, black-skinned plums, honey tangelos, tasty tarty kumquats—and sat down on the bed. But he seemed to find it difficult to sit still.

"Lena, ya got to understand, she wa'n't tryin' to *kill* you so much as to make you dead," Herman explained as he fingered his palm-sized buck knife.

"Kill me. Make me dead. What's the difference?"

"Big difference to her. It wasn't the killin'. It was the havin' you on *her side*—dead. Anna Belle had been watchin' me get closer and closer to you and to the livin'. Everybody had seen it. Couldn't help but watch. And she didn't think it was fair. That you had a body and a pussy and was livin' and everythang that you had on your side."

"Not fair?!" Lena was incredulous. "Not fair???"

"Uh-uh. As a matter a' fact, when she swung that plank at you, that's what she said: 'Fight fair, gal!' I'm surprised you didn't hear her."

"And you just calmly sitting there peeling apples in my bed telling me all this, huh? You weren't going to mention this, Herman? This wasn't ever gonna come up in conversation?"

"Shoot, baby, the way I feel 'bout it is don't trouble trouble 'til trouble trouble you.

"Besides, Anna Belle knew what she was up against in you, Lena. Baby, you the one. You the 'oman. Everybody livin' and dead that know me know that."

Lena wanted to reach over and just sink into this man. But she didn't. She was still scared.

"Well, it looks like trouble's troubling us, huh?" she said. "I repeat, you just calmly sitting there peeling apples in my bed telling me all this?"

He stopped his paring and turned to her.

"Lena, at some point you got to finally understand that thangs ain't all like it seem here on earth, here with the livin'. Ya'll ain't got a clue. Ya just don't know 'bout everythang."

Maybe not, Lena thought, but it seemed she had a fight on her hands with Anna Belle. And Lena *did* know about fights. She had seen fights of one kind or another all her life. Although she had never been in one herself, she certainly knew the drill from The Place.

Call someone out of her name, date someone's man, talk about they mama, steal someone's job, purse, song. And your next step better be pulling off those big gold hoop earrings and snatching off that wig because a fight would be about to ensue.

Lena had even seen a nun fight, but she had never witnessed a ghost fight, and she didn't look forward to being a participant.

"Anna Belle had done had her eye on me fo' fifty or sixty years," Herman continued. "And even before that, when she was 'live in Mulberry."

"Well, good God, Herman. If I got some woman—dead or alive— out there ready to waylay me with a two-by-four to my skull, what should I do? Start carrying a knife?"

Shoot, Lena was scared.

She recalled all the women over the decades downtown at The Place and at juke joints all over the lower South who had threatened to "sharpen this knife all over" some other woman's face. She had seen the scarred women themselves, the victims of these big brassy, bodacious women and their smaller sneaky, sprightly sisters, with ropes of keloid around their necks and crisscrossing their chests and down their arms and hands.

"Um, that woman cut everywhere but on the bottom of her feet," Nellie would say with heartbreaking empathy as she stood in The Place with her flawless skin and her high-heeled pumps.

Lena had hardly been able to look at the victims without feeling the original pain of the knife wounds.

She didn't want to wind up like one of those women, with scars on her face from fighting over a man, even a man like Herman.

Even Cliona from Yamacraw, who made her young cousin drive her out to the river again in late summer to see about Lena, seemed to sense Lena was worried about her safety.

"Lord ham mercy, Lena, what in the world done happened to you?" the old woman inquired as they sat on a teak bench under the trees by the driveway drinking some decaffeinated iced tea. "You look fine, but can't nobody get a hold of you. You dodging a creditor or somebody, baby? You don't need no protection, do you? Ain't no man's other woman after you, is she?"

Lena just smiled as reassuringly as she could and shook her head.

After that, Lena seemed to see knives and recall fights everywhere.

There was a woman who had been coming to The Place ever since

Lena was a child who was supposed to have a shiv still in her stomach from an ancient lovers' quarrel.

Lord, she thought as she sat on her bed rubbing the chill bumps from her arms, is that how you got it planned for me to end up?

But Herman calmed her fears when he came over to the bed and took Lena in his arms. "Lena, you know I wouldn't let no harm come t' *you*," he said.

Lena could not help herself. She had to work hard not to let Herman become her Savior, her Emmanuel, her Jehovah, her Redeemer. But right then she just sighed in relief and put Anna Belle right out of her mind.

25
BLACKBERRY

Mr. Renfroe had been the McPhersons' trusted "yardman" for decades.

But before Lena knew anything, Herman had turned into *her* yardman.

She even started going around her house taking care of business or cooking Herman a little "som'um-som'um," shaking her shoulders and singing about her yardman like Alberta Hunter.

"Now, my ice man is a nice man, 'cause he brings me ice every day. And he says I ain't got to worry. I ain't never got to pay.

"My wood man is a good man, 'cause he loves to keep his baby warm. And when his wood don't burn to suit me, then he takes me in his arms.

"My coal man is a old man almost ninety-two. But that old man sho' knows what to do!!"

Herman was her nice man, her good man, her old man.

As he took her grounds under his capable hand the same way he had done with the horses, Lena found she had to improvise:

"Now, my yardman is a hard man, steady, sweet and young. And when his tool don't satisfy me, then he does it with his tongue."

Herman *was* her yardman. He noticed everything on and around her and her property. Lena once saw him stooped down in the grass studying an insect alit on a cane of a descendant of the St. Luke's Hospital roses. He must have squatted there for seven or eight minutes before he backed off from the bug and turned to call Lena.

"Hey, Lena, baby, come here," he called. When she joined him, he took her arm and guided her up to the rosebush. "Look at this dragonfly," he said. "Don't you have a dress like that?"

Lena looked down at the blue-black dragonfly still as a drawing on the tip of the rose stem, its gossamer wings thrown back in a show of pride, and chuckled.

"You don't miss a trick, do you, Herman?"

"Well, I thought I remembered you wearin' it or seein' it or som'um." He tried to sound casual, but Lena knew he liked to walk through her closet and touch her beautiful clothes as much as he liked sitting up on an impossibly high limb in the pine trees, his feet dangling like a boy's, outside her glass shower watching her suds and rinse herself.

After that, when they danced together on the deck in each other's arms in the moonlight, Lena often wore the tight black Todd Oldham gown with the long gossamer sleeves she had bought for some charity ball or another just for the pleasure of hearing him say, "You look as pretty as a dragonfly in that dress, Lena, baby."

Herman, with his ghostly observant eye, was the one who started her to keeping a serious gardener's journal. She came in on him in her office sitting by a window in the fading light of a late day in summer writing in a book of fragile handmade vegetable paper one of her godchildren had sent her. It had sat for ages on one of the bookshelves there. She turned on a lamp near him, but only one.

"What you writing, Herman?" Lena asked, intrigued. Other than some figuring and ciphering, as he called it, Lena didn't think she had ever seen him write.

"Oh, just jottin' down a few thangs. How Keba doin'. That she measure seventy-two inches around in her fifth month. What new we been plantin'. Yo' land takin' on a whole new look with all we been movin' around and puttin' in. Just thought we oughta keep up with it.

"I wrote down 'bout them hummers we saw today, too."

That morning, as they roamed around her property on their daily adventure, they had stopped to give two ruby-throated hummingbirds room to pirouette, do-si-do, twirl and spin around each other in the air right in front of them. The tiny birds were jousting over a cluster of fiery-red fire spike.

"Look at 'em, Lena. Is it two males? He ain't givin' it up w'out a fight," Herman yelled.

Lena found it fascinating but difficult to watch. She just knew that at any second one of the tiny birds was going to impale the other on the prong of its beak. Lena did not realize she was sinking to the ground until Herman quickly reached out to catch her.

He carried her to a cool spot under a juniper tree by the river and splashed a little Cleer Flo' water in her face to bring her around. He had to put his hand in his chest and start his heart to beating again. It had stopped when he saw Lena falling to the ground.

"Then, too," Herman said, "I find, when I read som'um I wrote a while back—no matter what it's 'bout—I see all kinds a' thangs I didn't even know I was recordin'."

"Um, I used to keep a journal," Lena said, laughing out loud at her innocence in those weeks right out of college before she knew what her true vocation in life would entail. She really imagined she would have the kind of time in her life to keep up a journal, even intermittently. It suddenly dawned on her that now she could do all kinds of things, had time for all kinds of endeavors.

"Hope you don't mind me usin' yo' journal and pen here," Herman said as he wet the nib of one of Nellie's fountain pens on the tip of his tongue, leaving a tiny blue mark there.

Lena smiled as she thought of how her mother would have responded to Herman's casual bid to use something of hers. When

Lena and her brothers were young, her mother had a way of putting an end to any litany of such requests from her children: "Mama, can I have the rest of your ice cream?" "Mama, can I have the funny papers you reading?" "Mama, give me some of those buttered pecans you toasted. Those the last ones." "Mama, what you eating? Gimme some!"

Nellie ended it all with one of her trademark tirades.

"Here!" she'd say. "Here! Take it! I can't have nothing in this house. I can't have nothing to myself!! Take it! Here, take my kidney! Take my liver! Take my blood! Take my jawbone! Take my gizzard! You want my heart? Here, take it! Take my heart!"

She would just be getting wound up.

"I can't eat a can of Vienna sausage in this house in peace," she'd complain.

Nellie overlooked the fact, little Lena always thought, that her mother could make the act of opening a can of Vienna sausages a grand occasion, could make anybody want some, too. Flipping off the tabbed can lid and safely disposing of it in the newspaper-lined plastic trash can. Pouring off the excess juice. Gently shaking the fat little firm sausages out of the blue can onto a pretty flowered plate along with the last of the juice. Then, separating the sausages from standing shoulder-to-shoulder with their little brothers and sisters.

Nellie had a way of making everything look elegant and desirable.

"Uh, Mama, that look *good!* Can I have some?"

Lena knew she didn't have to tell Herman that he was welcome, *welcome*, to all that she had, all that she felt, all that she could give. With all that he had given her, Lena felt she could joyously say, "Here! Take my liver! Take my gizzard! Take my heart!"

She smiled and said, "You can have anything I got, Herman."

"You got so many beautiful and useful thangs, Lena, that you don't even know up in this house. And out in the barn and buildin's, too. Shoot, it look like you ain't *never* got to go to the sto'."

"You gotta start payin' more 'tention, Lena," Herman said seriously.

He sounded so stern, so professorial, that Lena was a little taken aback and anxious to understand what he was advising.

"Pay attention to what, Herman? My yard? My house? My things?" She knew Herman didn't care about things.

He didn't have any attachment for much of what Lena had purchased. Oh, he loved the feel of silk or 100 percent cotton sheets on his bare back, butt and legs. But he was just as happy lying on the rough, heavy, locally woven rug in front of the fire in the Great Jonah Room, as content nestled in sweet-smelling hay that he had just pitched in the loft of the barn, as satisfied stretched out on a bed of leaves down by the river, as fulfilled sleeping between the rows of Silver Queen corn he had planted himself. Happy, content, satisfied and fulfilled as long as he had Lena sleeping next to him.

He *never ever* wanted Lena to stop ordering from the catalogs that specialized in silk and satin lingerie—bawdy to demure. But most of all he liked her naked. He was just as excited when she walked buck naked to their swimming hole as when she waited for him on handkerchief-soft white cotton sheets dressed in a black lace bodysuit from Barneys. Herman could take or leave all that Lena had. It was Lena he couldn't do without.

Lena couldn't believe her luck one day when James Petersen announced that he was just going to stay out of her house anytime she might be there. He said he was just tired of walking in on her without any clothes on.

"Well, Lena, if you gonna insist on walking around here butt-naked, I guess, I'm just gonna have to stay down there in my own little home and read my books."

He waited a beat or two for Lena to renounce her hedonistic ways and promise to at least try to remember to throw something over herself. But she didn't say a word. She was afraid of upsetting a very good turn of events with anything she might utter.

"You and that *new man of yours* that don't nobody ever get a chance to meet keep this place so clean now. It look better than it did when you wasn't never here."

He waited again for her to say something. Lena just held her breath.

"Well, from now on why don't you just call me when you need me and keep leaving me my lists?" he said. Then he added, sounding a bit like his brother, "Shoot, I can go back to my reading." He left Lena grinning and pleased with herself.

James Petersen did not say it, but he wanted to go back to his writing as well. One day in the spring, soon after Herman had come, Lena heard James Petersen say under his breath as he picked up a new stack of mysteries she had gotten for him, "Shoot, I betcha I could *write* one of these things."

"You think you could, James Petersen?" Lena had asked seriously.

"Well, Lena, I done read a million of 'em. And now I not only know how they end before I get there. I can end 'em better than the writer do sometimes."

That same day, Lena had Toya from Candace bring out a manual typewriter, a couple of reams of twenty-pound copy paper, some pencils and some pads. She left them on the doorstep of James Petersen's little cottage in a peach crate. Lena guessed that James Petersen wouldn't want any kind of writing instrument other than a manual typewriter. A computer of any kind was out of the question. He didn't even like to dust in Lena's office around her computer.

"I might set something off," he would explain.

Now in early September, Lena and Herman would stroll down the road past James Petersen's house and smile at each other as they heard the *tat-tat-tat-tat-tat* of James' typing.

With James showing up only now and then while she was away, Lena had her privacy *and* Herman. She felt *she* had died and gone to heaven.

Herman stopped writing in his journal and looked at her, long and hard. It reminded Lena of how Frank Petersen used to stare at her before deciding to enlighten her nine-year-old or eighteen-year-old mind. And like Frank Petersen, who always chose to inform her, Herman smiled and his whole wide face softened. But his voice was serious.

"Lena," he said. "You need to start payin' 'tention to everythang you think is important enough t' give ya some peace or some wisdom or some kinda new tack on the world that might be what you s'posed to see.

"You didn't see nothin' in that fight with the hummers this mo'nin'?" Herman hated to sound that way with Lena, direct and incredulous, but time was moving on. As he told her when they were trying to plant some beans before nightfall and the good soaking rainstorm Herman felt coming, "We burnin' *daylight* here, Lena."

Lena went right over to the shelves by her worktable and selected a thick journal bound in leather with endpapers of hand-painted birds in flight in colors of red and gold. Then, she turned to her mother's pen collection displayed in a glass case atop Nellie's marble-topped dresser and picked her favorite—the lacquered Cartier Panther pen.

Settling in a rocking chair with a cotton blanket thrown over her bare legs, Lena opened to the unlined paper of the first page and wrote in the upper right-hand corner: *Tuesday, Sept. 8, Home.*

By late summer, when an albino hummingbird got in the screened porch, Lena didn't panic for one minute as she thought of her dead grandmother's drained, sweaty face as she raced around the house on Forest Avenue in pursuit of a bird the day before she died. Lena stood watching the trapped ghostly-looking bird swing back and forth in front of an amaryllis bloom for a good long while. Then, she calmly and gently shooed it out the door with a flat straw basket and went right to her journal to record the incident.

Lena began to realize what an unexamined life she had been leading before. She had given herself so little time to just sit and think, without planning and fixing and scheduling her day in her head. Now, some days she found herself sitting alone under a sycamore tree in the woods just pondering. She was beginning again to think freely and comfortably about her mother and her father and the other dead members of her family, chuckling to herself how she was like this one or that one.

Lena started noticing all kinds of things. She discovered that her garden and woods were full of volunteer plants this summer—those that had been borne as a seed or a spore on a wisp of the air or on the wing or beak or claw of a bird or in the stream of rainwater formed by a sudden heavy downpour or even cunningly attached to the antennae of a buzzing insect. All along the banks of the Ocawatchee River on Lena's land new and unusual plants foreign to Middle Georgia were taking root and flourishing. Little mountain orchids with lady's slipper-shaped flowers brought downstream in the Big Flood of '94 bloomed in a crevasse past the woods on the other side of her stables. She wouldn't see them for five or six weeks, but the sprouts that would become a colony of wild Venus's flytraps were just coming up at the foot of hickory trees in a woodland meadow south of the creek. Mushrooms were growing everywhere.

Right outside her workroom window facing the river and the western sky, there on an antique oak drafting table where she made drawings that came to her sometimes, she noticed for the first time that the Mirandy rosebush dead in her sights had split at the root and reverted back to two earlier unhybridized breeds of flower, a big fragrant red rose on the left, a tiny pink unscented climbing rose on the right.

Taking the time to look, to smell, to recall, to touch, Lena began to see the earth in the way she had as a child. The way she had before everything around her seemed to turn sinister. She had eaten the earth around her house when she was three and four if her mother didn't prevent her. Now, with no one around to stop her, and with Herman there thinking it was cute and natural, she ate a small amount of Middle Georgia clay and black-belt loam from the cupped palm of her hand whenever she felt like it.

Just the simple act of sitting on a wooden bench out by the barn and watching the wind gently disturb the fronds on the clumps of lemon grass all along the path down to the river became as moving, as prodigious, as phenomenal, as snatching up family land from the bank and getting it back in the hands of the original black owners.

Now, there was a symmetry to her life that she saw reflected in nature on her property, in the stories Herman told, in the crape myrtle leaves that he crushed in his hands and rubbed all over her exposed skin to keep biting bugs away.

She was even beginning to see some harmony in the death that always seemed to crop up all around her.

The longer Herman was with Lena, the stronger she became. It got to the point around the end of September where she first noticed that she could think something without Herman smiling and agreeing, or disagreeing and gently guiding her onto another path.

She liked the new feeling of awareness and confidence this ability gave her.

She and Herman would be walking in the woods or along the bridle path or through the fruit orchard, and they'd both stop in their tracks and lift their noses in the air. Rain, each of them would think. They would look at one another and smile as the intoxicating scent of rain on a patch of dirt in the next county drifted over their bodies and entered their bloodstreams through inhaled oxygen.

Although Herman often encouraged her, "Put yo' bare feets to the earth, Lena," he wouldn't let her ride Baby or Goldie without good heavy boots.

"I done spent too many nights rubbin' those feets to see 'em messed up in a twisted stirrup," he joked. Then, he turned serious. "I couldn't stand to see you hurt none, Lena, baby. Havin' to go to the doctor or the hospital."

Lena had never been in a hospital overnight. And her body reflected that.

Charting her body, Herman would go all over it with the tips of his fingers examining, looking for any mark or scar or blemish other than her vaccination mark on her left upper arm and a chicken pox mark on her nose.

"Got a pretty stomach," he would say almost to himself as he traced her body like a blind cartographer feeling a relief map. Lena laughed and thought of her gynecologist, Dr. Sharon, who addressed all her patients as "Boo." She had said the same thing as she examined Lena the last time. "You got a pretty stomach, Boo."

Lena laughed when she remembered Dr. Sharon's routine questions about premenopausal symptoms on her last checkup: "Any soreness of your breasts, Boo?" "Any vaginal dryness during intercourse, Boo?" With Herman around, her breasts were always a little sensitive. And just kissing Herman made Lena as wet as a sixteen-year-old girl slow-dragging in the dark for the first time at a basement party.

She thought of old men and their stories of old women sitting in tubs of hot water and alum to tighten up loose and overworked vaginas. Lena would hear the jokes as she passed a cluster of men her father's age chuckling at the bar. "And when the preacher got up to the pulpit the next morning, he said, 'Ummmmphhh-uuhhhhhhu.' "

Herman reminded her of those old men sometimes.

He had an old-timey way of talking, of saying things that she had only read in books. He said "cipher" or "figure" for add. He called a purse a "satchel," and pants of any kind—even her panties—were "britches."

And although he understood the inner workings of a computer better than most experts because he had actually been inside one, Lena would still hear him say to himself as he figured the amount of pig iron he would need for his blacksmithing: "Nought from nought leaves nought."

Lena had never heard Mr. Renfroe refer to his penis as his "Georgia jumpin' root." Still, Herman's speech continued to remind Lena of her gardener.

Walking through her grounds with Herman by her side, his arm draped over her shoulder, Lena would come up on Mr. Renfroe and stop to chat a bit about a fungus on the roses or a new clematis she had seen in a magazine.

"Eee-bah-ning, Lena," the gardener would say.

"Good evening, Mr. Renfroe," Lena would reply.

"Good eee-bah-ning, Mr. Renfroe," Herman would echo politely.

Herman would stoop down beside them and examine the plant in question, then stand and offer Lena his own seasoned advice.

She wanted to ask Renfroe, "Did you hear that? Did you see that? Did you?" But she knew he hadn't heard or seen anything. Only she had.

By the end of summer, Mr. Renfroe had cut down drastically on his time out at Lena's. She was his only client, and he had continued to work there only because it was such fun, though he saw from week to week how much she was doing on the property with her "friend."

Mr. Renfroe had finally demanded to know who was building all those trellises for moonflowers, who was turning the compost piles before he and his assistant could get to the job, who was planting that old-fashioned shooting star primrose all over the property. Just who was her new yardman?

"I got a friend who's real handy," Lena told the old man honestly. "And he enjoys doing things around the place. He hasn't messed up anything, has he, Mr. Renfroe?" she asked, trying to hide the talons she was going to use to rip the old man to shreds if he criticized any of Herman's work.

"Naw," Mr. Renfroe admitted. "He done okay. And some of that stuff, like the trellises, is *fine workmanship!*"

Lena retracted her claws and just beamed at her man's compliment. Lena knew where this conversation was going. She had been down this road before with James Petersen.

James Petersen had seen things: Lena dancing in the moonlight. Lena sitting naked in the sunlight with her feet stretched out in front of her just chattering away. He had caught her a couple of times running from the direction of the barn, laughing and glowing, as if someone were right on her tail.

He had seen all this, but he hadn't said a word to anyone.

To begin with, whom would he have told? If his brother Frank Petersen had been alive, maybe, but Frank hadn't liked hearing anything that even sounded like it was against Lena, and there was no one else with whom to share it.

Anyway, what would he have said? "I keep catching Lena talking to herself and singing to herself even when her lips aren't moving. I saw Lena dancing naked out on the main deck of her house. I'mo say that?" James Petersen muttered to himself time again as he moved about cleaning Lena's house and considering what his duty was as her only in-house guardian.

James Petersen hadn't yet spied "The Man," as he called him, but James knew he was there. Practically moved in, it looked like. The housekeeper had washed enough of Herman's shirts and jeans and brightly colored cotton underwear; fallen over enough of his big work boots; dusted around enough of his dissected handiwork to know that there was a man around. A man who felt comfortable in his surroundings.

"But then, who wouldn't be comfortable out here?" James Petersen asked the empty house. It was what he said about his position at Lena's with his own stone house and his own hours when someone remarked on his good luck. "I'm quite comfortable with my situation."

"Yeah, fine workmanship, Lena," Mr. Renfroe had repeated, waiting as James Petersen had for her to say something, then continuing.

"Yeah, like to meet the man sometime. Talk to him face-to-face 'bout the work he done. Yeah, sure would like to meet him."

But Lena just said, "Um," stroked her throat and looked down that "long, long country road" the way her mother had when she no longer wanted to discuss something.

Although she relished her privacy, Lena missed the old man being on the property so much.

For years, she and the old gardener had moved among the vegetable plants and weeping willow trees and ivy and yew and hibiscus bushes together for a little bit practically every day. But after her parents' death, she had had to get Mr. Renfroe some help of his own because she no longer had the time to be of any assistance to him.

She couldn't remember all the great-looking animal-print Manolo

Blahnik high-heeled mules and Charles Jordan pumps she had ruined trying to squeeze some gardening in on the way to work.

Before the spring when Herman came, she just didn't have *time* for gardening or any of the things she had enjoyed most of her life. Over the last decade, it had happened so gradually, so slowly, that she hardly noticed that her life revolved around doing for others.

"Shoot, I don't even have time to turn my own compost pile or cut flowers in the evening," she had complained to herself for years.

Now, when she walked with Herman on the grounds, he'd even look at her every now and then and say, "Time, baby."

The long daylight hours of summer somehow agreed to continue on through the shorter days of early fall. For Lena, Herman had all the time in the world. And she felt that she had all the time in the world. Sometimes, he even seemed able to stop time. One day in September, he took her back to the berry patch where he had taught her how to really pick blackberries. When she saw where they were headed, she said, "Herman, it's too late in the summer for those blackberries now."

"Yeah, baby, but not fo' us," he said as they rode up to the massive mounds of vines covered with juicy purple-black fruit. He jumped off his horse, picked the biggest juiciest berry Lena had ever seen and coming back to where she sat on Baby, said, "Open yo' mouth and close yo' eyes."

At Herman's sweet shy insistence, they had even made love one night in August under a big full moon and the stars of the Southern Crown in the furrows between the rows of Silver Queen and Golden King corn growing in a high area near the river to enrich the soil and ensure a good harvest.

Herman paused in licking her breasts and rolling her hard nipples gently, carefully, between his strong teeth to say, "Well, we sure as shootin' gonna have us a splendiferous harvest at this rate."

Between moaning and kissing the crown of Herman's bushy head under the tassels of the sweet white corn, Lena had to agree. She knew a good harvest was ensured as soon as she lifted her head from the rich black loamy soil where she lay naked on her back and watched Herman slowly sink his thick tight penis deep into her wide-open purple and pink vagina like an ancient handmade farm tool sinking into the earth. Herman had not had to change shape or form or essence at all to make them both groan as he rested in her a moment—a long moment—then pulled out as she sunk her short nails into his clenched firm butt, and he sunk his into the rich dirt around her.

In the grip of a sweet, soul-rattling orgasm, their eyes met, and they smiled at each other. Then, they both fell back to the earth.

Even Mr. Renfroe remarked on how rich Lena's garden soil was becoming.

From the first, Herman just wouldn't allow her *not* to have a full garden on her property.

"Good God, Lena, you got soil like down on the muck in Flor'da, and you ain't even gon' plant no *beans!?*"

Using old-time and Native American techniques of planting in nothing but hills of rotting compost from Lena's kitchen, Herman grew so many ripe, sweet, juicy watermelons that he loaded some in the back of Lena's dark green Wagoneer for folks downtown at The Place.

Perfectly round, nearly blue-skinned Cannonballs; long pale Charleston Grays; round, sweet Sugar Babies; oblong lime-striped Crimson Sweets.

A couple of her teenaged children from the corner, thrilled to see Lena for a change, trooped in with her with the melons on their shoulders and placed them on the counters and in empty sinks and half-full soda coolers.

Coming into The Place, Lena warned, "Be careful. You know, liquor and watermelon'll kill you," and old men and women looked up to make sure somebody as young as Lena was repeating such an old-timey belief.

Then, as quickly as she had appeared at The Place, she was back in her Wagoneer and gone.

"Guess she gone back out there by the river with her 'friend,'" Peanut said as he watched everybody's face fall when they realized she had disappeared before anybody got a chance to say anything to her.

Herman, Lena discovered, was tied not only to their own cultivation. He would eat out the woods in a minute if what he wanted was not being grown in the garden. One day he stopped during their walk and looked over in the direction of a dark damp cluster of poplar trees nearby. Taking her hand in his, he led her to the trees and stooped down at their trunks by a stand of dark brown mushrooms.

"Those toadstools, Herman?" Lena asked as he picked one, turned it to the light and smelled it.

He just smiled and popped it in his mouth.

Lena held her breath and waited for some kind of ghostly allergic reaction, but none came, and she, satisfied of their safety, started selecting the safe mushrooms Herman pointed out from the poisonous varieties.

Herman never said it in so many words, but Lena knew she was being drawn closer and closer to the earth. And she knew that it was somehow Herman's doing. The further she pulled herself away from the things of the world—her possessions, her businesses, her shoes, her dependents, her visits, even her gifts and acts of kindness—the nearer she drew to the peaceful, serene spirit of the world itself.

"You need to be mo' like Mary and less like Martha," Herman would tell her gently when she still went off to take care of somebody. "Choose the better part, baby."

When Lena didn't come to church four or five Sundays in a row, folks there began to sound the alarm. Church folks were the first to notice that Lena McPherson was slacking off!

Lena would have been stunned if she had known people in Mulberry were saying that. That she was slacking off. She felt just the opposite.

"You want to come join me for Holy Communion, Herman?" Lena asked him one morning as she was heading to Mary and

Martha's grotto down by the river with a bottle of champagne, half a biscuit Herman had made that morning, a few tiny Sweet 100s tomatoes from the kitchen garden and a little honey from the field hive.

"It's *all* communion, baby," Herman had called back to her as he headed for the barn with brush and pail in hand. "It's all good."

26
DOWNTOWN

When Gloria came up on Lena sneaking out of the grill side of The Place at five in the morning, Lena jumped as if a strange ghost had brushed up against her.

"Um, um, um," Gloria said. "Poor thing. Now they got her sneaking around her own place." Lena was so surprised, she nearly dropped the bulky cardboard box she was carrying on her hip like a country woman toting a baby. She laughed as if she had been caught with her hand in the cookie jar.

"I'm just trying to get a few things out of here before everybody gets in and catches me," Lena explained sheepishly. Her box was filled with a bottle of old brandy, some papers she needed and her father's small adding machine for Herman.

"Um, um, um," Gloria said. "Got the nerve to be trying to have a life of her own. Lena, girl, you *know* you 'un tore your drawers with this town now," Gloria laughed in her slow Mulberry drawl as she helped Lena lift the box onto the bar.

It was something Lena had often heard the still-sexy manager say when she felt somebody was in serious trouble.

"Lena, this town just now beginning to see that you feeding them out of *a long-handle spoon*! And, girl, they don't like it one bit. A few folks ain't even noticed yet 'cause you done took such good care of them before. It ain't hit 'em all yet. But enough of them talking."

Lena smiled at Gloria, whose Maybelline mole had disappeared years ago in the bustle of running the business, and said slyly, "I have a friend who says, 'Our folks are smart people. They'll get the message.' "

"Well, you know what your mama always used to say," Gloria replied.

Both women chimed in together, " 'You can show a Negro quicker than you can tell 'em.' "

Then, they laughed good and loud at the memory of Nellie Mc-Pherson.

"Come on, girl, sit for a while," Gloria said. She took a pack of Tareyton cigarettes from her purse as she and Lena settled in on a couple of The Place's vinyl barstools.

Lena watched Gloria lean on the counter and light a cigarette. Oh, that's the way a whore smokes a cigarette, she thought. Lena couldn't help it.

It had always been difficult for her to get an image out of her head once it was there. That was what had made her attempts to exorcise the memories of her childhood demons and ghosts so hard. And that was how it was with an image of Gloria stamped in Lena's memory from forty years before.

Lena had been playing among the cases of liquor on the floor of The Place one Saturday when she heard her mother chuckle to herself: "Humph, only a whore blows her smoke out like that."

Lena had clambered up on the counter, using the shelf underneath for a stepladder. She made it to the top just in time to see Gloria take another drag of the cigarette, hold it in a while, then blow it out with her bottom lip, directing the smoke in a wide stream toward her flared nostrils.

"Oh, *that's* how a whore blows her smoke out," little Lena said softly to herself, her tongue playing lightly in the corner of her mouth trying to imitate Gloria's. She had already disturbed the whole car one Sunday morning as the family drove to Mass by asking exactly what a whore was. So, she didn't dare say the word out real loud. But she stored away that bit of information with the certainty that she would find it useful one day. Even now, forty years later, she could not break herself of the habit of thinking, Oh, *that's* how a whore blows her smoke out, whenever she saw a woman exhale that way.

For years, that's what people at The Place had thought Gloria was—just a whore with a steady job. Even Jonah, who had relied on Gloria so much, had treated her as if it were her ass that made her valuable. After Nellie just had finally, quietly, flatly refused to keep running The Place for Jonah's convenience, it was Gloria who kept his business running smoothly—opening up in the morning so he could stay out late and gamble and carouse; staying later and later in the evening while he went about his other business and businesses. Yet, Jonah continued to have talks with Gloria about what was proper juke-joint employee attire, what she should and shouldn't wear to work, how she should conduct herself with customers, how not to lean too far over the customers' plates and drinks.

"Gloria? Shoot, she giving it away out of both drawers legs," folks would say, summing her up.

But one of the first things Lena did when she inherited The Place at the deaths of her parents was to make Gloria the manager. "One of the smartest things I ever did," Lena said to herself whenever her mind turned to the business.

When Lena came back from her last year of college, it had amazed her how much Gloria seemed to have changed. Even though she had encouraged and even bullied and embarrassed her father into giving the barmaid more responsibility and an appropriate pay raise, Lena was herself surprised at how quickly and easily Gloria had handled the duties. Gloria even initiated changes and plans she had obviously had in mind for quite some time. And they worked.

It was Gloria who centralized the ordering for both the liquor store and the bar and grill side. It was Gloria who finally and successfully set up a real work schedule that included regular employees, gofers and roustabouts. It was Gloria who reorchestrated the deliveries of beer and wine and sodas and snacks and linens and liquor from the hodgepodge Jonah and his managers had made of it when Nellie had thrown her hands up in surrender.

But even before Gloria proved herself an astute businesswoman, Lena had respected her on many other levels.

Gloria was only eighteen years older than Lena, but the younger woman thought Gloria was as old as the ages. Certainly not because she *looked* old. But because Lena thought she had lived, really lived, forever.

Nellie had always prefaced just about everything she said about Gloria with the phrase "Considering how long she been out there . . ."

"Considering how long she been out there, she look good."

"Considering how long she been out there, it's a wonder she can get up in the morning and come to work."

"Considering how long she been out there, it's a wonder she ain't got a houseful of children."

Lena had once seen Gloria push an ardent but unwanted suitor out of her face with a firm friendly shove. Her admirer, a nice-looking young man wearing a freshly pressed short-sleeved white shirt, just stroked his thin mustache, sort of laughed and sat down at the end of the counter. He ordered an orange Nehi, biding his time until his next chance with her came around.

Gloria had looked at a teenaged Lena and confided wearily, "Girl, it's so old it's new."

Lena thought Gloria wasn't as young as she looked but that she just looked good for her age, as everybody, including her mother, said.

A straying boyfriend of Gloria's stood at the end of the counter at The Place one night, dap-daddy hat now crushed by his own hand, his chin on his chest, his shoulders slumped. Lena heard Gloria tell him: "You play with fire you get burned. You play with pussy you get fucked."

The soon-to-be-ex-boyfriend hadn't looked burned anywhere that Lena could see, so she assumed from what Gloria said, he must have been fucked. Ever since then, when Lena saw someone looking like Gloria's dap-daddy friend, she'd say to herself, "Um, um, um, bless his heart. He's fucked."

Gloria and Lena sat in the dark by the big plate-glass window at the front counter of the L-shaped bar and grill for a while in comfortable silence. The orange glow of Gloria's cigarette and the weak light from the corner streetlight were the only lumination there. Gloria put out her butt in a tin ashtray on the bar and got up and flipped on a small light over the front door.

"Lena," she asked suddenly, "you want to split a beer?"

Lena smiled at the thought of sharing a beer with Gloria at five in the morning. "Sure," she said.

Gloria took a good look at Lena in the dim light. "You know, Lena, you look so good." On her way back from the cooler, she stopped and looked Lena right in the face again. "I don't think I seen you this happy since you was a girl. You smile all up in your eyes now, girl. I was telling Eva just that the other night."

Gloria was pretty happy herself these days, Lena noticed. She and Eva and Eva's two children from her first marriage were living happily in that beautiful two-story house Lena had found for them out in what everybody called "Bird City."

Folks wanted to be as blind about Gloria's true sexuality as they were about her business acumen, Lena thought as she watched Gloria make her way to the cooler in the back of The Place in that slow, easy, hip-swaying walk. Lena and everybody else downtown had admired her gait since Gloria first started walking Broadway, strolling up and down the street from bar to bar, from shop to shop, accepting a drink from this one and that one, going home with *some-body*.

Now, no one believed that Gloria was a lesbian.

"She sho' ain't gay. Miss Thing is serving *pussy*!" folks quite confidently declared out loud when Gloria walked by.

"Shoot, she 'un lay down with just 'bout every man in Mulberry. She was even married for, uh, ten years or so, wa'n't she?"

"Yeah, she sho' was. Hell, I had her myself years ago. Let me tell you, she ain't no bull dyker!"

"It's a feeling and a lifestyle choice, Miss Lena," Gloria had told her. "I love women. I don't love men. So, what was I supposed to do?"

Gloria had said it nonchalantly, as if it were the kind of thing said all the time in Mulberry, Georgia. With all the complexities of a woman who had seemed to fuck everything in pants all her life being a lesbian, choosing to live that way, to love women exclusively.

"Shoot, Lena, I don't care what folks think 'bout me. Hell, that would be like jumping from the frying pan into the fire for real. I didn't care when I was married to Harry. And I don't give a damn now that I'm with Eva."

Gloria hadn't been married in over fifteen years, but folks with hope in their voices continued to explain, "Gloria and Harry ain't together no mo'. They estrangled."

When Gloria overheard this, she would laugh and say out the side of her mouth to Lena, "Damn, were they there for the last fight?"

"But that's what I like 'bout living in a little town," Gloria had told Lena. "Once people get over the initial shock, they kind of accept all kinds a' things. Now, they may go on talking 'bout it for the rest of their natural-born days, but they do seem to go on and accept it. That's what I've found."

And folks did talk.

"Naw, she sho' ain't no lesbian. Miss Thing is serving much pussy!"

"She may be. But she sho' ain't serving it to you boys," one of

Gloria's friends would offer to the group. And even the men would have to join in the laughter that gently put them down.

"I guess you are right 'bout that," Alfred or Peanut or one of them would say, shaking his head in amazement. " 'Cause we ain't had none in years!!"

Over the years, she and Gloria had shared all kinds of talk: business conferences to circumvent Jonah's biases; girl talk about men and women; family chats about emergencies and achievements. But this early conversation now was feeling better than anytime they had talked.

Gloria split the tall can of Colt .45 between the two frosty mugs from the cooler, and they sat at the bar sipping their beer as Gloria lit up another Tareyton, blowing the smoke out of her mouth like a whore.

Then, reaching in her jacket pocket, Gloria pulled out two quarters and spun on the stool, hopped off and went over to the jukebox.

"Shoot, I don't ever get to hear *my song*!" she complained lightly, and punched two buttons. "I started coming down here early to open up, but now I come down early just to get a little quiet time to be by myself and get myself together."

"Humph," Lena said. "I used to do that."

Lena was talking to herself, but Gloria heard her.

"I know, Lena, I seen how you changed your life, baby. Ain't no need for me to go down that same road.

"We ain't *all* got to go cross the burning sands to know what it's like and what's on the other side. Shoot, Mulberry can take a lot out of you. Some folks got the nerve to be mad you ain't still pretending to eat their food."

Although Lena had laughed it off, what Gloria told her about the people in town was true.

Sometimes, Lena would spy someone she hadn't seen in ages standing on the corner waiting for the bus, and she'd pull up to offer a ride before she thought about it. Or sometimes, she'd just pull up to someone's porch to say hey. But she would always end up regretting it.

Folks were beginning to feel they were well within their rights to get Lena straight. When they could catch her, they had the nerve to say, "Well, yeah, Lena, you have been, well, I won't mince words, sugar, distracted lately. Like your full mind ain't on what it s'posed to be on."

She would listen to them chastise her if she had time and Herman wasn't waiting for her and just shake her head and chuckle at their presumption.

Some people still insisted on trying to stop her as she breezed infrequently through The Place, trying to slip in a litany of needs. But Lena had learned a thing or two in the last few months with Herman at her side. She would just calmly stop talking with Gloria or one of her children and suggest that the needy person get in touch with someone at Candace Realty or at the church or at the bank or at one of the service organizations she supported. She even gave them the name of the specific person to see to get the job done.

The response was usually shock, followed by disbelief, then indignation. Folks would stomp away from Lena muttering, "If you ain't gonna do it *for me*, then don't *tell me how to do it!*"

Sometimes, she'd call out, "My mama always said, 'You can't dance on every set.' "

But most times she would just smile, shake her head and put them in the hands of the Lord, remembering Herman's words, "They ain't in yo' hands. They in the Lord's hands."

Gloria was more mildly amused than anything else by Lena's new way of handling her business and her life. She was right happy to see Lena pay more attention to her own life.

But everybody was not as happy with Lena McPherson.

Some of the phone messages and notes she began to get when folks saw they *really* could no longer get their hands on her at will sounded truly plaintive.

"I sure will be glad when you get back to normal," Miss Birdie told Lena's answering machine. Like so many older people, Miss Birdie hated answering machines and usually refused to speak into them

when they beeped. Or the old folks would just start talking as soon as
the greeting began, so if Lena heard anything, it would only be the tail
end of their message or maybe just a word she could use to try to
decipher the identity and message of the caller. Sometimes, when
there was no message at all, Lena would have to sit and try to guess
which of her older friends was hanging up without leaving any message at all. She'd call all those people until she found the true caller.

Lena knew Miss Birdie was fairly desperate to talk on the machine.

"I used to be able to do my own shopping and errands and even go
to church regular," Miss Birdie's message said. "Now, I can't even get
out of my house without you."

It was laments like Miss Birdie's that tore at Lena's heart and
made her sometimes question if what she and Herman had—the
childlike freedom to play and love and laugh and eat and explore as if
they didn't have a care in the world—was theirs at too high a price for
everyone else.

For a while, Lena seemed to be almost as busy delegating all her
duties as she had been fulfilling them herself. And of course, *nobody*
was satisfied with the arrangements she made because none of the
arrangements involved *her*. Herman watched her go through this futile dance for a couple of weeks. Then he reminded her—again:

"Lena, baby, you need to be more like Mary and less like Martha."

But she still worried about her people. Miss Birdie's call preyed on
her mind, worrying her so, that even after Lena had made arrangements to handle her errands, she drove into town one afternoon at the
end of the summer to check on the old lady.

When she walked up the cement steps to Miss Birdie's house in
Pleasant Hill and found the front door closed and locked, the television in the front-room window off, her heart leapt into her throat.
Lena didn't know whether to head for the hospital or the morgue. She
was just about ready right then to repent her new ways, recant her
devotion to Herman, and put on her designer nun's habit again, when
the woman next door recognized her and waved.

"Hey, Lena, ain't seen you in a month a' Sundays! Birdie ain't home. She gone on the church picnic out at Lake Peak."

The neighbor fanned herself, waved again and went on back in her house to sit up under her air conditioner.

Lena's legs turned to jelly in the late summer heat. She had to lean her behind on Miss Birdie's porch railing to keep from sinking to the rough wooden floor. She regrouped and headed slowly down the concrete steps toward her car.

As she made a U-turn in front of the old woman's empty house and headed on back out to the river and to Herman, she kept saying to herself in wonderment:

"Miss Birdie gone on a picnic!"

"Miss Birdie gone on a *picnic!*"

"Miss Birdie *gone* on a picnic?!"

"Miss Birdie gone on a picnic?!"

"Damn, Lena," she said to herself as she slipped onto the interstate. "You *are* a little foolish fool like Mama used to say!"

Herman was waiting for her at the back door. He smiled his big welcoming smile and accompanied her to the kitchen. Lena knew she didn't have to explain anything to Herman.

"I made some lemonade, Lena. Want some?" was all he said then. He poured two tall glasses and sat down across from her at the long shiny picnic table by the window in the corner. They sat in silence. Then, he spoke:

"Lena, baby, I done seen peoples like you just sucked dry like a plant wid bugs by other folks' needs and their own good intentions and bein' taken fo' granted. 'Specially womens. I seen all their life and liveliness and spunk sucked right out a' them.

"I couldn't bear ta see you like that."

In the growing light, Gloria leaned her head back, drained her sweating glass of beer and got up to get them another one. When she came back, she glanced out the front window at the breaking dawn and leaned over toward her boss and friend. Gloria spoke seriously.

"Lena, there's something I been meaning to talk to you about."

"You can talk to me about anything you like, Gloria. You know that." Lena felt she was speaking with a relative on some serious family matter.

"Well, you told me last spring that that new door and lock leading from the storeroom didn't have nothing to do with The Place. That it was private. And you know that's good enough for me."

"Oh, it's nothing illegal, Gloria, you know I wouldn't put you or The Place in that kind of jeopardy."

"Oh, shoot, I know that. I just didn't know whether or not you had noticed, but around the edge of the doorjamb, it looks like some-body been hitting it or kicking at it with a steel-toe boot or some-thing. Dude the Second noticed it last week when he was stacking liquor by the wall, and he showed it to me so I wouldn't think *he* did it."

Lena felt a sudden little shiver and remembered Anna Belle swinging a two-by-four. Herman had made her sound so determined. Lena was just glad that Gloria was sitting there with her in the slowly advancing dawn. She knew Gloria could take care of herself and would do what she could to protect Lena in a fight, too.

Lena tried to hide her concern and sound casual. "Um, let me take a look at it." Picking up her ring of keys, she went out the front door of the bar and grill and unlocked the front door of the liquor store. Gloria did not follow her, and Lena was thankful for that. She didn't know what she was about to see or how she was going to react, but Lena could still see Gloria through the glass partition, and felt reassured.

She grabbed a long silver flashlight from under the liquor store counter among *Jet* magazines, breath mints and boxes of condoms that Lena and Gloria encouraged the staff to give away to customers and headed in back. It was dark and clammy in the back storeroom, and Lena felt uncomfortable when she realized she was out of Gloria's sight. She flicked on the flashlight and let out a gasp. In the lower portion of the extra-strong burglarproof steel door Mr. Jackson had placed at the entrance to Herman's secret room, there were deep rounded dents.

Gloria was right. It did look as if someone or something had been banging at the metal door with a heavy blunt object or kicking at it with steel-toe boots.

When Lena stooped down and hesitantly ran her fingers over the marks in the heavy steel door, she felt another shiver run down her spine. The metal door felt icy to her touch along the depressions. Lena snatched her hand away, but then she steeled herself and checked the heavy double-gauged-steel bolt lock. There was not a scratch on it. When she took the doorknob in her hand and tried to rattle the door in its hinges, it did not budge.

The door seemed secure, but she rushed out of the empty liquor storeroom just the same and back to the safety of Gloria's company.

"Oh, I think it's okay," she reassured Gloria as she gave her a quick hard hug, gathered up her box and headed toward the front door. "I'll have Mr. Jackson come down and take a look at it."

Lena made her voice sound light, but when she reached her car, she checked the locks and the interior before opening the door and sliding behind the wheel. Lena thought she sensed Anna Belle's presence skulking around the frame of the car all the way home. It was nothing real or concrete like Herman's breeze and touches, but it disconcerted Lena just the same.

When she saw Herman leaning on the fence waiting for her, Lena breathed her first sigh of relief. She hurried from the car to tell him about the dents on the door of his room down at The Place.

"Was the do' broke into?" he asked Lena like a private investigator as he escorted her into the house.

"No," she said, going into the Great Jonah Room with him.

"Was the lock broke?"

"No, Herman, it was still secure."

"Was there anythang stolen or disturbed?"

"No."

"Ain't nobody been hurt, have they, Lena?"

"Oh, my God, no," Lena replied. She hadn't considered the possibility of one of her people, Gloria or Peanut or Miss Cliona from Yamacraw, being injured or terrorized by Anna Belle.

"Well, then, I don't think it's nothin' to be bothered 'bout if nothin' wasn't disturbed."

"Nothing but *me*," Lena said, trying to make a joke.

"Aw, baby, don't be concerned. It sound like Anna Belle, but it ain't nothin' to worry 'bout. I wouldn't let nothin' harm a hair on yo' head."

"Yeah, Herman," Lena said warily, "but you didn't see those marks on that steel door. And you didn't feel how cold it was. Hell, this is a woman who tried to kill me a few months ago, Herman."

"Make ya dead," Herman corrected her.

"What the fuck ever," Lena replied crisply.

"I know, Lena, I ain't tryin' ta make light of it at all. But there a few thangs here that sets my mind to rest. First, Anna Belle ain't shown up as herself. And since that first day down at yo' place last spring, she ain't even tried to touch a hair on yo' head. She cain't. 'Cause if she could, she woulda by now. I guarantee you that. She just tryin' to upset thangs 'round you. Spookin' the horses, kickin' the locked door to my room down at yo' place. It's kinda sad when ya think about it. But she ain't hurt a soul."

Lena sat down next to Herman on the sofa and leaned back on him.

"Why, Lena, I didn't say nothin' 'bout it to you, but last month I went down to the river and found yo' favorite wood bench th'owed over in the drink."

"My teak bench?"

"I took it on out and washed it down. But I knew it war'n't no wind or nothin' that took it over in the water. It was Anna Belle. But it didn't do no harm."

"This happened last month?" Lena asked, a little surprise, a little hurt in her voice. "We aren't keeping secrets now, are we, Herman?"

"Wa'n't no secret, baby. I just didn't see no cause to go and upset you, is all. Everybody ain't got to know everythang. In fact, don't *no* nobody know *everything*.

"Anyway, ain't no way I could keep no secret from you, Lena, baby. We ain't got that kinda relationship."

He took Lena in his arms and pulled her cradled in his lap.

"And as long as I'm here wid ya, I swear, ain't nothin' gonna hurt ya. Not Anna Belle, not a bolt a' lightnin', not nothin'.

"Baby, I'd stand 'tween you and eternity if I had to. Don't ya know yet how I loves ya, Lena?"

"I know how you love me, Herman."

"Then you hafta know I mean what I say. I won't let Anna Belle hurt ya. As a matter a' fact, I'mo get it straight right now. *I'mo* handle this, Lena, baby, head-on."

Lena knew Herman could do just about anything.

"You promise me, Herman?" Lena asked.

"I promise you, baby," he replied.

With all her heart, she believed him.

27

LIVIN'

But then, Herman was an unusual man.

Lena knew he was from another world when she first noticed that he picked up after himself. It wasn't as if he went around dusting out ashtrays, but if he smoked his clay pipe stuffed with sweet-smelling tobacco, he didn't leave ashes all over the chair arm.

He agreed with Lena that making a bed every day was a waste of energy and time. But he never thoughtlessly threw a damp towel across the tousled linens because he knew Lena couldn't stand to fall into bed on a wet spot.

He never even turned right over and fell asleep right after making love to Lena. He *expected* her to fall asleep in his arms, lying on his chest with his arms tenderly encircling her like the prongs of the bed's headboard. She often awoke to Herman singing a little tune under his breath in her ear.

Lena heard Herman singing the most unlikely things. Sometimes, it was a nursery rhyme put to music or a song from a game Lena had played as a child.

*"Jump back, Sally, Sally, Sally
Walkin' through the alley, alley, alley."*

Herman found pleasure in simple things, quiet endeavors. He had looked at a few shows on television when he first came. But if Lena never turned the TV on, he never bothered with it.

"I can't stand that noise on all the time," he said.

Mostly, at night, if they didn't go fishing, walking or stargazing, on the lookout for Venus in the sky, Herman liked to sit out on the deck with Lena and just let night fall. He could pick a tune pretty good on a box. And, of course, Lena had wanted to run out and buy him a handmade acoustic guitar from Tennessee, but Herman demurred.

"Lena," he said with a laugh in his voice, "I ain't all that good. Just go down to a pawnshop and pick me out som'um that'll be even wid my talent."

Lena had picked a rather plain shiny guitar from the ones on the wall at the pawnshop. "If the man can't get his box back, least somebody'll be playin' it," Herman whispered in Lena's ear and strummed the guitar one time as she got in her car with the instrument in her hand.

After that, she heard Herman's guitar music all over the place, all times of day. First thing in the morning, she awoke to notes and half notes playing all on the covers around her. In the late morning, while she prepared supper for Herman, he sat in his favorite white pine chair, watched her and played. At midnight, Herman stood outside her bedroom window and serenaded her, with the frogs and crickets playing backup.

Some evenings, they'd have music outside on the deck—a little song from back before the turn of the century like "Don't Let the Devil Ride."

Sometimes, Lil Sis would join in the song.

One day in early October, Herman stopped his strumming to say: "You know, Lena, you really freed me up to do some thangs I like anytime I want to. Thank you, ma'am."

"I freed *you up?!*" Lena whooped.

Lena felt that Herman had unlocked doors all along the route to *her* freedom. With just a suggestion or even a look, Herman had made Lena question so many things that she had found it impossible not to change.

By the time the weather had started getting a little chilly, he had stopped saying, "God don't want burned offerin's, Lena, He want mercy," because she had finally gotten the message and taken herself off the altar. She had discovered that with one phone call she could delegate a chore to one capable person she was paying to do the job anyway and stop worrying about the outcome of the job at the same time. Sometimes, she didn't even have to make the phone call.

"Don't worry 'bout the mule goin' blind, Lena, baby," rang in her ears.

As the two of them tromped through the woods, Herman would mutter to himself every now and then, "It sho' feel good to roam free. It *still* feel good."

Herman helped Lena *claim* her land, her spot of earth as her own. She thought she had already claimed it—plotting the buildings, sur-veying the land with Mr. Renfroe, keeping as many people out of her inner sanctum as possible. But Herman showed her she hadn't really *claimed* it. She couldn't do that until she *knew* the land and the spirit under it.

Then, back inside the house, winded and exhilarated from a hard fast ride on Goldie and Baby to the end of her property nearly ten miles away and back, he would set about helping her claim her soul.

Most evenings, Herman shared a recitation with Lena. He prided himself on his memory and recitation. He loved to recite poetry he had learned over the years . . . all the years. Some nights, it was Langston Hughes and Paul Laurence Dunbar; other nights, it was Sonia Sanchez and Mari Evans.

"I really like verse from the last twen'y-five, thir'y years, Lena," he said.

Spying a rare American eagle in the sky over the Ocawatchee River, Herman would quote the Temptations *and* Nikki Giovanni, "I mean I can fly like a bird in the sky."

He was impressively familiar with a wide range of verse.

Back in the spring when Herman first appeared, Lena would walk through her big comfortable house worried about somebody who was about to be evicted and arrested for bad checks and mutter to herself, "Life is real and life is earnest."

And Herman would yell from some other part of the house, " 'And the grave is not its goal,' Lena, baby. 'Dust thou art, to dust returnest, was not spoken of the soul.' "

He always remembered Lena's recitation that first night they loved each other, and it became a tradition for her to stand and recite "The Stars" before the night was out.

Other nights, Herman told stories. Some stories Lena had never heard. Stories about animals mostly and how they got to be that way. Why a rabbit hops. How God made butterflies. Why the mockingbird is away on Friday.

Lena told him stories of her family and her past. She told him of her family's trip to the Georgia coast when she was seven, and he told her the story of why the porpoise's tail is on crossways. She told him of meeting a ghost named Rachel on the beach. And he told her the story of his family's flight for freedom.

Herman's stories about funeral wagons and about cats wearing diamond rings, showing up after a man's wife had died wearing the same rings, and sticking their paws into the open campfire to retrieve pieces of sizzling fatback reminded Lena of her grandmama's lurid tales.

Lena would ask him questions about everything: the afterlife, his own time, how computers worked, had he ever run into her favorite author, Zora Neale Hurston, in the hereafter. She was voraciously inquisitive. He would look up at her and say in wonder, "Damn, baby, ya don't know *nothing*!"

"Well, Herman," she would say, throwing her head back and laughing, "you won't know if you don't ask."

"Yeah, Lena, baby," he'd say as he pulled one of her braids or reached up under her skirt and tugged at her silk panties, "but you don't have a clue. A 'oman like you." But he laughed when he said it—proud that she was learning. Then, he'd break into another story that would answer her question.

Sometimes, the stories he told were of his life and sometimes of his experiences since he'd been dead.

Herman told stories of Africa—West African tales that *his father* had heard from *his father* about the meaning of honor and the creation of the sky. He talked of Geronimo, who had surrendered in 1886 when Herman was nearly thirty. He had heard of the warrior around campfires with other Maroons and Seminoles in Florida. Sitting with Lena in front of the ingenious hearth he had built on the deck, Herman retold all those tales.

He spoke often of his life in and around her own home county just before his death.

"Here in Mulberry, Lena, you could get a room, nice room, for fifty cents a week. Others ain't so nice cost less. My room down there in yo' place was the best in the city I ever had. I lived right in that room 'bout two years, Lena.

"Some folks 'round here thought I was a country boy 'cause I was raised out in the wilds of Flor'da. But livin' the way we lived was different in some ways, some important ways, from just livin' out in the country. Now, I could find my way 'round in a town, not a big old city like Boston or Atlanta. But Jacksonville, Mulberry, Savannah, Dublin, them towns I can get around in 'thout walking into a buildin'."

But Herman let her know he wasn't "citified." He took pride in being of the earth, in being from Maroons.

"Now, it take some smarts to run off from the plantation and make it. Lena, I never had mo' respect fo' anybody in this world than my ma and pa. To run off like that when both of them wasn't hardly grown. And my ma just showin' with my big sister. And my pa not knowin' nothin' but the stars and what somebody had told him 'bout freedom bein' Nawth and South, too.

"My pa didn't have no fam'bly other than my ma. And she was the same. They'd both been sold off from they fam'blies and they bloodline. My ma—her name was Mae—didn't know her own ma and pa. My ma said she heard her pa had been a stockman, had a hundred and some-odd children when he died. But she didn't know if that was true or not."

The Mulberry stories were some of Lena's favorite.

"You know where Greenwood Bottom is, Lena?" Herman asked one day as she dressed to make a rare trip into town to tie up some loose ends on a deal she was working.

"Well, now, Herman, it seems I have heard Grandmama speak of Greenwood Bottom," she said as she slipped into a pair of red tap panties that matched the snug-fitting camisole she was wearing.

"Greenwood Bottom," Herman explained, "was a section of Mulberry when I lived 'round these parts. A nice section. I wonder if it's still around."

Lena made a mental note to research Greenwood Bottom. It seemed to her that her Grandmama and Granddaddy Walter had at one time lived in a section with "Bottom" in its name.

Everything Herman said seemed worth noting, Lena thought. He didn't always talk so much as a rule, but everything seemed to interest him a bit. And he liked to comment on what was passing by.

"I been 'round, Lena, baby," he told her.

"I even was able to pop in and hear Robert Johnson play some music, Lena. Couldn't pat my feets, didn't have no feets then. Couldn't even bob my head to the music. Didn't have no head. That was before you, Lena."

He smiled at her and continued.

"That blues-playing man died in a place called Baptisttown. You warn't even born yet, Lena. Shoot, he warn't much more than a very young man himself."

Herman loved the blues.

"So, ya'll gon' just go on and lose the blues music altogether," he came right out and said to her one night as they listened to a newly released CD of Johnson.

"What you mean by that, Herman?"

"Well, if you don't 'ppreciate som'um, you lose it."

"And who are you talking about?"

"You know, Lena, black people in this country."

"Herman, you trying to say we don't care nothing about the blues?"

"I ain't tryin'. I'm sayin' it. Ya'll gon' lose it. Gon' look up, and it ain't gon' be part a' us no mo'. It gon' be a part of somebody else, and we ain't gon' have nobody but ourse'fs to blame fo' it. Shoot, if it wa'n't fo' that trumpet-playin' boy from New Orleans, ya'll woulda lost Louis Armstrong. Lena, you gotta claim stuff to make it yo's. But we black folks gon' mess around and lose the blues. You watch."

Herman was serious about his music.

Music had always been a part of Lena's life. A part of her family's life, a part of her community's life. It infused every event, crisis, decision, love affair, heartbreak, everything.

Herman felt that way about music, too. It was a part of his natural life.

Out of the clear blue, he would look right into Lena's eyes and sing, "Do I love you? Oh, my, do I! Do I! 'Deed I do."

Herman sang to her like he was singing for his supper. And Herman loved to eat.

He'd start off singing to her from across the bedroom or the Great Jonah Room or the barn.

"Do I love you? *Oh, my, do I?* Do I? 'Deed I do."

Then, he'd move closer to her, singing the next chorus.

"Do I want you? *Oh, my, do I?* Do I? 'Deed I do."

Then, he would come even closer, his face inches away from hers, and sing:

"Do I need you? *Oh, my, do I?* Do I? 'Deed I do."

He would take her in his arms, strong country hundred-year-old arms, and kiss her all over, her face, her neck, her back, her stomach, her thighs, her feet, pausing to nuzzle her throat with a gnawing sound, then, he'd turn her around and bite her on her butt.

Herman serenaded Lena with bawdy songs from every decade of the last century. Seamlessly, he moved from performing some thoughtful domestic chore like washing the dishes in the sink to doing some erotic, raunchy song and dance from some vaudeville show right down to an achingly slow and suggestive bump and grind.

He had no shame.

He would sing an old blues number like "Hoochie Coochie Man," and Lena would be moved to roll down her silk bikini panties, slip them off and throw them at him as if he were on a stage.

Herman's voice was a soft baritone, like Brook Benton's or Jerry Butler's. And it would just insinuate its way into Lena's heart. She would close her eyes and see the eighth notes and the quarter notes float from his lips and drift toward her in a wave. The fluttering little notes, each one carrying his love for her, would rest on her chest, then disappear into her heart.

He saw how natural and happy she was with him, and it brought him close to hubris.

"You know what, Lena?" Herman said casually one day. "Every time I come near you like I did just then, you open yo' legs to me. Look, just like that."

Lena was more than mortified at Herman's revelation. "What business a ghost got lyin'?" he said often. She looked down at her legs where Herman was pointing and saw that she had indeed opened her legs as he approached.

Every image of every nun she had ever known came back to her from grammar school to college, speaking of Mary-like dresses and occasions of sin, which were mostly women, and their clothes and their smells and their breasts and their lacy underwear.

The principal at Blessed Martin de Porres School had explained it quite vividly: "Girls," Sister Louis Marie said in her thick Irish brogue, "your chastity, your virginity, your very virginal essence, is like a magnolia blossom. The beautiful creamy white flower of the South, so fragrant, so sweet. Yet!!! If you dare to lay a finger on that pure white chaste blossom it is *forever* marked!! Oh, girlies, there's no getting away from the truth.

"Well, you might as well throw it away, throw it in the trash heap. What good is it now, this once pure blossom, I ask you? All sullied and bruised? Might as well throw it away."

For a fleeting moment, Lena felt like one of the nun's allegorical flowers. Have I really become so carnal, she pondered, so lustful, that I can't even keep my legs together in this man's presence?

Lena had thought she was now truly a lusty woman, one who slapped her pussy at will, but Herman's observation embarrassed her. She lowered her head a bit, but Herman would have none of that.

"Oh, Lena, baby, I didn't say that to shame you. Shoot, I'm proud a' the fact. In fact, thank you, ma'am, fo' the honor." And he bowed his head a bit and let his eyelids drop briefly in her honor.

It was a new way of life for Lena—this living in the moment with a loving man who might disappear at any moment. She wanted to revel in it, throw it on the ground and roll around in it the way her horses did in a nearby field of clover in spring.

All Lena had to do was think about this world of hers without Herman and tears would start to well up in her eyes.

Lying in bed with Herman beside her, her grandmama's quilt spread over them, Lena felt blessed. Truly blessed. The way everyone in Mulberry always thought she was.

28

MULES

With her summer-reddened braids and her golden-brown skin, to Herman, Lena looked like autumn itself walking through the woods in October, dry leaves crackling under her boots. She had grown so strong in the few months since he first appeared in April. She had not been anything like weak before. But now she was lusty.

With his ghostly vision, Herman could see it in a way that Lena couldn't appreciate. Though Lord know, Herman thought as he stretched his stride to catch up to her, she sho' do appreciate it as much as she can.

"Uh, uh, uh," Herman said under his breath to himself as he shook his big head and continued walking. "I wish I had somebody I could tell 'bout this 'oman."

Lying naked next to him in bed or just in shorts out on the river deck in the low bone-warming sunlight, Herman would see Lena look down at her body and smile. She was surprised to see how toned and strong she looked when just a few weeks before she had remembered looking at herself naked in her grandmother's old standing full-length mirror and seeing a different person.

Lena had started out with a good God-given build and stayed active, riding her horses, turning their manure into the compost piles for the gardens, swimming laps every day in Rachel's Waters. She had seemed to effortlessly keep her great S-shaped figure into her early forties. But in the last four or five years, she dropped much of her physical activity as her responsibilities to her people grew. So, for quite some time now, she no longer rose and rode or walked or swam. Instead, she rose and got on the phone to begin taking care of business, business and duties that didn't seem to cease until way after dark.

To Lena's chagrin, her body had begun to show the lack of activity, sagging a little in the hips when she sat on the edge of her granite bathtub with just her panties on. She was almost beginning to thicken in the waist the way old dowagers did. The seldom-massaged skin around the base of her breasts was threatening to become crepey; her shoulders, forearms and breasts were beginning to think about becoming round and soft.

The word "flabby" had come to mind. And it shocked her. She had seen other women who had obviously had cute bodies as young adults, but hadn't yet realized that they no longer looked cute, little and toned the way they always had.

Just weeks before Herman arrived, Lena had said, "Oh, Lord, I'm on the road to looking like one of those women!"

She had intended that very day to leave The Place and her business meetings in the hands of her staff a couple of hours early and saddle up Baby for a flat-out run the way she used to every morning. But when she got home, there had been a note on her door or a person at the door or a phone call from somebody in need, and she had never gotten around to her ride or any other exercise.

But now as the autumn days grew shorter and Herman pointed out the Swan constellation each night to remind her, "You know, they mate for life, Lena," she thought, Damn! Look at my body!

She hadn't noticed the gradual change over time. How could she? She had been too busy to take a look at her own self. All that ripping and running with Herman in the woods, exploring caves on her land that extended into the next county, racing their horses, betting blow jobs and massages on who would win.

And then, she thought, there was the lovemaking.

For Lena, that activity covered everything she and Herman did or planned to do to give each other physical, that sometimes verged on spiritual, pleasure. Fucking, licking, sucking, scratching, fondling, tickling, holding, pumping, biting. All of it meant lovemaking to her. And she had to credit her incredibly strengthened inner thigh muscles as much to riding Herman as to riding horses.

Gloria teased her when she came in The Place, "Look at her. Think she cute again."

The truth was Lena didn't *think* she was cute. She *knew* she was cute. And she hadn't thought *that* since she was a child prohibited from crossing Forest Avenue by herself. Herman thought she was pretty cute, too. He hád caught her admiring her strong, healthy, fit body in the old warped mirror and hat rack in the barn.

"It's hard to believe that that's Lena McPherson standin' there, eh, baby?"

Lena couldn't get the small pleased smile off her face quickly enough, so she turned around and let Herman see her pride.

"Things are so different. I'm so different, Herman, sometimes I can't even take it in. If I didn't know better, I'd think this was one of my dreams."

Their passion for each other had not cooled at all from spring to fall. At night, in their bed under the covers like old married people, they still made love like dancers in a Salt 'n' Pepa video, moaning and grinding and humping and caressing, the music from Lena's matchbox playing furiously to their rhythm. Some nights when they made love, champagne corks popped in the wine cellar. And through it all, Herman never forgot to stop and kiss and lick the cherished mole on her neck that he called a "beauty mark."

"This isn't a dream, is it, Herman?" She knew Herman wouldn't lie to her about it.

"Naw, baby, this ain't no dream," Herman said straight up.

"Good," Lena said, heaving a big sigh. She gave herself a nice firm pat on the seat of her jeans and went over to a rough wooden table to pick up a currying brush.

Keba's rich brown coat glistened with the attention she was getting, and Lena felt the quickness of life each time she gently stroked the mare's tight rounding belly.

"I *am* different now, Herman. My life is so different," Lena said as she continued currying the horse's thick mahogany mane. Both she and Herman gave Keba as much love and attention as they could now that Keba was expecting. In the next compartment, Baby began softly kicking the side of her stall.

"Hush up, Baby, I'll get to you," Lena said, quieting the horse for a while. "I look back just six months, Herman, and I truly think, How could I have done all that shit? And it's not that I was miserable. No, Herman, really I wasn't. I know it looks like I was trying to take care of the world but . . ."

Herman wouldn't even let her finish.

"You were, sugar. Ain't no buts 'bout it. You *were* tryin' t' take care a' the world. And you *were* miserable. Yo' yoke, baby, was hard."

He didn't even give her time to reply.

"You mighta been pretty on the outside right along. But on the inside," he declared, pointing a long sturdy forefinger at her head, "Look at yo'se'f! That's how you felt!"

The currying brush fell to the floor from Lena's trembling hand as if someone had just read from the Gospel of Luke. "You fool! This very night your soul shall be required of you!"

She looked down in surprise at her bare arms and went over to the old warped mirror. She was shocked by her reflection. There were long thin scratches on both her arms as if she had gotten caught without a long-sleeved shirt among the rosebushes in Miss Zimmie's garden. On the left side of her face along the faint fading scar that a hot curling iron wielded carelessly at Delores' Beauty Parlor before her favorite beautician Mamie arrived had caused when she was a child was a long thin scratch as if she had fallen on a cat.

When she saw the unexplained scratches on her face and arms she looked at her ghostly lover and teacher and said, "I know, Herman, I *needed* to get rid of that cat."

Herman just sighed and smiled, then went back to work.

Lena didn't seem to notice, but the longer Herman stayed with her, the more her childhood powers—powers of the caul—were returning to her. The random voices she had heard as a child were now the inner voices that guided her. Now, she put the magic on declining plants and revived them. She began to be able to look at strangers and familiars alike and sometimes read their thoughts and intentions.

Not many people drove up Lena's road anymore to knock on her door in the night. She was proud of herself for having made it clear so many times that they couldn't anymore, and she was proud of her folks for how well they were taking the change in things.

Herman had punctuated her resolve for privacy by building a wide locked gate of Middle Georgia pine a few hundred feet before James Petersen's house. He set a huge mailbox in the posts beside the gate, and he didn't install an intercom system to Lena's house or to James Petersen's.

"When folks come to a locked fence, they oughta turn 'round," Herman said.

He also made a long wooden sign with the initials "LLL" etched into it and hung it at the back door where most of the traffic entered.

"What's that stand for, Herman?" she asked when she came in that afternoon.

"It stand fo' 'Leave Lena 'Lone,' baby. That's what it stand fo'. Thought I'd put up a sign just in case I ain't 'round right then to say it."

Then, he marched right down to the new wooden gate and posted another handmade "LLL" sign there.

When someone *was* coming, Lena could always feel it. She would call James Petersen at his house and alert him. Then, she and Herman would make themselves scarce while James Petersen dealt with the visitor or delivery.

Where Lena used to envision pictures of her people stranded and suffering without her, she now saw flashes of folks helping each other out.

Nothing interrupted her and Herman as they lay in the grip of her big bentwood bed—surrounded by a sea of books and papers, his guitar and her laptop computer. It felt like a Sunday afternoon, but Lena really didn't know what day it was. They lay up in her bed like that mornings, afternoons and evenings on end sometimes, the sky changing above them through the skylight. With the French doors open onto the screened-in section of deck and the grounds and river beyond, with small yellow sulfur butterflies flitting along the surface of the Ocawatchee like patches of sunlight, it was their favorite place to lounge.

Now that she had delegated most of her business to others, her days out at her house by the river ran together like the creeks that fed the Ocawatchee.

She and Herman did just about all the work with the horses now, finding work elsewhere for the stable hand and the gardening crew except Mr. Renfroe. Ever since the Fourth of July, Lena had counted herself among Renfroe's staff whom he directed to weed and haul and dig and turn. It was part of the reason she had gotten her body back. Even the weak left ankle that had required her to wear an elastic brace from time to time seemed to have grown stronger over the last few months. For the spots that still gave her pain, Herman heated his molecules up and wrapped himself around her entire foot and leg.

Lena had watched Herman study her—her body, her expressions, her moods, her body language, her secrets—until she finally realized what Herman was doing. He was charting her body, as if she were a body of water he planned to navigate over and over, and he wanted to know landmarks.

He would delicately—and sometimes not so delicately—plant little baby kisses all down her body, from up under her underarms, past her breast, down the curve of her waist, then back around to kiss the round of her butt. Then, a kiss on the spot above her hipbone, a sliding kiss down the outside of her thigh, another detour up to the curve of her belly above her vagina, then back down the other thigh until he stopped to suck gently on the meaty indentation behind her knee. Herman's big bushy mustache tickled her along the whole route, giving her even more reason to laugh.

In summer when she wore sleeveless cotton blouses and at night when she wore nothing, Herman liked to plant a kiss like a flag on the tip of her shoulder and then kiss all the way down her arm, stopping momentarily at her fading wrinkled vaccination mark, and continue on to the bend of her elbow, where he planted another kiss, like a marker for an explorer.

In fact, that was what he was doing: exploring Lena just the way that they explored the woods surrounding the river and her house.

Herman had his favorite parts of Lena's body like special points of interest on an adventurer's hand-drawn map. One was her behind. He cupped her butt in his big hands, as much of it as he could hold. He held it up, lifting Lena into his naked lap like an offering to the big ass goddess.

He was always talking about her butt, speaking of it in the third person.

"Would you sit yo' pretty ass down?!!" he would say as close to exasperation as he got with Lena.

"Lena, would you please stop dawdlin' at every flower you see," he'd tease, "and bring yo' big butt on so we can be in the water by sunset. We burnin' daylight here, baby!"

"Miss Lena, would you do me the honor of bringin' yo' fine ass on to bed and let those papers wait 'til mornin'?"

Herman was always looking for an opportunity to prove how hot her butt was. He liked to sit in chairs after she had alit, then jump up as if burned, yelling, "Ooo, hot butt! Hot butt!" If she wasn't vigilant, Herman would take a big kitchen match—he couldn't stand the smaller safety matches—and run its red and white tip along the curve of her hip, pull it away and light it with his ghostly magic, pretending Lena's hot butt had set it on fire.

Herman felt he could worship at Lena's back. The curve of it, the small concave spot at the base of her spine, the gentle slope of her shoulders.

He could do the same thing at her hair.

Herman would take a fistful of her thick brown braids in his hand and inhale so deeply that Lena would think, He needs that scent to live, just like I need air.

"I need all of you to live, baby," Herman said one time in response to her thoughts. And then he regretted it. He noticed that if he didn't say anything to remind her, Lena forgot from time to time that he could read her mind. It was one of the few things that he did that made her angry.

"Damn, Herman, if your thoughts aren't private and personal and protected, then what part of you is?"

Stung at the suggestion that he was in any way invading her life or her privacy, Herman told her, "Well, shoot, baby, you just there, hanging out fo' the whole world to see. You ain't got to be no spirit with special powers to invade yo' life. Look at all the folks in Mulberry. And you got the nerve to be mad wid me 'cause I don't pretend not to know yo' thoughts sometimes."

Lena was stunned at his bluntness with her.

"Herman!" she said.

"Aw, Lena, baby, you don't razz me!" he said, coming over to give her a kiss.

"You old-timey Negro! What that mean?" she asked, laughing in spite of her hurt feelings.

"Oh, yeah, I'm old-timey when you don't know what 'razz' mean. But you expect me to know what yo' matchbox is!!" Herman was in rare form, indeed. And his joke and kiss smoothed over her hurt feelings and their little rough patch like his hands smoothing over her hair.

Herman loved Lena's hair. The hair on her body, the hair under her arms, the hair on her arms, the hair on her legs, the hair on her pussy and the hair on her head.

"Why you shave yo' legs and up under yo' arms?" Herman asked early on as she stepped out of the shower. "I don't think I ever heard of a 'oman shavin' her body atall."

"You don't like it?" Lena wanted to know as she raised both her arms in the bathroom mirror to get a better view of her armpits.

"Oh, it's okay," Herman said easily.

Lena vowed right then not to shave again, just as she decided to stop using deodorant because Herman liked to lick under her arms. But these were the least of the changes in her toilette.

With Herman, Lena did something she had never done in her life. She went two, three and sometimes four days without showering or bathing. At first, she was just too busy playing with Herman to keep up with her usual hour-long toilette. She tried to squeeze her toilette in sometime during their days or nights. Then, when she didn't feel like making time for it, she just stopped trying.

Riding her horses with Herman, working in the garden, she would stop, bend her head down and sniff up under her raised arm. "Now, I know I ought to by rights smell a lot worse than I do. I ought to be smelling like a Montana mule, as Mama would say, 'round about now. But I don't."

Lena didn't fool herself into thinking that she smelled like the fall-blooming jasmine twining with the wisteria around the sycamore tree. She didn't smell that sweet. No one would confuse her scent with that of honeysuckle.

She smelled like earth. Like dirt. Like Herman. Like the rich black loam she brushed from under her nails each night. Like the dusty red roads out on her property when the rain showered down on their hard-packed surfaces and sent the scent of Georgia earth throughout the air.

She smelled like the earth the way Rachel, her ghost at the beach, had smelled like the ocean.

As the weather had warmed in the summer months, Lena and Herman had not bathed more than for their own entertainment. They almost hated to see cool weather come because in the steamy days of July, August and September, Lena and Herman regularly had washed each other's hair outdoors with big buckets of Cleer Flo' water from the streams that were now flowing copiously through her property. It was a ritual they reveled in.

They enjoyed hauling the water from the nearest stream, a good two hundred yards off from the stables.

"I even like totin' this water wid you, Lena," Herman told her with a wide proud smile one day as they hauled two buckets each, Lena's smaller than Herman's, from the stream to the barn. That's where they liked to perform the hair-washing ritual.

It made them feel good.

Just messing in Herman's great Samson-like mane made Lena feel good. Herman knew it.

"Hey, Lena," he'd say to her, coming up to her seated at her desk with a big red bush comb and brush in one hand. He'd gently push her legs apart. "Scratch out my head some fo' me, hear, baby?"

He would never wait for an answer. He knew what it would be. He'd fall to the floor at her feet and turn to settle his broad shoulders in the lacuna between her knees. He fell to the floor like a young boy. And Lena had to chuckle at how agile her "pig meat" was.

Lena would always smile when she'd feel the muscles of her inner thighs strain and ache sweetly at the pressure of him between her big legs. His first weeks in her home, in her bed, inside her, she couldn't believe how sore her entire body was from making love regularly to a husky man. Not just the insides of her thighs, but muscles and sinew and sections of her whole body ached from rolling around with Herman on the decks off her house and over the river, on and off the padded throws onto the wet soil, rubbing against each other in a corner of the sauna until they were faint from the heat, lying with their heads between each other's legs on her mama's long shiny shellacked breakfast table in the sunny corner or the kitchen overlooking the exercise grounds of the stable.

At first, the outside of her hips ached, the muscles under her behind ached, her pectoral muscles ached, the arches of her feet ached, the small of her back ached, her titties ached.

The women at Candace got sick of seeing that little wince, then that little smile on Lena's face every time she moved. Once, Precious even heard Lena go, "Ooo," when she stooped down to pick up the reading glasses she had dropped.

"Been working out, Miss Mac?" Precious asked, reaching out a fleshy arm to help Lena up.

Lena had just smiled a big old wide grin and said, "You could say that." And Precious was sure for a moment that she heard lovely music playing over the office sound system.

In the still-warm days of autumn, when Lena had to go into town to check on a business transaction or to purchase something for Herman, she slipped on some of her beautiful soft underwear that smelled of the herbs and potpourri James Petersen strewed in her dresser drawers, put on one of her mother's sleeveless linen shifts that just skimmed her body and threw a cardigan sweater around her shoulders against a sudden chill. The outfit looked right with the flats and sandals and low-heeled boots she only wore now.

Herman loved these dresses of Nellie's from the summers of the sixties. "You look like you naked under those shifts," he told her appreciatively, even though he knew full well what she had on underneath.

Most likely, he had picked out her lingerie.

Herman appreciated all of Lena's clothes—underwear *and* outerwear. He appreciated the material, the feel, the workmanship, the stitching, the decoration of the clothes *on Lena*, but he especially enjoyed taking the items of clothing *off her*. He kept his nails short, clipped and clean with his buck knife just so he would not accidentally scratch or injure her. He favored unhooking, unfastening, unbuttoning, unzipping, unlacing, unscrewing, unsheathing. He loved unbuckling her hose from their garters and slowly rolling them down her thighs, over her knees to her ankles without one single snag.

He reveled in undoing the hooks of her satin bra, holding the ends together with one hand while he used the other to dip her breast out in one handful into his mouth.

Lena had clothes that gave Herman an erection when he saw them just lying on a chair or on the floor or hanging on a padded satin hanger in her long walk-in closet. She had a pair of thigh-high, glove-soft doeskin slate-colored boots that he said he didn't even allow himself to touch when Lena wasn't around.

Just weeks before she and Herman met, Lena had purchased a red and orange and teal-blue satin Chinese robe. The first time she wore the kimono, she had let the wrap slide off her naked shoulders, her arms, her back and down her hips in one fluid motion, landing in a vermilion pool at her bare feet. "Lena, baby, I can't get that picture a' you out my mind," he told her.

When Lena did think to bathe or shower after that, she never did it alone. If she even thought about taking her clothes off to take a steamy shower or if she decided to take a real long soaking bath in a tub of hot soapy water, Herman would magically appear right there next to the tub.

Look at him standing there with that eager grin on his face, Lena would think as she checked out Herman leaning against the doorjamb of the bathroom waiting expectantly and unapologetically for the floor show to start.

"Herman, you aren't even ashamed!" Lena would chide him regularly. "You act like you paid for that box seat and you ready for the ten P.M. show."

He'd just throw his head back and laugh. Then, right before Lena's eyes, Herman would become water, warm soapy water, and splash into the marble tub, raising the level of the water in the tub to near overflowing.

Once a part of the water, he submerged and enveloped Lena, swirling around every part of her body like a gentle whirlpool.

When Herman heard Lena moan, "Umm," he heated up his molecules right there in the tub and reactivated the almond-paste bath emollient floating on the surface, suddenly filling the tub with bubbles.

Herman's appreciation of Lena was so natural, so open, so guileless, that Lena never felt turned into an object by his watching and his presence. He watched because he liked to watch her. She liked it, too.

Any number of times during the day, Lena would stop and just laugh at how much she loved this smart, kind, extraordinary man. Throughout the day and night, she would say prayers of thanksgiving to God for Herman. It was amazing to Lena to note the blessings she gave thanks for now compared to months before. Then, it was thank you, Father, Mother, Yemaya, Oshun, for the roofs over people's heads in Mulberry. Thank you for the last business deal. Thank you for the new flooring at The Place being done so quickly.

Now, it was thank you for the way Herman smells in the morning. She gave thanks that the collard greens that day tasted sweet. She thanked the universe for the rain that their gardens needed. She thanked her maker for the time to sit and read and for the blooming of the moonflower.

Lena was truly thankful for the way Herman smelled: the way The Place had smelled the morning she had danced through the renovated juke joint, like a man's underarms, like the musk of activity, like the scent of outdoors.

Lena loved to lay her cheek on his thigh and bury her face in the thicket between his thighs. He had a pungent odor there that Lena never tired of smelling.

He faced each new day renewed, refreshed. Like a new man. You would have thought that he had gotten a full eight hours of shut-eye. But Herman had no need for sleep. He had so wanted to be with Lena, he had so wanted to be alive again just for Lena, that she would forget from time to time that he was a spirit, with no need for anything, it seemed, but her.

Herman said, "I'm glad I got a body, not just fo' us, baby, but so I can *feel* thangs, *appreciate* thangs again." He stopped to touch Lena's stationery, her flowered hand-painted cards, her Japanese paper in cream and red, her mother's collection of old fountain pens. "You forget how good life is."

Lena loved to watch him move and touch things and stretch his new body.

In the days after he first appeared, his stretching was a part of his becoming real, becoming whole. As he threw his generous-sized head back and extended his palms toward the sky, arching his elegant back with his expansive chest thrust forward, his pants and shirt pulling at the seams, Lena could see and sense the muscle and sinew pulling and appearing, becoming stronger and leaner and more real with each "Ummm" Herman uttered.

"Feel good to stretch," Herman would say.

When Lena dropped hints about her forty-sixth birthday coming up in a month, Herman couldn't stop shaking his head in amazement.

"Lena, baby, you don't look like no 'oman in her middle forties to me. Shoot, in my time, you'd be a grandmother many times over and ready fo' yo' grave. God, Lena, when my own mother was that age, she was a tired 'oman even though she had enjoyed her life in the settlement. Life was just harder then, especially for womens. And look at you with yo' Victory Secrets underwear and yo' fast car and all yo' property . . ."

"Um, Herman, you almost sound like you resent I got the kind of life I got." Lena was a little hurt by the tone in Herman's voice and didn't try too hard to hide it.

"Oh, no, baby," Herman said seriously. "It's just so amazin' t' me that thangs coulda changed so much in less than a hundred years."

Lena chuckled.

"I know you think that's a eternity—a hundred years—but it ain't hardly a tick on the clock or a cycle a' the moon.

"In just a hundred years, a black 'oman like yo'se'f in her mid-forties is in her prime. And you damn sho' in yo' prime, baby. All in just the tick a' the clock, Lena."

Lena smiled looking at Herman because he, too, despite being into his second century, was also sure in *his* prime.

29
REAL

Lena thought Herman had a beautiful dick.

The first time she saw Herman's semen on the tip of his penis, she was awestruck. She reached out and took a drop on her finger to examine it more closely. She brought it to her nose and smelled it, rubbing the silky liquid between her thumb and forefinger.

"Herman is *real!*" she said softly to herself in wonder. Not that Lena had actually doubted Herman's existence there in Middle Georgia. He had been with her seven months and was now such a complete part of her life that there was no doubt in her mind that he was no dream.

Just looking at the seed on his penis, Lena knew that Herman was no incubus. He was real and he was good.

Herman's uncircumcised penis was a new one for Lena, who had never been a real dick woman anyway. She hadn't seen that many, but she didn't think she needed to have seen a lot to appreciate Herman's penis in the same way she appreciated him.

Lena had as much interest in tongues and fingers and ears and minds as in penises, and all things considered, she had seen her share.

But next to Herman, all those men she knew before—the passionless ones with cushy jobs, the ones who were wastes of time with good bodies, the ones who continued to look at a football game while you talked—seemed lifeless, dead, empty as an ancient robbed tomb. Herman was boyish without being puerile, fun-loving without being silly, manly without being overbearing, foolish without being a fool.

Herman prided himself on seldom having to rely on his ghostly power to impress, please or take care of Lena. Even as an ordinary man, Lena knew he wasn't any ordinary man.

He didn't seem to have time for what she and Sister called "manshit, one word." The name encompassed all the strange, foreign, foolish, unrealistic, annoying, spirit-crushing things men, *all men*, did naturally, it seemed, without a thought. Things that regularly drove women crazy. "Manshit" included everything from leaving the toilet seat up to not stopping to ask for directions.

"Lena, baby, I got a powerful pocketful a' tenderness stored up in me from the last hundred years," he told her. He showed it to her every chance he got.

Then, he punctuated his statement with a deep, long, lush kiss.

When Herman kissed Lena, deeply, tenderly, gently, insistently, urgently, she often thought of Moms Mabley and the comedy routine of the hysterically funny toothless genius Lena had heard as a child.

"And that man kissed *me*!" Moms had explained about an amorous encounter with a prized younger man. "My toes curled up just like that!!"

That's what Herman's kisses did for Lena.

They made her toes curl up just like that.

And although he was technically nearly a hundred years older than she, Lena realized when he sprinted out to the shed and back before she could finish peeing, when he grabbed a bale of hay with the huge iron tongs and slung it on his back, when he sat in a chair sometimes with one of his legs thrown over the arm like a teenager, that Herman was indeed her younger man, her pig meat.

"Look at that old lightbulb," Lena's mother would say about some aging Romeo, especially ones who *had been* lovers in their day, the ones who were really old. "Old men when I was a child still out there trying to be sweethearting like they certifiable pig meat—young and tender," she'd say. Nellie called them "flambeaux."

I wonder what Mama would call Herman, Lena thought with a smile. She said a quick prayer for the repose of Moms' and her own mother's souls whenever Herman kissed her like that.

Herman kissed like Tommy Davis, the first boy Lena knew who really could kiss. Lena remembered sitting in the parking lot of M'Lady Cleaners after the James Brown and the Famous Flames Show and Revue at the Mulberry County Auditorium. Tommy was all gangling arms and legs and pretty, smooth brown skin—just fifteen himself then, like Lena. But Tommy had not kissed like a fifteen-year-old boy. He kissed, Lena thought, like a man. He kissed with passion.

Before Herman came and put his magic on her, Lena had a *powerful amount* of compassion. What she didn't have was passion. Her wild, raging passion had been depleted by all her duties, her responsibilities, her gifts, her wealth, her business dealings, her property, her life.

She still had to struggle to keep Herman from becoming her god. Seeing him jealous made him more human, more real to Lena. One day in mid-October, she got her chance.

Herman eyed the young man coming up the driveway by the river in his old beat-up electric-blue truck for a good long time. Longer than he usually took to look at someone, Lena noticed.

"This boy, what he atta?" Herman wanted to know.

Lena, headed to the back door, stopped in her tracks and turned to look at her man. She laughed.

"Herman, he's not *after* anything! He's just someone's son come to pick up some papers for their farm."

Herman didn't seem totally convinced. Lena had to smile.

"With so many people taking care of their own business now, folks need their papers. It's hard to believe I had that many deeds and wills and stuff in the safe."

Herman disappeared into the bedroom without another word, but Lena could tell he was not convinced.

She couldn't believe she had to reassure Herman, *her man*, that she had no interest whatsoever in this other pig meat who was indeed trying to flirt with her. The young man—she thought he must have been about twenty-seven or twenty-eight—craned his head around her a couple of times as they stood in the Great Jonah Room to see if there was anyone else in the house before he spoke.

"So, eh, Miss McPherson, Lena. I can call you 'Lena,' can't I?" the young man had asked, eyeing this woman who looked like the title character in *Carmen Jones* he had seen on cable the night before. He had sat through the credits just to learn that Dorothy Dandridge was the name of the beautiful actress.

One of Lena's undershirt straps had even slid off her shoulder like one of those *Carmen Jones* blouses. And, the "boy" noticed she wasn't wearing a bra. He could see the outline of her nipples under her shirt.

Lena went about her business quickly and professionally, but she saw him watching her and looking for an opening. She smiled at the flirting, but she didn't give him a chance.

When the young man left, frustrated at having made no headway with Lena, Herman appeared, really miffed, walking around the house with a heavier-than-usual footfall.

"You don't see me being jealous of your otherworld friends, do you?" Lena said.

When she didn't get a rise from him, she continued, digging deeper.

"You don't see me being jealous of Anna Belle, do you?"

Lena suddenly shivered as if someone had just danced over her grave. She knew she had hit her target.

She had not really wanted to bring up the spirit of the woman who was out to get her, but she just *had* to ask. Herman had not mentioned Anna Belle in the month since Lena had found the dents in the door down at The Place.

Actually, now that Anna Belle's name was out in the open, Lena felt better. There had not been one sign of Anna Belle in more than a month. Lena needed to know what had happened.

Herman was silent so long, Lena thought, Oh, shit, I done gone too far with this man. Why the hell did I have to mention that woman's name?

However, when he turned to her, he didn't look a bit bothered.

"I was wonderin' if you was gonna mention her again," he said.

Lena shrugged her shoulders, pretending to be unconcerned.

"Lena, baby, right after you saw those marks on the do' downtown, I did just like I said. I took care a' that thang. I wouldn't no mo' have you—of all people—walkin' 'round here scared a' some 'oman I done brought in yo' life for nothin' in the world, this one or the next."

Lena knew he was serious.

"So I had me a talk wid Anna Belle."

Lena sat there in the heavy silence waiting for Herman to continue. When he didn't, she asked exactly what she wanted to know.

"You saw Anna Belle? You met with her?"

"I don't know if you would call it a 'meetin',' 'xactly, Lena baby. I just went out in the yard and called her. The wind stirred up a bit in a familiar way, and I started talkin'."

Lena leaned forward waiting for the details.

Herman chuckled at his woman and her curiosity.

"All I said was you was the only 'oman fo' me, you *the 'oman*, now and fo'ever. And nothin' was gon' change that, ever."

Lena just smiled. Then, she asked, "And that was it?"

"What somebody gon' say to that?" Herman wanted to know, coming over to Lena to close the space between them. They kissed, dismissing Anna Belle and the "boy" who had been trying to flirt with Lena.

Before Herman came, Lena had gotten off on flirting. She did it with just about everybody. It was an inherited natural gift. Jonah, when he really put his mind to it, could charm the sweetness out of syrup. And Nellie could get anything she wanted by opening up her face and smiling. Lena could, too.

But Lena didn't need that kind of fake passion anymore, flirting with a bag boy, a liquor salesman, a fellow passenger on a quick flight out of Mulberry.

Herman rekindled her passion, unstopped its rush and gave it a number of new directions in which to flow.

He did it with love. He did it with concern. He did it with wisdom. He did it with laughter. He did it with sex. And he did it with surprises.

Herman loved to surprise Lena.

He would walk up to Lena while she curried and cooed to Keba, who, halfway through her term, seemed to be getting big with her foal so quickly. Herman would have his hands behind him and say, "Baby, close yo' eyes and stick out yo' hand."

Sometimes she'd squeal as she shimmied her shoulders, dropped the currying brush and pulled off her short leather work gloves and, with her eyes shut tightly, offered her palms to Herman.

There was no telling what he'd drop in her hands. A juicy piece of fruit, a small wiggling salamander that immediately turned the color of her palms, a velvety Mirandy rose that he had stripped clean of thorns with his new buck knife.

Herman was thrilled with himself for being able to surprise Lena—"Surprising a child like you, born wid a veil and all," Herman would say, pretending to be incredulous. But actually, he was proud that Lena wasn't surprised by nearly as much as she had six months earlier when she truly did not have a clue.

Now, when he came up behind her suddenly, she knew he was there. He had seen her do the same thing lately with people who came by for a rare visit to her house.

Lena was becoming sensitive about all kinds of things. A number of times, Herman had heard her say, "Umm," out of the clear blue sky and go to the phone to make a call to discover it was just the thing to do. She knew when the weather was about to change. And now that she was about to change life, she was just beginning to understand her own menstrual cycle.

But Herman could still surprise her with his acts of love.

"Shoot, Lena," he had said back in September, sweating and digging in the sun outside her office, "you favor these hummers so much, it ain't too late in the season for yo' land. I'll plant some mo' of these fire-red cannas fo' you here in the sun. And you'll have mo' of the little creatures than you can shake a stick at."

Herman had watched Lena sit for hours at the big windows in her workroom watching and waiting for the tiny emerald birds with the slash of nail-polish red at their throats. Since Cleer Flo', a couple of rufous hummingbirds up from the Gulf Coast and one with a purple head from Mexico had joined their East Coast family at the flowers. The bird's tiny tongue darting in and out of the deep full throat of the canna flower made Lena and Herman both hot.

When Lena's birthday came around in mid-November, he celebrated as if it were the beginning of time. He trained the telescope on Mars so Lena could see the planet flashing red, then green, then white in the night sky.

"My day a' birth was that day in April when I kissed you and you kissed me back, Lena. That was my birthday, thank you." But Herman wasn't an Aries. Lena just knew that he was a Cancer. A child of the moon. Drawn to water. A sweet home-loving homebody.

Lena had put her newfound passion for her homebody lover into nesting, into making her cabin out by the river as soft and as cozy, as inviting and hard to leave, as she could. Leafing through a home furnishings catalog, she would see an outrageously overstuffed down comforter and immediately picture the two of them wrapped up in the cover together.

As the nights began to grow cooler and cooler in the fall, Lena made sure that every chair and sofa they used had a thick cotton or wool throw on it so Herman would have something handy to throw around his shoulders if he got chilly as he sat and read or strummed his music box or her matchbox.

Lena watched Herman lying at the broad foot of her creepy-looking bed, wearing the bright red long johns she had ordered for him buttoned all the way up to his neck, against the cold of a near-winter night in Mulberry, running his big hands appreciatively over the various patterns of her grandmother's quilt—the homey blue and white flowers with yellow centers, the elegant red satin, the twining green vines with purple hearts hanging from them, the black and white checks, the pink and white gingham.

"It feels good to be real again, Herman?" she asked him. And he just snuggled in and smiled.

Most nights, before or after making love, they'd swim a few laps in the heated pool, then race to the sauna to lie naked, one above and one below, on the wide cedar benches. Surrounded by billowing clouds of eucalyptus steam rising from the hot lava rocks, they let the heat soak into their pores, their worked muscles, their tired bones.

Each night, Herman remarked, "This feel good, Lena."

Then, before crawling into bed, Herman would take Lena's hand cradled in his, close his eyes and repeat the first prayer he had ever invoked with Lena.

"I do thank you, Lord."

Before Herman came, Lena would lie alone in her bed night after night after night and pull her Grandmama's heavy quilt up over her body and into her arms like a child for warmth and love and assurance. At those times, she could almost hear her grandmother's voice assure her, "Grandmama always here, baby."

Lena had always slept with one of her Grandmama's quilts at the foot of her bed. She would feel its weight, like her grandmother's hand, resting on her feet while she slept, and she didn't feel so alone.

Nearly thirty years after her grandmother's death, the handmade quilts she had stitched with such care still smelled like the old woman and her bedroom in the house on Forest Avenue—a little bit of dust, a little bit of talc, a little bit of age.

When the first chill set in, Herman had shivered and teased her that in his day, folks had called her part of Mulberry County "Cold Neck."

"Cold Neck!" he'd say as he walked through the house after checking on the horses for the night, his feet toasty in the shearling-lined brown leather slippers she had bought for him back in the summer when she discovered he was cold-natured.

"On a night like this un, I guess you can see why they called it that!" he'd say.

Then, he'd shiver.

In the nearly winter nights of late October and early November, the heated pool, the sauna and their bed were Lena and Herman's domain. They took turns running from the bedroom to the kitchen from time to time for snacks in their red plaid flannel pajamas and long silk underwear. Herman was always ready to eat.

"I could eat a little som'um-som'um," he'd say as if the idea just came to him.

Lena would pretend to suck her teeth and say under her breath loud enough for Herman to hear her, "I bet you could!" But she reveled in getting up and fixing him a little something.

When Herman couldn't stand being inside any longer, he'd get them both up from their cozy nest and go outside—day or night—for some fresh air and excitement. "Can't stand it no mo' bein' cooped up in here."

Lena would sometimes stretch and moan and pretend to protest, "Awww, Herman, we comfortable here." She'd point to the hot drinks in thick ceramic mugs and the chessboard they had set up.

"We so comfortable," she repeated, stretching out in her long red underwear. But she only said it so he'd come over and tease and coax and play with her a little before she got up and started donning her outdoor gear.

"Come on, Lena, baby, we sitting up in here like *old people!*"

Chuckling to herself as she pulled on her heavy insulated socks, she'd think, Shoot, you were born in 1855. You *are* old people!

Herman just laughed at her thoughts.

"I ain't as old as all a' that," he said, and made her laugh even more, grabbing at her "stuff" as she tried to dress.

Once outside, Herman would stop at the first bend in the trail to lean Lena against a tree, and they would dry-hump each other through their heavy warm clothes. Hot, sweaty and musky inside their layered clothing, he would rub Lena slow and hard against the rough bark of a live oak tree, then turn to enjoy Lena doing the same thing to him until they both came.

30
HER MAN

Talk of Lena and her mystery man had been buzzing through Mulberry since the end of summer. But the week of Thanksgiving, it was being discussed all over town. Who was this man who was so important Lena couldn't seem to leave him for a minute? And what? We little folks in town ain't even good enough to *meet him*!? they asked each other. Even an unexpected Cleer Flo' in mid-November could not push Lena and her mystery lover to the back burner of the town's gossip mill.

"And by the way," folks asked each other, "didn't *he* show up about the same time Lena started acting so funny?"

Some of her father's old poker and skin buddies swore it was an older man Lena had fallen for.

"It *has* to be a man with some age on him. Got to be a old man. You notice how she been talking lately?"

"Hell, she ain't been around long 'nough lately for nobody to be noticing how she talking.

"How she talking?"

"Shoot, you ain't noticed all them old-timey expressions Lena McPherson been using? Man, you must be blind *and deaf* in your old age."

"Well, since you so clued-in, clue me in."

"That's just what I'm talking 'bout. When's the last time you heard somebody 'sides us say something like that?"

"Like what?"

"Like what you just said. 'Clue me in.' When's the last time you heard somebody Lena's age say that?"

"Humm, you are right."

"Know I'm right. All you didn't say was 'Daddy.' 'Clue me in, Daddy.' You old sona bitch."

"Yeah, and what a young chippie like Lena know 'bout whiskey and watermelon killing you? She may a' heard it when she was a child, but when the last time somebody her age say something like that?"

"She did come in here the end of the summer talkin' 'bout whiskey and wallermelon, didn't she?"

"She sho' did."

"Naw, can't be no old man."

"Why the hell you say that? You think a man with a few years on him can't get a woman like Lena McPherson?"

"Naw, hell, I'm as much of a *real* man as I was thirty years ago. My manhood ain't in my hambone. But I hear her new man doing all kinds a' work out there on her property. Shoeing the hosses and planting scuppernong vines and building rose trellises all 'round the house."

"Yeah, even put up a big old wooden gate 'cross the road near James Petersen's house. I went out there and seen it myself. Damn good piece a' work. But what Lena McPherson need with a gate? Got a lock on it, too."

"Yeah, well, irregardless, all that building and hauling and stuff. That ain't old man's work. That's young man labor."

"Maybe that's what it is, then."

"What?"

"She might not have no old man out there, she might have her a boy out there."

"You think that's the reason ain't nobody seen this Very Important Man who done *took* Lena 'way from us?"

"Could be. Could be he just a boy."

To this group of old flambeaux, "a boy" could mean anyone from a teenager to a man in his mid-forties.

And that was just the men. When the women in Mulberry discussed the possibilities, they brought infinitely more insight and incisiveness to the subject.

Women down at The Place tried to draw Gloria into the fray, but she stayed above it and refused to even discuss her employer and friend with them.

"Now, a woman don't look that good in her mid-forties unless *something* is going mighty good in her life."

"Yeah, Gloria, I even heard *you* asking her, 'Lena, who you fucking?' I heard you way back in June or July or August, one of them hot months, right down here at The Place say that. So don't be acting like you don't know what we talking 'bout . . . woman like you."

Gloria just shrugged her shoulders, smiled the way she had seen her mentor Nellie McPherson do when she didn't want to get involved in the politics of The Place and looked down that long long country road.

"Well, ya'll can sit around here crying in your beer wondering what ever became of *our Lena* and such. But I'mo do something about it. I'mo corner her and ask her. Next time I see her, I'm just gon' corner her and ask her."

"Well, I wish you luck 'cause the last time *I* saw her—can't even hardly remember when it was now—I tried to tell her what was going on with me, and she just smiled and didn't say a mumblin' word. Not 'Can I help you get on your feet?' Not 'What can I do for you?' Not 'Don't worry. We'll get it straight.' Not nothing. Not a mumblin' word. She just shook her head, all sympathetic-like, and walked off.

"Then, she had the nerve to turn around, come back and say, 'I'll be sure to pray for you.' That's what she said.

"Hell, I needed a little piece a' money. I don't need her fucking prayers."

Things sure weren't the way they had been when everybody could really count on Lena McPherson. That's what folks noted to each other with incredulous shakes of their heads.

"Ain't like it used to be before," they said.

"Yeah, me and the children used to go out right regular to pet the horses and ride 'em sometimes. Shoot, now I wouldn't *think* of going out there without getting *permission* first. Wouldn't feel comfortable."

"Yeah, and Lena used to *always* make us feel comfortable!"

"Humph, *better not* go out there unannounced now. Rick Little said he learned that the hard way. Say before she got rid of him and found him a job out at that new riding club up by Macon . . ."

"She *fired him*??!"

"Um-huh, said she didn't need so many folks working out there now."

"Damn, what's this new man's name? Clark Kent?"

"Yeah, think just because she found Rick a job—good job, too, pay's as good as she was giving, I hear—everything okay."

"And who she think she is getting rid a' people and then finding them jobs, anyway?"

"Well, Rick say before he was fired, he happened to go by early one evening to pick up some of his equipment, and he heard her up there in the loft moanin' and screwin' and singin' like she didn't have a care in the world!"

"Up in the hayloft??!"

"Uh-huh."

"She and that man up in the hayloft?!"

"Uh-huh."

"Rick Little say he always thought Lena McPherson look like a woman who could throw down, but he never thought she'd be a screamer like that!"

"So you better not be taking your children out there unannounced. Ain't no telling what you gon' walk up on."

"Ain't like it used to be before," they said.

They picked Lena apart as if she were a holiday turkey and feasted on her business. Even the customers and clients at The Place or at Candace Realty Co. tried to get away with dissecting Lena in her own places of business. But they did not get much play. For the employees and staff there, things were moving along rather smoothly with their boss's attention elsewhere.

Lena had just about turned everything loose to devote her time to having fun with Herman, but her businesses didn't go to hell in a handbasket as everyone had predicted.

Even Lena could see clearly that God and the universe were taking care of things.

As Herman said, "Right is right, Lena. And right don't wrong nobody. When it happen the way it's s'posed to, eve'body come out on top, baby."

It seemed to Lena he was right.

Gloria was in all her glory being the true Boss of The Place now. But even Gloria questioned how The Place would fare without a Mc-Pherson at the helm.

"Lena, you know how places change when the owners change."

"Shoot, Gloria, what are you talking about? You been the real boss of this place for a long time now and ain't nothing changed except for the better."

James Petersen, freed up from taking care of Lena and anticipating her every need, found time to polish up his mystery-in-progress.

He was pleased as he could be that Lena was acting like she was part of a world that didn't extend beyond the perimeters of her riverfront property. He had never seen her so sunny and happy. Even though he didn't see her much anymore, it was okay with him.

"She always did too much and saw too many anyway," he said to himself many days as he buzzed to see if there was anything for him to do or if now was a good time to do it.

James figured that after so many years of having people all up in her face twenty-four hours a day, seven days a week, Lena deserved a bit of peace and solitude.

But by the week of Thanksgiving, the townspeople were so through with Lena and the way she had deserted all of them, they could hardly make sense.

"I never woulda thought it of Lena McPherson," folks down at The Place said. "The one we could always count on. Shoot, I let my burial insurance lapse years ago 'cause I knew she'd see to me being buried proper . . . Guess I'mo have to end up in Potter's Field now."

With Thanksgiving so close and Christmas coming on and the idea of empty stockings and no honey-baked spiral-cut hams or smoked turkey breasts and "dry" Christmas cards or maybe no fancy hand-painted, suitable-for-framing cards at all, the townspeople's anger at Lena whipped up to new levels.

"I always knew she was doing too much. Trying to be a saint or something. Serves her right."

"Who the hell she think she is to just drop us like that? Going to church all the time. Humph, she ought to learn how to be a true Christian."

"She shun me like *she* owe *me* money!!"

"Yeah, bringing us watermelons like we the yard niggers, and still can't return our damn phone calls."

It wasn't that folks in Mulberry were just talking about Lena and her new odd "self-centered" behavior. It was that they were now calling themselves worried about her, ready to take action. Asking among themselves at The Place over their beer and wine, "What we gonna do 'bout Lena? What we gonna do 'bout our girl?" Meeting at intersections, leaning out of their cars pointed in opposite directions under the changing traffic light, "Don't she seem strange to you?" Lifting the hood dryers in beauty shops to ask their salon partners, "You think she having a nervous breakdown?"

"Ain't none of *ya'll* met The Man, neither?" the women would inquire, trying to lead the women of Candace on.

But none of them, not Precious, not Wanda, not Marilyn, not Dorothy, not Brenda, not Carroll, not Lois, not Caryl, not Mrs. Jeffries, the receptionist, not Toya, the office assistant. No one wanted to upset the applecart at Candace.

The called themselves being loyal to Lena, and, in their way, they were. They knew she had been a good friend and employer to them.

"I don't know anything about Lena McPherson's business except her *realty business*," Precious would say, stopping the gossipers in their tracks. "And as good as she been to all of ya'll, I don't see why you, of all folks, don't let her have her own life."

Lena had not made it public knowledge, but all the women at Candace were now part owners, and Lena's magic still seemed to flow in and out of the realty office doors just as it had when she was sole owner and in and out the doors herself every weekday.

She had been thinking lately of turning the business entirely over to her partners and getting out of real estate altogether. Strange as it seemed for a woman who had made it her business to know about every property transaction in Mulberry, she no longer had any interest in acquiring land.

"Good God, Lena McPherson, ain't a hundred acres enough?" she would ask herself when she came across the death notice of the last member of a large landowning family in the *Mulberry Times*. She would start to pick up the phone to call Precious to tell her to pass the information along to Wanda, who was now handling acquisitions. But then she remembered how Herman always said, "They smart people. They figure it out," and she laughed at herself, and went off to find him and check on Keba.

When Lena told Herman she couldn't believe that things had settled down at the office and everyone was taking her place doing what she did best, he wasn't a bit surprised.

"Lena, right is right, and right don't wrong nobody. It's like when a miracle happen. Don't nobody get wronged by it. It works out fo' everyone."

That's what Lena began praying for right then. A miracle to keep everyone happy and blessed just the way they all were.

31

THANKS

In honor of all her blessings, Lena planned to cook a huge feast for her first Thanksgiving with Herman—her main blessing.

Besides the twelve-pound Butterball turkey and her mama's corn bread dressing, she was fixing pole beans, onions and little new potatoes; crookneck squash casserole; rice and gravy with giblets and boiled turkey egg chopped up in it; turnip greens and their creamy sweet roots; sliced tomatoes from plants they had hung upside down in the loft of the barn; Herman's mother's china briar bread; sautéed green onions; cranberry sauce; a sweet-potato pie; her own bourbon pecan pie; her grandmother's cream cheese pound cake and her mama's ambrosia.

She had gone over to the house on Forest Avenue to retrieve the huge turkey roaster that Nellie had stored on a top shelf of the pantry. Now that the ghosts and demons had settled down since she had found her mother's recipes, her family's house was peaceful and serene. The house now called lovingly to her every few weeks, and she'd go by and sit in the kitchen or on the forest-green screened porch or upstairs in her parents' bedroom on the floor.

With a pad and pen in her hand, she had gone over the menu with Herman two or three times just to see him lick his lips in anticipation of the huge meal. James Petersen had said he would be busy Thanksgiving Day and would appreciate a plate late in the evening. So plans were for Lena and Herman to dine alone on Thursday evening.

As the holiday week rolled around bringing with it a sudden warm spell, Lena felt she had so much to be thankful for: her privacy and the time to enjoy her life, Herman and their still-hot lovemaking— still hot and hotter seven months into their relationship.

On this Wednesday afternoon just as Lena was enumerating the blessings of her new life and peeling fat Valencia oranges for ambrosia, she heard car horns beeping down at the new gate Herman had erected near James Petersen's house.

"Now, who in the world could that be the day before Thanksgiving?" she asked Herman, who sat cracking soft-shell Georgia pecans for pies and roasting with butter and a little salt the way he liked them. Herman said nothing. He just kept cracking the nuts into a red glass bowl in a piece of newspaper on his lap.

Lena rinsed her hands off in the sink and walked over to the intercom panel in the Great Jonah Room. When James Petersen came over the intercom, Lena was struck by the force of his voice.

"Lena!" James Petersen said with real incredulity. "You ain't gon' believe this, but there's four, naw, five cars a' folks out here. They say they come to visit.

"And they got *food!*"

As the holiday season approached, it seemed that everyone in Mulberry had reverted to old familiar habits, routines, forgetting what he or she had learned over the last five or six months about Lena no longer being the hand everyone fanned with.

It reminded Lena of so many people who can't afford to give their families the kinds of Christmas they want suddenly saying, "Aww, fuck it. Buy it anyway. Hell, it's Christmas!"

Lena had heard that phrase repeated hundreds of times at The Place or at the realty company during the holidays. "Hell, it's Christmas! Give me that fifth a' Chivas. And throw in a bottle of that Harvey's Bristol Cream for my old lady. Hell, you right, man. It's Christmas!"

"Here, take this little rent money and get the children's Christmas out the layaway. Shoot, it's Christmas! And Christmas comes but once a year!"

Old women who had not brought Lena cooked food since the summer were riding up to her gate with their sons and daughters and grands as if they had been invited for the entire holiday weekend.

Folks brought so much holiday food out to her house on the Wednesday before Thanksgiving and all that Thursday morning that Lena had to send James Petersen to head them off and send them back to town.

James Petersen was mad, not at all in the holiday spirit. The unexpected, unneeded, unwanted, unsolicited visitors and food *really* interrupted his writing time. He had learned a thing or two himself from Lena in the last couple of months about claiming his own time for himself.

That week, James Petersen was just getting to the climax of the mystery novel, *The Way the River Flowed*, that he was writing. And the last thing he wanted to deal with was a bunch of folks from town with a bunch of food that wasn't needed.

Any minute now, James Petersen felt, he was about to come up with the key to his southern murder mystery.

Then, "honk, honk, honk" at his gate.

He wasn't going to have it.

He threw down his pen and stormed out to the gate.

Students home from college for the first time in the semester came streaming out to pay respects and show off grades.

"Mama said don't bother to call Miss McPherson first," the eager young people said to James Petersen. "Mama said just to come on out."

James Petersen called with each new arriving car.

Buzz.

"Lena, it's Cliona from Yamacraw."

"Well, James Petersen, please tell her I'm getting ready for my own Thanksgiving. I'm just not in any position to receive company right now. And tell her I said Happy Thanksgiving."

Buzz.

"Lena, it's Peanut and Dude Sr. and Dude Jr. and Dude the Third and some more of your daddy's friends. They say they come to share a little holiday cheer with you." James Petersen did not even try to hide the sardonic tone in his voice. "They got a fifth with 'em, but it's 'bout empty."

Lena finally told him to put up a sign.

"And what do you think the sign oughta say?" he wanted to know.

Lena was baffled, too, for a minute. It *ought to* say, "Leave us the fuck alone," she thought.

"Just say, 'Do Not Disturb,' " Lena said.

She thought a moment and added, "No, James Petersen, write, 'Please, Do Not Disturb.' "

She paused to think, then said, "Write, 'Please, Do Not Disturb,' then add the name, address and phone number of the soup kitchen downtown, the one where my children go. Okay?"

"All right. Good idea," James Petersen muttered, almost to himself. "I got some work I want to get back to."

"Well, after you put the sign out, you're through. And thank you, James Petersen."

"You welcome, Lena," he said. Then, he chuckled and added, "Happy Thanksgiving," sounding just like his brother.

Lena had tried to sound calm as she spoke, but she was mad as hell.

"Happy Thanksgiving to you, James Petersen," she said.

Herman had disappeared into the woods. Lena had to go looking for him. She found him down on the river deck with his fishing pole and line dangling in the chilly waters of Cleer Flo'.

Lena came storming down the deck's wide walk past the blooming pink and red and white camellia bushes.

"Herman, I'm mad enough to spit," she said, coming up to him.

"Uh-uh, Lena, don't be spittin' mad in the river. Cleer Flo' started for the first time when you did that. Ain't no telling what'll happen this time."

Herman's revelation stopped Lena right in her tracks.

"What do you mean, Herman? Cleer Flo' happened last time?"

He chuckled and said, "Right here where you caused Cleer Flo', hey, Lena?"

"Herman, what in the world are you talking about?" she demanded.

"Good Lord, Lena, baby." Herman's voice was mildly irritated with a splash of love. "You don't even know you caused Cleer Flo'?"

Lena had forgotten that spring morning when, in her irritation with the world, she had stood on her deck and spat out the words "You old muddy nasty river!!"

Then, like an old woman, Lena had spat in the murky waters of the Ocawatchee. In a flash, Herman's comments brought it all back to her.

He looked at her with those clear sharp eyes with a little blue in the whites like a boy's and no trace of red. He sighed deeply and lay his cane fishing pole down.

"Lena, this ain't 'bout folks botherin' you. It's 'bout you knowin' yo' own se'f, baby.

"Baby, you got the power to get mad and cause som'um like Cleer Flo', and you don't even know it? Yet you 'round here getting heartless mad just 'cause some folks come when it ain't convenient. Lena, baby, you got to do better."

Herman had not meant to sound so chiding. He picked up his

pole again and went back to fishing as he talked, trying to sound casual.

"All them folks comin' out here from town just people bein' human. That's all they doin', Lena, just being human. What you gonna do? Fill in all their spaces fo' them? Be mad all the time? Abandon them altogether?, They just tryin' to love you best they can."

"I guess you're right, Herman," Lena said, trying to forget her annoyance at folks intruding on her private holiday with her man. She sat down beside Herman on the dock, rested her chin on her hands and looked out over the rushing Cleer Flo' waters. Herman made things so clear for her sometimes.

Lena hated to feel angry and hurt. She had even started to feel a little sick to her stomach as she had stomped down to the dock. All she had wanted was to enjoy a quiet Thanksgiving repast alone with Herman.

Now, she could feel her stomach settling down as if she had taken one of Sister's calmatives with leaves from Lena's stand of two-hundred-year-old bay trees. Lena was more than glad to toss off the old heavy dirty-feeling cloak of anger that had begun to settle around her shoulders. She watched the tiny peaks on the surface of the river begin to disappear and took a good deep breath.

"You know, Herman, I don't know the last time I have been mad," she said with surprise.

32
FUCK YOU

The moment Lena walked in the crowded front entrance of The Place the Saturday after Thanksgiving dressed in soft jeans, one of Herman's shirts, short boots and an oversized riding habit jacket, she said to herself, "Something's up."

A sad old blues song was playing on the jukebox that struck Lena as an odd choice for folks on a holiday weekend morning. Usually, something like "Let the Good Times Roll" would be blaring. And for there to be so many people present, there was hardly another sound in the joint. Lena heard her mother's voice say, "You can hear a rat piss on cotton in here this morning."

When Lena had called the day before to tell Gloria she was coming into town the next morning so she could say "Happy Holidays" to some folks she had missed on Thanksgiving, Gloria had been pleased. "Oh, folks will be happy to hear that, girl."

Now, however, Lena sensed a distinct chill in the air. She did not feel that usual quilt of warmth, love and affection that had always greeted her at the door. In fact, now that Lena noticed it, people standing and sitting around seemed suddenly to find a piece of lint on their lapels or take an interest in an old sputtering neon beer sign.

Since the cold November morning Jonah and his poker buddies had toasted her birth there, Lena had gotten nothing but love from The Place. On the wall of her office at home, she had a photograph of herself as an infant, bundled in a soft yellow blanket her grandmother had knitted and propped up in an Old Forester bourbon box on the counter of the liquor store.

But that was not how it felt this holiday weekend morning.

Through the glass partition, Lena could see Gloria waving at her as the strong little compact woman tried to push her way from behind the counter of the liquor store. But there were so many people on both sides of The Place that Gloria could not get to her. Lena noticed, however, that a path seemed to open right up for *her* to get through the crowd.

"Morning, Peanut. Morning, Bubbles. Morning, Miss Jessie. Morning, Miss Etta. Hey, Dude Jr., how you doing? Miss Cliona, what you doing down here?" Lena greeted folks. No one said a word.

She didn't get one single response. Folks were as tight-lipped as deacons.

Lena stopped in her tracks and looked around at everyone. Peanut wouldn't even look her straight in the eye. And Dude Jr. picked up a broom and started sweeping in one spot.

"What's wrong with ya'll?" she asked lightly. "Cat got your tongues? Or did everybody have too much Thanksgiving celebration?"

At that, Lena heard two or three people in the crowd suck their teeth in disgust.

Gloria had reached the partition dividing the liquor store and juke joint and was loudly rapping on the glass and motioning for Lena to come to her. Now!

It was too late. Lena was encircled by a gang of regulars. She noticed, too, that there were some faces there that did not belong to the usual customers. In fact, there were some folks present whom she had never seen inside The Place before.

There were a couple of people from St. Martin de Porres Church who she knew approved of neither drinking nor juking nor the McPherson family. Clara, the only woman she ever fired from Candace, was standing near the back of the crowd with her arms folded. And Lena thought she recognized some people from Sherwood Forest who owed her back rent from the eighties.

"What's going on?" Lena asked, still smiling but quizzically. The crowd of Mulberry citizens tightened around her and ushered her over to a tiny table and sat her down.

Despite signs to the contrary, Lena thought for a second that her people had planned a little belated surprise party for her the way they sometimes did when they forgot her birthday. But the sober tone of the gathering dispelled that illusion.

"Now, Lena, don't get yourself all upset," Cliona from Yamacraw stepped forward and said soothingly.

"All upset? All upset about what? What do ya'll think you're doing?"

"It's what's called an 'intervention,' baby," Cliona from Yamacraw explained slowly as if she were talking to an idiot.

"*Intervention??!!*" Lena laughed. "An intervention for what? For who?" She was really puzzled.

"For you, sugar," Miss Cliona said.

Lena was struck dumb.

In the silence, the crowd opened again and a white man who looked to be in his eighties wearing a dingy white shirt and shiny blue serge suit made his way slowly to the table and sat down in the other chair next to Lena. Seeming to ignore Lena, the man took a few wrinkled sheets of paper from his weathered briefcase.

"Don't we know each other?" Lena asked politely of the man with the ashes and burn marks down his shirtfront.

Lena knew she had seen the man somewhere before. Then, it came to her.

"Why, you're Dr. Byrd. From the hospital in Milledgeville!" Lena exclaimed, remembering the strange jumpy white man who had shown up one night when she was a child to borrow money from Jonah. She had started to say "the crazy house in Milledgeville" instead of "hospital in Milledgeville."

Nellie had threatened all her children at one time or another to commit them to the state hospital for the insane if they continued "to act so damn crazy" and get on her nerves.

"Do it on a Sunday, Nellie," her father would put in with a laugh. "Then, you'll get thirty-five dollars instead of twenty-five for each."

But no one was laughing in The Place this morning. Especially not Lena. She was just understanding that this was not a joke. These folks were serious.

"You mean you actually got this man up in here to put me away in a padded cell?" Lena was incredulous.

"Well, just to observe you for now," Miss Cliona explained. "That's the first step in the commitment process."

Lena just sat there in The Place in shocked silence. She had to rest her spinning head in her hands for a moment. She could hardly form words.

"Okay, let's make a deal," Lena said evenly to Cliona from Yamacraw. "You don't commit me, and I don't send your black ass back to Milledgeville."

"Well, now, you have been acting mighty strange, Lena," someone in the circle said. There was a buzzing in Lena's head, and she couldn't place the voice.

"Yeah, we know Nellie and Jonah worked too hard to give you all a' this just to have you th'ow it away on some kinda change-a-life craziness."

Lena spun around at the sound of the familiar voice. Peanut? She truly could not believe these words were coming out of his mouth.

"I beg your pardon!" Lena said to the tiny man. "Surely, you don't want to talk about 'change of life.'"

Peanut dropped back into the crowd.

Lena was just dumbfounded.

"Have all of ya'll taken leave of your senses?" She was serious. "You all ought to be ashamed."

But they weren't a bit ashamed. Lena could tell that from their faces. They were self-righteous and serious. But not a bit ashamed.

"I tell you what," Lena said to the concerned and curious faces around her. "Kiss my crazy ass!"

And she stormed out of The Place, brushing past Gloria, who had finally made her way over, but knew enough to leave Lena alone.

Lena felt she had been hit in the head with a two-by-four. She saw stars. And she heard voices.

As she sped away toward Riverside Drive, she heard somebody back in The Place ask, "You think she sane enough to drive?"

It feels like Anna Belle and all those spirits or whatever in that locked room down there just got loose, Lena thought, crowding out the cacophony of the complaints and conversations that was ringing in her ears.

Lena was too mad to cry. She had not driven ten blocks before she found herself embroiled in a Mulberry-sized traffic jam of cars on their way to the biggest sale of the year out at the town's mall.

She banged the steering wheel with the palms of her hands and laid on the horn.

Burning down the whole town of Mulberry seriously crossed her mind. "I know what Mama meant when she used to say we children made her very asshole tremble!" she said fiercely to herself.

The entire torturously slow way home, Lena could hear the towns-people's talk in her head:

"What the hell is wrong with Lena McPherson!!!"

"Yeah, she even stop eating our food. Out there cooking so much herself, don't even appreciate what *we* been doing for her."

"I don't know what she out there cooking for. Hell, *her time* sho' could be better spent conducting some of her business."

"You know why she out there cooking. Trying to keep that *man*!!"

"Ain't *no telling* what's going on out there since nobody can't just drive up like normal people."

"Have the nerve to go sending us to somebody else when we need to talk to her."

"Lord ham mercy, I sho' am glad Jonah ain't around to see how his girl is running things now. It woulda broke his heart."

"And what about Nellie? Now, *that woman* was a saint!!!"

"Not even eating our food! What she think? We gon' pizen her!!??"

"Think she too good?!"

Caught up in traffic with carloads of ravenous shoppers ready to acquire more stuff, Lena could not block out the voices.

"Look at her, dressing like a ragamuffin."

"Running away from all her responsibilities. I've never seen such a selfish thing in all my life."

"What does she expect us to do?"

"Yeah, she's there for you when *she* want to be. But don't have a emergency, 'cause she off gallivanting with her crazy self with God knows who, doing God knows what."

"Her mama would turn over in her grave if she knew how Lena was neglecting her people. Like she ain't got no upbringing."

"Yeah. And if Lena McPherson ain't got none of that, ain't none of us got it."

"*My mama* died and we didn't hear a word from her. Not a word. Didn't come to the funeral. Didn't send no flowers. Didn't do nothing. What about *my mama?*"

"Uh-huh, did all that good stuff for the public eye when mama was alive, but where was she at the funeral when we *really* needed her?"

"Shoot, that ain't hardly nothing compared with the fact she done turned her back on God, too, they say."

"On God???"

"Uh-huh. Don't even go to church no more. And, you know, St. Lena used to wear out the pews at St. Martin de Porres."

"Yeah, *St. Lena.*"

"Just go to show you. Her heart ain't in the right place. Never was."

Lena thought her very heart would break. By the time she got home, she had heard it all.

"And Herman, now Cliona from Yamacraw got the nerve to be going around saying I'm crazy. *I'm crazy?*

"Shoot, maybe I *am* crazy to put up with this shit. And then take all this grief for it. Shit. I guess I'm crazy as a betsy bug *and* a little foolish fool, too!!"

She was the only one who was surprised by the townspeople's anger and resentment toward her.

She knew folks in town were calling themselves worrying about her and her new cavalier ways. But to actually have some white man, some jackleg quack, ready to tie her up in a straitjacket and cart her off to a padded cell like some madwoman. To say that she had no heart. To say she was selfish. It was just too damn much for Lena.

She was so hurt and angry she threw things. She didn't think she had ever felt this way before, and she certainly had never shown her anger in such a manner. She destroyed a number of items precious to her before Herman stilled her hand as she was about to chunk her mother's delicate white-flowered china face-powder bowl with little rounded gold-leaf claw feet. The very act of touching her, stopping her in midthrow, brought her up short and made her look around the house at the irreplaceable things she had shattered.

"Shoot, Lena, you at least gonna need a old plate to cut collards up on," Herman tried to reason with his woman. His plain-spoken sense did give her pause to gather herself and her rage, but only for a second.

"It's just like Mama said, 'They start out wanting your friendship, just wanting to talk, and they end up wanting your heart, soul and liver, chopped up fine and spoon-fed to 'em.' "

She mimicked Nellie and said, "Here, take my heart, take my liver, take my soul! Take it and be done!"

"Yeah, why don't these damn people just do that?"

Outside, little white peaks were beginning to form on the Ocawatchee River. Even from the deck, Herman could see that Cleer Flo' had suddenly ceased. And the wind was whipping up the pine straw on the ground.

Seeing how furious and hurt Lena was, he tried to make a joke to lighten her mood.

"Hey, take it easy, greasy. You got a *long way* to slide," he said.

Lena, however, was not to be played with this day.

"Herman, listen to me, they actually had some jackleg doctor who used to work at the crazy house in Milledgeville down there at *my place* to observe *me*!

"Cliona from Yamacraw sitting up in there just as big with her certifiably crazy self talking about 'Now, stay calm, Lena.'

"Saints preserve us, Herman!

"They actually talking about the process of commitment. For my own good!

"Said they made some phone calls and had collected some 'pertinent information' about my 'recent strange behavior.' Herman, they called the bank and down to Candace!

"And *they* got the nerve to say *I* lost *my* mind!!"

While Lena came up for air, Herman just said, "Umm." Lena continued.

"At least the folks at the bank and my friends at Candace didn't fall for this and throw in with them. Now that I think about it, Gloria was trying her best to head me off when I walked in this morning.

"But the rest of those folks . . ."

Outside, Lena's anger was wreaking as much havoc on nature as it had on her prized possessions. A storm had come up suddenly over the Ocawatchee and tall muddy red peaks were beginning to form on the surface as the wind whipped up foam. A lightning bolt struck a tree in Pleasant Hill, melding a baby doll, a brand-new Schwinn bicycle and a red hairpin to its trunk.

Herman felt the tension in her clenched fist flowing through her wrist, up her arm, through her chest and down to her heart. When he felt it in her heart, he had to steel himself and stop himself from crying like a baby at her hurt.

He moved closer to her on the sofa in their bedroom and put his arm around her shoulder.

"Shit, I can't believe I've been such a fool. Everybody ain't happy for me. After all I've done for them, they don't really give a damn about me. Herman, they *mad* at me!!!

"Where I been? How come I ain't answered their phone messages? What they s'posed to do waiting for me to get around to them? They got a pain in their chest, and I won't make it go away. Don't I care about nobody but myself?

"And where was this little foolish fool? Ripping and running all over creation trying to do what I could. And here I am thinking I'm the one who has to *save* everybody. If I don't do it, the world will fall apart. What a fool I was!! Some of them making fun of me and calling me *St. Lena.*"

Lena was cut to the quick when she understood that the people of Mulberry were truly angry with her, talking about committing her, talking about her deserting them, talking about her betraying her family name.

She suddenly heard James Petersen's voice cut through the other noises in her head.

"Yeah, Gloria, it woulda broke Lena's heart if she knew how some of those folks just threw that food against the fence when Lena didn't invite them in yesterday.

"I got it all cleaned up, so when she came out this morning she didn't know no better. But I wouldn'a let her see that for nothing in the world."

Herman took Lena in his arms and held her there.

Her big brown eyes filled with tears at the thought of people she had loved all her life talking about her like a dog and treating her like one, too. Throwing food at her gate.

Her! The baby! Used to being instantly loved.

"You expect people to love you, don't you, Lena?" Sister had asked once. And Sister was right.

Lena had always gotten what she expected. What she measured out, she seemed to get back, pressed down, shaken together, running over. Everybody in Mulberry could testify to that. She had done that with her town and had not really judged them for always pulling at her skirt tail and taking her for granted.

But she was the baby. She wanted to tell folks who made mean, thoughtless statements, "Oh, you must not know I'm the baby."

Herman held her as if she were the *only* baby. He held her and rocked her and kissed her and made over her until she began to feel better.

"I think these people can get on just fine wi'out Lena McPherson's constant 'tention," he said as he gently patted her back. "Everybody can. But Lena could stand a little 'tention, too. That's what I think."

But Lena was not so easily pacified. She was deeply hurt.

"They know I ain't got no family but them," she said softly. And realized again suddenly how hurt and mad she was. Outside, it began to rain softly.

Her senses so sharp, her emotions raw, Lena could not seem to block out the conversations people had been having about her for months.

She discovered they were mad about everything. When the women in town had gotten wind of Lena packing up her clothes, they had had a fit. The clothes had gone into pools of professional attire that young women from Spelman College, Fort Valley State College and Xavier could borrow for job interviews and conferences and social occasions.

"Giving away her designer clothes."

"Giving away her high-heeled shoes."

"Ain't no telling what else she giving away. Wouldn't be surprised if she gave away Jonah and Nellie's home over on Forest Avenue before it's over. Giving away everything she own and still won't return an old lady's phone call."

"I hear she kept that little pink Chanel job, but all the others—the black and white Chanel suit, those little black Ungaro silk dresses, the Versace blouses and jackets, the Ralph Lauren slacks and sweaters, those Jil Sander cashmere and wool suits, that brown leather suit by Calvin Klein—all that went off to some strangers!"

"Yeah, I guess we little country folks in Mulberry wasn't *worthy* and *sophisticated* enough to get her little designer castoffs!"

"Uh-huh, and I had my eye on that brown leather suit for years!"

"Yeah, what she want us to do? Get down and paw the ground just 'cause she did a few things here and there for folks? What we got to do, paw the ground at her feet?"

When Mrs. Jeffries, the receptionist at Candace, overheard one of these talks, she had snapped back, "Maybe what you got to do is give her a little credit and a lot a' breathing room." Precious and the other women at Candace had just smiled and kept on working. "We all make a good living here at Candace," the receptionist added, "and if we want designer clothes, we can buy our own." That had really shut the grumblers up.

It eased Lena's pain a bit to know that every damn body in town was not poised to stand outside her gate with flambeaux and pitchforks.

Gloria left a message of support on Lena's machine.

"Lena, girl, I know this town 'un tore its drawers with you," the message said. "Call me when you feel like talking."

Even days after the incident down at The Place, Lena still did not feel like talking with anyone in Mulberry but Herman. The storm on Saturday had finally passed on down the state, but Lena's stormy feelings did not abate.

For hours, Lena would just sit—her elbows on her knees, her head in her hands. Then suddenly, she would slowly raise her head and shake it. "Um, um, um," she'd say to herself with infinite sadness. Many times, tears would just roll down her cheeks. Remembering what Herman had told her, when she was out on the deck, she was careful not to let any of the salty drops fall into the now muddy waters of the river.

Lena could still hear women all over town discussing the possibilities of just what was wrong with Lena McPherson. Even people who didn't know her personally itched to get into the act.

"You know she had a lick to her head just last spring according to Bubbles down at The Place," one of the secretaries at the East Mulberry High School office told another.

"Did she really?" the other asked from her brightly painted cubicle.

"Friend o' mine work in the emergency room of the medical center. No, she didn't see her come in, but she heard that Fred Jackson, the man who *own* the construction company, brought her in and was plenty worried. She say he *swore* she had been hit in the head with something even though they couldn't find no bump."

"Maybe it didn't take no bump."

"What you mean?"

"You know some womens go crazy when they reach the change of life. I know it's hard to think of Lena going through that but she *is* at that age."

"Lena McPherson, I know exactly when she was born. It was 1949. In the fall, I think."

"Anyway, like I was saying, Lena 'bout at that age. Maybe that explain it."

Each time she heard another Mulberry conversation, she grew angrier and angrier.

She was so mad, she even reverted to her five-year-old self and wondered how they'd all feel if she were dead. "Yeah, if I was laying up in a coffin somewhere, they'd have to get the Mulberry city *and* county police to direct the crowds.

"Yeah, like Mama say, 'Gi' me my roses while I'm still alive to smell 'em.' "

If Herman had not taken her keys away from her, Lena would

have jumped in her car many a time and driven into town to confront each and every one of the folks who were so through with her.

For days, Lena would stand out in the garden near the stables and scream in the direction of Mulberry.

"Bump you!!!!!" "Forget you!!!!!" "Screw you!!!!!" She said everything but "Fuck you."

"Yeah," Lena shouted to the woods and the bridle trail and the road and the river leading into Mulberry, "why *don't* I just wait? Wait until I'm, say, forty-seven, or forty-eight or forty-nine or fifty-nine to get a life of my own. Yeah, why don't I just fucking wait until it's convenient and comfortable for all of you?!!" She balled up her fist and shook it in the direction of town.

She thought Yahweh must have felt like this about the Israelites about the time they had been in the desert for a few decades. And they were still turning against Him, doubting Him, blaming Him.

"*Fuck* these people!!" Lena imagined the Father turning to the Mother and the Holy Spirit and saying of his chosen people. Then turning to his people and adding, "I brought you out of Egypt. Parted the Red Sea for you. Dried up Jordan. Rained manna and birds on the desert so you could eat. I closed my ears to the pleas of your enemies, the Ammonites and the Hittites and the Canaanites and the Girgashites and the Perizzites—and made you my people, victorious.

"Gave you land you didn't have to clear and till. Gave you vineyards and olive trees you didn't have to plant. And just listen to you.

"*Fuck* these people!"

Herman just looked at her.

"So now you up there wid Yahweh, huh, Lena, baby?

"Good God, Lena, just 'cause people loves ya don't mean they won't wear yo' ass out day to day. Why you so surprised?

"But if folks truly loves you, they be there for ya. They don't let you run yo'se'f completely in the ground doin' fo' them. They like children who don't know no better, if they do that, Lena. But regardless of what *they* do, you gon' have to give it up, baby."

"I have given up as much as I could, Herman, and you see what's happened. You see how people acting now!"

"Naw, baby, I don't mean givin' up the work. I mean givin' up the control. The decidin' who gets what, who needs what, who can't survive wi'out Lena McPherson's he'p.

"You don't know the meanin' a' the word yet, but, baby, you gon' have t' *surrender!*

"Once you do that, you'll be able to love folks again."

"Love them?!" Lena sucked her teeth.

"You know, baby, you can tell Mulberry and all its people, '*Fuck* you!' and still be able to love them.

" 'Cause no matter how much you hurt, all they done is just be human. It's just people bein' human. You ain't in control, Lena. No matter how sweet ya want to do it. Doin' fo' people don't make 'em yo's. Everybody responsible fo' they own se'ves. Just like you.

"Damn, baby, you don't have a clue, do you?"

Herman said it with such power and emphasis that it had hurt Lena's already wounded feelings. It was spoken almost as an indictment, a grand jury charge. Herman felt the weight of his words, too, and tried to soften them a little.

"Lena, baby, you got t' do better. You can't afford not to have a clue. You got thangs t' do. And ya ain't got to sacrifice yo'se'f on the altar of doin' and goin' and fixin'.

"You ain't got to give burned offerin's of yo'se'f to be good. God don't even want that. That's all yo' hush mouth is . . . burned offerin's. And yo' good works, too. Burned offerin's."

Lena was hurt to the quick by Herman's judgment. Tears welled up in her eyes.

"I ain't judgin' you, baby, I'm try 'na he'p you.

"I been dead a hundred years, Lena, baby, I do know a thang or two.

"You done forgot to look out fo' yo'se'f. Shoot, Lena, baby, even iron wear out! What you make possible fo' Lena to do? See, you might be able to come up wid som'um, but you got to think, don't ya?"

She listened to all that Herman said and then settled down to hurt. He wrapped himself around Lena in a stream of warm loving mist night after night when she finally fell asleep angry and spent.

Things began to settle down with the folks in town and in Lena's heart. She felt as if God had replaced her heart of stone with a heart of spirit, of love.

She couldn't believe that with Herman's direction, his help, she was beginning to forgive folks and herself.

She was understanding how to say, "Fuck you!" and not let it end her love.

Before Herman came and opened her back up to the earth and the universe, she would have just ignored the feeling. But now she tried to be attuned to everything, every thought, every prayer and wish that came across her path. Not to just solve the problems or even to alleviate the suffering. But to take note and learn.

For a while, she felt she could do anything with Herman by her side.

Finally, one night in early December, Lena got up out of her nice warm bed and walked naked out onto the deck. She left Herman lying in bed among their rumpled flannel sheets, but he rose on his elbows and watched her through the French doors. There was another meteor shower lighting up the night sky over the river. Herman thought Lena looked like a goddess as she stood naked in flashes of celestial light comfortable and natural. Facing south toward Mulberry, Lena stretched her arms high over her head and took a deep breath of the crisp air. She leaned forward a little bit over the cypress railing of the deck. Then, at the top of her lungs, she screamed, "*Fuuuccckkk* you!"

The invective rang out through the woods and over the river, all the way to town, Lena imagined.

"*Fuuuccckkk* you!" she screamed it again. Lena imagined folks in town being awakened by her directive.

She paused and said it again. This time she didn't scream or yell. In a normal voice, she repeated, "*Fuuuccckkkk* you!" Then, she chuckled. Lena liked the sound of it.

"*Fuck* you." Now, she was really laughing as she looked out over the waters of the Ocawatchee.

Lena lifted her hands over her head, stretched her chilly naked body in the light of the moon and said it one more time as Herman got out of bed and, picking up her heavy wool robe, joined her on the deck.

"*Fuck* you!"

Herman draped the warm robe around Lena's bare shoulders.

Then, she and Herman sat on their deck, snuggled together inside her robe, and laughed and laughed and laughed.

33

SHELTER

For the first time in fifty years, it snowed in Mulberry on Christmas Eve. The frigid weather had blown in out of the north suddenly one day in mid-December. One minute, it was still fairly comfortable, the next, it was freezing.

However, after the floods of the year before, the recurring Cleer Flo's, and the unseasonable storm that Lena's anger had caused back in November, no one in Mulberry was really surprised at the weather anymore.

But everyone in Middle Georgia knew that Christmastime could bring balmy sweater weather. So, that's what folks were expecting. Everybody except Lena and Herman. They had seen the signs.

First, Keba, little more than halfway through her pregnancy, began nesting. The second week in December, she started kicking straw into the clean brick corners of her stall as if she were a bird or a squirrel. Lena and Herman would stand and talk to her for hours, combing her mane, rubbing her big belly when she would let them, and reassuring her that the vet knew her due date.

Then, around that same time, Lena could feel a difference in the air. She looked like an old country woman stopping in her muddy tracks between the kitchen garden and the stables to lift her nose and smell the air. Sniffing two or three more times, she detected something new there.

"Herman," she called, his name ringing out in the crisp strange-feeling air.

"Hold on," he hollered from inside the stables.

Suddenly appearing next to her, he asked, "What ya want, Lena, baby? If you got the money, honey, I got the time."

Herman said the same thing whenever or however Lena called him for his assistance, his perspective, his opinion, his touch, his kiss, his love.

She'd yell it aloud, whisper it or think it. Sometimes, she just felt the need for him, and Herman would appear.

"Herman, can you come here a minute?"

"If you got the money, honey, I got the time."

"Herman, doesn't it feel strange out here to you?" she asked.

"Uh-huh," he replied without even pausing. "I been feelin' it, too. Feel like we in fo' some sho' nuff cold weather."

"Cold weather? Um, that's what it is. But it feels so balmy now, almost warm. I bet I'll know it next time."

"Bet you will," Herman said proudly. "I think it's gon' get real cold, Lena. Let's brang in the last of those punkins from the field."

They brought in the pumpkins and the last of the gourds, too, and put them in the barn just in time, before the first snow fell.

The Ocawatchee did not freeze over completely during the snowstorm, and folks marveled when Cleer Flo' occurred about the same time. "In the middle of winter, too." Puffs of frozen mist rose off the surface of the river like spirits. The children in town started calling them "snow ghosts" and stood on the bridges over the river to watch in wonder and try to catch the cold vapors in their little gloved hands.

The area was truly living up to its old nickname of Cold Neck.

Lena's log cabin looked like an old-fashioned Yuletide postcard covered in a heavy snowfall with smoke billowing out of its chimneys.

The grounds looked like a wonderland indeed, and Lena and Herman cavorted in the snow like children until they were nearly frozen. They'd come back inside, tossing their wet clothes everywhere, and make love—naked and damp—in front of the fireplace at the manger Herman had built by the foot of the Christmas tree covered with heirloom family ornaments. Their cold skin tingled as the fire's heat radiated off their naked bodies. The whole time, Donny Hathaway and Charles Brown and Otis Redding sang of Christmas on the sound system all over the house.

It was the best Christmas Lena had ever had. Even better than when she was a child.

Since reaching adulthood, she had not known the joys of a simple Christmas: a good-sized tree, a good meal and a good mate with whom to share it. That's what Lena had this Christmas.

No extravagant, mad, feverish shopping for everybody in the world she knew to have a little Christmas. No writing a hundred individual checks to everybody who knew her name.

Instead, this Christmas, in place of all the hams and turkeys and poinsettias and gifts, she sat down in her office at home and wrote notes—some with checks and some without—of love, gratitude and forgiveness.

It was difficult for her to stop giving. She had so much. But now it didn't feel so like an obligation, so like a boulder on the small of her back pressing down insistently, constantly.

Suddenly recalling the story Peanut had told her every Saturday when she was little, she wrote it down and sent it to him. She even sent Cliona from Yamacraw a pretty card with a note inside saying Lena was sorry she had yelled at her and that she loved the crazy old woman. She did not know how her little notes would be received, but she sent them in love.

Looking at her snow-covered estate made her happy she had. The ice hanging from verdant spruce and fir limbs made her think of all the folks who were not as cozy as she and her man. Snuggled in front of the big fire in the Great Jonah Room with the ten-foot-tall Christmas tree over by the French doors, Lena couldn't stop thinking of the folks in the world, in Mulberry especially, who didn't have simple shelter during this unusual cold snap.

It surprised her now that she was not still through with the town of Mulberry and its people after her rage a month before. But with each day, the grace of forgiveness seemed to shower her with peace.

There was no way she could greet the birth of the Prince of Peace without making peace with her people. And the thought of anyone, especially those she held dear, being out in this weather with no warm dry place to call home made *her* go all cold inside.

That's when the idea for the shelter popped into her head.

She jumped up from her toasty seat still wrapped in a soft cable-knit cashmere throw she had bought for Herman for Christmas and snapped her fingers.

"Herman, I can't believe I didn't think of this before," she said. "The house on Forest Avenue would make a perfect shelter for my children!"

The very idea of her little ragtag throwaway teenagers, who stood on cold street corners braced against the wind, who slept in alleyways and deserted buildings, who did anything to keep from going back to situations they had fled, residing in the big, cozy two-story brick house on Forest Avenue where she grew up warmed her heart *and* lit a fire under her.

Lena didn't wait for the beginning of the year to put her plan in motion.

"Shoot, I wish I could have gotten them in there for Christmas," she said to Herman as she dashed about her home office, writing faxes and making calls all over town. Lena called the women of Candace. She called her lawyers and her banker. She called an organization she knew would be perfect to help run the place. She made calls about home furnishings at a good price and industrial-sized kitchen appliances at cost.

And Herman just smiled at her excitement.

"Folks sho' gon' be able to pay fo' they Chris'mas this year," he teased as faxes came into the house from plumbers and carpenters and electricians with estimates and plans.

Lena laughed, too. "Daddy used to say, 'Money make iron float!' Shoot, Herman, what else is it good for but spending?"

The shelter was the first thing she had been truly interested in outside of Herman and her own property in almost a year, and the first thing having to do with the folks in Mulberry since she had stormed out of town the weekend after Thanksgiving.

It did his heart good to see her flurrying about happily and efficiently making plans and phone calls and faxes because she wanted to and not because she felt she had to. She brought the papers and plans to bed with her along with snacks for the both of them. Leaning back on Herman like a strong backrest and sitting happily between his legs, they sketched out plans for the house on Forest Avenue, shared their thoughts, figured on her laptop and his adding machine and wrote in their journals late into the night.

Finally, Herman, sounding like Jonah, would say, "All right, now, ain't it 'bout past yo' bedtime, baby?"

"One more minute, Herman, one more minute," she would plead. She knew he loved to hear her beg.

"Uh-uh, Lena, baby, I don't need no sleep. But you do! 'Specially now you doin' again."

Then, he would cut out the power to everything in the room, even the fire burning low in the hearth, plunging the room into darkness and quiet and startling Lena to shivers and giggles. She could not see him, but she could feel him getting closer and closer on the bed. Like a warm mist, he slipped around her, enveloping her until she fell asleep.

Getting the house ready for its new residents, buying furniture, picking up a couple of her children on the street to go pick out paint colors and wallpaper, made Lena feel like a mama. The last of the McPherson clan was mothering and sheltering in a way she thought she would never get to do.

She and her children—proud and happy to have a permanent address—decided to name the shelter "455 Forest Avenue."

The house had stood empty for nearly six years.

A couple of months after Jonah's and Nellie's deaths, when Lena realized that her life was pulling her more and more toward her own house out by the river, she had tried to rent 455 Forest Avenue. But even the new couple, their four children, one dog and two birds didn't last a month.

Mrs. Robinson came to Lena after two weeks and said plainly, "Ms. McPherson, we can't stay in that house."

Lena immediately understood the look of controlled panic in the woman's eyes. She had felt that way some nights herself as a youngster waiting for God knew what to come to her in her sleep, to lead her down dangerous paths in the waking hour, to pounce on her whenever.

It seemed so wasteful to have a beautiful house standing empty when so many people yearned for shelter, but she and the other three families who tried to live there soon discovered that the house only wanted Lena.

Now, as Lena made plans for the runaway shelter, she didn't worry once about the physical, mental or spiritual safety of the young people who would live there. Four fifty-five Forest Avenue seemed to welcome and accept the teenagers in a way it had never done before.

The young folks filled the six second-floor bedrooms. And the construction crew created six more private rooms in the basement. The kids complained when they moved the big heavy pool table out and built the rooms and two baths there. But Lena gave the pool table to St. Martin de Porres for its rec room and teased, "If ya'll want to play pool, take your little asses to church."

The first time Lena entered the house after the young folks, supervisor and counselor had moved in, she just stood in the warm foyer of the house, threw her head back and laughed. She breathed in the new life that ran through the house, from the second floor to the first, down to the remodeled basement, and up to the unfinished studios in the attic.

The only demons in the house seemed to be the two-legged kind who raced up and down the stairs two at a time.

"Hey, Lena," they called as they passed, "nice house."

It *was* a nice house.

The children had already put their stamp on everything. Lena noticed that the beautiful hat and coat rack she had bought for the wall near the door was loaded with every kind of coat and wrap imaginable. And one of the children—probably Damon, who prided himself on his muscles—had brought in enough wood for the two fireplaces to last the final two months of winter.

The young people used the official front door of the house that her family never used. She saw their heavy shoes and boots, caked with ice and slush, dumped outside the door on the porch like forgotten playmates.

Demons don't stand a chance in *this house*, Lena thought as she heard an altercation over creative differences break out in the music room. Lena had added a synthesizer to the baby grand piano, and the enlarged music room became the most popular room in the house.

In the big yellow kitchen, next to a schedule of house duties, the young folks had hung coffee mugs on the wall near the stove with a resident's name on each cup. When she saw a large copper-colored mug with "LENA" written on it, Lena felt as if she had been given a kindergartner's handmade Mother's Day card.

"Now you can come have your tea with us some mornings," little Chiquita said when she saw Lena studying the cup and fighting back tears.

Lena found she had to work hard not to let the shelter for teenagers take over her life. But with Herman waiting for her back out by the river, there was only so much time she was going to put into anything else.

Lena tried to keep everything as low-key as possible, but the shelter was big news in Mulberry. And there was plenty of talk. Four or five folks who hadn't learned their lesson at Thanksgiving felt called upon to comment.

"What?! You mean to tell me that she gon' turn that beautiful house over to some dirty homeless people!??"

"Not even grown homeless people, I hear. Teenagers!"

"That's what I hear."

"Oh, you got to have heard wrong."

"I don't think so. I heard it from someone who saw the papers turning the house over to 'the children of Mulberry.' "

"Giving it to the homeless children!!!??"

"Homeless and runaway teenagers."

"Teenagers??! Shit, that's worse. Well, I be."

"Can't get over it, can you? I feel the same way. And I'm sitting up here can't afford to pay my apartment rent month to month, and she going 'round giving big old beautiful houses away to the homeless, of all people."

"Hell, those folks—and teenagers, too—don't know nothing 'bout taking care of no house like *that*! And she know it."

"Lord, I can just imagine what that place gon' look like in two or three months."

"My people. My people."

"Lena McPherson must a' lost her mind."

"Jonah and Nellie, especially Nellie, must be turning over in their graves."

Everybody was silent for a moment realizing that Jonah and Nellie had no graves.

"Well, ya'll know what I mean."

"Lena McPherson just giving away her inheritance. And how many a' us got one of those?"

Lena could hear them just as well and just as clearly. But she didn't let it bother her now. She knew it was just people being human, like Herman said. And after a while, she was able just to tune the voices out.

Being with Herman for almost a year had sharpened Lena's senses to a right sharp edge. Conversations being conducted in the next county came through to Lena's senses now just as clearly as radio signals. It had taken her a while to learn to filter out the extraneous talk and thoughts and feelings that swirled around her. Herman had helped a bit at first to straighten out the din in her head.

"Ya hear *that*, Lena?" he'd ask, forcing her to block out all other sounds except the snatch of conversation he was talking about. He even helped her to hear and heed her own voice when it spoke in her head.

Herman was such a blessing to her.

He said things that made her shiver with love and lust for him. Sometimes, there was an element of sadness mixed in, too.

"I love you so much, Lena," he would say out of the blue. "If you had any children, I'd love them, too."

It made Lena want to weep. Just thinking about children and her age and the changes even Herman with his prodigious powers didn't seem able to stop, made her want to question why she was put on this earth.

God, I can't believe I just let my line end here, she would think. My DNA ends when I die. Oh, God, what kind of little foolish fool was I not to have a child.

It was what she had thought when she examined the semen at the tip of Herman's penis. She had imagined that she could actually see the sperm, quick and alive, darting about searching for a fertile egg.

"Lena, baby, don't worry 'bout the mule goin' blind. Just hold him in the road," Herman would tell her.

She always winced a bit at the statement. Not because she resented him gently chastising her for worrying needlessly—she didn't do too much of that anymore—but because the old saying conjured up pictures of Herman's accident and death.

As they lay quietly together after lovemaking, Lena couldn't resist reaching out and running the tips of her fingers over the faint scar and indentation on the side of Herman's head where the mule's hooves had landed. She would lean over and kiss the mark hoping to heal it and make it better the way she would whenever children came to her with their scrapes, cuts, bruises, boo-boos and hurt feelings.

Lena said the same soothing, healing things as she rubbed and kissed the little grimy, swollen spot: "Aw, she hurt herself" or "Aw, he got a *bad cut* here" or "Aw, they don't love her like they should. They don't give her *nearly* enough attention. She's hurt for real. Come here, sugar." "Heck, I might just have to get in my car and take this baby to St. Luke's Hospital."

Most of the children had never heard of the private black hospital where Lena and her brothers were born, but they could tell from their Auntie Lena's voice that it must be a special place.

The small children loved it, snuggling in closer and closer to Lena's body, feeling better and better, throwing a look that said, "See, this is how you supposed to make it better. Auntie Lena know."

Lena was one of those on earth who understood that it was as bad to be a childless mother as a motherless child. Whenever her children on the street would ask when she planned to have some children of her own, Chiquita, one of Lena's favorite children, would always pipe up, "You can be my mama anytime, Miss Mac. I'll be your little girl." Chiquita didn't care that someone among her cohorts would always chide, "Big old rusty girl like you don't *need* no mama no more."

Lena thought many times it was a wonder that children liked her at all. Folks made her sound like such a fussy old maid.

"Now, Lena ain't got no children, don't be going over there getting on her nerves."

Or "Child, you got any idea how much that dress Lena got on

cost??!! Don't be getting your old dirty hands all over her. Lena don't
want those old sticky kisses!"

Or "Naw, you can't go home with Auntie Lena for the night. She
ain't got no children. Messing up her house. Going in her refrigerator
a million times. Naw, stay your butt home."

Even well into her forties, Lena had still felt she had time to have
a child, to get pregnant, grow large, eat too much, and deliver a pretty
little healthy baby girl.

Now, on the cusp of menopause, Lena looked at her flat unmarked
stomach in the mirror and felt remorse, shame, guilt at not having
brought her own sweet little girl into the world. Lena could see her fat
little bottom and her cute little handmade dresses that she would
create on her mother's old Singer sewing machine.

Lena could hear herself say, "Hold still, baby, just one more minute so Mama can get this hem straight."

"Didn't you ever want no children, Lena?" Herman had asked her
back in September as they lay in a shower of leaves under the chinaberry tree.

Lying next to the man she loved more than life itself, whose child
she would gladly die to bring into this world, the question stung her to
the quick, bringing sharp salty tears to her eyes.

Herman looked truly baffled at her reaction and took Lena in his
arms before her tears had a chance to overflow down her face.

"Oh, baby, don't ya weep," he soothed her as he rocked her on the
grass against his solid chest.

"Every 'oman ain't got ta have a baby out a' her own body,"
Herman said casually, looking down at Lena's wiggling feet.

"How many babies have you had out a' your own body, Herman?"
she asked tightly.

Lena felt like Sarah speaking to Abraham, sitting there with her
old self talking to Herman with his near-140-year-old self about having babies.

"Well, baby, you ain't got to have a baby out yo' own body to
know how it feel to have a baby, to be a mama or a papa."

Lena had heard that platitude so many times that she wanted to spit at the sound of it coming out of Herman's mouth. Herman heard her suck her teeth.

"Lena, one a' the reasons my pa run off to Flor'da was so he wouldn't have to spill his seed all over the place, wherever somebody told him to. He taught me and my brothers to be careful 'bout where we planted our seed 'cause that was our legacy to the world. And we couldn't just plant it. We had to cul'ivate it and care for it, too."

He paused and looked at her.

"I don't mean to be just givin' you words, Lena. I know it's a rock in yo' heart, not havin' no children of yo' own, Lena, baby. And I ain't pretendin' I knows how ya feel. I ain't no 'oman.

"I just want ya to know I feels wi' ya."

Lena felt his empathy and love flood over her as if he had just made her come.

"Lena, baby, the end of yo' menses ain't nothin' t' weep 'bout," Herman said. "It's a might powerful time when a 'oman's menses, monthly cycle, ceases. Almost as powerful as when they start. More powerful, really, 'cause you know so much more then."

Lena just sniffled. Herman kept talking.

"Shoot, all those womens you got altars to 'round here. Most of they menses had stopped when they did they best work. And see how powerful they was."

As with so many women, menopause just seemed to sneak up on Lena.

Miss Naomi, who continued to come to The Place long after most of her cohorts were in nursing homes and graveyards, told Lena early one morning over breakfast at the front of the grill how menopause sneaked up on *her*.

"Lena, I had just had me a *good* piece of tail the week before, so when my period was late, I said, 'Lord, you mean to tell me you let me get this far in life,' I may have even been close to fifty, 'and here I come up pregnant? Lord, ham mercy.'

"When I went to the doctor's office, he laughed right in my face."

Lena, premenopausal, on the cusp of the symptoms of irritability, mood swings, missed periods and hot flashes for a couple of years, had felt as if life had laughed in her face.

But she had Herman, and now she had her children to care for. She was happy.

34

FORGIVE

In creating the shelter for her children, Lena gradually moved happily back into the life of the town, and gradually, the town welcomed her back in.

Nothing big, nothing intrusive, nothing that she didn't want to do. She did not ever intend for Mulberry or anything else except Herman to swallow her up again.

Her love notes at Christmas had softened so many hearts and sparked so many tears that forgiveness could not be stopped. They had hurt her feelings, but she had forgiven them. She had hurt their feelings, and they had forgiven her.

As February turned into spring, so much was forgotten and forgiven. March came in like a lamb, warm and gentle long before anyone in Middle Georgia expected it to be.

Keba was so round and swollen and heavy with foal that she could barely move herself out of the stables and into the sunshine in the exercise area. But Baby and Goldie were actually cavorting in the pastures and meadows around Lena's house in the early balmy weather every chance they got.

Lena and Herman, too. They went for morning walks, watching the wind move through the fields of tall wildflowers like a solid creature, bending down swaths of grass. They'd climb up on the fence to watch Baby and Goldie frolic and roll around in the clover. Then, Lena or Herman would climb down and go back to the stables to visit Keba.

"Life follow life, Lena," Herman said one day as he patted Keba's fecund stomach. "It's gon' be excitin' when this here colt decide to come. Life followin' life."

Then, Herman and Lena went on in the house and sat at the table in the kitchen, drinking glasses of his favorite banana-orange juice.

Herman always insisted that they clink their glasses together in a toast.

"We need to mark this moment a' bein' together, Lena, and give thanks fo' it," he'd say.

It wasn't anything formal like a toast at a wedding reception. But it was just as heartfelt.

"To us," Herman would say with his eyes shining.

If they were outside, he would pour a splash of his drink on the ground and add, "Fo' all the brothers and sisters who went down."

They were a couple, a real couple, even though one of them was a ghost. They sat there like an old married couple, their feet touching under the table, and discussed the day, what they were going to do in the yard and on the grounds, how Keba was coming along with her pregnancy, what the vet said when she came out to see her, what things were like in the settlement when he was a child.

In February, Lena and Herman made love every single day. Lena kept count. He just could not seem to get enough of her. In the night, she would stir to feel Herman pulling her body to his. Then, all through March, with winter's back completely broken, they lay in bed under the stars and snuggled and loved each other tenderly.

Some nights, he couldn't seem to hold her close enough. And she'd have to say, "Herman, I can't hardly breathe."

"Oh, I'm sorry, baby," he would say. But he'd have to give her one more squeeze before he let her go.

Lena had let go of a few things herself. She remained a silent partner in The Place, but she sold Candace outright to the women through some creative financing.

Relinquishing those acquisitions and their control felt so good and freeing, Lena decided to turn some other things loose. She packed up Nellie's antique fountain pens each in a long narrow wooden or velvet pen box and wrapped them up in stiff, shiny forest-green paper sandwich style like something from Tiffany, so each gift-wrapped package seemed to spring open the moment someone pulled the end of the pale green grosgrain-ribbon bow.

Months before graduation, she gave a pen to a graduating Mulberry girl to take off with her to college or a job or life. She tucked a little check in there, too. Then, she set up a fund to continue the tradition.

With the vast majority of her contemporary clothes out in the world on other black women's backs doing some good, she took a look at the beautiful vintage clothes that had belonged to her mother, Mrs. Williams, Miss Zimmie and her other Grandies. She funded a new wing of a local black museum and set up a permanent exhibit called "Women of Color in Mulberry," that preserved and cared for the clothes while allowing the public to enjoy them.

"Right is right," Lena said at the exhibit opening.

So often since her parents died, she had wondered what she was going to do with the pens and so much else she had when she herself died. Now Lena felt like Osceola McCarty, a washerwoman in Mississippi, who never married and never had a child. She had saved $150,000 over her lifetime and gave it all to a scholarship fund for local black students when she was eighty-three years of age.

"For the children," the newspaper article had quoted Miss Osceola.

Now, Lena felt so much like a mother she wanted to cry.

When Lena and Herman surveyed her linens and china and flatware and crystal, they looked like a bride and groom checking out their booty. Lena had never noticed before that folks had been giving her gifts every year as if she were getting married. But she was not in the business of collecting, she was lightening her load.

New and recent brides in Mulberry weren't the only recipients of gifts from her storerooms. Folks starting households of all kinds received beautiful never-used items that would become heirlooms in their families.

It felt good for Lena to give and to forgive.

Herman tried to make it sound like a casual question as they walked in late March among the budding fruit trees, but Lena's head snapped up when he spoke:

"Hey, Lena, baby, what you want to do with yo'se'f?"

She had turned loose so much of her business holdings and possessions she realized that for the first time since she went away to college, she was free to choose what she wanted to do with her life.

She didn't have to ponder Herman's question.

"Oh, keep my legs wrapped around you for the rest of eternity."

And that is just what she planned to do.

35

TELL

When Lena woke in her big cozy bed with the huge bentwood headboard, she reached for Herman, but he wasn't there. It was the anniversary of his coming to her, and, although Herman did not mark too many earth days, Lena suspected he was around somewhere preparing a surprise for her this April morning.

For days, Lena had known something was up. From the way Herman had been going around the property, shoring things up, digging up new garden space, leaving his Herman touch just about everywhere inside and out, Lena knew he had a surprise for her.

She rolled over into the gaping hole her man's absence left in his side of her wide bed and rubbed her face into his sheets to inhale the scent of him.

"Well, okay," Lena said as if she had just gotten a much-needed fix.

The night before, she had played with him and tickled him, teased and seduced him, but all they had ended up doing for a while was holding each other and cooing to each other of their love, with Lena's pussy singing strains from "He Called Me Baby, Baby All Night Long" while mourning doves cooed on the edge of the skylight over their bed.

But Lena wanted to do more than kiss and touch.

When she had had all the stroking she could stand without exploding, she stretched in Herman's arms, kissed him and, pulling him into her arms, whispered, "Come on, Herman, I want you inside a' me."

He chuckled at Lena's insistence and said, "Proud to oblige, Miss Lena." Then, he proceeded to love her as flesh, as smoke, as heat, as steam, as rough hide.

In the dark morning hours under the covers, Lena murmured, "Oh, Herman, you always know what to do for me."

"Yo' pleasure is my pleasure," he assured her. And he made it sound like the words to a song.

Herman's guitar box was still leaning against the silk-covered mauve ottoman to her big easy chair by the outside doors where he had left it the night before. She had sat inside because the night air had been chilly to her, even after Herman had thrown his cashmere blanket over her legs. But he had stood on the screened porch, serenading her while she dozed.

"I can't seem to get enough a' this night air," he explained as he came inside.

He picked Lena up in his arms as she came awake with an "uhhhmmm."

"It's just me, baby. Herman," he said, lifting her over to the bed and gently placing her down among the lightweight comforters and her grandmama's quilt.

This morning she put on his favorite red and orange silk robe and went in the bathroom to splash cold water on her face. Then, she went barefoot in search of Herman in the darkened morning. As she passed through the pool room, she looked up and smiled at the stars over her. She recognized the Virgin right away and thought, I'll have to remember to thank Herman for showing me so much.

He was standing by the kitchen table looking out the back window at the stables and the river, drinking a cup of day-old coffee. She saw he had made her a pot of tea—chamomile, probably, she thought—and thrown a heavy yellow linen napkin over it to keep it warm. He was so deep in thought that Lena went to the counter and poured herself a steaming cup of the tea without saying a word. She took two or three sips, but she could not place the variety. She took another small taste, then put the cup and saucer down with the thought, That tastes odd.

Herman still had not moved.

She looked over his shoulder from where she stood and could see Venus rising in the dark morning sky. That's what Herman was looking at, she thought.

She started to say, "I'll make you a fresh pot of coffee, Herman," but he was so still looking out the window with his big red mug in his hand that Lena hesitated to disturb him.

But the longer he stood there in the morning silence, with his back to her, the more disturbed *she* became.

Her mouth was growing dry, and she felt a little dizzy.

Lena's eyes suddenly started filling with tears at the sight of his back. He was wearing the same shirt and pants he had worn when she first saw him in her bathroom.

Slowly, she moved toward him.

He felt her approaching and without turning around, he spoke.

"I gots to go, baby."

"Oh, God," was all Lena was able to get out before her legs went out from under her.

Even though the big, rough, white pine chair that Herman liked was right there at her elbow, she fell right to the cold Mexican-tile floor.

"I watched you all night, baby," Herman said, still facing the kitchen window. His shoulders appeared set, determined.

At the sound of his voice, Lena felt her heart begin to break.

"Oh, God," she muttered again.

"I thought if I watched you good and long, whether you knew I was watchin' or not, whether you knew I was there or not, then I could capture all a' you. Not just how you look. But how you feel in my hands and 'gainst my body, too. And how you smell. Lena, you know how good you smell? You smell like almonds, even yo' matchbox smell like those nuts you eat all the time."

Lena was dizzy from trying not to hear what Herman was saying, and she felt herself getting sick to her stomach.

Finally, Herman took a deep breath and turned to look at her. She thought she saw him weaken at the sight of her, but with the tears running down her face, she couldn't see anything clearly.

He walked over to where she sat crumpled on the floor and stooped down to her. Lena noted how light he was on his feet, how light he was in his old black rusty boots. She closed her eyes a moment and saw them dancing together. The first night they met and made love, down by the river to celebrate Cleer Flo'. She saw them on Christmas Eve in the snow and out on the deck beyond her bedroom in summer.

She didn't know how to handle the pain and shock she was feeling now. It was so deep, and she was completely unprepared for it. She kept hearing Herman's words: "I gots to go, baby."

"Come on, baby," he said, pulling her up onto his lap as he sat in his pine chair. He put his long callused hand on the bright silk over her breast. "You know you can feel it in yo' heart. You know you can feel it's time fo' me to go. One of the thangs I'm most proud of is I *know* you can feel it. I *know* you know it."

"Oh, Herman, I don't know nothing but if you leave me . . ." She couldn't go on for a moment because the words "leave me" had never occurred to her.

"Oh, Herman," she begged. "Don't leave me."

He just repeated it. "I gots to go, Lena, baby."

Lena rocked in his arms and wailed, "No, no, no, no, no."

"God, Lena, I done had two shots at life as it is. That's one mo' than most ev'ybody else get."

"It's not enough for me, Herman. Stay with me."

She grabbed his hand and brought it to her lips. Then, she took his hand and slipped it inside her robe and down into her panties.

"Don't go, stay here, Herman, stay *here*," she pleaded as she took his fingers and began massaging Lil Sis. "Oh, Herman, stay right here.

"Come on back to bed with me. It's early. The sun's not even up. You don't have to go yet. Come back to bed with me. Come on make love to me one more time.

"Come on, Herman," she pleaded, standing and attempting to drag his body toward her boudoir. Remembering his favorite Al Green song, she begged, "Come on, Herman, love me one mo' time, for the good times."

Herman took both Lena's hands in his and kissed them gently.

"You do know me, don't ya, Lena, baby, I gots to gi' ya that. You sho' do know me. 'Cause 'bout the only thang that could keep me is you in that bed up under me.

"But even after that, baby, I still gots to go. No matter how many times we go back to that bed, no matter how many times I touch my tongue to yo' tongue, my lips to yo' titties, my mouth to yo' sweet pussy, I still gots to go."

Now, Lena was sobbing like a two-year-old who knew what heartbreak was. She grabbed Herman's hands and tried to pull them into her chest. Then, she sank to the floor again because she didn't have the strength to stand. Herman sank to the floor with her and took her in his arms.

He held her as tightly as he could without bruising her tender McPherson skin, but she got no comfort from his tenderness. She could feel him slipping away, getting less and less solid, less and less Herman.

She buried her face into his chest and bit the sweet skin of his dark dark nipple. She rubbed her face on his green cotton shirt, leaving tear and mucus stains on the spot above his heart.

"Herman, if you knew that you were going to leave me, why didn't you tell me? Why didn't you tell me yesterday or last week? Or when you first come here? Why you string me along like this?"

"Tell you? What fo', baby? So you could be this miserable and cryin' and heartbroken longer?"

"Longer? Damn, Herman, I'm gonna be heartbroken forever."

"Aw, naw, you won't, baby." Herman's voice was so soothing and reassuring that Lena almost believed him for a second. But the next moment, it hit her anew that Herman was really leaving her now, in spring, with the wisteria blooming and the jasmine and the honeysuckle about to break into flower. And she broke down again, moaning and begging and screaming in Herman's arms like a woman who had lost her only child in a drive-by shooting.

She was inconsolable.

He started to tell her, "Good God, baby, you knew I was a ghost when I first rode up." But he knew she was in no condition for an old-time saying right 'long through there. Instead, he said, "You always knew I was a spirit, baby."

He kissed her face and neck and stroked her braids and forehead and rubbed her breasts awhile.

"Shoot, baby, if we s'posed to be t'gether, then we be t'gether fo'ever. This life ain't it. This ain't nothin' but a vapor, baby."

A vapor. Lena remembered him as nothing but a vapor when he first appeared to her in her bathroom, and she wept all the more.

"I been here so long now in yo' time that folks in my world startin' to question thangs."

Lena wiped her runny nose with the sleeve of her silk robe. "*Fuck* your people asking questions, Herman! You ain't got to go. We don't have to follow no rules. You said most spirits don't get to come back like you did. So, maybe you don't have to go, neither."

"I gots to be honest Indian wid you, Lena. I don't know how I got this time wid you. I don't know. I know I ask fo' it. Folks ask fo' a lot a' stuff between here and there, and don't usually get it. Ain't s'posed to have it, I guess.

"But I looked up, and you was callin' me, Lena. You was callin' me to come on into yo' world. And I been happy, deep-down happy, ever since. And, Lena, I will be happy for all eternity.

"You the cause a' that, baby. 'Cause God, who I may be 'bout to meet, knows I love you."

"Oh, Herman, I know you love me. I know that. Just don't leave me. You know I don't have nobody else. Please, don't leave."

Herman kept on talking as if Lena were not sobbing and begging him to stay. He appeared nearly unmoved, but Lena, even in her state, could feel his deep sorrow.

"Whether I gets to stay a extra year or fifty years, I'mo or you gon' haf to go. And this life gon' end. But, baby, what we got ain't gon' end, never, ever."

"Oh, Herman, is this what I get for loving a ghost? Just some metaphysical bullshit and you *gone?*"

"Lena," he said, looking at the sun rising low out of the Ocawatchee for his last day on solid earth, "look, baby, I can't love you enough. I can't suck you enough. I can't kiss you enough. I can't massage you enough. I can't eat you enough. I can't touch you enough.

"If I had a million years on this earth, it wouldn't be enough time to love you the way I want to. But be that as it may, Lena, baby, I gots to go. And that's just the pure-T truth. It's time.

"Time. It's the answer to everythang. Time, baby.

"It's my time now. It don't make me love you no less. But I gots to go."

Lena had no shame. She didn't give a damn about shame. She was so weak, she couldn't even stand. All she could do was beg.

"Don't go. Don't leave me, too. Hell, every dead body say I can do anything. Now, I want to do this! I want to keep you. Oh, Herman, don't make me beg and cry like this."

"Baby, I don't want to see you hurt. It hurt my heart to see you hurt."

"Then, dammit, Herman, don't go! Just don't go!"

"Gots to, sugar. I been here a year . . ."

"A year! A year??!! Herman, a year ain't shit. You were dead a *hundred* years! You had a hundred years to love me. I only get *one year* to love you? That ain't right. Oh, God, that ain't right." She could feel anger building with her shock and pain.

"Baby, right is right and right don't wrong nobody."

"Oh, Herman, I don't even know what that means. Save that old-timey bullshit for somebody else."

Then, Lena stopped, still as the grave. She wiped the snot and tears from her face once more.

"Herman, is that it? Is there somebody else?" She could barely whisper the words.

"Aww, baby, even feelin' the way you feel you gotta know better than that! You still the 'oman whether I'm goin' up under yo' skirt every chance I get or not, whether I'm shoein' yo' hosses or not, whether I'm rubbin' yo' feets or not . . ."

"Stop! Stop!" she cried, closing her eyes and dropping her head into her hands at the images his words called up. She could not bear to think that all of that was over. Lena had been certain, *certain*, that she and Herman would live and love out at their place by the river for years and years. She had imagined them growing old together like Ossie Davis and Ruby Dee, like Nellie and Jonah. Then dying together. She could not imagine a future without Herman.

"I got friends, and they been holdin' thangs off fo' me. Ain't all a' them like Anna Belle, bless her jealous heart," he was saying.

Lena broke down crying again at the thought of Herman slipping away to others who probably didn't even appreciate him the way she did.

"Oh, Jesus, Herman, don't go!!!"

She looked right in Herman's face and kissed both his beautiful high cheekbones, kissed his chin that looked so resolute and strong, kissed his straight black black eyebrows, kissed his curly black eyelashes. By the time she got to his lips, she could not bear it any longer.

"Herman, didn't you promise to always be there for me? Didn't you?"

"Baby, I ain't got t' be up inside you to be wid you."

Lena burst into new tears at the thought: Herman ain't never gonna be up inside a' me again.

She was the very picture of every obsessed, crazy, crying, hysterical, out-of-control, want-her-man-back, want-another-chance woman in history.

She cried for Herman like Nellie had at the thought of Jonah going off to fight World War II.

She cried for Herman like Carmen cried for Joe in *Carmen Jones*.

She cried for Herman like Lena wanting her man back.

Lena just wanted to *cleave* to Herman. And as he stood, she did just that. "I ain't got no damn shame, Herman. Don't leave me," she implored as she grabbed him around one of his long strong legs and clung to him. When Herman tried to turn and reach down for her, he just dragged her limp body a bit on the floor. But he seemed to steel himself against the pitiful sight and dropped again to the floor beside her.

For Lena, April was indeed shaping up to be the cruelest month.

"Ya gotta do the work you called to, Lena. But you ain't gotta be miserable. In fact, that's just what you ain't supposed to be. But yo' deep unhappiness, no knowledge of yo'se'f, who you was, what you could do, what you was called to do. Ya just didn't have no knowledge 'bout yo'se'f."

The more Herman told her, the more it hurt.

"I had a duty when I come here, Lena, to he'p you along a little bit. Baby, yo' unhappiness was causin' such havoc in the otherworld ya wouldn't believe it. Then, yo' broken heart start causin' disturbance in this world, too.

"Yo' anger callin' up storms. Yo' loneliness extendin' over the county. Yo' spittin' causin' Cleer Flo'. Like you som'um from the Old Tes'ament, Lena.

"That's 'bout the time I showed up."

"So, you just took me on to teach me a thing or two? You took me on as a job, a task, an assignment?" Lena felt that someone had grabbed her by her ankles, turned her upside down and shaken her.

Herman didn't drop a stitch. He asked quietly, "Did you ever feel like a task in my arms?"

And Lena had to break down again at his feet. "I'll never feel myself in your arms again," she wailed, and threw her face into Herman's lap. Looking down, she noticed his boots were not as hard and leathery as a few seconds before.

"Oh, God, Herman, you're really disappearing." She screamed like the goblins had her. "I'll never feel the breeze without loving you. I'll never come without feeling you in my bloodstream.

"Is that the way you want me to go on? How the hell am I supposed to do that?!"

Herman didn't answer. He began strobing, disappearing and reappearing right there in Lena's arms like a hologram.

"Oh, my God, Jesus, don't do this to me. I don't want to lose my man," she sobbed. Her breath was coming in short frightened gasps. "Oh, Mary, mother of God!" she cried. She felt as she had as a child when a ghost or spirit or demon had her in her sleep and wouldn't let go. She wept the way she had on a Georgia beach when she was seven and realized she was the only one in her family circle haunted by visions and voices.

Sitting there, she called his name. "Herman. Herman. Herman."

He had *always* come before when she had called him or even *needed* him.

"If you got the money, honey, I got the time." Herman had said it, and she had taken it as a promise. Now, that promise was broken.

When he appeared solid, Lena grasped at him with all her strength. She felt that merely by the power of her love, by the power of her *wanting*, she could keep Herman within her grasp.

But the next second he was just a vapor. She could not hold onto him.

"Lena, baby," Herman said, looking into her eyes with his fading gaze, "I am much in love wid you."

Then, he was gone.

36

CRAZY

Lena just about lost her mind lying there on the kitchen floor by herself.

After Herman disappeared, really disappeared, Lena just wanted to dissolve right where she lay and follow him back into his dead world. She wanted to close her eyes and just will herself to die, too. But she couldn't, even though she felt she might die of the pain anyway.

"Oh, Lord, don't do me like this. Please God, you know I've tried to be good, tried to be a true Christian. Jesus, you know that, you know everything. You know that."

Lena pulled herself up onto her knees and prayed to every deity she believed in.

"Oh, our Mother who art in heaven, don't just take him away like this. Please, don't do that. Didn't I forgive when you wanted me to? Didn't I? Didn't I love the way you wanted?

"Now, I'm asking this one little favor. Give me back my man."

Lena started making deals with the Lord.

"Okay, Jesus, if you just send him back to me for one more month,

This is what I'll do. I'll be aware of every single thing around me. I swear I won't let my anger and emotions get out of control. I'll learn more about the gifts you've given me and how to use them. I swear if you'll just send Herman back to me.

"Oh, Yemaya, please hear my cry. You're a woman. You know how it feels. Let me have Herman back, and I'll never ask another thing of you."

All she could think of was Sister Louis Marie telling her and her female classmates in their senior year not to think they could fornicate, then make deals with God not to get pregnant.

"Girlies, you can't make deals with God, you don't have the ante."

She stood shakily on the cold kitchen floor and stumbled into the Great Jonah Room. "I swear on my Grandies' graves that I'll do *anything* if you help me find Herman," she said aloud to the rafters.

She stopped dead in her tracks.

"Oh, God, I don't even know his last name!"

Then, she fell to the floor crying and wailing.

When she rose, she got up feebly like an old or pregnant woman—first on all fours like a dog, then one foot flat on the floor, then the other, and finally, with her knees bent, she pushed herself slowly upright from the floor with the palms of her hands. She moved to the oak French doors overlooking the deck. Our deck and our stables and our garden and our ground, she thought achingly, bracing herself against the door with the palm of one hand.

Lena knew she had to gather all her wiles if she was going to be able to do any good and get her man back.

"Not knowing his full name won't matter, I don't think," she mumbled to herself as she moved toward her bedroom, pulling her braids back out of her face. Herman had told her that the rites or ceremony of conjure or voodoo or hoodoo or Christianity were just outward signs, like a sacrament, of inward grace or belief. She wanted to show that she truly believed.

Her mind raced to remember concoctions she had overheard

down at The Place, to recall what Sister had said was used to hold onto a wandering husband.

Now, was it Adam's root or valerian root she told me to use? Lena wondered desperately. Her heart was pounding and her ears were ringing as if she had a steel band around her head. She just couldn't think.

The word "root" reminded her of Herman's Georgia jumpin' root, and she had to fight images of Herman's beautiful penis.

"Let's see," she said to herself as she stumbled around her big deserted house, "I think you add some ginger lily root and some rabbit tobacco. Now, where would I get some rabbit tobacco?"

Lena remembered that she had taken a piece of thread from Herman's trousers one night, not to try to hold him, but just to have it. But when she checked the tiny peach and purple trunk-shaped box where she knew she had placed the threads of dark green cloth, the box was empty. A small knot from his hair had vanished, too.

She put on the red silk underwear that Herman liked under a pair of worn jeans and one of Herman's long-sleeved shirts.

She sprinkled salt and pepper around all the doors of her house and stuck a fork in the ground in a vain effort to keep Herman there with her. But she knew it was too late for that.

When she thought of the chinaberry tree and its aphrodisiac roots that Herman had teased her about, it had begun to rain hard, coming down in sheets across the river. Still, she walked into the woods without a raincoat and got soaking wet sitting at the foot of the chinaberry tree on a stump.

Lena was truly torn about eating one of the mushrooms growing at her feet. She didn't want to go on living. Sitting there, she composed her obituary, "She died after eating poisonous mushrooms she found in the woods near her home."

Fuck that obituary, she thought, I don't think I want that to be my epitaph. I don't want that to be the last thing I do on this earth. She got up and headed back to the house to tell Herman of her decision, but when she realized Herman was gone and that she'd never be able to tell him anything again, she fell right to her knees on the mucky, muddy ground and began crying again.

Worn out from weeping, Lena walked back to her house and stripped out of her clothes—wet to her panties—at the back door. Lena felt chilly in the house and thought she would never feel warm again without Herman. She sat naked at the shiny breakfast room table, the wood of the shiny benches cool against her butt. Recalling the first time she and Herman had fallen back onto the table, knocking a tall vase of daffodils and yellow roses to the floor, and made love there, Lena rubbed her hand across the slick surface. She lay her face, still wet with tears, against the table's top and thought for a moment she could detect their scent.

But it was gone as soon as she sensed it.

Lena suddenly shivered and thought of going to get one of Herman's big cotton sweaters that she loved to wear. Herman's clothes!

Stumbling and bumbling, she ran to the closet and saw all his things there in her house, some lying on top of her freshly laundered things, some still smelling like him.

Lena was so happy to see something of her man still in her possession, to touch and smell, that she sank to the floor and burst into tears in the doorway of the closet. Each time she collected herself, she broke down again, until she was spent and drained. She finally gathered her strength and walked in.

She entered slowly, stealthily, quietly, and buried her face in the cotton and wool and silk of Herman's things, still full of his smell.

Then, right before her eyes, Herman's clothes began to disappear, dissolving just the way Herman had. She could hardly believe it was happening.

"Oh, God, don't do this," she said, feeling anger amidst her grief.

She started grabbing the clothes off the shelves and hangers and hooks, holding them in her arms as tightly as she could, as if her will could keep them real, solid, there with her. It could not. They all disappeared: his boots by the back door, his rain and outer wear hanging in the laundry room, his undershirt on the back of the chaise longue, his jeans and leather belt hanging on a hook behind the bathroom door. She raced around the huge house looking for just one sock or undershirt that Herman had worn.

By noon, all of Herman's personal belongings had vanished, even the white shirt she was wearing. Lena was desperate. She could not even find one of his short hairs among her rumpled sheets.

Lena knew she couldn't perform any kind of ceremony without some personal artifact of his. And other than the things he had built around the property—the gate, the signs, the carved-seat chairs, the trellises, the altars—there was not a shred of physical evidence of him.

Lena was willing to try anything to get Herman back.

She began seeking out ghosts for help: burning white candles, calling out Rachel's name in her pool room until blue and gray and purple forces swirled around the room so fiercely that waterspouts appeared in the pool.

But she received no answer.

Lena thought of other ghosts she could turn to.

"Let's see," she said shrewdly as if she were planning how to get some money together quickly for a business deal, "there's Mama, Daddy, Grandmama and Raymond and Edward. There's Granddaddy Walter, even though we never met. And my baby aunt who died. We already know each other. Then, there's Frank Petersen."

She ticked the names off until she had to note that just about everyone she cared about was dead.

"I'll ask my dead baby aunt where Herman is," Lena said, forgetting how the infant's ghost, in a photograph over her Grandmama's bed, had terrorized Lena when she was three until her grandmother moved the picture to the attic on Forest Avenue. "I'll ask her how I can get hold of him. She will know, and she'll know how to get him back, too."

She raced to the velvet jewelry case in her dressing room and put gold hoops in all four holes in her ears. She had read that gold improved one's sight for ghosts.

Thinking of her best friend, she said, "Oh, God, I wish I could get my hands on Sister. She could really help me."

Sister had always told Lena, "White women may go crazy quietly in their homes. But black women, little girl, like to get out in the street and go crazy."

Sister was right.

Lena put on dry clothes, grabbed one of her suede jackets hanging by the door and a khaki wide-brim hat hanging there, too, and made her stumbling way to her car. It was storming seriously outside, and she was just about soaked again by the time she passed the wooden sign Herman had made to try and protect her.

"It stand for 'Leave Lena 'Lone,'" she remembered Herman saying. She traced each letter with the tips of her fingers and crumbled against the wall of rosebushes to wail some more.

"Oh, Herman, why you have to leave me? Lord, take me, too."

When she got in her little Mercedes, she took a deep breath. Even though he was rarely in the car, the interior smelled to high heaven of Herman. His sweat, his saliva, his oils, his funk, his musk, his semen. She threw her head down on the steering wheel and sobbed.

She cried so deeply and heartily that she began to feel relieved. She cried the way she had cried when she was a child, with all her heart and soul.

All the way into town, to 455 Forest Avenue, Al Green sang on the CD player.

Don't look so sad, I know it's over
But Life goes on and this old world keeps on turning.

Lena didn't think she could bear to continue listening to the heart-rending voice of the now-preacher singing a country boy's song, *her country boy's* favorite song. But she couldn't make herself turn it off. It made her feel still connected to Herman.

Let's just be glaaaaddd
We had this time to spend together
There is no need to watch the bridges that we're burning.

By the time she crossed the wooden bridge over the river, she barely had strength to shift gears. When she got to 455 Forest Avenue in Pleasant Hill, little Chiquita was at the piano working on her music and saw Lena through the window coming around the side of the house. Chiquita cheerfully opened the door for her with a big, wide grin.

Lena calmed herself enough to give the tiny girl with the big low butt a quick hug and say in a near normal voice, "I just came by to get something from the attic," and hurried on up the stairs.

Chiquita gave her a funny look. Damn, Miss Mac look *bad!* the teenager thought.

Lena's pretty face was bloated and puffy from crying, her big brown eyes were red and swollen.

Chiquita watched Lena disappear up the steps and went on back to her music, promising herself she would call Lena the next day to make sure she was okay.

By the time Lena got to the last flight of steps leading to the top floor, she noticed how hot it was already up there in April. She felt a little dizzy. The attic was where she had loved playing as a child among the boxes and relics of decades of her family's life.

When she got to the top of the stairs and into the hot dark dusty attic, it was silent and empty except for some building materials. She had forgotten where she had told the carpenters to store her family belongings—including her dead aunt's picture. There was nothing to do but turn around.

Lena slipped out the house without anyone seeing her face tear-stained, her hair barely contained in their braids, her hopes dashed, her heart broken.

Lena felt she had no one on earth to turn to. So, she headed for church. She didn't know how long it had been since she had driven to St. Martin de Porres. Her car seemed to drive there under its own power. She sat in the parking lot awhile waiting for the torrential rain to let up a bit, but it seemed only to get heavier. As she climbed the cement steps in the downpour, Lena felt like a ninety-year-old woman who had watched all her loved ones die before her. She didn't think she had the strength to go on by herself.

Now that Herman had vanished, her heart, her soul, her special powers, had seemed to evaporate with him. And she wanted to throw herself down in a pool of mud that she could slowly sink into and die.

Her soft suede jacket was soaking wet against her skin, and heavy drops fell from the ends of her long fat braids. It was chilly in the church, but Lena didn't feel the cold. She felt numb, the way everyone said her father was after his mother died. Lena had heard Nellie say over and over after Grandmama's funeral, "Jonah, he just numb."

Candles flickered in their Mary-blue glass holders on the side altar. Lena sat nearby with her head resting on the back of the pew and heard a rustling noise at the back of the church near the entrance like the ringing of delicate golden chimes. When she looked up, she saw a procession coming down the center aisle of the church. A family procession. Leading the way was her Grandmama. Right behind her was Nellie, and gently holding her mother's elbow as if it were a monarch butterfly was her father, Jonah. Then came her brothers, Raymond and Edward.

They were only there for a second, but Lena did see this ghostly congregation clearly. And she felt better for the sighting.

Seeing her family, her people dead—and she thought gone—proceeding down the aisle of her parish church gave her a sense of peace, the way she felt now when she entered 455 Forest Avenue and felt only serene spirits, safe at home. She remembered Herman's words— "Shoot, baby, if we s'posed to be t'gether, then we be t'gether fo'ever. This life ain't it. This ain't nothin' but a vapor, baby"—but she was too angry and hurt to take any comfort from them. For a second, she felt that she could almost feel him reaching out to her. But by the time she thought to extend her hand and spirit back to him, the feeling had vanished, and with it her hope of getting her man back.

She just ran from the empty church sobbing and feeling more barren than when Herman had said, "I gots to go, baby."

By the time she got onto U.S. 90 heading back home around dusk, it was raining so hard she could barely see the road. And when she *could* see the road, she could hardly keep her little car on it because the wind had whipped up to a lashing velocity.

Lena could tell the river's waters had begun to rise. As she drove over her wooden bridge, she noted that it was nearly swamped. For the first time in fifteen years, the span didn't feel all that secure.

"This is a *bad storm*," Lena muttered to herself.

Lena's anger at the townspeople and the town at the end of the year had stirred up some trouble in nature. But her devastation at Herman's leaving was causing real destruction. Lena had cried a river of tears. The flooding of the Ocawatchee proved that. Even her land seemed in danger from the swelling torrent.

She heard Herman's voice. Not the way she had heard it when he was with her, but now only as a memory from far away.

It was what he had said to her before he began disappearing.

"You can't be the hand *everybody* fan wid, Lena. Then, you ain't nothin' fo' you'se'f. Shoot, everybody want you. You special," and then he had laughed at his understatement.

"Everybody want some a' you, want *you*! Shoot, baby, if I had my way, it'd just be you and me and a couple of those fine horses you got fo' eternity. That's what *I want*. But hey, as they say over on my side—and the other side is my place, baby, I do know that—people in hell want ice water. You don't always get what ya want and most of the time, you ain't s'posed to."

Lena cried and carried on for most of the evening, pacing around her house, dark from the storm that was raging like a crazy person outside. Lena carried on until she was sick of herself.

When she did finally fall across the bed, exhausted, disheartened and lonely, it was early evening, but Lena felt as if she had not rested in years. The fury of the storm raged outside, and she instinctively reached to the bottom of the bed for one of her grandmother's heavy quilts. When her fingers touched the thin voile swatch at one end, she felt a spark of comfort spread through her body. She pulled the quilt up to her chin, wrapped it about her body and cradled one end in her arms like a baby.

She fell asleep hearing:

> *He called me baby, oh baby, all night long*
> *Used to hold and kiss me 'til the dawn*
> *But one day I awoke, and he was gone*
> *There's no more Baby, Baby all night long.*

37

STORM

When Lena awoke a few hours later in the night, she looked on Herman's empty side of the bed and began to weep onto her soft blue pillowcase. She could still feel the space he took up inside her, like an echo of his penis, and its absence left a dull ache.

Lena thought at first that sorrow must have roused her, but then she heard a strange sound. She did not think it was the storm, even though it was raging outside. Then, she heard it again. The sound was coming from the stables.

"Oh, God. Keba!" she said, and threw the covers back. "The foal is coming. It's time."

She reached over to turn on the light in the darkened house, and with the click-click sound, she realized the storm had knocked the power out. She reached for the phone to call the vet, but there was no dial tone.

Lena had slept in her underwear, socks and shirt. She grabbed her jeans from the bottom of the bed where she had tossed them and shook her braids around her neck to clear her head. She felt as if her braids were standing around her head every which a way.

"Well, damn, nothing but static," she muttered as she slammed shut her small cellular phone. She pulled on her jeans and grabbed the flashlight Herman kept in the folds of the handmade quilt hanging from the table next to her bed.

As she ran through the house, she heard the storm moving across her land, sailing down her river, striding into her yard. Looking out the windows and doors, Lena could not tell if the storm was tall and thin, slicing through the woods and the town, or if it was wide and low, barreling through and flattening everything in its path. But she knew it was doing some damage.

"My God, where did this storm come from? It's gotten so bad."

When she got to the Great Jonah Room, she could see that the storm was no longer just raging outside. It was now in her house. She must have left the big French doors unlatched because the wind and rain had blown them open and swirled through the room soaking and upending everything all the way to the big stone fireplace.

Water was everywhere. Flowerpots and vases, books and papers were strewn all over the floor. Her silk-covered chaise longue was tipped over and halfway across the room. Quilts and rugs were ripped from the walls along with Lena's prized photograph of her Grandmama and Granddaddy Walter on their wedding trip.

It took her a while battling against galelike winds, but she managed to close the doors. Then, she struggled through the mess to the kitchen. She started to buzz James Petersen on the intercom but remembered all the power was out. Instead, she grabbed a lantern, took a set of keys from the wall inside the pantry and headed for the back door.

Her head was throbbing as she put on her heavy khaki rain slicker hanging in the laundry room. And her stomach was upset. She tried not to pay any attention to the empty peg where Herman's slicker had hung before he and it disappeared. She knew she would not have the strength to go on if she started thinking about her man, her friend, her lover . . . gone.

At the door, she pushed her pants legs into her boots and opened the portal to a raging tempest. Lena, who had come through the Flood of '94 unscathed, was awestruck by the power of this spring storm. As she ran to the garage, tree limbs crashed down around her. Pieces of loose fencing whizzed past her head. In a flash of lightning, she saw a huge branch fall within feet of her stone grotto to her mother and mothers. She realized that she had been praying since she awoke. All the while, she could hear Keba whinnying and crying in the stables above the babel of the storm.

She breathed a deep sigh of relief when she finally sat safely behind the wheel of her sturdy old Wagoneer.

"I'll just get James Petersen to drive into town and get the vet. And I'll stay here with the horses. Keba'll be okay. She'll be okay," she reassured herself as she made her way down the debris-cluttered road. Fallen limbs and uprooted bushes were everywhere.

She had a funny feeling and slammed on the brakes so hard she bucked in her seat. Two seconds later, a tall Georgia pine tree came crashing down in her path just inches ahead of the Wagoneer's front bumper. And there was no driving around it.

Lena was grateful she was only a few hundred yards from James Petersen's house.

He met her at the door.

"We can't go nowhere for now, Lena," he informed her as he took her wet things and led her to the gas heater logs. "I heard a big crash a couple of hours ago and drove down to the bridge. It's gone, Lena. Washed away, just like that."

"You mean to tell me our bridge is gone?!!" Lena was astonished. Even with the force of the winds and rain she had just faced, she could not imagine one of her structures being destroyed by the elements of nature.

"Uh-huh," he said.

"James Petersen, you mean we completely cut off?"

"Uh-huh. And the water is rising fast, not like the last time. This look different, Lena. Real different. I'm gon' stay down this way and keep an eye on the waters."

Lena thought her heart would leap from her chest.

"James Petersen, I think Keba's having her colt right now. We got to get a vet out here! Now!"

"Ain't gon' be able to do it, Lena. Even if we could get a message to Dr. Diehl, she couldn't get out here with the bridge out."

"Oh, God, what we gon' do?"

"We ain't gonna do nothing. I'mo stay here like I say and watch this water. If it starts rising any more, we gon' have to move to higher ground, fast! You *and* your man up at the house."

"Oh, Jesus, so it's just me and Keba," she muttered to herself.

"You hear me, Lena? We may have to move *fast!* Now, when it happen, when I say so, I don't want no Lena talk, I want all us to move to safety. You hear me, Lena?"

But Lena was thinking about Keba having her baby all alone up in the stables. She knew Baby and Goldie were freaked out by the storm, too. She grabbed her slicker and hat and headed out the door before James Petersen could stop her.

"I'll be at the stables, James Petersen!" she shouted as she headed back down the road to her Wagoneer.

She had to take it slow and easy, but she was able to turn the four-wheel vehicle around and drive all the way back to the pecan trees by the stables. Two of the tall trees had toppled over into the clearing where she usually parked her car.

The storm was striding the earth with a vengeance. Ahead, Lena could see lightning striking the surface of the Ocawatchee River, sending up sparks and electricity into the stormy night air. She had never seen so many lightning strikes. Thunder crackled all around her as she climbed down from the high seat of the big Jeep and headed for the stables.

She could hear Keba kicking and whinnying inside, and she rushed on to the wide swinging doors of the structure, cracking the stormy darkness ahead with the beam from her big flashlight.

Keba was already lying on her side in the pile of new clean straw that Herman had laid the day before. Lena had watched him do it. Keba lay with her head up listening and crying. Lena stopped right inside the door and said a little prayer.

"Help me, Lord. Help me, Herman."

Then, lighting the battery-powered lantern she had brought with her, she went on inside toward the whining horse.

"Hey, Keba, girl, how's it goin'?" she said, trying to sound upbeat and assured like Herman. "Looks like that time, don't it, girl? Well, it's going to be just fine. Better. I'm here and your baby's almost here. And that's the truth, period."

Lena put down the lantern and pulled off her rain gear and tossed it in a corner. She looked just like Herman as she rolled up her shirtsleeves and knelt down beside the big struggling mare. When their gazes met, Lena was sure she saw terror in Keba's huge bulging eyes.

Right then Keba's water broke, sending torrents of blood and fluid flooding the brick floor where Lena knelt.

She turned from the prostrate mare and said to herself, "Lord have mercy, Herman. I can't believe you left me with this mess on my hands."

Then, she turned back to the task at hand and went to work examining the braying animal, pulling some blankets down from the shelves behind her, speaking soothingly to the mare. It was a daunting task.

Shit, I can't do this, she thought five or six times. Her heart was racing so.

"Oh, Keba, I don't want to let you down," she said to the struggling mother. "But I don't think I can do this. I don't think I could do this on a *good* day, Keba, and this sho' ain't no good day."

Lena thought of her mother and her grandmother and her

Grandies and all the women who had been through this ordeal to bring a child into the world. "Oh, Mama in heaven, help me! Help your child!" she cried. "Mary, *you* had a baby in a stable. Help me!"

As she knelt in Keba's blood and water, Lena heard something heavy slam against the roof of the stables, and the thought crossed her mind, "Maybe, if I calm down some, this storm will do the same thing."

She took deep slow breaths, and placing her hand on her heart, she willed it to slow down and stop ramming against her chest.

The wind did seem to settle down a bit outside, and she tried to calm herself further by recalling Jesus in raising the little daughter of Jairus from the dead. We don't need hysterics and lamentations here. We need faith. Believe!

Then, she thought of Herman. Herman sitting in a field of wild gladioli covered with yellow sulfur butterflies. Herman lying naked next to her in bed with his hand over her matchbox. Herman astride Goldie exploring her land. Herman astride her.

Each image of the man she loved rent her heart but also calmed and centered her. Each time she saw him in her head, all big and strong and sexy, all up and through her property and her house and her soul for the last year, she recalled his love and his wisdom and his gentleness. Surveying the birth scene before her in the barn, she repeated, "Don't worry 'bout the mule goin' blind, Lena, just hold him in the road."

So, that's what she did. She called on all her powers of faith and belief and love and gratitude and did the work before her. She called on all that Herman had told her and taught her and shown her since he had shown up a year before and concentrated on Keba and her predicament.

Then, like a breeze, Herman was right there at her shoulder. She thought she could feel the heat of his breath on her neck inside her shirt collar.

"Take it easy, Lena, baby, take it easy," his voice whispered in her ear. Then, "Shoot, Lena, you can do *this*. Now, you gon' hafta get her started, but don't you worry, 'cause then, Keba gon' take over and yo' job be almost finished."

The sound of Herman's old country voice in her ear, the feel of his ghostly breath on her neck made her very heart melt.

Lena took a deep breath and turned to get a good look at him. He was there! He was still wearing his light green shirt and old work pants. He had his old black boots on. And his beat-up old hat was set back far on his head. He was just a vapor, but it was enough for her.

"Oh, God, Herman, I'm so glad you're here," Lena whispered, nearly breaking down on the stable floor.

"Lena, baby, I'mo *always* be here fo' ya. I tol' ya that."

Then, Herman smiled at Lena and turned his ghostly attention back to the horse. Keba seemed sedated by Herman's voice.

"Come on, Keba, it's gon' be all right," he said. "Everybody's here that needs to be here."

Lena looked around the stables and saw that everyone *was* there. Her whole family was around her.

"Hey, Lena, you old pop-eyed fool, you can't do this," her younger brother, Edward, chided. "You better go get some help."

"Don't pay him no attention, Lena," Raymond said reassuringly. "You can do this. Edward don't know what he talking about. You can do this."

Keba made a kicking motion, and Lena saw something emerging from the mare. Lena was thrilled until she realized it was the hind portion of the colt. "Shit," she muttered.

But she heard Herman's voice at her ear. "Oh, Lena, it ain't no big thang, baby. You know what t' do. We talked 'bout the time I delivered that colt. 'Member?"

"Uh-huh . . ." Lena said uncertainly.

"Well, what ya think?" Herman prodded. "You know ya can do it, Lena."

Lena's mother was as encouraging as Herman.

"Look at my child," Nellie said from way off in a corner of the stable. She was dressed to kill in an all-seasonal cream and caramel wool Chanel suit with ropes of gold chains and pearls around her neck and waist. Lena heard the click of her low-heel cream and white spectators on the stable's brick floor as she stepped back farther into the corner.

Nellie looked beautiful. In death, she had more than "kept her color."

Lena knew Nellie wouldn't get much closer because her mother was delicate and had a weak stomach. And looking down at herself covered in the mare's blood and mucus and such, Lena knew this was no place for weak stomachs.

Jonah appeared and put his arm around his wife. He looked good, too.

"Look at her, Nellie, delivering that colt. Shit, probably gon' be a thoroughbred racehorse. Probably gon' win the Triple Crown or something. Damn, my baby girl lucky!"

Lena's first-grade teacher, Mrs. Hartwick, was there, too, her face and body unravished by the cancer that had taken her away from this world in her sixties.

Lena smiled when she saw Nurse Bloom, dressed in her spotless white St. Luke's Hospital uniform and cap, cheering Lena, the pretty little special baby girl, on.

"I was there when you were born, Lena, and I'm right here now in case you need me. Kinda feels the same way in here it felt in your delivery room. Things are alive out here at your place."

Dr. Williams was standing next to Nurse Bloom, just as he had at Lena's birth. And it made her feel better knowing a physician was around.

The next time Lena looked up, she saw a small light-skinned woman with fluffy white hair and a bright red scarf tied around her head standing over in a corner trying to look around somebody's shoulder. She was such a nice, gentle-looking older lady that Lena couldn't believe her first thought was, I bet that's Anna Belle.

Lena took a deep breath, lay her head against Keba's extended belly and reached her right hand up into the mare's birth canal. She almost fainted when she felt the live colt inside its mother's womb.

"Jesus, keep me near the cross," she prayed.

She panted a few times as if she were the one having the baby, grabbed the colt above the tail, and tried to give it a little turn.

It was not easy to do. The colt, eager to enter this world, squirmed and thrashed about in its mother's belly, making Keba snort and cry with each kick. She was ready for this baby to be born, too.

As Lena got her hand inside Keba up to her armpit, the baby started and kicked back, grazing Lena's forearm.

"Oww!" Lena yelled, but she didn't withdraw her arm. She could feel the open gash on her arm bleeding inside Keba's womb. And at the wounding, Keba started to kick back, too, right toward Lena's pretty face. But something stilled her hind legs. Lena felt it. Probably Herman, she thought automatically.

"Shoot, we up there now, Keba," Lena said, resolutely praying to the Mother Spirit. "Let's do it!"

She placed her slimy palm firmly on the colt's hind portions and gave a push, a hard push from her shoulders, and spun the baby around. That's all it took. She barely had time to pull her hand out and sit back.

With a rush of birth fluids and mucus, the colt came out front legs first, first one then the other, then the head. The rest of the body, covered with slick, wet chestnut-brown hair, and part of the birth sac followed quickly. The white membrane made the newborn horse look like a ghost emerging. It was all over in less than ten minutes.

Lena sat back on her heels and went, "Whew!"

The sound of her relief in the stables seemed to break a spell of some kind, and Baby and Goldie, who had been quiet as nurses during the whole delivery, began kicking in their stalls. They lifted their huge heads in the air, whinnying their welcome to the newborn male colt.

Lena stood for the first time in over an hour and stretched her weak-feeling legs. She realized she was bone-weary from the events of the last twenty-four hours. Holding onto the stall, she walked over to the wide closed barn doors and swung them open.

Outside, the furious storm had passed so suddenly, leaving the air wet and warm and still. Crickets were singing a cappella, and from the stable doorway, Lena saw early fireflies on the other side of the river.

Over her shoulder, the colt—Lena thought his name should be Emmanuel—lay next to his mother on the straw in the corner of the brick stable floor. Lena thought it was a lovely sight, mother and son together. But the restful scene didn't last long. Within just a few minutes of his birth, Keba's baby began struggling to his feet. Herman had told her that was normal, but seeing new life stand and walk so soon after birth right before her own eyes stunned her.

He was wobbly on his thin, new slender legs, legs almost as long as his mother's and as wobbly as Lena felt. Right away, he had found his mother's milk and stood nursing while Lena was still trying to catch *her* breath. And she wasn't even the birth mother. Just the midwife.

Lena remembered Herman saying, "Life follow life, Lena," as he had brushed and babied a pregnant Keba. It made even more sense to Lena now.

As she marveled at the birth of Keba's foal, she marveled at the wonder of her own transformation and the gift of her family of ghosts.

It surprised her just how comfortable she was with all these ghosts appearing and disappearing around her. Some were family. Many were friends. A couple she did not recognize right off, but she was not a bit afraid of or confused by any of them. They all seemed to have a place. And she did, too.

The specters she now saw all around the stables did not seem to upset the horses, even the newborn, one bit. And she couldn't remember just when she had become so comfortable with the spirit world.

"Well, lovin' me fo' bre'fast, dinner and supper might have had som'um to do wid it," Herman's voice said at her ear. Lena raised her hand and touched the ear where his words still echoed.

Feeling the love and strength and warmth she received from this community of ghosts, she felt she would never again want to keep these gentle spirits at bay.

When Lena went outside and stood under the night sky, the wind, just brisk now, was pushing the clouds away in a rush, exposing a golden moon. She saw the Virgin in the sky and thought of Herman. Automatically, she reached for a fence post, feeling she was about to break down again, but she found she did not need the support.

Softly, sweetly, she felt Herman right there next to her, gazing up at the stars along with her. Not in the same way he had for the last year, real and solid, ready to slip his hand inside her panties first chance he got, but next to her all the same.

"How I do, Herman?" she asked.

"You done fine, Lena, baby," he replied, his spirit leaning against the wooden fence post, sinking into it, becoming a part of it. "But then, I'm always proud a' you."

They stood there in the cool, wet night air together, and it felt good. Not the way it had felt when Herman was real, but good.

"Herman," Lena said finally. "It's not ever gonna be the way it was before, is it? You're not ever gonna be here like all this past year, are you?"

Herman spoke, but it was as if the fence post were speaking.

"Naw, baby. Not like it was."

What he said broke her heart anew, but he spoke so plainly, so like her Herman, that she had to take the news in the same honest way.

"I didn't think so, but I had to ask," she said.

"I know ya did, baby."

"You know what, Herman?" she asked, stroking the rough fence post with the tips of her fingers.

"What, Lena, baby?"

"I am much in love with you, Herman." She didn't want to start crying again. But she couldn't stop the tears or the weeping in her soul. Lena reached for Herman and the fence pole for strength and support and held on.

She heard Herman take a deep breath, then reply:

"Lena, baby, I am much in love wid you."

"I'm still your woman," she told him.

She could feel Herman smile.

"I'm still yo' man," he replied.

They both sighed. Then, Herman moved out of the fence post and into the stables.

When he had vanished, other spirits came out of the stables.

The spirit of Mamie, the beautiful amazon of a woman who did Lena's hair when she was small and taught her how to be nosy, wafted out first.

"Are you okay, Lena?" the healthy-looking ghost asked. "You know Herman's being here this past year was a gift. Have you been paying attention to what's been going on this last year? Then, he *still* here!!" Mamie smiled and wandered off in the direction of the river.

Rachel came out of the stables next and walked right on past Lena with a smile and a wave. Lena could smell the deep, salty ocean scent on Rachel's skin from yards away. Rachel didn't stop. She went right on down toward the waters, catching up with Mamie.

Nellie followed. She seemed eager to speak.

"I told you wrong, Lena, when you were young. About how you could get away with a lot in this life, but you couldn't get away with acting crazy. And you been trying so hard not to be crazy. I know I told you that folks won't allow you to be crazy in this world. But life ain't about what folks won't let you do. It's about what you *choose* to do. I wish I had told you that. If you don't let yourself be crazy sometimes, baby," Nellie said, "then you go mad."

"I shoulda' told you that, too."

The ghost of her mother looked as if she felt better just having had the opportunity to say that to her baby girl.

"And, baby, I didn't know what I was doing when I poured out your caul water and burned your caul. I just didn't know. But Mama always loved you."

Then, picking her way through the muddy trail in her great-looking spectator pumps, Nellie headed for the deck on the west side of the house.

Frank Petersen came out of the stables just ahead of Grandmama, who had paused at the barn door looking out on the night. Frank Petersen was walking and looking back over his shoulder like something was after him. His beat-up old felt hat pulled down over his brow made him look like an elegant fugitive ghost.

"Hey, Lena-Wena, you done good in there. But then, you been doing good for a while."

He touched his hand to the brim of his hat and disappeared off into the woods.

Lena felt as if she were having her own private family reunion, without the fights and petty squabbles and struggles.

Grandmama sailed over and began speaking as if they had talked that morning.

"Hey, baby, you look good under all that crying and blood and misery," the old woman said. She looked good, too. She wore a lovely long lavender gauzy gown like the ones she wore in Lena's dream.

"Okay, Lena, I know you been having the time of your life. But that part of it is come to an end. But just that part. It's got to be, baby. Lena, you can't say you didn't get any warning. You just weren't paying attention.

"But it's going to be okay. It's going to feel okay, too. It just doesn't seem that way now. But how things *seem* don't mean nothing.

"We think we know so much while we alive, Lena. Deciding stuff, fixing stuff, saving people, settling turbulence. Especially us black women. We think we can fix it all. And we don't know shit, baby. We think we know this one and don't give 'em nothing. And we think we know that one, and we give 'em everything."

Grandmama's ghost leaned forward and chuckled a little as if the joke were on her.

"Lena, baby," she said finally, "I didn't have a clue."

"What do you mean, Grandma?" Lena asked.

"When I was 'live, I thought I knew a thing or two. Knew how things oughta be. Thought I knew 'bout life and death, too. But, Lena, I didn't have a clue."

Lena was dumbfounded. From the first time Lena remembered being held in the old lady's arms, she knew that her grandmother was the very essence of power and wisdom. As powerful as her mother and father. As wise as any of the nuns and priests at St. Martin de Porres, as any of the winos and whores down on Broadway and Cherry.

"Good God, Grandmama, *you* didn't have a clue?? If *you* didn't have a clue, then what about *me?*"

"Exactly, baby!!!" Grandmama said and, rising like a soapy bubble into the night air, burst and disappeared.

38

PERIOD

It was a day in late May when Lena first noticed the sound of her own laughter. It truly shocked her to hear the throaty giggle coming out of her own mouth as she watched Emmanuel prance importantly around the corral right behind his mother. Lena realized that she was no longer in deep mourning for Herman the way she had been throughout the month of April, breaking down each time a spring breeze ruffled the hairs at the back of her neck.

Remembering all that Herman had taught her, Lena just didn't feel right being miserable.

She could hear his voice as clear as anything.

"Ya gotta do the work you called to, Lena. But you ain't gotta be miserable. In fact, that's just what you ain't s'posed to be."

Now, Herman whispered at her ear when she had a question, or he swung open a gate when she reached it. He still spoke to Lena all through the day, just the way he had before, asking her questions and pointing out new signs of spring along the river. And she talked to him, just as she had before, seeking his advice, sharing an interesting thought or pangs of love.

He had promised her that he would always be there for her. And he was.

But Herman no longer walked her property as a man. He was there as mist, as breeze, as a feeling, as sunshine, as a hunch, as the Ocawatchee River, but not as a man.

And Lena missed Herman's body.

Every single thing reminded her of Herman. The gate he built. The trellises he erected. The steps he repaired. The signs he made. The seeds he planted. The bed they shared. With the sound of her laughter, she realized she had reached the point where she was grateful for nearly every single memory.

For a while after Herman first disappeared Lena had tried to be angry with him. For loving her and leaving her. For teaching her everything except how to live without him: without him eating her food, without him eating her pussy, without him taking her hand as they walked through the woods.

She had stood on her deck many a night cursing and screaming at the darkness for enveloping her Herman and taking him away.

She had even tried one night to yell, "*Fuuuccckkkk* you!" in the direction of the stars, but the words evoked such hot sexy images of her and Herman together in the cornfield, in the shower, in the hay-loft, in their bed, that she could not even get the whole curse out.

Lena found it impossible to sustain any anger at Herman. She loved him too much. And the ache she felt when she could hear him but not see him, when she could see him but not touch him, was not as sharp as it had been at first.

It seemed a waste to spend time being angry at Herman for doing what it was time for him to do. For not doing what she wanted him to do. She knew that her time would be better and more happily spent remembering and smiling and living and continuing to love him whether he was there in body or in thought.

Herman wasn't the only ghostly presence around Lena's place nowadays. Her grandmother, mother and some of her other Grandies came regularly now to sit on the deck and talk or to stand in the kitchen and watch her make dressing or a hoecake of corn bread. They offered comfort and gentle guidance.

Even the ghost of Herman's mother—Lena called her "Mama Mae"—had come a few times to smile on Lena and help her with her recipe for china briar bread. She spoke just like her son, and she didn't even make Lena nervous. Her talks helped Lena appreciate Herman the spirit in the way she had loved Herman the man.

Lena's brothers just about lived in the woods on her grounds now. She had seen the two of them dashing down to the river one morning. Lena was looking forward to talking to them sometime soon. She found that she really did not know her brothers at all.

And Jonah, she discovered, enjoyed just sitting on her deck in the warm spring sun.

Lena even began to think that her birth caul had indeed been a gift.

Almost against her will, she found herself moving on with the life and plans she and Herman had set into motion. She carried the dull clump of pain with her, but she moved on. Not as a martyr. Not as a widow. But as someone who had a life to live. She was just beginning to understand what Herman had told her about "surrendering" and reveling in what she had right then.

She was thankful for a great many things in her life: Herman and her ghostly family; her faith and the right she claimed to her own privacy and choices; 455 Forest Avenue and her children; her garden and horses, and the freedom and time to enjoy them.

Lena found laughing in the morning with Herman a difficult habit to break. She woke rested now with a smile on her face, remembering one of Herman's songs or one of his stories or one of his sayings. Her day was so full of things she was eager to do on her land or at 455 Forest Avenue that she also awoke smiling in anticipation.

No one, not even James Petersen, who saw that all of Herman's personal belongings were gone, dared ask what had happened to Lena's man. The town of Mulberry respected her privacy and did not treat her like a grieving widow to be smothered with sympathy.

She was grateful for that.

Lena felt as if she had been given a treasure each time she heard Herman's voice or caught his scent on the wind. But she was even more grateful that his ghostly presence had not yet shown up in their bed. Just hearing Herman's voice, or remembering the touch of his callused fingers all over her and up in her, Lena would come some-times standing at the sink or stooping in the garden. Sometimes, she thought she could feel Herman's fingers strumming the hairs on her matchbox.

Her pussy, as lonesome for Herman's body as she was, had not sung a note since he first disappeared. Lil Sis didn't even sing the blues. And Lena was glad of that.

Sister had completed her sabbatical in West Africa and planned to swing through Mulberry on her way back home from the continent that week.

"Girlfriend, do I have some talk for you," Sister's wire had read. "And I bet your hair looks like the devil's doll baby danced in it."

Lena's thick copper braids were loose and messy, but her hair, in Herman's agile hands for a year, now looked better and healthier than when Sister had last oiled and braided it.

She heard Herman say, "I loves yo' hair like that, Lena." And she tossed her head and smiled.

Lena hadn't decided how much she was going to tell Sister about Herman. It really didn't matter. Lena found she did not need to tell anyone else about Herman. She liked having him all to herself.

There was hardly a sign still around her house of the fierce storm that had blown through the county the month before. Lena and James Petersen got the house and grounds straight faster than she would have thought. They retrieved outdoor furniture, resecured trellises and replanted uprooted bushes. All the while, Herman's spirit kept pop-ping up to guide her.

Lena discovered more things she owned that she did not use, things she could get rid of or share. She could hear Herman say, "Good God, Lena, ya got so much." Her cabin out by the river was not Spartan now. But it was indeed free of much unneeded plenty.

Chiquita from 455 Forest Avenue was Lena's first choice to help her sort through the goodies she and James Petersen unearthed in their cleaning. The teenager, who was just discovering Dinah Washington and bebop, said the two of them—she and Lena—were "simpático."

Lena found that was true soon after Herman disappeared. Chiquita had tried calling a couple of times, concerned about how bad Lena had looked the last time she had seen her. When Chiquita didn't get a response, she sent Lena an envelope.

Inside, there were lyrics and music to a love song Chiquita had composed about her own mother and a note that read:

"When you feel better, Miss Mac, I'll play it for you."

The image of little fifteen-year-old Chiquita, who had not seen her own mother or father since she was two, trying to comfort Lena brought tears to her eyes. She called and invited Chiquita out to visit that very week.

Lena found that even after giving Herman all her love, she still had love to give. And her children needed as much love as they could get.

Lena and Chiquita would sit for hours at 455 Forest Avenue or out on the deck at Lena's house by the river and discuss everything from boys and birth control to poetry and clothes. Then, they would switch to a serious discussion of Chiquita's artistic aspirations. Sometimes, James Petersen would sit down and join in the discussion—from a writer's point of view.

When Chiquita bounded into Lena's house with her short dark hair braided in an abbreviated version of Lena's hairstyle, Lena had to smile at the imitation. Chiquita had blown in like a new breeze and put on Dinah's "What a Difference a Day Made," singing along the way Lena had in the house on Forest Avenue when she was a child.

"What's this, Miss Mac?" Chiquita asked as she dug through the closets in the sewing room. "Some kind of instrument stand?"

"Oh, that's for the telescope," Lena said from the other side of the room. And she smiled thinking of the first time Herman had looked through its lens. Some nights, Lena could feel him looking over her shoulder as she scanned the heavens.

"I'm a little hungry. You had lunch, Chiquita? Let's take a break and get something to eat."

Having her children around her house from time to time felt so right.

"Okay, I'm always hungry. And you always got something good to eat in your refrigerator, Miss Mac. You the only single grown person I know who cooks like that."

At the mention of food, Lena felt Herman's presence enter the room. He seemed to be around all the time now.

"Can we eat down by the river?" Chiquita asked. "It feels good down there."

"Uh-huh, moist air, good for your skin. You got pretty skin, Chiquita. Now, you have to take care of it, okay? Be gentle with it. Pat it dry when you wash your face. Don't ever rub it hard. Pat it dry, do that for me, okay?"

"Okay," Chiquita promised as demonstrated. "You're always showing me something good, Miss Mac."

"Am I telling you too much? Am I getting bossy?" Lena asked with a chuckle.

"*Uh-uhh,* I love to learn things. 'Specially from you."

Lena smiled again. "Come on, let's take that lunch break. Eating down by the river is a good idea."

"I need to go to the bathroom anyway, Miss Mac. Can I use your great big bathroom?" Chiquita asked.

The teenager said she wanted a bathroom just like Lena's when she built her own house.

"You got a Tampax, Miss Mac?" Chiquita called from the bathroom off Lena's bedroom.

Lena thought a minute. "I'm sorry, sugar. I don't think there are any."

"You don't have a tampon in this whole house, Miss Mac? In *this house?*"

Lena smiled when she thought how Herman had called her house the "got house."

"Uh-uh, Chiquita," she answered. "I don't think I have any in my purse, either."

"You don't have any? No panty liners either?" Chiquita was not convinced. "What *you* been using, Miss Mac?"

"I don't know," Lena said more to herself than to her young visitor. It seemed she had not had use for a tampon in ages.

Lena glanced at the Varnette P. Honeywood calendar on the wall in the kitchen. Lifting the pages, she looked back through to the beginning of the year where she had drawn the last red star. Lena realized she had not used a Tampax since February.

She looked through the calendar once more, counted back again, and pondered the date with a quizzical smile playing around her face.

"I made do with some Kleenex," Chiquita explained as she came into the kitchen ready to eat. Taking containers of leftovers from the refrigerator, the girl continued to chatter away. But Lena wasn't listening.

A slight change in the temperature of the room told Lena Herman had just entered. Then, she felt him at her ear looking over her shoulder and counting with her under his spectral breath:

"Nought from nought leaves nought."

Standing with her hands on her hips, Lena chuckled and, sounding like her dead grandfather about to set off on an adventure, said softly to herself and to Herman, "Well, Lord."

ABOUT THE AUTHOR

Tina McElroy Ansa's first novel, *Baby of the Family*, was named a Notable Book of the Year by the *New York Times* in 1989. Her second novel, *Ugly Ways*, was published in 1993. She lives with her husband, Jonée, a filmmaker, on St. Simons Island off the coast of Georgia.